ATOMIC HORRORS

ATOMIC HORRORS

TIM CURRAN

WEIRD
HOUSE

ISBN: 978-1-957121-63-5

Text and Afterword © 2007-2023 by Tim Curran

THE SHAPE (originally appeared in Dark Animus 10/11, 2007)

Cover and interior artwork © 2023, by K. L. Turner

Interior and cover design by Cyrusfiction Productions

Copy edited by F. J. Bergmann

Editor and Publisher, Joe Morey

Weird House Press
Central Point, OR 97502
www.weirdhousepress.com

CONTENTS

Furnace	1
Ground Zero	7
King Of Flies	29
Rat Trap	49
Doll Parts	67
Black Widow	87
Worm Cast	101
Fallout	119
Coffin Birth	139
Brain Death	153
Crabmeat	179
Bride of the Termites	203
Conjoined	217
Little Monsters	239
The Shape	259
Afterword	297
About The Author	303
About The Artist	305

ILLUSTRATIONS

Atomic Horrors	vi
Ground Zero	6
King Of Flies	28
Rat Trap	48
Doll Parts	66
Black Widow	86
Worm Cast	100
Fallout	118
Coffin Birth	138
Brain Death	152
Crabmeat	178
Bride of the Termites	202
Conjoined	216
Little Monsters	238
The Shape	258

FURNACE

J ust before the world ends, the woman, the chosen one, awakens screaming
with a froth of white foam at her lips. She shakes in the darkness, the
pains in her belly excruciating like hot knife blades being jabbed into
her guts. Lathered with oily sweat, she grips the mound of her belly with
straining, white-knuckled fingers, loving what's inside her and hating it at
the same time. As the old hags mutter ancient words, their faces cadaverous
in the guttering candlelight, they try to hold her still.

"*It's ... it's biting me,*" the woman says in a hissing voice. "*It's tearing me
apart....*"

The old man looks on, the flaking leather book in his hands trembling.

"Tell us," he says. "Tell us what you see."

The woman jerks with clonic spasms, blood leaking from her nose and
staining her face like red wine. Her voice is garbled, but they hear what she
says, what she sees in the narrowing perception of her mind. The prophet,
she tells them, the dark one, the holy one, the abomination before the
Christian god. It stands in the broken ruins of the cities of men and calls out
its plan for humankind. Multitudes gather at his feet ... burnt, puckered
with gaping sores, eyeless and deranged, they howl like animals and lick
his fingers like dogs. As the abomination speaks the forbidden words that
make the world tremble and the blackened masts of trees sway, the sun goes
black as a charcoal briquette in the sky and the earth splits open with great,
seething fissures. The writhing vermin of hell crawl free with leggy, slinking

profusion to rise up and walk the gutted landscape. The stars are different now. They laugh in the sky as the land grows cold and ashes blow on the moaning winds in a great, screeching dust storm.

"It is the prophecy as we understand it," says the old man. "Let the world become a graveyard, let the cities be tombs, and let the jackals gnaw at the bones of the fallen god and his followers...."

The woman contorts and squeals, her belly shuddering as what's inside her stretches its limbs.

The child is coming.

And the world is about to die.

In the first seconds, there are two suns in the sky.

One is yellow and ancient, the other a brilliant burning red exploding with impure light. The sky is no longer blue, no longer scudded with puffy white clouds. It becomes a yellow-orange tangerine and then an odd shimmering rose—the color of burgundy held up to firelight. The atmosphere is a flickering, iridescent blue-green with pockets of phosphorescent crimson.

This is followed by an instantaneous, blinding white flash that sears the world, scalding faces and burning out retinas. For a moment. The world is X-rayed in white brilliance ... and then death comes, on a scale that is literally unimaginable, with a resounding, rumbling sonic boom.

Close now, so damn close.

The agony the woman feels ratchets up from zero to a hundred in bare seconds. It feels like she's being peeled raw inside by razors, dull surgical blades, and rusty crosscut saws. She screams and thrashes. The old hags, the midwives, nod their heads and call out forgotten words that were ancient when the world was young. They anoint the woman with salves and balms and liniments made from the fat of boiled infants.

"Make ready," one of them says.

The old man prepares the sacred cloth. He unfolds it with shaking fingers. It is scarlet with yellow piping. He has waited for this moment his entire life, but now that it is happening, he is not sure how he feels. Scared. Excited. Hopeless. Overjoyed.

One of the hags with a face like a yellow, shriveled skull places her ear against the moist, warm belly of the woman and nods her head. Inside, she hears something like the low bubbling of a cauldron and a scratching sound like a dog outside a door.

"Make way for the Lord," she says.

The other hags listen now with cupped ears. They grin with toothless maws, for they hear the sound of the child … like the guttural lowing of an alligator in a swamp.

The woman is out of her mind by this point.

She is a husk of breathing meat that sweats oil and blood and slimy excretions. Her mind is filled with grotesque shapes that dance with ritual movements. The hags crowd around her, touching her with fingers sticky as rotting peaches. They exude a foul perfume, a sweet and gassy smell of dead squirrels trapped in the walls of old houses. Their formaldehyde breath is sickening to the extreme. They wear black, musty shawls that rustle and flap like the wings of crows. Though they are living, inside they are rotten like the hearts of old stumps.

One of them, her face dark as coffin wood, says, "He comes now … you must surrender your flesh, for it is his nest, his food and drink and spawning grounds.…"

The woman no longer understands words. Thought and reasoning are alien to her. She is an animal now, a pink and fly-specked sow about to farrow. There will be nothing beautiful about the birth; it will be brutal, organic, and unpleasant, a blood sport like a cow calving in the straw of a stable.

The hags hold her tighter now, fighting against her manic muscular contractions. The flesh of her swollen belly has become membranous and sheer. They can see the nightmare fetus within her turning and turning, a larva preparing to break free of an egg sac.

The gushing, spinning fireball rises above the city, becoming a vast crimson, mushrooming shape of clear, evil delineation. It looks like a skull, a demon, a laughing face—all depending on who sees it. There is no doubt what it is to those who dare look upon it. The Devil of man's construction has come to earth. Its explosion creates an initial, devastating shockwave that lays neighborhoods flat, grinding concrete and brick to dust, reducing the city center into a gutted, scarred landscape of rubble, jagged girders, and mountains of steaming slag. Hurricane winds follow immediately, destroying buildings still standing and reducing houses to kindling, all of which gets sucked up into the raging, funneling dust storm of the fireball and then dropped to earth in a deadly, blazing barrage.

Huge, bloated blood-red clouds seem to dip down over the skyline, rupturing like brilliant scarlet tapestries, lightning arcing earthward in dancing chains that play along the rooftops, blasting free chunks of concrete and roofing tiles, starting fires and splitting trees. The resulting heatwave turns streets into rivers of molten tar. Sidewalks split and heave, water pipes bursting with eruptions of boiling steam. Rubble flies through the air, static electricity crackling and popping, exploding with acrid bursts of blinding light.

The firestorm comes next.

The superheated city center erupts with great licking fireballs that spew greasy black smoke in roiling, churning clouds above the ruins that flash with veins of brilliant red. Fed by broken natural gas mains, ruptured propane tanks, and gasoline wells, the firestorm rolls on and on, propelled by hot, dry windstorms. The flames leap up several hundred feet and then cascade down like napalm, incinerating everything in their path.

The city has become a huge crematory, as an incinerating blanket of heat turns the world to ash.

In birth, there is death.

In spawning, biological obliteration.

The woman's body is pulled taut as a bedspring, a coiled and elastic thing that stretches with the sound of an overinflated balloon. A sharp, septic smell like necrotic wounds rises from her. Her lactating breasts ooze a pink foam, fluid splashing from between her legs in a uterine flood that inundates the bed and splashes to the floor like the cold guts of a fish.

The hags can barely hold her in the grasping claws of their hands. She writhes and fights, twisting and jumping as if she's thrumming with high voltage. If there was anything left in her mind to think with, she would have likened herself to a rubber band that was stretched beyond endurance.

As the old man shouts the words from his book, the woman undergoes contractions that tear her skin open with pinpoint, blood-bubbling fissures. The pain is white-hot and unbearable. It tears her mind out by its pink, shivering roots.

And then, from anus to vagina, she splits wide open in an expulsion of gore, tissue, and afterbirth. What emerges is a worm-like mass that pulsates and quivers, splitting open the birth-sac with black talons, a scaly, monstrous fetus with corrugated flesh the color of blood. It squeals and mewls, a suckering gray mouth pulling in air with a wet, gulping sound and exhaling a fetid mist of corruption.

It squirms between the macerated, shorn pubis of its mother, flapping like a freshly-landed carp, an undulant, mutating, embryonic horror that is smoldering with the stench of roasted flesh and burnt hair. It cries with a cacophonous, shrill noise like millions of buzzing insects and whining buzz saws.

Its mother is dead, collapsed into herself like a melted candle. She bleeds ropes of tallow. It crawls from her anatomical wreckage, unfurling itself from a web of sticky excretions like a fetal wasp, staring out at its wailing worshippers with pink, blood-seeping eyes like skinned toads.

As the world outside is ground beneath the heel of nuclear annihilation, the Devil has been born. Its congregation is wiped out as the blast flattens the house and their bodies burn like candle wicks.

The gigantic mushroom cloud towers above in the sky, purple and red and hot as a smelting oven. It was born at the very exact moment as the child.

In the flaming wreckage, the abomination crawls forth, crying out for its mother, its true mother. And from the smoke and debris and fuming sparks of the furnace, a tall, gaunt woman steps forward. She has the green, slit eyes of a cobra. She holds out her hands.

"My child," she says. "At last. Now, let us remake the world in our image...."

GROUND ZERO

THE DEMON

When the bomb detonated above the city, there was an instantaneous release of kinetic energy equivalent to 100 kilotons of dynamite. A blinding white flash burned brighter than a thousand suns as nuclear fission released a deadly saturation of neutron and gamma rays. The sky went a brilliant, bruised purple, then the blazing fire-red of a supernova. A shockwave of greater than 500 miles per hour lashed out with devastating force, convection currents sucking dust, smoke, and debris 30,000 feet into the atmosphere, creating a boiling mushroom cloud millions of degrees Fahrenheit.

And it was only the beginning.

SURVIVOR

Penn came out of his underground shelter outfitted in an olive-drab military-grade NBC suit. Through the goggles of his hood, he saw the wasteland that had once been the city: an endless maze of heaped rubble, overturned cars, bodies rotting in the gutters. What a pretty picture it made. Dust storms were still blowing off and on, all of them cooking hot with fallout. He knew he had to be careful. The suit would protect him only if he was careful. And smart.

And I'm both, he thought. *Hell, yes.*

And he was. While everyone else pretended in their naïveté that the

7

Cold War as such was over, Penn knew better. He prepared. He built the shelter under his basement. He stockpiled it with food, water, medical supplies, weapons … all the goodies needed to survive a worldwide pandemic or, in this case, a full-out attack by the Russians. It had taken years and thousands and thousands of dollars, but he'd done it. He didn't give a damn what his family said or what those headshrinkers at the VA told him—he was not paranoid; he was prepared.

There was a difference.

As he stepped out into the hell zone of the new world, he moved carefully, stealthily, like a stalking animal. He'd been waiting for this. He hadn't wanted it any more than anyone else (at least, he liked to tell himself that), but he was a survivor with a survivor mentality. He was going to live through it.

Humanity, what was left of it, was in shambles now. Society had collapsed. But, of course, it was only a matter of time. He'd known that for years. As Captain Kane had told him in the war, the peaceniks and liberals were to blame. Love and peace, racial equality and gender neutrality. *It makes me sick, troop. It all makes me sick. We're over here fighting for their freedoms while they run the country into the ground.* And Kane was right; Kane was always right. The only equality in this world was who had the gun in their hand and how willing they were to pull the trigger. Survival of the fittest.

If we'd have nuked the Ruskies years ago, this wouldn't have happened.

"Damn right, Captain," Penn whispered.

Goddamn Putin. He was to blame. Penn had counted on Trump to put an end to that sonofabitch; instead, he'd climbed into bed with him. Which only proved that all politicians were corrupt little maggots.

Wait.

Something was moving over there behind the bus. He'd seen it skitter away. It could have been a victim, even a dog, but Penn trusted his instincts. The goddamn Russians didn't bomb the shit out of the USA for no reason. They were probably already here in numbers. It was something he and the other patriots had debated at length out on the message boards: the likelihood of a full-out Russian invasion once the United States was crippled sufficiently by thermonuclear weapons and neutron bombs.

Oh, they're here, all right.

As Penn moved closer to the burnt hulk of the bus, he saw that all the windows were gone and inside were dozens of blackened corpses still sitting upright. They had not even fallen over. Probably welded to their seats by the intense heat of the initial blast. They grinned at him like melted rubber fright masks, lips burned away so all he could see were teeth and gums. In the distance, he heard screams and then gunfire.

Slowly, controlling his breathing, Penn brought up his M4 carbine, his finger glued to the trigger. Through the earpieces of the suit, he listened. He heard something move. Someone was trying to be quiet; he knew that. He could sense that. Suddenly, they burst into a fit of coughing.

Penn moved fast.

Maybe it was a trap.

Easy, troop. Real easy.

He ducked around the bus. He saw a woman crouched there. She was dressed in burnt rags. There were gaping sores on her face. She looked at him with one bleary eye.

"Water," she said, holding out a dirty hand to him. "Water."

Just a victim. That's all. She was no threat, just a pathetic thing that would probably be dead from radiation poisoning within twenty-four hours. He stepped closer to her … then stopped.

A bead of sweat rolled down his face.

A chill went up his spine.

Something clicked in his head and he saw that there was a knife in her hand. Sure. He'd read about that. The Russians had developed a special adaptive camouflage that could make their soldiers look like ordinary men, women, and children. That's how they were planning on infiltrating American cities after the bombings. You'd see them and think they were no threat, then the camo screen would go down and you'd be looking down the barrel of an AK-47.

Now you're thinking like a soldier, troop.

Penn kept his gun on the woman. He licked his lips. "Nice try," he said. "You make one move and you're dead."

"I need water."

"Don't fuck with me, bitch. Where's the rest of your unit? What's your strength?"

9

"Please."

"Tell me the name of your commanding officer. You got about five seconds, Svetlana."

"Please, oh dear God ... please help me."

Penn wasn't fooled. Oh, they'd tried to fool him at the VA hospital, too, when he'd been shipped back from Iraq, telling him all kinds of crazy shit about how he'd had a breakdown over there and had wasted some women and children. Ripe bullshit was all it was.

"Last chance," he told her.

"I just need ... water," she muttered and he had to hand it to her: she was good, real good. Her camo was perfect. She definitely looked like an old lady and she acted the part convincingly, but she was no doubt part of an advanced recon unit.

Where was her knife?

It had been right in her hand, but now it was gone.

She's playing head games, troop. Don't hesitate. Just like them dune coons in Iraq—they smile to your face and put a knife in your back first chance they get.

She inched forward and Penn stepped back two paces, then he fired. *See how good that feels, troop? Just like in the war. Nothing sweeter than pulling the trigger. It sorts out all and any problems.* He gave her a three-round burst dead-on. One round blew a chunk of meat from her shoulder. The second cored her throat. And the third shattered her jaw. Moaning, squealing, she writhed in a pool of blood that jetted steadily from her throat.

"You can't fool me," Penn whispered inside his hood. "I defend freedom."

Somewhere in the back of his mind, Captain Kane laughed with a shrill, grating sound.

As Penn watched her die with a soldier's clinical detachment, he remembered the heavy fighting in Mosul when he was with the Deuce Four. They bagged insurgents all day long, wasting those fucking reptiles in numbers. Some of them looked like women and kids, too, but they were animals, dirty, sneaking, conniving animals that worshipped a degenerate god and bathed in the innocent blood of Christians. Nothing but crawling vermin that needed to be stepped on.

And we sure stepped on 'em, didn't we, troop?

Staring down at her, feeling his American blood running hot, Penn realized he should have interrogated the woman or turned her over to command. He knew from experience that it was amazing how they'd start talking when you used your knife on them.

Kane was going to be pissed that he didn't follow procedure.

Then Penn recalled that he wasn't in Mosul.

This was America.

He had to keep that in mind.

THE DEMON

The glowing fireball in the sky did not dissipate, it expanded, a glowing incubus of destruction, fuming with rolling smoke and irradiated vapor and a roiling tornadic storm of debris. Its nucleus was a fiery red eye, hot as the guts of a sun, a glowing furnace of fissile material and subatomic particles. It churned and boiled with burning isotopes and hot gas, spinning into a luminous mushroom cloud waiting to rain to earth as deadly fallout.

Those on the ground were awestruck by its beauty. Its towering stem and mushrooming mass whirled and coalesced with a violent explosion of colors—red and orange, green and yellow and purple.

Though it was hell at ground zero below and above, the rising mass was like seeing the face of God and feeling his primal wrath.

PATRIOT

When he got out of the VA hospital, they diagnosed Penn with acute stress disorder, delusional disorder, and paranoid schizophrenia. All of which existed under the greater banner of PTSD. They jammed him up with the other crazies and made him go to weekly group therapy and one-on-one CBT, Cognitive Behavioral Therapy, with a google-eyed psych named Dr. Shirani.

Penn distrusted (and disliked) him immediately because he looked like an Iraqi insurgent, even though he claimed to be Pakistani. Shirani loaded him up with volume prescriptions of Paxil, Effexor, and Adderall, which sank his mind into a fog.

"The war is over, Corporal Penn," he told him. "You must let it be over. Terrible things happened, but we can get beyond that if we really want to. Do you understand what I am saying?"

Penn told him that he did: he knew how to play the game. The only way he was going to get his life back was by agreeing with Shirani, so he did. Even then, he was careful. He knew damn well that the headshrinkers from the VA watched him constantly. He figured they had planted cameras in the walls of his house and that more than one of his neighbors was spying on him and reporting in.

So he played it cool.

Very cool.

That's how you did it.

By the time of the big boom (as he liked to call it), he had gotten off most of his medication, and even the ones they gave him, he didn't take. He didn't need them. After all, he wasn't crazy. He figured he was one of the few sane people left, and after the Russians attacked, well, that pretty much proved it.

Quit ruminating, troop. Continue mission. You want to win this war, then you've got to do it like we did it in Mosul: house to house. There's no other way.

Oh, Captain Kane was right. He was always right. Penn had fought at his side in Echo 1/24 and he'd been with him ever since, some twenty years now. He knew if there was one thing he could trust, it was the captain. Fuck Shirani and the rest of those headshrinkers; Captain Kane knew the score and he'd never let him down.

But you're letting me down, troop. We got a job to do. Hump it, let's go! Lock and load, goddammit!

"Roger that," Penn said.

He moved deeper into the city, block by block by block. Everything he'd known all his life had been destroyed. Landmarks were gone. Buildings crumbled. Entire neighborhoods burned to cinders. Fire-blackened corpses filled the streets. Packs of hungry dogs fed upon them.

All in all, it was like some medieval hell.

He moved among the smoldering ruins, taking in the victims, searching for Russian infiltrators. They were here and they were smart. Captain Kane told him so. He came upon another woman. The clothes had been burned right off her along with most of her flesh. Her eyes were gone, the skin of her face hanging in ribbons. She had to be dead. Then she moved, mouthing some words that were incomprehensible.

Penn thought about capping her, but he figured she was no threat. He stepped around her. Before long, he started seeing people everywhere. Many of them, those that were capable, ran away when they saw him coming. Others didn't. He wasted two men because they were obvious infiltrators.

A group of filthy, ash-dusted toddlers were crying out for their mothers.

Penn wanted to help them, give them some water, but there was that odd clicking sound in his head again. Captain Kane said, *Don't be a bleeding-heart liberal, troop. It's a trap, you pussified sonofabitch. Can't you see? Just like in the war, they're using kids to draw you in.* Yeah, yeah. Of course. It all made sense. There were probably bombs, IEDs, hidden among them. Some Russian prick was probably hiding in the rubble. Soon as Penn got in close, he'd detonate it. That had happened in Mosul. It cost Ramirez his fucking legs.

"Not this time," Penn whispered.

Do the deed, troop. Maintain mission profile.

The children's tear-filled eyes watching him, seeing an adult that would help them, they reached out to him … and he gave them two three-round bursts, greasing them. They blew apart like rag dolls, their stuffing scattered in every which direction.

It sickened Penn, but he turned away quickly. He couldn't be vomiting in his hood. He was trained better than that.

He made a grid search through the wreckage, but he couldn't find the infiltrator. Some of them were very, very good. And why not? They'd been training for this eventuality for years. He remembered reading in *Soldier of Fortune* how the Russians had built an entire city they called Little America. Soldiers and intelligence operatives lived there, immersing themselves in American culture. They watched American TV shows and listened to American music. Spoke only English and ate only American food. They *became* Americans for the day when they would invade the United States and set up regional puppet governments.

Trust no one, troop. No one.

Deeper into the city, he saw groups of soldiers in NBC suits like his, dragging corpses around. They pulled them from gutters and creeks and even the river itself. They were blackened, swollen things. They didn't look like people, more like mannequins that had been turned into charcoal. They flaked away and fell apart as the soldiers manhandled them. They tossed them atop great heaps and then doused them with diesel fuel from a tanker and lit them up. It was probably the only way to dispose of their radioactive remains, which were now essentially nuclear waste.

Penn ducked away from them, hiding in the ruins, not really certain they were American soldiers at all. It was hard to know, hard to tell. Those fucking Russians were crafty as hell. As he watched them from his hide, he had trouble controlling his breathing. His gloved hands shook on his rifle. He kept hearing that odd clicking noise in his head that reminded him unpleasantly of wet fingers snapping.

After a time, he slipped away, putting some distance between himself and the soldiers. He did not trust them. They wore American-issue rad suits, but that didn't mean anything. His enemies were many, and they were crafty.

THE DEMON

The heat wave from the initial blast spread with hurricane force as the fireball opened like a burning eye in the sky. It was hungry to burn, seeking out any and all flammable materials and igniting them instantly in a deadly firestorm. The incinerating heat blasted through the streets, melting steel and baking the paint right off of cars. Heaps of wreckage that had once been houses or buildings went up in flames. People were instantly vaporized; some melted like wax, others carbonized into blackened, twisted shapes. Many left only smoky smudges and shadowy outlines against brick and concrete walls as they were flash-fried. The shockwave had stomped everything to ruin from the initial blast like Godzilla laying waste to Tokyo, and like the big fellah, everything burned under the saturation of its atomic breath.

And the fires kept burning, fed by exploding gas lines and propane tanks, reservoirs of gasoline and diesel fuel. Downed electrical lines added to the unleashed fury of the devastation. In the end, the very things that fed the city destroyed it.

BODY COUNT

It was hard to know where he was in the city because everything had been so radically altered. Landmarks were flattened. Entire streets heaped with rubble. Nothing was recognizable. Twice, he heard a chopper flying over the city. He wondered if it was Russian.

He came upon a man who was giggling. He had nothing to laugh at because most of his face was burned away. Yet, he kept giggling, pink, foamy drool running from his mouth like soap suds. He pointed at Penn with a hand that was more bone than hand. The flesh hung from it like Spanish Moss.

"Where's my weapon, soldier?" he asked in a scraping voice, spitting out a glob of blood. "I'm ready to fight for the good old US of A! Gimme a weapon! You hear? *Gimme a fucking weapon!*"

For not the first time, Penn trembled with fear. The dead. The dying. The insane. The maimed. There seemed to be no one else left.

"I wanna fucking weapon!" the wraith demanded, clawing out with his hands, snapping his teeth as if he was ready to bite.

Penn wasted him. Despite his condition, it took two three-rounds bursts to take the life out of him. When he finally collapsed in the dirt, barely any blood came out of him.

The shooting drew the attention of a group of soldiers and they fired in his direction. The rounds were screaming around him, thudding into bricks and broken walls. Penn didn't fire back because Captain Kane told him that would be a bad idea. *Evade, troop! Evade and escape!* So that's exactly what Penn did. He leapfrogged through the wreckage, darting into the teetering skeleton of a building and crawling over a mound of corpses and burnt furniture. He managed to lose them, but it had been close.

You'll want to be careful in the future, numbnuts, Kane snapped at him. *Don't be drawing in the enemy. Shooting is too loud. Use your knife.*

"Yes, sir!" Penn snapped in his hood, knowing he was only as good as his leadership.

Sweating in his suit, his dosimeter telling him he was skirting a very hot section of the city—it was cooking at something like 600 roentgens—he backed away, ducking from one smoldering heap of refuse to the next, pulling back through the maze of destruction until he was getting a reading of 300. He had to be careful: the suit could only take so much exposure before its shielding broke down.

He finally rested in the ruptured shell of a convenience store. He thought it might be the 7-11 on 27th, but there was no way to know for sure. He sipped water from the tube in his hood, thinking of the chili dogs he used to get there. God, it seemed like ages ago now.

Then Captain Kane's voice cut through his thoughts, *Watch it, troop!* He looked around. He saw nothing.

Behind you!

The mountain of debris at his back shifted and he saw a woman coming at him. He tried to get his rifle up, but she attacked. She had something in her hand—a piece of rebar—and she cracked him in the head with it. He saw stars and dropped his rifle. She crawled her way to him, muttering unintelligible things through a mouth filled with blood. She swung at him again and he avoided it. He tried to scamper free, but it was hard to move that quickly or that decisively in the suit. She took full advantage of the situation and cracked him in the leg. The pain was intense, but the force of the blow sent him sliding down the hill of debris. Otherwise, she would have had him.

She was an absolute horror—her clothes had been burned off and the flesh beneath was cured to fissured, black leather. Her lower jaw was missing, a rib bone jutting from her side, her eyes bright white. All of that was bad enough, but what was worse was the incinerated baby she cradled in one arm.

Penn had no idea how she still moved.

But she did and she was on him before he could pull his 9mm. *The knife, troop! The knife!* Penn pulled it, avoided the rebar and stomped her kneecap. She fell, but did not drop the baby. He was on her immediately. He drove the knife into her belly, her throat, finally right into her left eye socket. She went through some kind of jerking, horrible seizure, vomiting out curds of flesh, then went still.

After that, he was very careful.

THE DEMON

The dead and dying far outnumbered the living. The lucky ones went in the blast itself or were killed in the onslaught of the shockwave and resultant firestorm. Like the city center itself, they were cooked, burned to ash, trapped beneath falling buildings or incinerated in their own living rooms. Those that somehow, freakishly, managed to live through that were caught in the backblast which made houses either implode or explode. They were tossed into the air, burning like matchheads, smashed against buildings, bodies ruptured and torn, pressure waves making them explode like deep-sea fish losing compression—internal organs and copious amounts of blood ejected from their mouths.

The city was a wasteland of mangled cars, trucks, and buses, shattered glass and rubble, mounds of brick and smoldering debris. Churning black clouds of smoke blew through the twisted maze of streets along with pockets of radioactive steam and deadly dust clouds of fallout.

The survivors dug themselves out hour after hour, emerging from shattered houses and fallen buildings, filthy and bleeding, cut and torn, many blasted white with concrete dust. They staggered about, most of them struck mad, many falling down to their knees to pray and others shouting out their hatred of the politicians who'd allowed something like this to happen in the first place. They shambled about mindlessly, stunned, in shock, stepping over burning bodies and parts thereof. But for every one that escaped, fifty were trapped screaming, crushed and mangled in the wreckage.

This was hell at ground zero.

And above them, the demon laughed.

DEATH DEALER

Even though Captain Kane warned him against it, he used his rifle to waste more infiltrators. They seemed to be everywhere—creeping, hulking, inhuman things that crawled out of the blowing smoke and dust, sliding free from the remains of buildings like snakes. They kept coming for him. Some ran, but many reached out for him, so he blew them away. At first, the killing sickened him. It was like fucking Mosul all over again, but after a time it was no worse than playing *Call of Duty*, if you thought about it in the right way.

Hell, the people he took down didn't even seem real after a time.

They ain't people, shithead, Captain Kane reminded him again and again. *No more than they were people in the land of the sand. Insurgents. Infiltrators. Fucking extremists. They're here to usurp us. To rape and murder and pillage and force us to worship their evil god.*

Question is: are we gonna stand for it?

Or are we going to fuck 'em where they shit?

Penn knew the answer to that because he was a patriot. He'd go down fighting like a real American, like Chuck Norris or Vin Diesel, wrapped in the flag with his finger on the trigger and blood in his mouth.

Now you're talking, troop!

Despite the filters in his mask, he could smell the roasted bodies in the street. They were everywhere. And scattered among them were the dying, swollen and broken, bubbles of blood bursting from their lips. Flies were all over them. Birds were pecking at them. Bodies were floating in pools of contaminated water from burst water mains and hydrants. Many streets were impassable with rubble, but others were crowded with the dead.

He avoided these as much as possible.

More than once, he was certain they were moving, masses of the dead wriggling like maggots.

It's all in your head, kid, Kane reassured him. *Forget about those drugs they had you on. Forget about bullshit like borderline personality disorder and aggressive anti-social tendencies. Double-talk. Bullshit. Spin. Ain't nothing wrong with you.*

Yet, despite what the captain said, Penn had the most disconcerting feeling that there was something wrong with him. He had a rising feeling of anxiety, a nameless sort of paranoia that he was not only being watched, but followed.

He was sweating in his suit, confused, turned around, led deeper into this twisted labyrinth of hell. He heard footsteps crunching through broken glass. He whirled around, but there was no one. He edged between two still-standing walls of cinder block. He caught movement out of the corner of his eye and fired.

Nothing.

Nothing.

Get your shit together, troop. Ain't no one after you.

But Penn was not convinced of that. Even the captain's voice sounded unsure. This wasn't how it was supposed to be. He was the hunter, not the hunted. He saw shadows move. Heard noises of shifting debris. Once, outside the burnt shell of a shoe store—amused that there were hundreds of shoes in the street waiting for feet—he heard a peal of cold, braying laughter.

Keep it together.

He saw a woman run into an alley, then cut through a gaping hole in the wall of a building. She looked back at him and smiled. She was taunting him, he knew, and everything he stood for. He went after her. He searched around through what looked like a Panera Bread shop. It had been exposed to great heat and was still smoldering.

Find her, troop. She's one of them.

But Penn knew that much. He moved behind the counter and a voice said, *"Close ... oh, so close now."*

He came around with his rifle, but she dove at him out of the shadows, knocking him down. He tried to get his M4 up, but the barrel snagged on a dangling pipe. By then, she was on top of him, naked and wild, the hair burned from her head, her face a contorted mask with feral eyes and a slobbering yellow mouth. She pounded and clawed at his hood, trying desperately to get at his eyes.

As she battered at him, he pulled his 9mm Beretta and put three rounds into her. She collapsed, bleeding and spasming on him. He shoved her aside, grabbed his rifle and scrambled to his feet.

Now he was in the thick of it.

A little boy peered from behind an overturned table and Penn shot him. His aim was perfect. He splashed the kid's face from the skull beneath.

There was a scream.

Another woman charged him. He wasted her, punching black holes into her chest. She spun around like a top, blood jetting from her in gouts. A man tried to race for the door and Penn took him out with another three-round burst.

Then he slipped back outside.

It was dangerous to get caught inside like that. He'd gone through some real hairy moments in Mosul when they were cleaning out buildings room by room. If you got trapped like that, it was an easy way to die.

He ran the best he could in the NBC suit, stumbling into a courtyard. He leaned against a van and caught his breath. There. That was better.

After a time, he decided it was time to get back to his shelter. He needed rest. He wasn't thinking so good, making one mistake after another. One of these times, he was going to get himself into a fix that even the captain couldn't get him out of.

Time to escape and evade, troop. You've done some fine work today. But there's always tomorrow.

Words of wisdom.

He lost the street. It was there somewhere, most of it buried beneath an avalanche of wreckage, but he couldn't get at it. He moved from the skeleton of one building after another. They weren't much more than standing walls housing mountains of debris and blackened corpses.

He ascended a hill of bricks and timbers and slid carefully down the other side, cutting through a hole in a wall and stopping dead.

Hell was this?

Three bodies hung by feet. Throats slit. Somebody had pounded nails through their feet into an exposed rafter above. They had inverted crosses painted in blood on their pale faces. The blood was still dripping from their throats.

Scared, shaking inside, Penn didn't know what to make of it. Had they been killed before they were hoisted up or had it been after, like a sacrifice?

Panic leaped inside him. It ran wild in his guts like mice on a wheel. Cold sweat beading his face, he let out a low, sharp cry and ran, vaulting over things, tripping, falling, getting up again. He crawled through a window into a small yard where a dog, still chained to a fence, was burning with a foul stench. Captain Kane shouted at him about all the racket he was making, but the panic and hysteria won out.

He found the street.

It was hip-deep in a sea of corpses. Dozens and dozens of people had rushed from shops after the initial blast and had been cooked alive into a smoldering, fused mass of reaching limbs and mangled bodies. An overpowering, nauseous stink like burned feathers hung in a dirty haze over them.

Penn froze there. He could not move because he could feel them watching him, dead eyes piercing him, impaling him, holding him fast.

Careful now, troop. Your mind is playing tricks on you.

But was it? He couldn't be sure of anything. In the ruins to either side of him, he heard things moving, shifting, crunching and grinding beneath footsteps. Sliding sounds. A muffled boar-like grunting off to the left. A moist sound behind him, like bones pulled from a ripening carcass.

He swallowed, his heart pounding in his throat, his face lubricated with sweat. He studied the bodies ahead of him. If he climbed over them, he'd reach the avenue on the other side which looked relatively clear and wide open. His instinct and training told him that was the best route. The safest route. After all, he sure as hell didn't want to go back, ducking around in shattered buildings. But to go forward ... to wade through those bodies. In his mind, he could see them moving. Soon as he was deep in their midst, they would start moving, creeping, mouths opening and fleshless hands reaching out for him.

He could hear Dr. Shirani's voice warning him against such things, about letting subjective impressions take on physical reality.

"I'm not afraid of the dead ones," Penn said out loud, almost as if he had to hear himself say it.

He moved forward at a low crouch, fanning his rifle back and forth, ready for action. When you were a patriot, you had to do things that were unpleasant. And when you were in enemy territory, you had to be ready to do the unthinkable.

Don't look at them, troop. They might look back.

The captain was fucking with him. They couldn't look at him because they had no eyes. Most faces were melted like tallow; it was hard to say where their eyes had even been. He stepped carefully, lightly through the corpses with well-placed steps. He bumped the husk of a man and he broke apart. A hand crunched like burnt plastic under his boot. The cadaver of a little girl, curled up like a dead spider, held a charred doll out to him.

A few more leaps and he was through them.

He cut down the avenue, feeling exposed. He got behind an overturned minivan. A flaking corpse inside still clutched the steering wheel.

"I've been waiting for you," a voice said.

Penn swung around, bringing up his rifle. Another madwoman. She was covered in layers of grime and dust, her clothes burned right off her. She sat on an overturned garbage can. She had dark eyes and white teeth.

"Sooner or later our paths were destined to cross," she said, far too calmly and smoothly for the condition she was in. "Soldier boy. The good little killer."

Something about her made Penn feel cold inside. He wasn't entirely convinced that she was real. Maybe she existed only in his mind. Nothing made sense. Yet, the chill she inspired was very real. He was certain that what she was on the outside, she was not on the inside. Something terrible lived under her skin. In his mind, he caught glimpses of it … crawling spiders, a hissing snake, a heap of maggots, then something like a steaming pile of vomit that became a shapeless animal jelly that smiled at him.

"Get away from me," Penn said, backing away. He tripped over the curb and went on his ass.

She laughed. It was that cold braying he'd heard earlier … a woman, but with the guttural laughter of a man. He felt himself swooning with terror. As he stared at her, her face changed. It melted, reconfigured itself. It was Captain Kane. No, it was Dr. Shirani. No, no, no … it was his mother, his sister. It morphed into the death-ravaged faces of insurgents he'd killed during the war. Then it was the face of a little boy in a pristine dark burial suit, his face shining like white grease. His eyes were huge and impossibly black.

"Do you enjoy killing, soldier boy? Does it make you feel complete? Hmm?" it asked in a gravelly voice.

"Get away from me!"

The boy shook his head. "But I won't and you can't make me." He grinned and his teeth were black and gnarled, standing out in great contrast to his bloodless face. "Did you like the bodies I hung up for you? I knew you'd appreciate them. They screamed your name as they died."

An Imp, a fucking devil from hell! The voice of Captain Kane warned him.

But that wasn't so. It couldn't be so. This was some type of camouflage Russian infiltrators were using. *Yes, yes, that was it!* Alex Jones had talked about it. BAC—Bionic Adaptive Camouflage. Using a spooky, high-tech photonic camo material, Russian Spetsnaz operatives could make themselves appear as anything. A colossal mind game to draw the enemy into killing fields.

"You've done fine and holy work, soldier boy, and I admire you," the boy told him. "Oh yes, and how much I admire your cold-blooded drive."

The boy giggled at this. As he sat on the garbage can, Penn noticed that he had no shoes. His pants were pulled up to the knee and his legs were matted with coarse black hair. His feet were the cloven-hoofs of a goat.

Penn fired.

He opened up on full auto, drilling the kid with a flurry of eight or ten rounds. Christ, it should have blown him right off the garbage can, but it didn't. The slugs passed clean through him as if he was made of smoke.

"It won't be that easy," said the boy.

His voice echoed in Penn's head, each word pounding deep into his gray matter like a spike with a burst of incapacitating red agony. He cried out, dropping his rifle. The pain was so intense, he could not think. He crawled away on all fours, whimpering like a kicked dog. Inside his hood, he drooled and tears ran from his eyes.

A group of survivors, a woman and a man holding up a third who was horribly blistered with burns, came in his direction.

"Help," the woman said in a pitiful, broken voice. "We need help."

"Shall we help them?" the boy asked.

He laughed and pointed his index finger at them. They screamed as they burst into flames, instantly cremated down to skeletons that broke apart as they hit the streets. The woman's smoldering skull rolled toward Penn.

When he looked back, the boy was gone ... yet his eyes still floated there, as did his grinning mouth. Penn jumped to his feet and ran. He moved drunkenly, tripping over his own feet. He could hear Kane's voice telling him that he was fucking up, that he'd lost his rifle. But he didn't care, he didn't care about anything.

"Together, we'll do great things," the boy's voice promised him.

Penn ran, shrieking and sobbing, his mind fragmenting.

THE DEMON

The mushroom cloud hung over the city, sparkling with fission-hot radionucleotides, sucking up radioactive dust and fuming atomic steam. It was a swirling, hungry, deadly vortex that should have dispersed, but did not. If anything, it looked larger and fuller. Its stem was like a mighty pillar, its ever-rotating cap fleshing itself out until it became a perfect sphere that was hot as a reactor core, blazing and shining and throwing out irregular bursts of ionized particles, weird blue-green forks of lightning, and glowing blobs of radioactive plasma. It was white heat and red death, a gigantic pulsating monster whose very core flickered with enriched uranium wrapped around a skeleton of lethal cesium-137.

This was the devil that mankind had made and it wasn't going anywhere.

SOUL STALKER

The night was bad.

It was worse than anything he could imagine.

When the sun went down—what there was of it with all the dust and smoke in the atmosphere—the mushroom cloud still had not dissipated. It should have been blown clean by then, but it hovered over the graveyard of the city, glowing orange and finally red, taking on the unmistakable shape of a leering skull. Penn was certain it was looking at him.

He tried to escape it.

He used every trick of escape and evasion he'd been taught, but mostly he was driven by instinct. And fear. Oh yes, a cold and inescapable terror that had taken root deep inside of him, filling his guts, spreading out into his chest, and blossoming like funeral orchids in his head. He had never known anything like it. It was debilitating. It fogged his mind. It made his body shudder. It drowned him in a cold, stinking sweat.

He hid in ruined buildings.

He lost himself in dark pockets of shadow.

He crawled on his belly through the rubble.

He wormed into the wreckage of houses.

He curled up inside a drainage pipe.

No good, no good, just no damn good. The skull was always there.

And even when it was out of sight, he could feel it looking at him the way the boy had—its gaze hot, burning into him.

All night long, he could hear things moving around him. Dragging sounds. Rustling sounds. Slithering sounds. It was in his mind, it had to be in his mind. And whenever a shred of rationality that still existed in his fevered brain convinced him of the same, he heard the voice of the boy taunting him.

You've done fine and holy work, soldier boy, and I admire you.

The voice came out of the darkness. It echoed through the pipe. It spoke inside Penn's hood. It came from the mouths of corpses.

By dawn, he was a trembling wreck.

Somehow, someway, he had moved deeper into the city in his delirium. The river was before him and it was crowded with blackened corpses, buzzards and crows pecking away at them. Penn knew he had to retreat. He had to get back to his shelter. What disturbed him was how alone he was. Captain Kane was no longer barking orders, no longer instructing, no longer leading him. Penn called out for him again and again, but he was just gone.

Alone, so terribly, horribly alone.

Then he discovered that he wasn't alone at all.

A thick, cloying mist was rising from the river and out of it materialized the boy. His eyes were like pools of glistening red ink that spilled tears of blood down his phosphorescently white face.

"Soldier boy," he called. "Oh, soldier boy."

Penn was hiding behind a broken wall. He could hear the boy getting closer. He brought up his 9mm. He'd kill him. He'd put every round he had into him. Then he'd stab him and keep stabbing him.

The boy stopped a good distance away. He looked up at the luminous red skull in the sky, then clapped his hands together. There was a sudden crackling like static electricity. The air grew thin and sparkled with energy. Shadows seemed to crawl. The mist boiled.

And in the river, the corpses began to move.

Shrunken, burnt things whose skeletons were bursting through their scorched hides, they stood up, a fetid army of the dead. Faces melted to bone, bodies puckered with decay; they stepped from the water with clouds of carrion flies buzzing about them.

"Find him," said the boy.

Screaming, Penn emptied his Beretta into them and then threw it. He ran, stumbling through the wreckage of the city, crawling over piles of rubble and splashing through ponds of standing water, moving, ever moving. And each time he dared to look back, the boy was closer. The dead moved around him in a maggoty throng, some walking, some crawling, some inching like worms.

Penn kept going, moving in a confused, circuitous path until, again, he was back at the river and the dead were all around him. As he screamed what was left of his mind away and they reached out for him with puffy hands, they suddenly dropped to the ground. He crawled through them. They fell to pieces beneath him, but he kept creeping until he was black with their drainage and splashed with their fluids.

"Enough, soldier boy. Quite enough," said the boy. "Come to me now so that we can get on with things. Daylight is wasting."

Penn fought with everything he had, but he could not run. He could hide no more. The boy had him. He was like a wind-up toy, and he walked towards him, shaking, jerking with contractions of terror. As the boy held out a hand that was the yellowed, scaly claw of a beast, he pulled his knife and tried stabbing him, but it was no good. It was like trying to cut fog. There was no resistance.

There was essentially … nothing.

The boy seized his arm with a crushing, vise-like strength, crushing the bones within. Penn pissed himself and dropped to his knees. His arm was smoldering … the boy's fingers had burned right through his suit with a stink of melted rubber and sulfur.

"Now, we meet on common ground, eh, soldier boy?"

The boy's eyes had swollen in their flayed sockets like blood-seeped eggs. He grinned and his teeth were fine and sharp like fish bones, the gums like raw hamburger.

"You've made a fine and merry work collecting souls," he said, black smoke rolling out of his mouth with every word. "But now I must have them. I collect such things as you might have guessed, my soldier boy."

The Devil, the Devil, the Devil, said a voice in the cauldron of Penn's mind. It sounded very much like Captain Kane's voice, but weak and anemic like the voice of an old man broken by long years of suffering.

"And there's only one way to do that, I'm afraid."

Without further ado, the boy took hold of him like a rag doll, lifting him off his feet and holding him in the air before him. Penn cried. He screamed. He shouted. But the hands bore down with devastating strength, squeezing Penn in an eruption of agony until his guts were forced from his mouth like those of a stepped-upon toad. Simultaneously, his bones were shattered, muscles torn free from their roots, tendons and ligaments snapped, organs macerated, lungs rupturing and heart stopping in a paroxysm of blood and meat, and his brain blew out of his ears and eye sockets in a gray-pink sludge.

As Penn was turned inside out to release the trapped souls he had taken, he was quite—and thankfully—dead.

KING OF FLIES

Misery is manifold.
The wretchedness of earth is multiform.
Poe wrote those words, and ever since the bombs dropped, Sparks had been living them. Day by awful day, he skulked in the shuttered darkness like a rat, his mind slowly decaying into a soft, warm pulp. There were no good days. No moments of optimism. There was only the endless night that wrapped its arms around him and held him tight like a lover.

By his own reckoning, he'd been trapped in the cellar for over two weeks now. He couldn't be sure, of course, because there was no separation between day and night any longer. So much debris and soot had been sucked up into the atmosphere by the blasts that it blocked out the sun, turning the world into a gray void.

But it'll pass, he kept telling himself. *It has to pass.*

Yes, that was true. That was what they always said in their doomsday projections. That sooner or later, the debris would fall back to the earth as deadly fallout. And when that happened, *if* that happened, a lot of those who'd survived the initial attack were going to die.

When the first bomb exploded over the city, Sparks had been going down the basement steps, bringing a box of books down for storage. He just didn't have space for them in his over-crowded room on the third floor. The shock wave had thrown him down the stairs and the entire house—one of those big old Victorian monsters near the university—had collapsed, sealing him up in the bowels of the cellar.

There was no way out.

God knew, he'd tried worming his way through the rubble a dozen times, but there were simply no spaces between the timbers and bricks and shattered walls big enough to accommodate a man. He'd even tried shifting some of the wreckage with a pry bar. Each time he did, what was above him began to move and groan, threatening to come right down on top of him and squash him flat.

The house had been big and so was the cellar beneath it. Some of it was blocked with debris, but much of it he could get to. The problem was, whenever he went exploring, trying desperately to find something to eat, he had trouble finding his way back to his little hidey-hole behind the furnace. It was safe there. A broken pipe overhead dripped water, enough to keep him from dehydrating. That was something.

But, oh Christ, he was so hungry.

So desperately hungry.

The second day, he'd discovered that if he crawled on the floor, he could squeeze himself beneath the heavy fallen timbers and jagged sections of floorboards. It was a bit nerve-wracking with the weight of the wrecked house teetering and creaking above him, but after about twenty feet, he came to an outer sandstone wall. A little more wriggling and he found a window. It was mostly blocked by hanging ductwork and a deadfall of rafters, but he was able to peer between two planks and see the outside world through the broken pane.

What he saw was horrifying.

The neighborhood had mostly been laid flat, and the only light came from fires that were still burning. They limned the destruction in some detail. But the worst thing was that the sky seemed to be glowing. He could see a gigantic, radiant mushroom cloud hanging above the city like a hideous face, a floating evil puppet that stared down at the graveyard of civilization with a sardonic grimace.

In his frenzied mind, it was Poe's *Crepuscularia*, the Death's-headed sphinx.

The very sight of it made him jump back and he tripped over the remains of an old bookshelf and hit the floor with a resounding crash. He struck his head, but the pain wasn't too bad. He lay there—beaten, hopeless, praying for death as tears ran down his cheeks.

There'd been a bit of luck at first. Over in the cage where all the roomers stored things they couldn't fit in their rooms—everything from bikes to camping equipment to furniture to Christmas decorations and wrapping paper—he'd come across a Rubbermaid container of Power Bars. He figured they'd belonged to Kelsie Noel, the cute redhead on the second floor. Kelsie was pre-med, and she hiked and backpacked in her spare time. There were only six bars and he'd made them last a week..

It had been four days now since he'd eaten … or was it five? He couldn't be sure. The only thing he *was* sure of were the damned flies. They seemed to be everywhere. He'd wake up and they'd be crawling on his face, nipping at his throat. Obviously, they were feeding well.

Not like me, not like me.

He'd always been pretty lean and now he was becoming emaciated. He could feel the rungs of his ribs and protruding bones at his wrists. It wasn't good at all. His skin was itchy all the time, flaking away like chalk. It felt like he was made of crumbling papier-mâché. His gums ached. His lips were split open from the dryness and he was coughing out blood.

Radiation sickness, that dire voice in his head kept telling him, but he refused to listen, he just refused.

One day, he heard a voice;

You're dreaming. You're losing your fucking mind, he warned himself.

But no, interestingly enough, he heard the voice again. A woman's voice, very dry and pain-wracked, but it was most assuredly there.

"... help me ... oh dear God ... help me ..."

It was coming from the far opposite end of the cellar. He figured it couldn't be too far from the window he'd looked out of the first night.

He debated going over there. It was a treacherous crawl through the wreckage. It was inviting disaster. He knew damn well that at any moment, the entire goddamn house could come down right on top of him. Who knew what was even keeping it from doing so.

But a voice ... a human voice.

Excited, afraid, desperate, he made the long crawl again and it seemed that the passage which was framed by broken sections of sheetrock and splintered joists was even tighter this time.

Finally, he saw a feeble light and knew he was near the window. He saw suspended dust in its beams. Whether that was from daylight, moonlight, firelight, or that glowing horror in the sky, he could not say. The voice came again, though it sounded significantly weaker, if that was even possible.

"Is ... is someone there?" he asked; a strange, inexplicable fear rising in him that there would be an answer, not from someone but some*thing*. It was irrational and downright silly, but he couldn't help himself. His brain was so programmed from watching godawful post-apocalyptic B-movies as a kid on Saturday afternoons with his mom—*The Day the World Ended, Panic in Year Zero,* and *The Last Man on Earth,* to name but a few—that he fully expected some slavering mutation would be hiding in the dark, baiting him in.

He heard a low, pathetic moaning.

It came from somewhere behind him. He would have to feel his way toward it. On his hands and knees, he did just that. He crawled under hanging wreckage and over heaped debris and he *felt* rather than saw that he was getting closer to whoever it was. He smelled a revolting odor of burnt hair and cooked flesh, the latter smelling quite like burnt chicken. It was nauseating and appealing at the same time.

"Help me ... someone help me ..."

That voice. *That voice.* It was very familiar, but his head was so filled with cobwebs that he couldn't place it. Then he did: Emily. Emily Impiri. She owned the building. Her husband (she'd told Sparks) had bought the Victorian and had it remodeled into a rooming house. He'd done the same with five or six other buildings.

"Emily?" Sparks said. "Emily? Where are you?"

That's when a light clicked on. It was not only brilliant, but blinding. It was like stepping into the sunlight after days in a cave.

It was Emily, all right.

She was lying on the floor about ten feet away, rubble scattered about her. A huge timber had pinned her legs. She had a flashlight in her hand. The beam was weak, but it was like daylight to him.

He scrambled over to her, waving flies from her face.

Oh, she was in a state. Most of the hair was burned from her head. Her face was scorched. Her exposed belly and breasts were charred and blistered. The smell of her cooked flesh was almost too much to take. And what made it all so much more horrible was that Emily was in her third trimester, seven months pregnant.

"... the baby ... oh, my baby ..."

Sparks was beside himself. He froze up. He didn't know what to do. She was dying and he knew it. Chances were, her child was already dead. *Oh God, oh God.* He had no medical training. He was an English Lit major at the U and an unabashed Poe nerd who also co-edited a small—*very* small—EAP-themed literary magazine called *Oval Portraits*. He could tell you at length about Poe's textural criticism, his re-tooling of the Gothics, how personal tragedy, poverty, and alcoholism sculpted the person (and writer) he became ... but he knew nothing about taking care of the injured.

But he had to man up and he knew it.

"It's okay, Emily," he said in a voice that did not even convince himself.

He was afraid to touch her. Partly because he thought he would hurt her and, partly because the very sight of her made him squeamish.

The timber had not only trapped her legs with its immense girth and weight, it had smashed them. There was dried blood everywhere, her legs swollen purple. A shard of bone jutted from her left ankle. He had to get the timber off her. He tried pulling on it, but the damn thing had to weigh well over 500 pounds. Okay. That wouldn't work.

As she watched him with one bulging, blood-matted eye (the other was lost in a mass of leathery, burnt tissue), he pulled the flashlight from her fingers and gagged when strings of skin came away with it.

She must have been out in the blast, he thought. *Somehow, she fought her way down here and the ceiling came down on her.*

Yes, that was the only explanation.

With the flashlight, he searched about for something to move the timber with. He had a pry bar behind the furnace where his dirty blanket was, but he didn't want to go back all that way. He had to get this done now. He found a section of old cast-iron pipe. It was heavy and solid. It was the best he was going to do under the circumstances.

"Emily … Emily? You have to listen to my voice," he said, panting not so much out of exertion but out of stress. "I'm going to try shifting this timber. When I do, you have to pull yourself free. I know you're weak, but you have to try. Can you do that?"

She muttered something that he decided was an affirmative. Her voice sounded like it was spoken through wet leaves.

He set the flashlight on the floor and wedged a good five inches of the pipe beneath the timber after some groaning and grunting. It shifted slightly and Emily jerked with agony. Her lips were bloated and rubbery-looking, her tongue like a swollen blue-black leech as it protruded from her mouth.

"Okay," he breathed. "On the count of one … two … three …"

He was certain he could move the timber. The rest would be up to Emily and that was what he worried about.

Tensing his arms and putting his back into it, he bore down on the pipe, using it as a lever. The timber moved an inch.

Two.

Three.

Emily tried to pull herself free, letting out a scream of pain in the process. Sparks moved it another inch … and then there was a groaning, grinding noise from above and a terrible rumbling. Dust and lathing rained down on him. A plank hit him in the head and he dropped the pipe, tossing himself aside as the shattered ceiling above came down.

Emily made a grunting sound, a sort of forced expulsion of air. He pulled debris away from her, finally freeing the flashlight. The beam was filled with dust.

"I'll get you out," he told her. "Just give me a minute."

But when he got her clear, he saw that it was hopeless. Another pipe had swung down—the timber must have been holding it up—and smashed right into her face, neatly splitting her head in two. Blood and pink-gray curds of brain pooled around her.

Sparks fell back and away, making a hysterical gibbering sound. She was dead. She would have died anyway, but he had hastened the process.

He sat there, shaking. "Emily … oh, Jesus Christ … Emily …"

Crouched behind the furnace, a filthy thing in ragged clothes, stinking of urine, body odor, and mildew, he listened to the flies. They seemed to be everywhere. He swatted them away, but they kept coming back. They liked to hover about his ears. *Bzzzzzzt! Bzzzzzzt!* It drove him crazy. God, how he hated them. How they disgusted him. Yet, despite the sacking of the world, they were thriving.

Thriving.

He thought about the rats. He heard them quite frequently. At first, he'd been appalled, worrying that they might try to eat him as he slept, but after a time, he began thinking of ways to catch them. *They're food. They're meat. Plump and juicy.* But they were fast. They were survivors. His night vision was better than it had been at first, but he still wasn't quick enough to get one.

There's always Emily.

No, no, no. He clutched his hands to his head to shut out that idea. He wasn't about to become a ghoul. The very idea made him feel unclean inside, the personification of human evil.

He listened to the flies.

It had been days now since he'd heard anything like sirens or screaming in the distance. Was that a good thing or a bad thing?

He had the flashlight, but it was getting low on batteries so he didn't dare use it. It was for special occasions only.

As the days passed, he became aware that very often his thinking brain was being overruled by something else, something desperate and dangerous that he figured was instinct. It knew very well how to survive. It was the only thing that mattered: keep breathing, keep fighting for another day. But to do that he needed to eat.

The rats, it told him. *If they're feeding on Emily's body, then that's a good place to hunt them.*

Yes, yes, that made sense. The idea of eating rats had once been repulsive, but now it didn't sound so repulsive at all. Meat was meat. He had to keep that in mind: die of slow, agonizing starvation or eat rats. Eating them was better than eating other things.

He waited in the subterranean darkness, hungry, so godawful hungry. There were claws in his stomach. Biting teeth. Immense hollows that could never be filled. He woke from constant feverish nightmares wringing wet with sweat, stinking and dirty, certain he had been buried alive.

How much more? he asked himself. *How much more can I take?*

If only he could get outside. But, no, what was the point of that? Out into that radiation-soaked hell zone to die like the others, curled up like a dead worm.

Yes, that would have been bad ... but wasn't it worse down here in this blackness, this awful cellar that stank of dankness and dark soil and rotting things? It was like slowly suffocating in a buried box and the more he thought about it, the more he could not breath. The air was being squeezed from his lungs and he cried out silently, gasping, rolling on the floor.

Alone.

Alone.

Alone.

Then a large meat fly landed on his face. Another settled on his ear, gently buzzing.

That's when he realized he was not alone at all.

How long had Emily been dead now?

A week?

Ten days?

Sparks wasn't sure of anything anymore. His brain did not seem to work properly. Everything before the blast was convoluted, a gray haze that made little sense. He hid behind the furnace, thinking, plotting, planning, but mostly dreaming.

But what do I dream about? For God's sake, what do I dream about?

He could never remember, only that they were very vivid and that he woke from them shaking and muttering terrible things under his breath.

He was slowly losing touch with reality, but the one thing that anchored him to the real world was hunger. As the days added up and he wasted away, the slow starvation had gone from awful hunger pangs to a physical agony that tormented him constantly. He could think of nothing but food, imagine nothing but sinking his teeth into something. The need to feed was overwhelming and absolutely uncontrollable.

Which, of course, made him think of Emily.

He told himself he needed to crawl over to her. The rats were probably feeding on her and the idea of that was revolting. He would go over there and cover her with something so they couldn't get at her. Maybe hide her somewhere they couldn't find her.

But that's all you'll do, he warned himself.

Despite the situation, he was still a man and he needed to act like one. He was not a dirty, slinking animal. He would not be reduced to some terrible creature that would eat anything to survive. Maybe civilization had bit the big one, but he wasn't about to become a monster.

After many weeks in the claustrophobic darkness, starving, shivering with fevers, it was hard to know if he was awake or dreaming or trapped in some leaden netherworld in-between. The only constant, unabating connection to reality was the hunger that would never leave him alone. His mind had become a gray fuzz. Images of friends and family seemed to have no point of reference and it got so he couldn't remember their names or if they'd even been real in the first place.

His only companions were the flies.

They were the only true reality.

Flies, he thought. *Oh yes, the flies.*

Marvelous creatures. They were here before us, Sparks got to thinking, and they'll be here long after we're gone. And it was true—civilization had crashed, but the flies were still healthy, breeding and eating and fulfilling their beautiful destiny.

They were a constant, nipping at him, crawling in his hair, droning at his ears. They fed off his filth and bodily secretions. He'd wake up and they'd be lighting off his face, tickling his lips and trying to investigate his nostrils. Then one night—or was it day?—he heard the buzzing, only it was much louder, growing in volume and intensity until he cried out.

And then a voice said, *"Do you want to live? Do you wish to survive?"*

"Yes ... oh please, yes ... I'm so hungry ..."

"Then, listen ..."

In his head, he heard the buzzing of flies, thousands of flies. They covered his face and filled his skull in a droning, reverberating mass until he could no longer think, no longer reason. There were only the flies and what they wanted him to do. They flew into his mouth and up his nostrils and crawled in through his ears, infesting his brain, laying their eggs in the soft folds of his gray matter until they all began to hatch with a terrible slinking, squirming motion as they gnawed and fed and glutted themselves with all that he was and would never be again.

"If you want to live, if you want to survive," the voice whispered with a steady, overpowering droning, *"then you must eat. You must feed. Only then can you grow strong."*

The smell of decomposition led him directly to Emily. He turned on the flashlight. Oh Christ, it was horrible. She was bloated and mucid, acrawl with maggots and attendant clouds of flies. Her left arm had been eaten down to the bone and much of the flesh had been stripped away from her throat and face. Her lips were gone and she grinned at him with a rictus of teeth and gums.

He saw no rats.

But they would come.

Oh yes, this was their banquet and it would draw them in. He just had to be patient. He turned off the light, biding his time, listening to the flies, content with the smell of his own waste and unwashed body. It was quite foul, but reassuring at the same time. Like the flies. Once your mind had descended to a certain state, you could appreciate the music of their constant, incessant buzzing.

The sweet music of the grave, the melody of the tomb.

"Are you hungry?" said the voice of his god.

"Starving, starving," he muttered, drool running from his mouth in foaming, copious amounts.

"I can offer you juicy pink filets, well-marbled loins, succulent breasts and thighs seasoned in their own savory juices ... "

Sparks was shaking, droplets of sour sweat the size of peas rolling down his grime-encrusted face. "Yes, please, *please* ... I'm so damn hungry."

"Rare tender cuts, candied sweetmeats, and delicate morsels meaty and rich in flavor ... will you partake? Will you eat?"

"Yes, yes," he said, the hunger pangs drilling into his stomach, piercing him, impaling him with swords that disemboweled him, laid him open and raw.

"Then accept me as your Lord High King," said the voice.

"I do! I do!"

The table was set, the feast was spread before him. In the wavering, narrow confines of his mind, he saw the food and it beckoned to him. It existed only to fill him and make him strong. He could no longer resist—he dove on it. Oh, the fried chicken was well-battered and crispy, the skin flaking and crunchy as he tore it off in thin sheets. The thighs were plump, dripping with juices. The breasts sumptuous with gooey strings of cheese. He stuffed his mouth with saucy meatballs and butter-soft goat cheese. Gnawed on salty slabs of aged bacon and licked the gravy from delicate tenderloins sprinkled with exotic seasonings, sucking creamy pudding between his lips.

He went mad with it all, biting and chewing, slurping up spicy gravy and sucking stringy meat into his mouth. Delicious. *Delicious. Oh, how delectable, how very delectable—*

Then he saw, he *really* saw.

His hands were black with rancid discharge, his mouth smeared with gore. It was disgusting and delightful, sickening and beautiful as he stuffed himself, swimming in carrion depths with the maggots, worming in a sewage of decomposition, feeding, feeding, feeding—

And then he began to scream, howling with anguish and febrile madness and he was not sure of anything but the fullness of his belly and the terrible buzzing of flies in his head.

His eyes looked down at what was before him … *a nearly liquid mass of loathsome—of detestable putridity* … and he began to giggle, then he began to scream.

It was at this point that Sparks ceased to exist.

And the voice of the Lord High King said to him, *"Now for what is mine. That precious thing I desire. Lay it at my feet. Render it in a way that I will find pleasing."*

Sparks did not hesitate.

When God called, you answered.

"We must please our King, Emily," he said to her, staring down at her ravaged, split cadaver. Noxious flies filled the air, celebrating the morbid rituals of their priest. They flew about him, forming clouds and black currents, buzzing and buzzing and buzzing, landing on his face, covering his arms and feeding upon what was smeared upon his face. They were well-fattened, juicy and full like ripe blackberries. As he worked with sure fingers, digging deep, separating carrion from substance, swollen pouches of flesh burst one after the other, releasing a delirious swarm of maggots. In a dying, diseased world, they were fat and healthy.

And he was one of them.

It took some time to get what the King wanted and present it in the proper manner. But when he had, he displayed it with all due reverence and realized that his Lord High King and the mucid dripping thing were one and the same and his hands, his precious hands, were now holy objects for they had touched the living god.

Emily, ravaged and sunken, grinned up at him with gruesome empathy. For she knew. She had always known that she was the keeper of the King of Flies.

Being the instrument of the Lord High King had its advantages, of course. The King knew many things and he was only too pleased to teach his acolyte exactly what living required in the new world. Like his brothers, the flies themselves, Sparks listened and learned, amazed that he had not realized before how simple it all was.

Hidden away in his own safe little lair that smelled like urine and shit and far worse things, he thought about his new god and only about his new god.

At night, Sparks could hear the King breathing with a terrible, rasping noise, hear the frightful whirring of his wings. He would whisper to him in his dreams, promising him great things and luxuriant, decadent feasts. His voice sounded very much like the buzz of a blowfly and that brought a deep and abiding peace.

It was good to have a friend.

It was good to have a lord and master.

"There are many rats and mice here in our kingdom," said the voice. *"If a man is careful and cunning, oh, so terribly cunning, they make for nice little snacks. If properly aged, you'll find them deliciously soft and chewy."*

"I will hunt them," Sparks promised.

"Good, good. You are one of us now. Find them and kill them."

"I will! I'll catch them! I'll cut their heads off!"

This made him grin in the darkness. He had already made weapons to dispatch them with: stakes of splintered wood that he would ram into their greasy bodies. But first he had to find them.

Patience.

Always practice patience.

Waiting was his specialty. He had been down in the cellar for two months by that point. Waiting. Thinking. Creating a strategy of survival with the assistance of his Lord High King. It was finely crafted and thought out.

Armed with a single stake, he crept out from behind the furnace, moving with a silent, animal stealth. He pawed his way through the debris, knowing every bit of it by that point simply by feel. He crawled through piles of his own excrement, some recent and some quite old. Like an animal, he sniffed them, searching for bits of undigested food. They broke apart beneath his hands, most crawling with the intestinal parasites that infested him.

His stealth and patience paid off—he bagged three mice and no less than five rats. As the King suggested, he stuffed them away behind the furnace to ripen. Oh, the King always knew. He was a god for a new world of survival.

The weather was warm, unseasonably warm, and after a few days his larder began to smell ambrosial. He could barely sleep he was drooling so much. His belly growled, his fingers begging to tear apart the well-softened little carcasses. The flies had gathered in great, hungry masses. That was his cue that his meat was properly aged and seasoned. Speckled with them, he selected a rat, peeling its skin free with almost surgical delicacy. Ah! Its flesh was leathery and well-salted like beef jerky, its innards joyously soft to the tooth, its bones deliciously crunchy.

As he feasted upon them, he didn't see them as rats or mice, but as a buffet of fine cuts of rare meat, warm slabs of buttered bread, bowls of saucy noodles, and tarts with cream-gushing centers.

It was rapture.

Simple, blissful rapture.

Sparks was not only living and thriving now under the tutelage of the Lord High King, he was living well.

But such things as rats were simple fare, snacks and little else. A man could not survive on such things. He required a more satisfying repast, a true banquet as befitting a disciple of the King of Flies. So, his master schooled him, explaining in great, verbose detail how there were much richer buffets waiting, but to get them would require daring and confidence. He showed Sparks how to carefully tunnel his way out of the cellar by removing the debris that blocked the stairs. He'd always been afraid to attempt it, but once he began, accomplishing it with great caution and vigilance, he opened a passage out into the world.

The soot and dust in the atmosphere were gradually dissipating, so there was light to see by. It was dim, but after the cellar, quite brightly-lit.

"*See?*" said the voice. "*It's all quite simple when you dispense with your fear, isn't it?*"

There was a bounty of meat to be had. There were dogs everywhere, bloated offerings well-stewed in their own rancid juices. The pathetic things had crawled from houses to die in the streets. Of course, they had been nibbled by rats and other ravaging dog packs, but he was able to discover several appetizing specimens for his larder.

"But you mustn't be satisfied with dogs," the voice told him. *"There are other things. Listen and you will hear them scream in their madness."*

Quite right.

After days of waiting, he did indeed hear one of them crying out. A woman was living in a pile of rubble down the street, shrieking day and night.

"Poor, pitiful thing," said the voice. *"As your Lord High King, I demand that you end her suffering. It's the humane thing to do."*

Encouraged by the King and only wanting to be made safe in his court, Sparks stalked the woman the way he had stalked the rats and mice. He watched her. Learned her habits. She was a terrible, ragged creature of indeterminate age, wailing out her grief. She seemed to subsist on anything she could catch, though most of her diet consisted of canned food she had purloined somewhere. Trapped in the web of her own madness, she was a harmless thing, but the King wanted her and so he would have her, as befitted his station.

Dispatching her was simple enough—Sparks bashed her brains in with the pry bar, then he dragged her body down into his lair. The King was pleased. His brothers, the flies, gathered in excited swarms, making a delirious, sweet music for him as they crawled over him, celebrating his existence and his membership in their guild.

"Now," said the voice, *"let her soften and simmer in her own juices for no less than five days. Then, you may present her, Our Lady of Worms, in a manner that I shall find pleasing. I will grant you culinary delights beyond your wildest dreams."*

At last, at last! Finally, Sparks was being granted an audience with the King. It was something he hoped and dreamed about. Though he heard the voice of his Lord High King quite regularly and often paid homage to him with the flies, he had never truly seen him in the flesh. But all that was about to change.

The following five days were nearly unbearable with suspense and hunger, the fear that he would somehow displease the King. During that time, the carcass of Our Lady of Worms seasoned nicely, sautéing in her own delicate juices. Down in the cellar, it was moist and stifling. The corpse flies bred with wild abandon, droning relentlessly in the close confines like swarms of bees as the mad woman became a writhing mass of white worms.

Finally, the voice of the King of Flies was heard. *"The time is now. Bring the lovely carcass to me so that I might look upon her. See that she is prepared with proper veneration and you shall wear the secret crown."*

The Lord of Vermin.

The King of Flies.

Oh, how many dreams of rapture Sparks had had, picturing the momentous occasion when disciple met master, priest met god, and groveling, starry-eyed worshipper was invited to the court of the Lord High King of Flies.

The King's royal chambers were opulent and well-appointed with offerings of carrion that wriggled with septic spawn, steeped with the delicate perfume of the charnel. His acolytes, the flies, were in attendance. They moved through the air in black mists and buzzing waves, all of them fat and juicy with life. They fed and fed well upon the noisome scraps and foul heaps of excreta on the floor. They covered Sparks in a flowing luxurious robe of vermin.

And when he made his offering of the flaccid remains of Our Lady of Worms—*does it, does it please thee, oh Lord?*—they gathered in whirring multitudes, buzzing their praises with such sweet, melodious volume that Sparks grew faint in his ecstasy.

Our Lady's body was a hothouse of decomposition. What a splendid offering she indeed made for the discerning, well-educated palate of the Fly King. She was exquisitely distended, oozing the sweet cream of decay and exuding a fine, tempting, vile gas of putrefaction. As Sparks prepared her, using cutlery he'd discovered in the storage cage, her skin came away in tender layers, the tissues beneath liquefied to a gray slop of aspic jelly. Her face was soft as green cheese, one eyeball brined in a pus-filled socket. She had been tenderized by colonies of worms. Even now, they rippled beneath her flesh with secret glory.

She was a gourmet's delight, and he knew his Lord High King would not be disappointed.

Finally, the King of Flies made his appearance and Sparks gasped with delight. Why, how regal he was in his golden robes upon his bejeweled thrown of gilded bones! A tumescent human fly with glittering, scarlet compound eyes, wriggling black mouth parts, and the brown, puckered body of a child corpse.

With a mere musical fluttering of his membranous wings, he set upon the offered victuals, appraising them, buzzing curiously. The Fly King was an epicure. The presentation of the food had to be as pleasing to the eye as it was to the taste buds. He ate not just for sustenance, but for divine pleasure. He wafted the aroma of the food towards his olfactory receptors with hairy black palps, shivering with gastronomic euphoria. Carefully, almost sensually, he extended a hollow feeding proboscis, savoring the temperature and texture of a single moist morsel. Pleased, he became ravenous with hunger—slobbering and sucking up the fetid human gruel before him.

"Pray, join me in this grand feast," he tempted Sparks.

Together, they lost themselves in gluttonous abandon. Our Lady of Worms' lips were velvety cake, her viscous eyeballs succulent oysters on the half-shell. Her belly was a bounty of luscious noodles and plump sausages dripping with rich, decadent sauce. Rib meat juicy and falling off the bone, her lungs spongy with sweet cream. They licked up her drippings, nibbling on her seasoned loins, sucking up every drop of spiced gravy from her abdomen, carefully snapping delicate wrist bones like the shells of stuffed crab for the white, salty nougat of marrow. Her muscles were sushi. Her tendons jerked beef. Finally, her skull was cracked open, exposing the fondue pot of her brain and all its buttery convolutions that melted in the mouth like marshmallow custard.

That day, Sparks was made one with the King. He had arrived. He had become. And afterwards, lying in the scattered, gluttonous remains of their feast in a mindless, rapturous fugue, the flies became a soft, silken blanket that buzzed him asleep.

It could have gone on that way for many more months, but all good things came to an end in their own time. As enchanting as was the macabre symbiosis between his Lord and Majesty, the venerable— and verminous—King of Flies, the ever-increasing congregation of hungry, gnawing meat flies and squirming maggots, and the degenerate ministrations of Sparks, their high priest, it ended with the invaders.

Oh, how stealthily and silently they crept down the stairs in their gleaming orange anti-radiation suits. They carried rifles. They made their way into the private chambers of the King without being properly announced. And there they found the King of Flies and Sparks.

"What the hell is this?" one of them asked; his face unreadable behind the darkened plastic shield of his hood.

Sparks shook his head angrily. *"You can't be here! This is a holy place! Your unclean eyes do not dare look upon the King! It is forbidden! Only I wear the split mantle of Our Lady of Worms! Only I speak to his highness and wear the crown of bones!"*

He was insane. A filthy, degraded human being with purple-red blood blisters for eyes, his clothes hanging in dirty rags, his long beard matted with human grease and yellow marrow. He wore the blackened, leathery skin of a corpse and its attendant flies, a crown of finger bones wired together on his head. He danced about, grinning with the brown peg-like dentition of a rodent, a human rat hopping and crawling about in a revolting warren of bones, rot, hair, and maggoty scraps.

All of which was gruesome and appalling in of itself, but what was worse was the shriveled, blackened fetus ensconced in a chair. It was draped in gold foil wrapping paper, a pitiful and flyblown thing whose flesh had rotted away, revealing the fine bones beneath.

"Do not look!" Sparks said, trying to block their view with outstretched arms, the tatters of his mantle hanging in shreds like rotten sailcloth. *"This is not for your eyes! You contaminate the altar of the most holy—"*

Since he was far beyond saving, the soldiers shot him down, the sight of him and what he had done sickening to the extreme.

Sparks trembled for a few moments, spilling watery blood, before curling up on the altar of countless rat carcasses and the well-chewed bones of Emily and Our Lady of Worms.

The King of Flies, looking down from his throne, watched with grim amusement as the flies set upon him in a buzzing, investigative profusion. In the weeks to come, long after the soldiers had departed, Sparks became a nursery for generations of their larva who fed, and fed sweetly, upon him.

RAT TRAP

If you were quiet and very careful, Johnny knew, sometimes you could sneak right by them. They were vicious and deadly, territorial to a frightening degree, but they were still fucking monsters and he was still a man. He'd gotten very good at outsmarting them. They knew it and they hated him for it.

Squealers, he thought. *Goddamn squealers.*

He survived by stealing and scavenging. Slipping into their territory by night and taking what he wanted. They'd killed thousands of survivors in their rise to the top of the food chain, but here he was, active as ever.

Stealth was the key.

Johnny carried a military-style canvas shoulder bag. Everything in it was taped or padded so it made no noise. He wore sneakers. Dark clothes. He even blackened his face.

If things got ugly, he had a sawed-off pump shotgun in a sling at his back and a .45 with a silencer, both of which he'd liberated from the digs of a gangbanger on 23rd and Vine. The .45 was always his weapon of choice. A few well-placed rounds in the head would drop any squealer.

The idea made him smile as he breached their lines yet again. *Just try and stop me, vermin. Just try it.* He saw several of them patrolling the sidewalks, monstrous hulking shapes the size of dogs. The moonlight shone off their greasy pelts and the palings of their teeth.

He knew they'd tear him to pieces if they got the chance, so he didn't give them one.

He crouched in the rubble, silently duck-walking across the street from them. They neither heard him or smelled him. The radiation had mutated them into a whole new species. Like men, they had gained intelligence, but in the process, they lost many of their animal attributes—their keen sense of smell, their acute hearing. And that's why they were easier to fool.

Johnny froze.

He heard the sound of running feet in the distance. Not the pawing sounds of squealers, but the footsteps of his brothers and sisters in the resistance.

The squealers became aware of it, too.

They stood up on their haunches, heads waving from side to side, still trying to catch a scent, perhaps, as in the old days. They made a few squeaking noises to each other and raced off.

Johnny moved the rest of the way down the block, cut across the street, a shadow moving within shadows. He slipped down the avenue, clinging tight to the façades of buildings that the moonlight didn't touch. He crept down an alley and paused at the very end.

Now he was near his destination.

Now he would have to be very careful.

He slid the night-vision goggles over his eyes and scanned the terrain. The NVGs turned everything to surreal green, but every detail was there. He saw a cat slink its way between two buildings. A mouse emerged from a sewer grating. The Salvation Army depot was just down the block. He'd heard about it from an old guy named Preebo. Preebs (as he was known) had found it and was planning on a nighttime raid on it. That was the last Johnny had heard of him.

The squealers must have gotten him.

But they won't get me, Johnny thought.

Gone were the days when the rats were fearful, sneaking things. Now they were arrogant, certain of their domination, knowing nothing dared stand against them. They were huge monsters, all right, their eyes gleaming in the night like ball bearings. They made chittering noises, perhaps some debased form of speech.

As he waited to make his move on the Salvation Army Depot, Johnny watched a pack of them moving down the street, scanning the shadows with their beady pink eyes, their serpentine tails twitching.

Squealers.

He called them that because when you killed them, they squealed like babies. It was the sort of sound that went right up your spine. Once you heard it, you'd never forget it.

He wished he had a machine gun because he could have wasted the lot of them. But that wasn't his way. He was silent and lethal, like a knife slitting a throat. He saw himself as a commando, sneaking in, accomplishing his mission, then slipping out again before they even knew he'd been there. A ghost.

In the distance, gunfire broke out. Screaming. Shouting. Ah, his brothers and sisters had engaged the enemy. The squealers stood up on their haunches, concerned, alert.

They raced off and Johnny took full advantage of it. He moved down the block until he found the depot. He kept his NVGs on. He had to be very cautious now. According to Preebs, there was a window around the side that was open. It was only a matter of sliding it up.

Again, Johnny scanned the terrain.

Everything was quiet. No movement at all. Good and good. He tiptoed around the side. He found three windows. The one at the end slid up easy enough. Standing on the bottom of an upside-down garbage can, careful not to make any noise, he pulled himself through, landing quietly on the floor. The NVGs showed him he was in an office. Desk. Chairs. Filing cabinets. A cross-stitched wall hanging featured a cross, and beneath it, *TRUST IN THE LORD.*

Johnny giggled. *Yeah, good luck with that.*

He opened the door and stepped out into the corridor. He looked around vigilantly, searching for any little booby traps the squealers might have left for him. Most of them were non-lethal things like empty cans scattered about that the unwary might kick and clatter or packing peanuts on the floor that would crunch under your shoes, alerting them to your presence.

But he'd come across worse things.

Food or booze used as bait with tripwires attached so if you grabbed them, a spring-loaded board with nails driven into it would swing out and impale you. Sometimes they left poisoned food or water. Johnny had found more than one survivor dead in a pool of their own yellow, foaming vomit.

Oh yes, the squealers were smart.

Very smart.

Constantly evolving.

Changing at a frightening rate.

But the depot appeared to be clean. And better than that, the food pantry was untouched. He stuffed his bag with boxes of mac 'n' cheese and dehydrated potatoes, cans of pasta and Spam, anything he could lay his hands on. There was so much stuff, it would have taken ten or fifteen trips to get it all.

No sense in being greedy.

He had plenty for the time being.

He slipped out the window again, slid it closed, and dropped into the alley. He found himself staring at a squealer. It had been waiting for him. A rogue maybe or a soldier out scouting for survivors.

A hot wave of fear exploded in his guts. There was a solitary moment of inaction when it saw him and he saw it. It was a huge beast with spiky, oily-gray fur and glistening pink eyes. Blood-sucking lice the size of nickels jumped on its hide. It was up on its haunches, easily five feet in height, claws extended for the ripping, jaws open, ribbons of drool hanging from them.

It made a hissing sound and leaped.

He brought out the .45 with a smooth flex of muscle and drilled two slugs into it. They punched into its chest and throat, enough to throw it off balance so that its bulk sailed past him and struck the ground. It rolled over, injured, trying to rise, teeth grinding, blood jetting from its wounds. It made one last drunken attack and he put a bullet in its head, shattering its skull and spraying blood and gray matter against the brick wall.

It shuddered, letting out an ear-splitting death-squeal and stopped moving.

Shit and shit.

Squealers in every direction would be coming now. They always answered each other's cries.

Johnny ran, backtracking his way across the city. The squealers were out in numbers, circling, searching. Did they know he was there? Did they know he had killed one of them? He began to think so. It took him nearly two hours to make it back to his place.

By candlelight, Johnny lay on his cot in his basement digs, studying his wall of provisions as he ate a bowl of canned lasagna.

"You're doing okay," he told himself. "Yup, you're doing just fine."

He decided he'd lie low for a few days. Maybe the squealers had been looking for him, maybe not. Either way, it wouldn't hurt to make himself scarce for a time. Take it easy. Eat. Sleep. Do some reading. Unwind.

As he ate the lasagna, he thought about Diana. She used to make some great lasagna. The real stuff, that was, not like this canned puke. Yes, she had been quite a cook. He'd been so happy with her for a wife. A great cook, good-looking, always said the right thing at the right time, and smart. God, she was smart. She was an accountant and she ran her business out of an office in the spare bedroom, made big money from over a dozen lucrative corporate accounts. Yup, old Johnny had had it all.

Then the war.

The devastation.

Half the city turned to rubble. But he'd survived and so had she. They were lucky, real lucky. Johnny's brother, Dennis, had survived, too. Good old Dennis, that dirty sonofabitch. The three of them had been careful and they'd managed to eke out an existence. Then came the day when Dennis said he was feeling low, so Johnny went out scavenging alone. The rats had been everywhere. He'd killed a dozen, barely escaping with his life. He'd returned early and found Dennis screwing Diana. At gunpoint, they admitted it had been going on even before the war.

Everything Johnny had trusted in, fought for, valued and held sacred had been taken from him. He put six bullets into Dennis. Then he marched Diana out and tied her to a post in a field. Her crying and desperate pleas did not move him. He left her there.

When he came back the next day, the rats had eaten her right down to the bones. And even those were well-chewed, scattered like dice.

Faithless bitch.

Conniving cunt.

Every day he went through it in his head: finding them, killing his brother, staking out Diana. It was his favorite fantasy. There was guilt, of course, but it was overshadowed by raw hatred.

That whore, that dirty no-good whore.

He finished his lasagna, but he didn't enjoy it because he couldn't stop seeing Diana's face, particularly how she'd looked when his brother was on top of her. The lust in her eyes, the hunger. Just another filthy, rutting animal.

The only thing that made him smile was the rack of bones the rats had turned her into.

"I hope you screamed, you bitch," he muttered under his breath.

He hit the Salvation Army Depot again four days later, made another good haul. This time, he saw no squealers. They had been there, though. He found droppings in the alley. Maybe they had better brains now, but they were still filthy vermin.

As he slipped back across the city, just before dawn, nervous but feeling empowered, he came across a guy in a trap. Poor bastard. The rats had baited him with food—a case of ramen noodles, of all things—and he'd gone for it. *Wham!* The trap was sprung. It was basically a large rat trap they'd fashioned using an old door and a spring-loaded crossbar. They'd camouflaged it with loose brush (sneaky bastards) and caught themselves a rat. The crossbar had crushed the guy's legs, pinned him down.

Now the rats trap us, Johnny thought, the irony of it not lost on him.

The guy was in agony, writhing, blood-spattered. "Oh, help me, oh Jesus, you gotta help me," he pleaded. *"Get me out of here! Please get me out of here!"*

Standing there in the moonlight, Johnny considered it. The human thing would have been to help him, but if he did, what then? He'd never be able to walk. Which meant Johnny would have to carry him, get him somewhere safe, take care of him. He'd probably never walk again without real medical attention and where could you get that these days?

Besides, Johnny didn't like him.

As the sun started coming up, he saw he was one of those guys like Dennis: buff and handsome, a real fucking dreamboat. The sort of guy who got any woman he went after. Johnny hated men like that, arrogant, confident, shit bags that would steal your wife first chance they got.

"If … if you can pry the bar back, I think I can slide my legs free," the guy gasped.

"Sure, might work," Johnny said.

But he wasn't interested in that. It would be a lot of work and he sure as hell didn't want to be taking care of an invalid. He had enough problems. Besides, the squealers would be back any time now to check their traps.

And I plan on being gone by then.

Johnny took the case of ramen noodles, but left that poor sonofabitch to his unpleasant fate. Life's a beach, as they say.

"NO! OH CHRIST, WHAT'RE YOU DOING? YOU CAN'T LEAVE ME LIKE THIS!" the guy shouted, gasping, choking. *"PLEASE! YOU KNOW WHAT THEY'LL DO TO ME! YOU'VE GOT TO HELP ME!"*

Johnny was not moved. Life was cheap these days and human life was the cheapest of all. He could just imagine nursing this guy back to health. First thing he'd do to thank him would be to rob him or put a knife in his back. Oh yes, he knew how these assholes operated. He knew very well.

"We all got our problems, bud," Johnny told him.

The guy was still screaming, calling him every name in his well-thumbed book, as Johnny faded from sight.

Since the war, life for survivors had been one tragedy after another. It was about two years after the bombs came down that the first giant mutant rats showed. At first, they were simply vicious and predatory. Smart, but disorganized, one pack preying on another. Not only had they gained the intelligence of men, but along with it had come mankind's oldest vice: *war.* The need to raid and conquer, murder and rape, subjugate and enslave.

It had gone on for years, one bloody reprisal after another.

Then they'd organized.

Johnny had no idea how, but, suddenly, it was as if they were under some kind of central control that coordinated their efforts. It happened fast and that's what made it so damned spooky. They went from mindless, violent, tribal packs to a unified, cohesive force.

And this seemingly overnight.

And in doing so, they achieved the very thing humans had not been able to in 5,000 years of civilization: they cooperated fully for the good of all. Maybe it was their colonial nature. Regardless, they had become one and their primary goal was to exterminate the only true competition they had: human beings. The very ones that had waged genocide against them for so many, many centuries.

Role reversal.

Rat extermination had become a multi-billion-dollar industry back in the day. Men fought rats with science fueled by irrational blind hate and blatant disgust, exterminating them in numbers because we were the dominant, intelligent species and they had no right to impinge upon us or scavenge our leavings.

Now they were the dominant, intelligent species. And, true to form, they believed it was their right to liquidate unruly, troublesome vermin. They went at it with wrath and pure hatred.

And they wouldn't stop, Johnny knew, until the last of the human race was dead.

The thing that bothered him to no end was that the squealers he encountered in the streets did not seem terribly intelligent. They were by no means the simple rodents that they had evolved from. But as he moved among them and hid from them, he studied them again and again—how they moved, the simple tactics they used—and it was as if they were being controlled like puppets. Whenever they fought over food, for example (a favorite pastime), it would only last a few seconds before they squeaked with pain as if they had been kicked. They'd separate, stumble about drunkenly, some falling right over and twitching (reminding him of lab animals that were shocked if they made the wrong choice).

Puppets, he often thought. *Like somebody is yanking their strings.*

He experimented with them again and again, leaving food out for them to see how they reacted to it. They seemed to favor rotting meat and sweets. He injected his baits with strychnine and they never seemed to catch on, going for it again and again. He killed dozens and dozens that way, watching them roll over and die with horrendous convulsions.

But they never seemed to learn: if it was available, they went for it.

So much for learned behavior.

The bottom line was that they were voracious and would eat pretty much anything. He carried poisoned bait pellets in the pockets of his cargo pants, stuffing them into anything he thought they might go for. And they did time after time.

He was certain that left to their own devices, they would have carried on like their ancestors, but something had intervened, something was doing their thinking for them.

And the idea of that was more than a little scary.

In retrospect, he'd made a good run of it. In a city overrun with a highly organized force of mutants, he'd survived month after month and year after year. And he'd done so by being a lone wolf. While survivors banded together into groups and ragtag small armies—believing there to be strength in numbers—and were exterminated in their bunkers and strongholds by an invasive, relentless army of squealers, he had lived and lived well.

He killed them.

He moved through their territory unseen.

He robbed from them.

He was a phantom in their midst: invisible, unknown. A force of one they could never pin down.

But it had to reach the tipping point sooner or later. The law of averages dictated as much. And as it was a big girl (Diana) who had destroyed his faith in humanity, it was a little girl that brought him ultimately to his knees.

He'd had yet another successful night of scavenging. Moving around squealer patrols, so close to them sometimes he could have spit on them. He followed groups of them just to see if he could, slipping past their sentries. He found caches of food and weapons. He even located a closely-guarded nest of them, a brooding center where he could hear the cries of their young (he made a mental note to return there some night if he ever came across an RPG or a mortar).

Then he heard the crying of a child.

It stopped him there in the shadows. Though he fully admitted by that point that he was a selfish prick who despised his own kind, the desperate and pathetic cries of the child tugged at something inside him. They made his throat tighten and his jaw clench tight.

A child. A crying child. You can't ignore that.

Oh yes, I can. It's not my problem.

You can't leave a child to die.

Fucking watch me.

No, you can't.

I stay alive by being cold-blooded. It's my strength. It's the cornerstone of survival.

Yet, despite what common sense told him, he followed the sound of the cries, moving with great stealth in their direction. Something inside him cringed at the very idea, but he could not stop himself. There were times in life, he decided, that you just had to do the right thing. This was one of them.

His senses at high alert, he found the girl in a little weedy lot between two buildings that had become teetering piles of rubble. She was just a little waif of a thing in dirty joggers and a t-shirt. Her ankle was caught in an animal trap, a leg-hold trap like the kind used to catch bobcats and the like once upon a time. The jaws had her ankle, but thankfully, they weren't spiked.

Be careful, he told himself. *Very, very careful.*

He crept forward with the .45 in his hand, NVGs on. In the pale moonlight, she saw him right away. There were tears on her cheeks. She was shaking, holding out her hands to him.

His survival instinct told him to run.

His humanity told him to stay and help.

He holstered his gun and went to her. He figured she was maybe ten. Had things worked out, Diana and he could have had a daughter like her. They'd tried unsuccessfully for years. His heart in his throat, he told her to be as quiet as possible. He gripped the jaws of the trap and forced them back until the lock clicked. There was very little tension on them.

The girl pulled her foot back.

He thought she would fall into his arms, profusely thank him … but that's not what happened. She pulled away from him and he noticed that she was smiling.

What in the hell?

She brushed herself off and stood up. Her ankle was not paining her in the least. "HERE HE IS!" she called out. "YOU WANTED HIM AND NOW YOU'VE GOT HIM!"

Johnny's mouth hung open, a dozen expletives on his tongue. But he never had time to voice any of them before the squealers rushed in and seized him, forcing him to the ground, pinning him there with their swollen, vermin-infested bodies.

When he woke some hours later, he was a prisoner of the rats. Something which made him sick to his core. He had done the right thing, he had helped the little girl, and now he would pay the price for it. The treacherous little witch had baited him in.

He would never know why.

He could never understand why.

He was trapped in a hideous massing of squealers, hissing and snarling monsters that radiated pure evil. They knocked him around, stomped him with their feet anytime he tried to rise, butted him with their snouts and nipped at him if he dared move. There were dozens and dozens of them. Some were as large as dogs; others were nearly as big as he was. They swarmed around him, covering him with their hot, repulsive stink and pressing their greasy pelts against him. He had the worst idea that they wanted to tear him into pieces, but for some reason they did not dare, and this drove them into a violent frenzy.

Then several nightmare mutants pushed into the pack. They were different, grotesquely so—their bodies were huge and distorted, nearly hairless save for gray spines, their flesh pink and flabby and oddly scaly. The others fell out of their way as they moved in to appraise their captive. They communicated with a weird, shrill whining that made his head hurt. Their eyes were huge and bright red, seeming to burn in their sockets. They examined Johnny roughly with double-clawed paws, flipping him over again and again, making that terrible sound among themselves. Whenever they directed that noise at the other squealers, they scampered away.

They're in charge, he thought with rising horror. *You've always wondered how they were controlled and organized. These are the ones that do it.*

Horrible mutants whose mental acuities were far in advance of the others. Whenever they put their burning eyes on him, he cringed and there was a sharp bolt of pain in his head as if they were trying to get inside his mind. Was that it? Was that how they controlled the masses? Using some kind of devastating telepathic power?

Not too far in the distance, he heard a human voice wailing at maximum volume: *"No! No! Don't ... oh please God don't! DON'T TOUCH ME! DON'T TOUCH ME!"*

The voice seemed to get louder and louder before it was cut off by a shrieking, squealing noise that was much like the death-cry of the rats, but far beyond that to a frightening degree: the howling, bestial cry of a beast. It was followed by a wet, tearing sound that made Johnny's guts jump into his throat.

The mutants made that whining sound and the others rushed in, engulfing him in their bristling bodies, first knocking him down and tossing him around, then pushing him forward to where the screaming had come from with their snouts. The sea of squealers parted and he saw a gigantic cylinder of glass like a laboratory jar in an old movie. It was about fifteen feet high with a mean circumference of about the same.

In it was a man in a tattered anti-radiation suit. He was broken like a discarded doll, limbs bent at unnatural angles, red liquid gushing from rents in the suit.

And poised over him was a gigantic black rat. A mutant, yes, but not like the others. This was a huge, feral beast, a filthy monstrosity of snapping jaws and curved yellow talons. It was much larger than the man it tormented, its jaws dripping with blood as it struck at him again and again like a shark. The man was nearly dead, making moaning sounds in his throat which sounded liquid as if his mouth was filled with blood and vomit.

Johnny knew he had not been brought there for no reason. The squealers wanted him to see this because his turn was coming.

As terrified as he was, he did not cry out or try to get away: this was an inevitability. He'd known for a very long time that his end was coming and that it would be horrible when it arrived. As the giant rat tore the man apart, he thought about Diana and how she had died and how it could have been avoided by a clear head that was not muddled by raging emotions and that inescapable sense of betrayal.

And she did betray you, he thought. *There's no way around that, just as you murdered her. You can justify it all you want, but you did.*

The man in the jar was in the blood-oozing jaws of the monster rat. It bit down with everything it had and his bones went with a wet snapping, gore running from him in rivers. It shook him from side to side and then ejected him with great force at the wall of the jar where he struck with a wet splat, leaving a red smear before he slid down, a ruptured mass that barely resembled a man.

His death excited the squealer and it stomped on him again and again, bringing all of its weight and force to bear, forcing his guts from his mouth like a squashed vole.

Now it's my turn, Johnny thought.

Under the direction of the hairless mutants, Johnny was fitted with a quick-release leather harness and pulled off his feet with a rope thrown over a beam high above. He was dangled over the mouth of the jar like a tasty treat. The giant rat went crazy, squealing and squeaking and gnashing its teeth. He thought it would eat the remains of the man in the anti-rad suit, but it seemed to have no interest in him.

It wanted only to kill.

To rend and tear.

It lusted for it.

It was a wild beast, one that was probably too savage for the mutants to control. But in their world, it had a purpose like the well-starved animals in the Roman arena. Johnny was placid. Maybe they wanted him to scream and plead, but he did neither. He just hung there, defeated and hopeless, almost glad in a way that it was nearly over with so he could finally close his eyes and rest.

With a jerk, he was lowered down.

He took a quick appraisal of what was in his cargo pants. Most of the pockets were stuffed with poisoned baits, but there was a lock-blade knife he kept there for emergencies. Maybe if he cut the giant rat, it would kill him that much faster.

It wasn't much, but it was all he had.

Interestingly enough, the monster did not attack him as he was lowered. It made no sense, considering the slavering horror it was, but maybe the mutants were holding it back. As his feet touched the bottom of the jar and the harness released him, the rat circled him warily. It wasn't exactly afraid of him, just wary. Johnny could sense its indecision. He was not acting like the others they'd put in the jar, no cries or wild attempts to scale the smooth glass walls.

No, he just stood there.

The rat did not like that.

It cocked its head to the side as if confused when his hand opened one of the Velcro enclosures on his pants and pulled out the lock-blade. There was a moment of searing agony in his brain and he nearly dropped it. *The mutants. The goddamn mutants.* They were trying to get in his skull again. He saw them pressed up to the glass like spectators, their membranous pink flesh stretched taut over ridged skeletons, eyes huge and scarlet, teeth jutting from their mouths.

Johnny opened the blade.

"Come and get it," he told the giant rat.

It seemed to cower away from him for a moment or two, hissing in its throat, then it lunged. He tried to jump away from it, but it seized his left arm in its jaws, easily snapping the bone with an explosion of agony. As it did so, Johnny buried the knife in its throat three times in rapid succession. The rat pulled back, making a low and pained mewling as blood ran from it.

Johnny staggered back.

The pain made him want to sink to his knees and go out cold, but he knew he couldn't allow that. If nothing else, he had to stay awake long enough to stab the beast two or three more times. He leaned again the wall of the jar, his heart pounding, his mind filled with warm fuzz. The glass vibrated with the appetites of the squealers pressing against it.

Now the giant rat came at him again.

It snapped its teeth and he slashed. Then it closed in and he could not avoid it—it seized his right leg, bearing down, snapping his femur as he drove the knife into one of its eyes, splitting it like a moist plum, fluid blowing out of the socket in an eruption of gore.

Agonized, hating, raging, the beast knocked him down and went after him with a frenzy. Now it was not just fighting for amusement, it was fighting for its life. It stomped him, bit him, tore him open with its claws. As he screamed, it ripped open his belly and then his throat. The knife was gone. The hand that held it was several feet away and Johnny, incapacitated now by blazing pain and a rising numbness, no longer fought.

It had him.

It really had him.

As his bladder voided and his bowels let go, the crackling pain seemed to lessen as the giant rat went after him in a feeding frenzy, yanking his viscera out and tearing open his throat. It tossed him in the air and smashed him against the walls of the jar.

Then it ate him.

And, ultimately, as his mind was blown out like a candle flame, this was what he had been waiting for. It took his legs first, wrenching them free and pulverizing them in its jaws. Then it went after his torso, ripping and macerating what it found.

And then it stopped.

It quivered.

Saliva dripped from its mouth. Something was happening to it and it mewled with pain. In the pockets of Johnny's cargo pants were some thirty poisoned rat baits. Five of them, he had learned, were enough to kill a squealer. The giant rat was tougher than them, more durable in just about every way, but hardly impervious.

The mutants began to whine and the squealers hissed as the giant fell over, its massive body contorting with rapid-fire convulsions as a frothing vomit of yellow foam was expelled from its mouth. It fought and writhed and finally went still.

Though Johnny was not around to see it, the last round went to him.

DOLL PARTS

He was a lone man in a ragged black coat and dusty trail clothes. He came through the blowing dust, his face covered in a gas mask, heavy gloves on his hands. His name was really Woodton, but people had called him Woody for as long as he could remember.

It had not rained in many weeks and the earth was gray, scarred, and parched, broken open with jagged rents like the flesh of a mummified corpse.

He had been walking the lone, hard road since the bombs came down. No day was easy. He scavenged. He hid. He hoped. Sometimes he fought and killed when others tried to take what belonged to him. He woke each morning, listening to the howling, dry wind, tears in his eyes because another day was upon him. And that meant many miserable hours of grim survival and awful deeds before he could sleep and forget again.

Had he been alone in the underground shelter that was now his lair, he would have slept around the clock until one glorious day when he did not wake at all.

But Adelia wouldn't have it.

"Get up," she'd say. "Get out there. Find food. Find weapons. Water. You won't stay alive if you don't. The sleeping wolf gets no meat."

She was on him all the time just as she had been before the final war that slit the throat of humanity. He did everything for her. Being housebound these many months, she could not shift for herself so he was her caretaker, her servant, her eyes and ears to the world. Some days he hated her so much, he loved her. And other days, he loved her so much, he hated her.

Adelia.

Adelia.

Adelia.

Regardless of how terrible it all was, she kept him going. She got him out of bed and saw to it he put food in his belly and didn't do anything stupid like eating any of the irradiated animals he came across or drank from wells that were poisoned by toxic runoff. She made him work. She made him think. And, God yes, she made him move. He was a wind-up toy and she held the key. Every morning she inserted it and wound it up tight and off he went to do her bidding.

"Praise the Lord, but I think this will be a good day," she told him that morning. "Good things will happen if you do as I say, Woody. Now get out there and do what has to be done." Then she grinned with her crooked, starved mouth. "And bring me a girl. You know what I like."

God help him, but he did.

When he found the ruined house, Woody stood there a moment getting a feel for things, casting out his mind for danger. He sensed nothing. His coat flapping around him like a cape, blasted by dust from the shrieking wind, he stepped inside. It was nice to get out of the storm. It never seemed to stop blowing through the skeleton of the town. He stood in a half-collapsed foyer. Timbers angled down around him. He could still hear the moan of the wind in his ears.

Taking off his mask and gloves, he checked his little battered notebook. No, he had not been in this house yet. There had been 30,000 people in the city before the war; now there were a few hundred. Lots of houses to be checked, even if most of them had been turned into straw from the shockwave of the first bomb.

Stuffing his gloves and mask into his leather bag, he took out his flashlight and began the search. Most of the house was still standing, though it creaked unpleasantly in the wind, seeming to move around him. Adelia had warned him again and again about getting trapped somewhere.

You fall through a floor and break your fool legs, what happens to me? I'll be all alone. Without your help, I'll never be whole again.

Not that she was exactly whole now. She'd always been a bit soft in the head, a bit neurotic. It ran in the family. And you sure as hell did not want to cross her—

Shit. The rattler.

His free hand went immediately to the .38 at his belt.

Outside he heard a low, dreadful hissing as something big passed the house. It made a rattling noise like a diamondback, but he was certain it was not a snake. Just what it was, he could not say because he had never seen it in the flesh, thank God. It moved out there with a slithering noise that went right up his spine. It rattled off in the storm like a weird percussion instrument, maybe a Vibraslap, then it was gone.

Holstering the .38, Woody wiped sweat from his face with a shaking hand. There were lots of nightmares out there sniffing around and hunting for food, but the rattler scared him the most.

It should, oh yes, it should—it's looking for you.

He shook that from his head.

Most of the upstairs was in shambles, so it was pointless trying to root around in it. Just too dangerous. But luck favored him: he found the cellar door. It was dark and dangerous going down into basements, but he'd made some of his best finds in them. Before the war, it wasn't unusual for people to keep a pantry in the cellar.

Swallowing, he went down the steps, shining his light back and forth. Inside, he was drawn tight, waiting for something to jump out at him. It had happened in the past. He bore the scars from dog attacks. Once, a colony of very large rats had gone after him. But there were much worse things and he knew it.

At the bottom, he scanned the flashlight about.

Motes of dust moved in the beam. He found a rec room with cobwebbed furniture, a TV thick with settled grit. Brown leaves had blown in and they crunched under his heavy boots. There was a bedroom at the back. Long before he stepped in there, he knew it was inhabited.

The .38 in his fist, his heart thumping in his chest, he stepped in there. A girl in a filthy jogging suit was hiding behind a rocking chair.

"I won't hurt you," he said. "I just came in to get out of the storm. It's really blowing out there today."

He had encountered lots of people in his search of the ruined city. It wasn't like the old days where most were harmless. Now they were nearly all predatory and you had to be careful. So, he made no sudden moves. He sat on the bed and its dirty covers. The girl—he figured she was about eighteen or so—watched him with bright blue doll's eyes set in a face imbedded with grime. As he did so, he kept talking in a soft, non-threatening voice, telling her about things he'd seen and how he'd stayed alive.

Finally, she said, "I haven't eaten in a week."

Her voice was raw, cracking as if her throat was made of split leather.

"I have food. Back at my place, I have a stockpile. Come with me, get out of this rattrap," he told her. "It's clean. There's food and water. Soft beds. I've got everything we need."

"Why should I do that?"

"Because you're hungry and I need company. We're both human beings. Isn't that enough?"

She eyed him warily. "And what are you going to want in exchange?"

He uttered a short laugh. "I have a gun. If I wanted to rape you, I would have done so. I'm not looking for a lover, just a friend to talk to and help me. Is that so bad?"

"I guess not."

"What's your name?"

"Abby."

Woody smiled. "Abby. I like that."

"I was named after my grandma."

"Come on then. You're safe with me. We got some walking to do, so get a coat, something to put over your face or the dust will blind you."

She stood up. Her joggers were torn and he could see that she had long, shapely legs. Adelia was going to like her just fine.

Adelia waited.

She waited like the Devil in hell waited for souls to spit and roast. She waited like bricks and sticks and stones do. Her nest was in the corner of the shelter, high up, shadowy and strung with cobwebs, a lair as silent as the spiders that threaded strands of casket silk around her. She was a gaunt mortuary sculpture of leather skin, yellowed bone, and rustling rags like dirty bedsheets set upon an angular crosstree, her shriveled lips grinning, her broken teeth protruding. She stared down with rapt fixation like an owl from a dead tree with a single eye of hot yellow glass.

Soon.

It would be soon.

In the sunless hollows of the shelter, she giggled with a scratching, reedy sound as she waited.

Poor, poor Abby. How hungry she was. How broken by life and death and day by day survival. Like an animal, she only knew desperation, scavenging for scraps of food. Anything that would keep her going another day even if she had no idea why it was she bothered.

Woody thought it was just a damned sad state of affairs.

When they reached the shelter, he watched her look about with amazement. She indeed saw that things were clean, comfortable, and warm, as he promised. The wind was blowing outside, but it did not get in. She touched the cushions on the furniture and they were soft.

Then she sat down and he brought her fresh water which she gulped down with great enthusiasm. She ate a can of pork and beans, some Ritz crackers that were only slightly stale. It was the best food she'd had in many weeks.

"Don't eat too fast or you'll get sick," he warned her. "Save room for a sweet. I've got some good ones."

Poor thing. She gobbled her food like a starving dog. It was a hell of a thing that this was what life had become for most, if not all, the survivors.

"Have you been alone for long?" he asked her.

"Months."

"No friends?"

She blinked rapidly and he could almost hear the wheels of her mind spinning backwards. "No ... I ... it's funny, but it gets hard to remember."

"It does."

"My old life seems like it faded. My boyfriend was with me. His name was Rich. He died of the radiation. He was in a lot of pain. His teeth came out. He bled from everywhere." She swallowed. "My sister. She was with us. But she died right away."

"You've had some real tough luck."

"Yes."

"But you're safe now."

She sipped more water. "What do we do next?"

"You get cleaned up. Get new clothes."

"I'd like that."

"Then you rest."

"That would be nice."

"But first, I want to introduce you to Adelia."

"Who's that?"

"My wife. She'll like you."

He led her to the back of the shelter, past the stacked cases of survival gear, bottled water, and food, through a doorway. He lit a lamp because it was dark in there, but even with it glowing and throwing out flickering yellow illumination, the shadows were thick and crawling. There was an unpleasant smell in the air and she wrinkled her nose—age and preservatives, tanned hides and faint decomposition.

"What is this?" she asked.

Her eyes swept the shelves of tools and bottles, the anatomy prints tacked to the walls. What looked like dummy legs and arms, armatures and jaw-sprung doll faces dangled from the walls. On a bench there were gears and cogs, swivels and jars of glass eyes.

"This was my workshop. I made puppets for collectors. Highly detailed, one-of-a-kind dummies that were very realistic. I made quite a name for myself before the war." He set the lantern down among a gathering of wooden puppet hands, all of which seemed to be reaching out to grasp in the guttering light. "My puppets were special, very special."

Abby looked very uneasy. Her subjective impression was that this wasn't a good place: it was in her eyes, a frightened animal gleam.

Woody lit a cigarette with trembling fingers. "You see, Abby," he said, blowing out a rolling cartoon balloon of smoke, "I have the gift. Other puppeteers *claimed* they had the gift, but only I did. My puppets were special because I could make them move. My life-force imbued them, made them alive. It was like ... well, like a transfusion of sorts. I could make what's in me go into them."

Abby was hugging herself. She was shivering. She could feel the grave coldness seeping from the walls and it set on her very wrong.

"I talk too much, don't I?" Woody said. "It's always been my failing. No matter." He took her by the arm, but very gently. "You need to meet Adelia. That's why we're here."

He lit another lantern and brought her further back into the depths of the long, shadow-jumping room, so she could see what was in the corner, hanging there from a peg.

Abby let out a manic cry, fighting free of him and falling down.

"Don't be afraid. It's only Adelia."

What the light revealed was a terrible eldritch figure hanging there, a corpse puppet in gray ragged cerements and split hide. It was made from the odds and ends of dolls and the raw materials of the grave. Joints were replaced by swivels and hinges, withered claw-like hands attached to skeletal wooden rods, chalk-white rib bones thrusting from a hollowed torso of gears and pulleys.

Abby screamed and began to crawl frantically from the room.

Adelia licked her leathery lips with a black tongue, her hinged jaw opening with a rain of dust. *Do not let her leave. She is the one.*

Woody went after her, grabbing a hammer.

Idiot, can you do nothing right? I don't want her damaged! She must be controlled, harnessed.

Woody did not want that. He knew the awful things Adelia would do to the girl. Yet, he knew better than to interfere. As Abby scuttled out the door like a crab, he felt Adelia focus her malign wrath at her.

Come. Back. Here.

Abby jumped to her feet and it looked like she was going to run, then she stopped. She went rigid. Her limbs did not move. She barely breathed. Then slowly, stiffly, she turned around. Her eyes were filled with tears, her mouth hitched in a scream that would not come. Like an automaton, she walked mechanically back into the workshop and stood there, blankly, like a toy soldier.

Adelia giggled. Her head was twisted on its pipestem neck like that of a hanged man. Her skull showed through her flaking, cracked scalp. Spiders spun their webs in the mop of her straw-dry hair.

The girl will stand ready until I say different, she said, her hinged jaw creaking. *She is my toy and I shall play with her.*

Abby whimpered slightly.

Woody was shaking. Adelia had a new toy. She would play with it until she grew bored with it, then she would toss it away. By then, it would be little more than a dummy itself ... mindless, broken, and soulless.

Adelia's face was cloven as if it had been struck by an axe. It grinned malevolently, the seamed flesh stretching on the skull beneath, split lips pulling back from yellowed teeth.

Now she must dance! Adelia's voice shrilled. *She must move and entertain!*

Woody stood there, cold as ice, sweat running from his pores. He shivered, head-spinning, pulse racing, but it happened: Abby danced. She swayed and leaped, kicking out her legs, holding her arms above her head like a ballerina as she spun in circles. She pirouetted and whirled, a pathetic dancing stick figure.

Adelia's laughter echoed through the shelter.

It went on for some time until Abby was so exhausted that she collapsed, panting on the floor. Her eyes were stunned and sightless like those of a dog that had been struck by a car.

As the days passed, Adelia formulated her plans, which Woody knew would be terrible to the extreme. There was a coldness in her, a frigid cruel streak in her that could turn warmth to ice. Inside the basket of her ribs beat a black heart of devilment and debauchery. When she was done with poor Abby, why, there wouldn't be enough left of her to stuff a pillow.

Such a nice girl, too, he thought, as he moved through the perpetual dust storm that blew and blew, howling like a wraith through the gutted town. Things creaked and shook, swayed and groaned. The city was like a mortally injured beast in its death throes.

In the street there was wreckage everywhere: overturned buses and vans, cars blackened from the extreme heat of the blast. Buildings had fallen into themselves, telephone poles and their attendant wires tangled in the streets like snares. He knew he was in a bad part of the city. The lingering radiation levels here had to be very high yet.

Are you exposing yourself on purpose? he wondered. *Hoping you'll die because you don't have the stomach to take your own life? Then take off your canister mask and breathe, just breathe.*

No, he couldn't think things like that. Adelia wouldn't like it. Even miles away, she could hear his thoughts.

He came upon eerie shadows on the sidewalks and still-standing brick walls: black images of men, women, and children. Their bodies had blocked the intense light and heat of the bomb, absorbing the expended energy for a split second before they were vaporized, their final moment on earth flash-blasted, captured for an eternity.

He cut through the storm to yet another street. Amongst the wreckage, were what appeared to be hundreds of bones that gleamed whitely. It was as if people had gathered out here to die that day.

As he moved among them, he thought about Abby again.

He knew that Adelia had to rest from time to time; even the surgical sharpness of that cutting blade she called a mind had to be honed. During these periods, she went dormant and she was essentially helpless. He swallowed thickly, plotting defiance, contemplating an all-out rebellion. He could destroy her then. Smash her into her component parts. Burn her remains. Then Abby would be free. He could give her food and supplies, tell her to run, run, run away as fast as she could and never look back. It was in his power to save her—

Woody tensed.

Something was happening. The atmosphere around him went kinetic, and it had nothing to do with the wind. The bones around him began to move. Ribcages rolled. Femurs and ulnas rattled. Vertebral segments clattered like dice. Skulls chattered their teeth.

"Stop it, Adelia! Stop it!"

He heard her hysterical laughter echoing among the ruins. It bounced all around him.

I hear your thoughts, you little worm! she squealed in his mind. *After all I've done for you, you would dare disobey me!*

The bones gathered around him, thrumming with stolen life. Disarticulated skeletons were made whole. They rose up around him, reaching out with metacarpals, screams coming from their sprung mouths. Crying out, Woody charged through them, scattering them into ossuary piles.

So easy, eh? I can make it worse, much worse, Adelia whispered in his head. *There are terrible things that I can call.*

"Please," he panted, stumbling away. "Please, *please.*"

Her laughter reverberated in his head. He had been warned. He dared not help Abby. If he did, oh God, if he did, the reprisals could be a horror beyond imagining. Adelia had the power. She could do the most horrible things.

Out in the moaning depths of the storm, he heard the sound of the rattler closing in. Adelia had summoned it and now it was coming.

"If only she had died when I killed her," he heard himself say. "If only she had lain still."

Abby had no idea how long she had been a prisoner in the shelter. It could have been days or weeks. Her pounding head filled with thunder, she opened her eyes. Her flesh quivered on her bones. She fully expected Adelia to do something awful to her, to punish her yet again as she did every hour of every day.

She did not move.

She barely breathed.

It was quiet in the shelter, save the sound of the wind blowing outside. She knew that Woody was gone. Things sometimes quieted down when he wasn't there to annoy Adelia. And when she got annoyed, Abby became her favorite punching bag.

Abby lay on the floor, her eyes alive and shifting. She was in the living room, next to the couch. Woody had made her take a bath. He filled a tub with hot water, had her shampoo her hair and scrub the grit from herself. It was nice to smell clean again. Then, upon Adelia's command, he had dressed her in a beaded chiffon party gown. It was the most impractical of outfits for the world they now lived in.

Even if she was to escape, how far could she get in something like this? She was barefoot. Every inch of her body hurt. Adelia made her dance. And when she didn't dance fast enough or grovel properly, she was pierced by invisible needles. She was scalded. Beaten. Hung in the air by her feet; Adelia had complete control of her. She could make her walk, talk, scream and cry. She could make her shake with manic laughter. Hit herself. Bite herself. And several times now, as Woody watched with shining eyes, she had made her touch herself, masturbate with such frenzy that she hurt herself.

Adelia enjoyed her pain, her humiliation, her degradation. She made Abby lift her dress and tease Woody. She forced her to her knees before him, making her take him in her mouth … always making her stop just before he reached orgasm.

You will not enjoy the whore! I will not let you! Adelia would shriek. *Oh, how you'd like to mount her and fill her with your man-seed! But you will not! There will be no satisfaction! You are a bad man and must be punished! You do not dare play with my toy unless I say so!*

By that point, Abby was not even sure if she was still sane. Her mind had been slowly going for months and now it teetered at the edge of a great black abyss. Adelia would break her. It was only a matter of time.

As she slipped back into unconsciousness, a voice she had not heard for a long time said in her mind, *It's not Adelia, and you know it.*

Woody woke up with fear in his belly. He was stretched out on the sofa, Abby sprawled nearby. In his mind, he could hear Adelia berating him, her voice criticizing him, demeaning him. But it was a memory from just after the bombing. Right before he took the axe and—

Listen.

It was not the nightmare that had woken him, but something else entirely. Outside, something was circling the house. It made a sound like dozens of baby rattles shaken at the same time and with incredible volume. *Dear God, dear God, the rattler.* Yes, it was out there, waiting for him. It knew that sooner or later Adelia would send him into its arms and then it would have him, then it would make him part of itself or pull him into pieces.

Go to it now, Adelia's voice taunted him. *Go out there and look upon the horror you have created, offer yourself at its feet. It dreams about you. It wishes to pick your bones. It cries out in the voices of the many....*

Woody forced her voice from his head. He would not listen. He did not want to know. In his mind, as always, he saw the faces of Adelia's many victims, her toys that she had played to death, tormented into madness and then crushed like insects under a boot. How many of them had he dragged out into the storm, cast into the street like bags of trash, shattered and ruptured things that were barely even human by that point?

Abby, he thought, *she'll break her, too. It's only a matter of time.*

He did not dare move, thinking the rattler could hear even the most subtle of sounds. After a time, the rattling disappeared into the storm. He sighed, wiping sweat from his face.

But it'll come again, bad boy, and you know it, Adelia promised him, then began to laugh and laugh, filling his skull with her deranged cackling until he screamed.

In the narrowing confines of her mind, Abby was guided mostly by animal instinct. She did what it took to stay alive. Yet, there was a reasoning part of her brain that was still operational. It studied. It learned. It finally understood. There was a pattern here. Whenever Woody came back from one of his scavenging trips, Adelia woke from dormancy and got worked up.

That's when Abby was tortured.

Made to dance and crawl and perform.

Always then.

But afterwards, as she lay breathless and beaten on the floor, Adelia had to rest. She had to gather her strength for the next round of humiliation. Her insane amusements took energy, lots of energy. The problem was that by the time Amelia rested, Abby herself didn't have the strength to escape.

Like now, for instance.

Hurting, contused and cut, Abby lay there in her torn, blood-stained gown. Her mind wanted to sink into oblivion, but she had to focus. She had to gather her strength. Woody had gone out. Now was the time for action. Another round with Adelia and she might suffer permanent damage.

Gritting her teeth against the pain of abraded skin and sore muscles, she crawled on her belly like a snake in the direction of the door. Every few feet, she paused. Listened. Waited. Then moved again. Within ten minutes of such stealthy effort, she reached the door.

Then she was free.

Adelia was in a rage.

A blood-maddened fury of absolute anger. Up on her peg, she shuddered and shook, fingers clawing and teeth grinding and cerements rustling like mortuary curtains. And as she grew angrier and angrier, a storm broke in the shelter: bottles shattered, shelves collapsed, boxes of dry goods exploded, and trunk lids opened and slammed shut. Puppet limbs flew from the walls at Woody like missiles. Disembodied puppet hands gesticulated in the air.

My toy! My little whore! She is gone! You let her escape, you crawling little worm! Find her! Bring her back to me bound and gagged! Adelia screamed. *I want her! I want her now! Go and get her, or I'll go get her myself!*

Woody donned his mask, coat, and gloves. He ran out into the dust storm that whirled and blew with incredible velocity. He had to lean into it, or it would have laid him flat. The wind came from every direction in conflicting, hot currents of searing air. The dust was as thick as goose down.

"ABBY!" he cried. "ABBY! YOU CAN'T GET AWAY! SHE'LL LAY THIS TOWN FLAT!"

The buildings shook around him, crumbling, crashing, spilling rubble in every direction. Bones flew. Cars flipped over. Trees split in half. The earth shook, great jagged cracks opening up and swallowing debris.

Woody knew it was coming to an end now.

Adelia would destroy the world.

She would shake its foundations.

She'd smash it like a snow globe.

Abby would be the end of everything. All that potential energy stored in Adelia's yellowing bones was being unleashed by degrees, approaching critical mass. When the dam failed and it was set free in a barrage of total destruction, even the nukes would pale by comparison.

He shuffled forward, stumbling, falling, but moving ever closer to his target. Yes, he was close. He could *feel* her out there, her terror spiking, what was left of her mind fragmenting in the pure devastating force of Adelia's doomsday temper.

There.

He saw her. She was clinging to the bent pole of a STOP sign. She was crying out, what remained of her gown blowing around her in ribbons and rags.

"Did you really think you'd escape?" he asked her when he was close enough that she would hear. "She'll never let you go!"

Abby's face was blasted white with dust. She brushed it away, coughing. "No ... no, but you can! You can let me go! I'll never come back! I'll go far away!"

"It's not that simple!"

"It is!"

"No!"

"It can be if you let it!"

He shook his head. Why was she talking in riddles and impossibilities? Didn't she see what was going on around her? Couldn't she feel the frustration, hatred, and twisted animosity of Adelia? Couldn't she see that Adelia was a very angry god that could not be denied? Every second they wasted chatting like this, she grew more and more enraged.

"Just let me go!" Abby shouted at him, imploring him. "Release me!"

Woody shook his head. He didn't have time to explain it to her, the way things were, the way they had always been. How Adelia had bullied him for countless years, insulting him and demeaning him, breaking him down piece by piece, cracking open his shell and yanking out his guts loop by loop until he was no longer even a man. Just an emasculated sycophant with no will of his own.

A puppet, oh yes, a puppet. Pulling your strings daily until you lost control and took an axe to the miserable hag.

Yes, and how he remembered that.

The blood, all that blood spattering and dripping, stinking foul and diseased like the witch it spilled from.

But even then, she was too wicked to die. What was in her—the sick, malicious mind, the diabolical will to survive—refused death. Sectioned like an engorged bloodworm, her various parts still lived, writhing and crawling. Her head still laughed at him.

You pathetic, pitiful little toad! You couldn't even do this right! she cackled, spewing her venom like a spitting cobra. *You'll never, ever be rid of me! I'll haunt your bones for an eternity!* Severed, gored, her sections moved around him, pressing in. *Now, puppet-maker, we'll see who the real puppet is and who is the puppet-master! You will recreate me! You will make me live and breathe and walk!*

Out of his mind with it all, drooling and delusional with the memory of the horror he had created and set loose upon the world, he seized Abby in his hands and shook her violently.

"There's no time! If I don't bring you back right now, she'll come for both of us! Don't you see that?" he shouted in her face. "It won't be just you that will be punished, but me—"

"No," Abby said. "She's a dead thing! She only lives because of what's inside you! You give her life! Your guilt gives her power!"

Woody fell back, stripping away his mask and covering his ears because he refused to listen to any of this. "IT'S NOT TRUE! IT'S HER! IT'S ALWAYS BEEN HER WHO DOES THE BAD THINGS! NOT ME! IT'S NOT ME!"

And then he realized it was too damn late.

Just too damn late.

He could feel the energy of the storm focus itself like a beam of light. The temperature plummeted and he saw his breath. Cold fingers climbed his spine. His eyes bulged from his head. Nameless shadows seemed to stride about him.

Oh, please! I was bringing her to you! I swear I was!

Out of the rolling clouds of dust and fine particulates, a figure appeared, shambling forward with a loping, uneasy gait. Abby saw who it was and let out a shrill, broken cry. And when Woody looked upon it, he began to sob, urine running down his leg.

Adelia came out of the storm. When she sighted them, she moved faster, almost daintily like a long-legged insect—a walking stick or, perhaps, a mantis. But there was nothing dainty about her. She was a grotesque, misshapen mannequin of horror, a synergy of disparate parts moving in a clicking, creaking symbiosis. A morbid fusion of wood and corpse matter, swivels and ball joints, ivory bones and animate sticks.

She paused ten feet away, the tattered remains of her graying shroud flapping around her like a bedsheet on a clothesline, revealing her inner workings: gears, cogs, and mechanisms whirring in her hollowed torso. Her head revolved on her crooked neck, her wired-together bones trembling, her puppet limbs shuddering with horrid life. She appraised Abby and Woody with a single glass eye yellow as piss.

Together, are we? My little puppet and my favorite toy have joined forces, have they? She threw her head back with a cracking sound, her long hair writhing about her piebald skull like gray worms. She cackled with obscene delight. *We'll see about that, won't we? My puppet-maker will not take up with a cheap whore like you, sweet missy! Now you're both my toys to play with!*

Abby screamed, jumping to her feet to run … but the blood ran from her limbs. Her legs went numb and her knees locked up. Down she went.

"Woody!" she cried. *"Make it stop! Please, make it stop!"*

But he was powerless and quivering. Adelia had once again yanked out his bones, reducing him to a flaccid pool of flesh, a squealing little boy with tears spilling from his eyes.

Adelia had to punish him and he knew it. She came on with murder in her heart. As Woody sobbed like the bad boy he was, she laid her skeletal hands upon him which smoldered in the wind like branding irons. When they touched him, his flesh sizzled like hot grease.

He screamed with absolute agony.

He was blind with it, and incapacitated, reduced to a bawling brat as had been Adelia's intention. The only thing that brought him out of it was the shrieking voice of Abby.

"Stop it! Stop it!" she shouted. "Take the life out of her, Woody! Make her stop! Let her die!"

And for a moment, Adelia did stop. She froze in place, a posed dime-store dummy. But then the machinery inside her began to turn, belts hissing and cogwheels spinning. Nerve endings filled with electricity. Muscles jerked. Limbs reacted. Her patchwork carcass lived.

She approached Abby with clawing fingers, her face pulled tight in a contorted death rictus. Her hinged jaw opened and closed, clattering like the lid on a boiling pot.

She'll be fixed and recreated, Adelia shrilled in Woody's head. *I'll hang her from the wall and it will be she that watches the terrible things I do to you!*

As her voice echoed in his brain like a sacrificial drum, he finally could take it no more. Hurting him was one thing—his guilt demanded it—but he couldn't allow her to hurt Abby the way she had hurt the others. She had to be stopped. Climbing to his feet, scalded and hurting, he blocked her from reaching Abby.

How dare you! How dare you interfere with my fun! Adelia hissed in his head like water becoming steam.

And to this, he mouthed a single word: "No."

Again, Adelia stopped.

Only this time, what was in her seized up. The machinery did not start again. Gears ground to a halt. Belts burned. Cog wheels threw sparks. Plumes of blue smoke blew from her corroding guts. With a final, agonized screeching, her voice echoing into nothingness, she blazed up. Mummified flesh melted. Hair burned. Connections fused. The wires that held her together snapped and she collapsed to the ground, a smoldering assemblage of human remains and crude doll parts.

Woody dropped to his knees, breathless. Head aching, blood coursed from his nostrils. He was dazed, emptied, and finally *alone* in his mind.

Staring with wide, unblinking eyes, Abby shook her head from side to side because she knew, she *sensed*, that something was terribly amiss. Adelia was finished, but the energy feeding from Woody was not played out just yet. Strange noises issued from the storm—the sounds of baby rattles, shaken maracas, rapidly-clicking castanets, and rattlesnakes.

The rattler had come.

She heard whispering and hissing, slithering noises and a bone-dry creaking. The storm stopped moaning as if it was holding its breath. And out of the dust clouds that gathered like fog, came the rattler. Woody went hysterical with fright, whimpering and shaking, sputtering out words that made no earthly sense.

The rattler was the very physical embodiment of his secret terrors, the incarnation of the seamless evil that dwelled in the dank cellar of his subconscious, the ultimate manifestation of the awesome, deadly potential of his twisted, telekinetic mind.

A puppet swarm.

A collection of macabre, broken dolls and dismembered window dummies welded into a single entity—a walking nightmare of marching, swollen plastic legs, bloated thermoformed bellies splattered with whorls of dried blood. Some lacked feet. Others lacked arms. Most were headless. Those that did have heads were bald and cracked, and had no eyes.

The swarm moved past Abby, whispering and hissing with the high, fractured voices of children. *The puppet-master. The puppet-master. He who makes and unmakes. With us. Joined to us. Becoming us.* As Woody screamed, they fell on him, burying him in their squirming forms, the living/undead personification of all the lives he had destroyed to please a malefic leech named Adelia that fed on his fear of being alone and the insecurities of his damaged psyche.

That very thing rechanneled into what he knew and understood best: *puppets.*

As Abby watched with escalating horror, they literally pulled him part, plucking off his limbs and wrenching his head from his neck, splitting him open and pulling out his stuffing.

And then, as he died, they died with him.

Almost immediately, the storm stopped. The wind blew itself out. The dust settled. And for the first time in many dire months, the sun came out and Abby could feel its warmth on her skin.

The world was still gravely injured from the war, but it was no longer haunted. It was set free to begin again and so was Abby.

BLACK WIDOW

O	*h, how they scream and scream,* Meyer thought as he crouched in the darkness, listening to the papery rustle of his own heart. He trembled. He perspired. He bathed in the high, sharp smell of his own glands. It was perfectly insane like everything else, but he'd noticed that sometimes his thoughts had odors. Whenever he had a strong emotional response, whether that was fear or surprise or elation, the scent emanating from his pores reflected it.

The screaming came again and he squeezed his eyes shut, pressing his hands over his ears. He wondered who it was this time. Bob Moholick? Kenny DuShein? Jimmy Kang? Maybe Denny Frechal and one of his boy toys? Could have been any of them. Their numbers were slimming by the day as the Widow took them one by one, her voracious appetite never satisfied.

But not me, Meyer thought. *No sir, not me. I'm too smart and that bitch knows it.*

Was it done?

Was the killing over for the night?

"Quiet," he whispered to himself. "Don't tempt her: she might be listening to your thoughts."

A perfectly absurd idea … yet, sometimes as he cowered in the dusty shadows of his apartment, he was almost certain he could feel her thinking about him, her own wicked thoughts scratching the inside of his skull like fingernails.

Scritch, scritch, skreeeeek …

Carefully, with infinite slowness, he removed his hot, sweaty hands from his ears. He listened at the air vent. The screaming was over. It had been replaced by something even worse: the sound of babies crying, bawling in shrill, shrieking voices like starving infants. It grew louder and louder into a cacophonous squealing that peeled his nerves back.

Stop it! Stop it! Dear God, make it stop!

It faded as it always did … as if … as *if* they had been given the food they needed. He could hear other noises through the vents now—sucking, slurping noises like kittens lapping up bowls of warm milk, like hungry mouths suckling teats. Finally, a perfectly awful, skin-crawling purring sound that made his stomach roll over.

After a time, it, too, ended.

There was silence below, beautiful silence.

Meyer sighed. Oh, how he loved the sweet silence: nothing moving, nothing breathing, nothing feeding.

Though it was dark in the apartment, he could see quite well. Surviving night after night, he'd gotten quite good at it like a cave-dweller. Against that wall were his meager, dwindling supplies. Over there was the barricaded door. Across the room, the boarded windows, a few milky fingers of moonlight shining through.

Now and again, he would light a candle or use his flashlight, but always sparingly because his supply of candles and batteries was getting low. Usually only when he was desperate. Or scared. States he was in constantly now.

He had not been out of the building in nearly three months now. Not since Marlene went missing. Occasionally, and only during the daylight hours, he removed the barricade at the door and peered out into the corridor. He often found things out there: canned food, bottled water, blankets, candles. Odds and ends he needed to survive. But who left them? Why were they concerned about him? And if they were a friend, why didn't they show themselves? That was the great mystery, of course. He rolled it around in his mind and could never come up with an adequate answer.

Marlene, an inner voice, so frantic with loneliness, would tell him. *She's in the building. She's taking care of you. She's showing her love for you.*

But it was ridiculous and he knew it. If she was still alive, she would have knocked at the door. She wouldn't leave things, then run off. What sense would that make?

In his mind, he could see her standing by the door on that fateful day she walked out of his life forever.

"I can't take it anymore, David," she said. "I can't handle being cooped up in this damn place."

"We don't have a choice. We can't go out there. Not yet. Maybe in a few months, but not just yet."

"I don't care. I have to see the sun."

He tried to warn her about the lingering background radiation, the gangs of crazies haunting the streets in wolf packs, but it did no good. She'd always been such a free spirit, a child of nature, athletic and independent and so very adventurous. He couldn't stop her or contain her any more than he could the wind.

"But think of the baby. Please, Marlene."

"And what's it going to be born into, David? What sort of life can our child possibly have?"

"You can't risk exposing it to the radiation out there."

"It's already exposed. We're all exposed."

She was three months along at that point, just starting to show. She was convinced the baby would be stillborn. Or, if it lived, its genes would be twisted up from the radioactivity. After a time, he talked her out of leaving. But that night as he slept, she slipped out.

He couldn't imagine her here now living in her own filth as he did. Everything was unsanitary. It was no place and no life for the child she carried. His greatest fear was that she had gone out and killed herself.

He searched for her, of course, but never found a trace.

The Widow had gotten her.

He was sure of it. She was one of the first, but certainly not the last.

Long before the Widow began purging the men, she'd brutally slaughtered

all the women. She came out of the night—formless, nocturnal, nameless, a stealthy living horror that hated females, any females, on sight. She attacked them mercilessly, cracking their bones, shattering them like peanut shells, completely immobilizing them. She took their eyes so they would not dare look upon her, licking them from sockets, tearing out their tongues by the bloody roots so they would not cry out. Then and only then, did she kill them ... slowly, sadistically, ripping off their breasts and goring what was between their legs. The very things that offended her most, that made them women: organs of reproduction and suckling. She could not abide another female.

They challenged her.

They could breed

And only she had the right to spawn....

There had been some debate among the men (long before she was called the Widow) as to what she was and how she could strike so silently and surgically, and whether she was male or female.

But Meyer knew.

He knew because he listened.

At night, he could hear her through the vents ... singing. Singing with that terrible, dissonant whirring like that of a droning locust. And there had been no doubt in his mind that her voice was feminine in caliber.

Listen.

Just listen.

The stairs. The stairs were creaking. Meyer's apartment was just down from the staircase that led to the second floor. He knew the sound of it quite well, the telltale creaking of its ancient steps. He heard them now as if some great weight was bearing down on them. *She* was coming. Oh, dear Christ, the Widow was coming.

He heard the sound of a huge, bristling body moving down the corridor, rustling against the walls. It paused outside his door and he did not even dare breathe. He trembled, muscles taut, his sanity threatening to break free of its tenuous moorings.

Control your fear.

You must control it.

She can sense it.
It'll draw her in.

Now she was thumping against the door, but not with any real force. It was insane, but it was as if she were *knocking* to see if it got a response. The idea was ludicrous. Surely, she could have bashed through it if she really wanted to. Now there was a gentle tapping as of many fingers, followed by what sounded like licking ... as if she was *tasting* the door. It went on for some time as he shook with fear, then it stopped.

But she was still out there.

He could hear her breathing with a low rasping that gradually became a liquid gurgling as if her mouth was filled with saliva, overflowing with it. He smelled a pervasive sickly-sweet odor like over-ripened fruit rotting to mush.

She wants in, he thought, *but she won't force her way ... it's almost like she wants to be invited. What does that mean? What does it mean?*

There was a sudden peal of anguished screeching that pierced his ears and he had to clutch a hand to his mouth so he did not cry out. It was definitely female in quality, echoing out, making his skin crawl. It faded, breaking up into a low, melancholy sobbing like the sorrowful sound of a woman crying over the graves of her children.

After a time he heard her moving out there, creeping off into the shadows and he sighed. For a long, long time, he did not dare move. He waited. He listened. The silence was nearly overwhelming. The danger was that she now knew exactly where he was. How long before she tired of the games and forced her way in? Because she would and he knew it.

What if he was the last one?

The idea was devastating. There'd always been others and they had been his buffer against her. Plenty of game. But now, yes, if he was the last one, it was only a matter of time before she came for him.

"You need to get out," he whispered. "You don't have a choice now."

He wished he had done it a month ago, but he hadn't because he was sure that Marlene would return. He had been waiting for her. Sometimes, he was certain that he heard her tread on the stairs and more than once he had woken, thinking she had called his name.

Other nights, it was the babies he heard. Their incessant, hungry, pitiful squealing. It seemed to go on for hours, gradually dissipating into a sort of a guttural cooing noise like pigeons, but unpleasantly moist as if through mouths filled with wet leaves.

It's all in your mind. You're imagining it. There are no babies. It's just your guilt, that's all it is. Your guilt over Marlene and the baby.

He told himself that again and again. But every time he thought he had banished it, it always came again in the night: the crying, the horrible crying.

It was a long night, but finally, he saw a few fingers of light coming through the cracks in the boards over the window. He grabbed his canvas bag, shoving everything in it that he thought he might need—flashlight, batteries, candles, bottled water, cans of food and crackers, essential items of survival.

The time was now.

He gathered up his shotgun, the few shells he had left. Carefully then, he pulled the barricade apart, loosening splintered boards with a claw hammer and tossing them aside, the entire time thinking about Marlene and how much she had meant to him, how he needed her and without her he was a house without a foundation that rattled in the wind, threatening to fall. These thoughts were painful, but they were better than admitting to the rising paranoia that made his guts clench like a white-knuckled fist. The fear that told him that the Widow might be waiting outside for him.

When he got to the final boards, he paused.

It was a necessary thing.

"You either do this," he told himself, "or you slink back in your corner and wait for tonight when she gets hungry again."

He removed the boards and they clattered to the floor. The noise was amazingly loud. If she was anywhere near, she would hear it. He threw the deadbolt and locks. This was it. This was where he either became a man and faced danger like a man or he crawled away and trembled like a whipped dog.

Grasping the knob with a shaking hand, he turned it and threw the door open. It was dim in the corridor. The sweet smell the Widow put out lingered out there, a nauseating pall, a hot fermenting stink of leeched prey. He saw dust and emptiness. Not much more. He stepped out there, his breathing ragged. It scraped the back of his throat like a fork.

Inside, he was quivering. His guts were churning with jelly. It felt as if his blood had cooled, been replaced by something that moved through his veins like sludge.

The building seemed alive around him, alert to his presence. He could almost hear it breathing around him with a low susurration that came from within the walls. In his mind, he sensed the muted humming of its nerve endings, the distant and sluggish beat of its heart. His eyes drifted to the ceiling. There was an attic above the third floor. That's where its brain would be.

He purged the idea from his mind. He couldn't afford to waste mental energy on dark fantasies. The windows at either end of the corridor were so filthy with grime that barely any light got in. What there was of it was a dirty yellow. He clicked on his flashlight to chase the shadows away. The beam peeled the darkness back. He saw a few shriveled rat carcasses that looked as if they had been there a long time.

As he moved cautiously toward the stairwell, his heart thumped in his throat. He stood on the landing. Motes of disturbed dust whirled in the flashlight beam. The stairwell was so dark, so clustered with eldritch shadows, that it was like a cave. The darkness was threatening. It seemed to be trying to warn him off. In his imagination, it was haunted by malignant spirits and malefic, ancient gods. It dared him to enter it. He played his light around in the passage. There was nothing to see. Nothing dangerous. The threat he felt was in his mind, playing around the edges of reality. His animal instinct was aroused. It had risen like the hackles of a hound.

Breathing through clenched teeth, Meyer started down. He had to keep his eye on the prize: the first floor and the door that led out into the sunlight.

Overhead, he heard something shift up in the attic. It was there, then gone. His heart raced with fear because he wondered if that's where the Widow was … up in the attic. Is that where she had been hiding all this time? Up there in the dusty, cobwebbed blackness? The very idea made him run down the stairs, knowing he was behaving foolishly, recklessly, but unable to help himself. The fear he felt was beyond anything he had ever known. It owned him. Pushed his buttons, jerked his strings.

From above, he heard a thumping, bumping sound.

Something was on the move up there.

She's coming.

She heard you and now she's coming.

There was no going back now. Either he escaped out into the light or she would find him, make him scream as she picked him apart.

He stumbled down the corridor of the second floor, knowing there was no point in stealth now. She was coming to claim him. The building was her hunting grounds, her pen, and she wasn't about to let any of her livestock slip away. He heard the stairs creaking. She was moving fast.

He came to the passage to the first floor and what he saw in the flashlight beam stopped him as surely as a hand pushing him back.

He saw a man.

Something like man.

It was floating in the darkness before him, a gauzy figure like a ghost. That's when he knew. That's when he understood. Revelation made him cry out, it exposed his nerve endings like bare wires. The man was cocooned in webs, wrapped up like a mummy. He dangled from the ceiling of the stairwell on a single elastic thread like a corpse on a gallows. Strands of the stuff webbed up the passage like fibers of spun glass. The walls were covered in nets of it.

Spiderwebs, he thought, filled with a crawling, inescapable horror. *They're spiderwebs.*

His light picked out no less than five other such mummies. They were shriveled, shrunken things. *Drained dry, oh Christ, drained fucking dry.* He could see their faces pushing out from thin veils of web and they were gray and puckered, barely enough skin on them to cover the grinning skulls beneath.

Meyer moved down the steps carefully, but quickly. He did so because he honestly didn't have another choice. This was the Widow's lair, her nest, and he was trapped in it like a fly. He either made his escape now or … well, his mind refused to consider the possibility. The world was filled with horrors now, but the reality of this was worse than anything he had seen or could possibly imagine: it was madness. There was no other word for it.

As he moved down to the landing, he tried desperately not to bump the strands. He knew how very important that was. He made it and recoiled in terror because the first-floor corridor was like the gossamer tunnel of a funnel-web spider. There was a narrow channel to move through and that was about it.

The Widow was on the second floor now.

He could hear the busy tapping of her many legs as he moved down the channel, sweating, gasping. His heart pounded so hard he thought he would have a massive coronary at any moment. In his mind, he could hear his voice screaming. It would not stop. It seemed to come with such volume he thought it would crack his skull apart.

You have to move! Get to the door!

Yes, he knew it, but his brain … there was something wrong with his brain. Although he urged his body to move, his limbs to walk, nothing happened. Tears rolled from his eyes and his teeth chattered.

And then he knew what it was: the Widow.

She had him as surely as one of the carcasses wound in silk. Though he needed to move, he struggled hopelessly like a fat, juicy fly in a web.

In his mind, he could see her coming for him: slow, deadly, a creeping black horror that would bind him with silk. She would press her swollen body against him, the fine hairs on it like spines, the flesh hot and feverish and loathsome. And then she would grin at him with a mouthful of yellow fangs. *You cannot move, because I do not wish it,* her hissing voice would say. *You must not leave. You must wait for me because I've wanted you for so long and you have responsibilities. You must fulfill them.*

No!

He broke free from the momentary paralysis, his limbs thick and heavy, but moving, propelling him down the webbed passage. There were more cocooned bodies, many of them. Cold sweat broke out on his face as he saw that they moved, that they were not quite dead yet. They writhed slowly, lethargically, in their envelopes of sticky mesh.

He saw faces he recognized—Jimmy Kang, George Holk, Dr. Gupta from the second floor—that were cadaverous, wrinkled, emaciated masks that smiled at him, eyes rolling drunkenly in their sockets. They didn't appear to be in pain or driven mad with terror … on the contrary, they looked like they were in the throes of passion, a secret rapture, beside themselves with sweet lust like men on the verge of orgasm. Their mouths were speaking, gasping out things about how he must wait for her, the delicious kiss of her lovely mouth.

Meyer stumbled back, snaring himself in filaments of web that seemed to crawl over him, strands moving over his face and tickling down the back of his neck. The stuff was alive. It was moving. It was trying to make him part of it. He fought free, the strands snapping. They made sounds like plucked harp strings, vibrating, singing out, until the sound traveled through the entire network, resonating from one end of the building to another.

Now the Widow knew exactly where he was.

Several spiders emerged from the web tunnel and they were like no spiders he had ever seen before. They had bulbous bodies the size of tennis balls, slate-gray and shining, propelled by skittering black legs like needles. They came right at him. Meyer did not hesitate … he blasted both of them with the shotgun. They exploded like water balloons, casting a squirming gore of spider guts into the network where they dangled, legs still moving. Three more showed and he killed them just as fast. The perfectly appalling thing was that they screamed in pain like scalded children when he did so.

His sanity was bouncing around in his head, fragmenting, coming apart in every possible way.

"I'LL KILL THEM, YOU WHORE!" he shouted with such volume that he startled even himself. *"I'LL CRUSH THEM AND SMASH THEM! BUT YOU WON'T GET ME! DO YOU HEAR ME? YOU WON'T GET ME!"*

More and more spiders rushed out.

There was something sinister and diabolical about that, how they seemed to come out of the vents, creep inside the walls, and crawl in the pipes. An army, an absolute army born from the webs, spawned in the revolting hothouse profusion of the Widow's nest, the web-world the building had become. Each strand of silk like a single nerve ending in a gigantic sensory network.

He could still hear the voices of the cocooned, hear their lustful cries, their moaning inside his head, all of it swirling around with lunatic imagery. He dropped to one knee, mad with it all, seeing … yes, *seeing* Marlene in his mind, sweet, beautiful Marlene and she was glowing as first-time mothers always seemed to. Standing there, smiling at him. Her lips pulled back from even white teeth. In her arms, there was a squirming pink child, so full, so fat, a wriggling grub with eight skittering legs.

"IT'S NOT TRUE! IT'S NOT REAL! I'M NOT SEEING ANY OF THIS!"

But as his voice reverberated down the passage, he could hear the singing, scraping voice of the Widow in his skull, whirring, droning, the voice of a siren heard through sea-mist. It was lost and melancholy, drawing him in, a voice of misery and dejection.

It was Marlene's voice.

As her song faded, she spoke to him, *oh, David, not the babies, oh please, not our babies....*

As his mind seemed to melt in his skull into a warm tallow and he whimpered and shook, he smelled that sweet odor again. It engulfed him. So sweet, so sickening, like shoving his head into a rotting beehive.

The shotgun dropped from his hands.

And the Widow came racing out of the shadows, a huge nightmare shape, a black spider the size of a cow with a bloated abdomen and gleaming eyes like rubies, her mouth opening and closing side to side, spilling out a black slime. Her body was covered with her young. They clung to her like fattened ticks … swollen gray horrors with perfectly round bodies like softballs, thrumming and palpitating with obscene life. They made shrill squeaking sounds that Meyer felt right up his spine. As they abandoned her and raced in his direction, they began making guttural croaking noises like huge toads.

They converged quickly, their spindly legs forever on the march— *ticka, ticka, ticka, ticka*—like metal pins tapping the floor. *Ticka, ticka, ticka, TICKA, TICKA, TICKA, TICKA....*

And in those last moments as his will evaporated and fate wrapped its cold, skeletal arms around him, he realized that the Widow was Marlene, that somehow, some way, in the radioactive cauldron of the city, she had been joined with the spider, formed into a single hybrid entity. And it was she who he heard screeching with loss in the night, sobbing outside his door, her heart broken, a woman on the edge of despair, reaching out to the father of her children.

Just as it was she who left the gifts outside his door.

"My darling," he wept. *"Oh, my poor, sweet lost darling...."*

The children fanned out, spreading across the network, trapping him, not unlovingly, in anchor strands of silk that were taut like fishing line. From them, they spun nets and plaits of web over him in complex geometric patterns, weaving, weaving like old women at looms. Industrious. Fanatical.

Hysterical laughter scratching in his throat, his mind a whirlwind of horror, Meyer listened to them crying, all of them so very hungry. They clustered over his body, hundreds of them, their greedy little mouths piercing his flesh and suckling the sweet, warm blood that gushed out. Making cooing noises of contentment, Meyer fed his children, listening to them slurping and sipping from him, feeling the special, secret joy of fatherhood.

WORM CAST

If there was anything funny about it—and what can possibly be funny about millions dying?—It was that God, in his cracked sense of propriety, had balanced the books, so to speak, by shoveling all the hard-working, industrious types into a big mass grave, but he left no-account stew bums like me walking the earth. Go figure. All I knew was that there was a whole lot of booze out there and I planned on getting my fill.

When the bombs laid waste to the city, I was sleeping one off with Blueberry Tom in the basement of an abandoned brewery on 12th and Elm. We heard the boom, all right—it shook the city to its roots—and all the commotion afterwards. People screaming and sirens. The world had dropped its shorts and we were scared shitless, so we hid out in the cellar with four bottles of the hard stuff and a couple cans of Spam. When we finally came up for air three days later, why, the world we knew was gone. Wreckage in every direction. Smoke. Buildings still smoldering. Blackened corpses everywhere.

Well, you know the score.

That was the world we inherited. Anyway, the thing I want to tell you about must have been four, five months later. My sense of time, of the passage of days, ain't much. If you'd been on the sauce for two decades (or was it three?), yours wouldn't be any better. Now, the day in question—I like that, I remember those words from court when the bulls ran me in for vagrancy and petty larceny—that day, anyhow, Blueberry Tom and me were dry. We hadn't had a taste in near on twenty-four hours, I reckon, and along comes old Gladys with Cincinnati Ox in tow.

"You boys," she said. "Oh, you boys is going to love me right to death when you hear what I know! Ain't that so, Ox?"

He nodded. "It would be so."

Ox had spent his glory days in the ring and his head wasn't so good from being used as a punching bag. But he had a good heart. No one could ever say he didn't. Sure, now and again he had one of his spells, but he never took it out on anyone—he just punched holes in walls, was all. God, but the fists on that boy. I swear they were the size of hams.

Soon as Blueberry Tom caught sight of Gladys, he knew we was going to get a taste. Our throats were full of dust and we needed something to wash them clean.

"Well, come one! Come all!" he called out, breaking into song as usual. "Sidle yourselves up, friends and neighbors, for the eats is on me! We got beans and wienies and corned beef hash! Yassir, chili mac and Vienna sausages fresh from the can! SpaghettiOs, pork hocks, and spiced deviled ham! Don't forget our Beefaroni and pudding in a can! Top it off with cheeeeese *raaaaaaavioli* and you'll feel like a man!"

Gladys and Cincinnati Ox came over, smiling, grabbing a few cans of food from our stash. We were only too happy to share. People could say what they wanted about us (and back in the day, boy, had they!), but we were a giving sort. A real community that the ma-and-pa types, stuffed shirts, and white-shoe wage slaves could never wrap their lily white, mass-produced, starched little brains around.

As Ox wolfed down a can of chili, groaning about his ulcers the entire time, Gladys decided against the canned food and gnawed on some stale Doritos.

"Well, I'm all ears," Blueberry Tom said, rubbing his callused hands together so fast I thought they'd throw sparks. "Yassir, lay it on me and don't spare the details."

Gladys offered us a grin. "Liquor store on Twenty-Eighth and Piper. Untouched. Unmolested. Ripe for the picking. Enough juice there to pickle us for six months. Ain't that so, Ox?"

"It sure would be," said Ox.

Good old Gladys. She had a real nose for the old Sweet Lucy: if there was a bottle lying about, you could bet that girl would find it. She was something. She had a real way about her. Back in the day, when some good-hearted Samaritan asked her about her drinking, she'd either laugh in their face or, if she sensed she could panhandle a few bucks off them with a sad story, she'd spin 'em a tale of woe that would have them crying nickels. A real melancholy number like something straight out of an Irish wake, some bit about her mother being a prostitute and her drug-addicted father dying with a needle in his arm and her not knowing anything but the streets since she was thirteen years old, God help her.

As we listened, Gladys laid it out for us.

All we needed were some shopping carts, which we had a-plenty in our little corral (thank you very kindly, Duane Reade), a bit of stealth, and a whole lot of gumption. Something, of course, that was never in short supply. Because if we lacked that, hell, we'd have been toes up long, long ago, our rat-picked bones bleaching in the sun.

It was very exciting because, hell, nothing got me going like a cache of booze. I'd been at it a long time and was still going despite bouts of frostbite and pneumonia, a game leg, arthritis, and a bad liver.

It wasn't an easy sort of life, of course. Even before the bombs fell, it was hard.

Some days back then, I came to with no idea where I was or how it was I'd come to be there. I'd wake up, blinking dirty sunlight from my eyes, smelling maybe garbage or dog shit or grass clippings, running crusty fingers over my face, trying to make sense of it all. Trying to remember. But my memory—even on the good days—had more holes in it than the *Titanic* and the more I tried to get a handle on it, the quicker it would sink down into that black abyss just south of my brain. Oh, I might remember a few things … bits and pieces that were yellowed and grainy like old snapshots tacked to a barn wall. Things about killing a few bottles with Skinny Johnson and Bobby Cupps, begging for quarters with the Hobo King or Gladys, maybe caging a few cigarettes from some out-of-towner or getting some sucker to spot me the price of a hamburger.

I wouldn't remember much beyond that, though.

Like a leaf, I blew from one gutter to the next. The wind would blow me into some damned odd places—a dumpster or under the loading dock of some warehouse or maybe in somebody's backyard. Now and again, I might find myself somewhere more exotic like in a dog house or squeezed into the steam vent of a restaurant.

But that was my life and I was too far down the road to think of making another.

Most bums, I knew, didn't last too long on the streets, maybe a decade or two. It was a hard life and nobody knew that better than me. Back then, I'd get picked up and thrown in dry-out at the hospital, and they'd tell me I wasn't long for this world, that my organs were swollen up and it was a wonder I was still going. But soon as they sprung me, I'd be back at it. Some mornings I'd have the shakes so bad I'd have to slurp my whiskey straight out of a soup bowl and more days than not, I'd wake up so stiff from sleeping under some shed or on the cold concrete that it would take me two, three hours to work out the kinks.

And none of it, you understand, had gotten any easier since the war.

Anyway, enough of my sad story. Gladys had a plan and we liked it. You had to be careful when you went out on an expedition like that. Very, very careful.

The world in general and the city in particular had changed in the worst possible ways since our Russian brothers seeded the country with death, raising mushroom clouds in our blue skies sea to shining sea. Those that had survived the initial attack, the fallout and pestilence that followed in its wake, had become downright predatory. Vicious animals that walked on two legs, but would tear your throat out for a loaf of stale bread. Some of them were simply mentally disturbed, or bat-shit crazy if you prefer, traumatized souls who had lost their loved ones, homes, and sense of reality, had become beasts in human skins. Everyone and everything was a threat to them. They were dangerous as a lap full of rattlesnakes. You surely had to keep an eye out for them.

But worse were the organized groups—gangs and rat packs and religious crazies. They clung together like snakes in a crevice, sharing the same fever dreams, mounting all-out blood wars against other such clans. They'd slit your throat for the food in your pockets or the clothes on your back.

Case in point: when Gladys and Cincinnati Ox discovered the

untouched liquor store, unearthing it from beneath a fall of rubble like archaeologists at King Tut's final digs, some of the locals were not exactly happy about it.

As Gladys put it, "I'd have been more surely fucked than a four-legged fox in a forest fire if it hadn't been for Ox here. Ain't that so, Ox?"

The big man grunted. "It's the truth."

What happened was that a trio of locals (pipe-heads with brains stewed like tomatoes), challenged them with knives and broken bottles. As far as they were concerned, my good friends were poaching on their turf. So, Ox smashed the first one in the face with that battering ram he has for a fist, dropping him pretty as you please into la-la land. The next fellah swung his bottle and Ox grabbed his wrist, snapping it like a green twig. Then he gave him two powerhouse jabs that shattered his jaw and freed him of no less than five teeth.

The other local ran off.

Good thinking, because I'd seen Ox in action before and, true to form, his left hook was coming next. The very one that had cold-cocked Mad Dog Kapinski at the Arena. Yes sir, if it hadn't been for that Russian maniac, Vasilev, who put Ox's lights out at the Garden—some of which never quite turned back on—he'd have gone all the way.

Anyhow, pushing our shopping carts, we moved deeper into the city, into unknown terrain, eyes peeled like green grapes. I'll spare you the travelogue. Suffice to say, the city I'd known all my life had been rearranged. Landmarks were rubble. Streets blocked by debris. Bones scattered in every which direction.

Finally, we arrived.

Ox scoped it out and gave us the all clear. Excited as nips at Halloween, we pushed our carts through the broken doorway of Maxie's Discount Liquor and Party Supplies. The store was in pretty rough shape: walls buckled, ceiling hanging down in places. The floor creaked and groaned as we walked on it … but, oh boy, what a bonanza! Vodka, gin, scotch, vermouth, rye, whiskey, brandy—name your poison, friend, and it was there in quantity. And not just the cheap hootch we were used to, but the top shelf stuff: Bushmills and Bumbu, Grey Goose and Bombay.

"Lookit all this Kool-Aid, chief," Ox said to me. "Yes sir, we're in the pink now."

You can bet we helped ourselves. We filled our carts, upper and lower rungs. Then to celebrate, we had a round or two for the road. Because, hell, it was on the house.

Yup, it was all laughter, good cheer, and fine company like in the old days.

And had it ended there, it would have been a sweet memory to lay your head upon at night. But it didn't end there. God help us, but it didn't.

It began with a bottle of booze on the counter near the defunct cash register. With all that hootch lined up on the shelves, who would pay attention to that lone bottle on the counter?

Blueberry Tom, that's who.

Back in the old days when we took a bed at one of the missions or grabbed some grub at one of the free lunch counters run by the churches, there'd always be some guy there, some old lush who'd reformed and decided he had to give us the spiel. Tell us drunks how he saw the light and quit the juice, praise glory. Sometimes Blueberry would laugh, tell that sumbitch, *I spilled more'n you ever drank, Slim.* He'd get a few laughs from the veteran winos with that, but it was true. Maybe he had more bed bugs in his shorts than most flophouse mattresses, and was so filthy you could never say honestly if he was white or black. Maybe he lacked common sense, but if it came in a bottle and was fermented, it was his kind of thing.

"Why, what do we have here?" he said, seizing the open bottle by the throat and holding it up to the rays of sunshine coming through the doorway. "Yassir, what indeedy? A rare juice in a green bottle!"

"Ah, toss it away," Gladys told him. "What you want with sloppy seconds when we got the good stuff? Never know what germs might be circulating these days. Ain't that so, Ox?"

"It would be," Ox said, completely fixated by the bottles of Widow Jane in his hands. Ever since Vasilev had given him that beating, he couldn't get enough of the sauce. It was in his blood. And if some bum asked him when it was he'd started drinking, he'd say, *Well, shit, what year is it, chief?* The last thing he remembered with any clarity was the fight at the Garden. Next thing he knew, he'd been on the skid for months with a bottle of sweet juice in his paws. And that was all she wrote.

Blueberry Tom ignored her advice. He gave the contents of the green bottle a sniff and his eyes went wide. "Whoo-whee! Now that's a strange bouquet!" He held the bottle up to the light. It was half-full, the label torn off. It could have been coffin varnish and he still would have given it a taste. "Yassir, and lookee here, friends, got a worm in it. Must be some kind of rare mescal."

I took the bottle from him and studied the shape in there. I'd seen the worms in tequila before and they looked nothing like this one. They were always stubby, withered little things. This one was longer, maybe three inches, sort of plump in the middle and tapering at both ends. 'Course, through the green glass, I couldn't see much of it.

Blueberry Tom thought he had a real find and snatched the bottle back from me. Before we could stop him, he took a taste. "Kind of fruity, kind of sweet," he said. "Good stuff! Yassir, the finest!" Upon which, he upended the bottle and drained what was left. "Does a body good! Got a kick, too! Yassir, it'll burn the shorts right off you! I'll be shitting blue-flame propane by this time tomorrow, but, hoo, it's tasty!" He upended the bottle again, sucking that fat worm between his lips.

"That's enough to gag you," Gladys said.

It was at that moment that I noticed that the fat worm between his lips was wiggling. Blueberry Tom made a gagging sound and tried to spit it out ... but the damn thing wriggled up his left nostril.

We all saw it.

It happened that fast. Whatever it was, it was no garden-variety mescal worm. It was something special. Something horrible that had been swimming in that bottle, maybe just waiting for a fool like Blueberry Tom.

Gasping and gagging, spitting out curds of pink froth, he threw himself against the counter, then hit the floor. His body was gyrating wildly. His bladder let go and I could smell it. *"Oh, Christ, oh sweet Jesus! Get it get it get it out of me! It's in me! It's in my fucking head! It's chewing through my fucking head!"*

We tried to take hold of him and hold him still. What we had planned after that, I don't know. But we couldn't hold him. His flesh felt hot and greasy, his eyes rolling in their sockets. Blood came out of his ears and nostrils. Even Ox couldn't control him. He flipped and flopped.

A sweet, sickening smell wafted out of him, like yellow cake, and then it was replaced by an odd fishy odor.

Finally, he went still as a stone.

I looked at Gladys. She looked at Ox. Then the three of us looked at poor old Blueberry Tom. I knew what was going through their heads because it was making the rounds of mine: he was infected, infected by some mutant worm, and we wondered if there might be others and we might get it, too.

"We better get him back," Gladys said, dispelling any notion we might have had of leaving our old friend behind.

We emptied out Blueberry's shopping cart and Ox scooped him up gently like a child and placed him in it. Bright red nodules were popping on Blueberry's face. They were about the size and general color of ripe cranberries.

It was about then, I figure, that the floor gave one mother of a pained groaning and collapsed beneath us, dropping us fifteen feet below. How we survived that without a broken limb was a miracle.

"Everybody whole? Everybody okay?" Gladys asked us. "Hang tight, I'll get some light going."

It was black down there. Gladys always carried a plastic Hefty bag tied to her belt. She called it her notions bag. I'd known her to keep everything from Band-Aids to extra socks to bug spray in it. She scraped a match and lit a candle and we got a look at the fix we were in.

We were in sort of a cellar or crawlspace. The ceiling above was a mass of wreckage, timbers and joists wedged between sections of floor. There was more debris to all sides, hemming us in. Our space was maybe ten feet by fifteen, at the outside. Enough to stretch our legs in, but not much more.

Our faces were pretty grim in the candlelight. No rescue party would be coming. And the most heartbreaking thing was all that good booze shattered on the floor.

Well, we were aching, coughing as we waited for the dust to settle. Now what? Being the enterprising lot we were, Cincinnati Ox and I began checking our situation out in detail. It wasn't so good. There was no way we were getting through the walls. Beyond the shattered sheetrock, it was a tangle of concrete and snaking rebar. Even if we had sledgehammers and picks, it would have taken weeks. Ox tried to shift one of the rafters above and more debris fell down.

We were in a real spot.

Entombed was the word for it.

By then, Gladys had Blueberry Tom out of the shopping cart that had come down with us. He was still out of it. I was thinking that he'd never wake up.

I'll cut to the chase: trapped as we were, we watched over him like hens over a chick. We couldn't bring him around, get him to eat what little we had in our pockets or drink a drop. He just lay there, sweating out this fermented sort of stink, the nodules on his face seeming to jiggle like Jell-O whenever we dared prod one of them. By then, his complexion had gone a jaundiced kind of yellow in color and his eyes, when Gladys parted the lids, were filled with blood.

"You ever seen anything like it?" she asked me more than once.

The truth was, I hadn't. I'd been on the bum a long time and had seen lots of terrible things, picked up more than a working knowledge of basic medical skills ... but what had Blueberry Tom was beyond what I knew and beyond what anybody knew, I figured. The radiation had done some strange things. I'd seen a few mutations and they were not pleasant to look upon. And I'd heard rumors about other things that crept out at night, preying on the unwary.

I'd never put much in any of that.

Now, I wasn't so sure.

But let me tell you what happened next.

Well, first things first: we were trapped, all right. We had a few unbroken bottles of vodka. Cincinnati Ox had a couple tins of sardines. I had two packs of cheese and crackers. And Gladys had one can of apple juice, one box of Kraft mac and cheese, five candles, and a box of matches in her notions bag.

That was our inventory.

We could probably stretch that much food for five days, being that we weren't much on eating regularly; we preferred to drink our meals.

The next question was: how much good air did we have? Using the candle, I lit up a dry sliver of lathing. As I figured, we weren't airtight. The smoke was sucked away up a crevice between a beam and a dangling section of roof that was anxious to fall.

So we had air.

Which brings us to Blueberry Tom. He was in some kind of state, that was for sure. He wasn't going to make it and we knew it. He was sweaty, more than a little swollen, and he'd shake with bouts of the chills from time to time. We couldn't even guess what that god-awful worm had done to him.

The lot of us were scared, and as it turned out, being trapped underground was the least of our worries.

Ox got it into his head that if we shifted one of the timbers above, it might open a passage we could squeeze through. I tried to explain to him that it wasn't just the store above pressing down on us, but quite possibly the two stories above *that*. For all we knew, the entire building had come down. But Ox, well, he understood things like brute strength, but careful thinking was beyond him. But I guess we had to try something.

He put his back into it and I joined him.

We managed to move one of those big old timbers maybe a foot and the shit hit the fan, as I figured it might. The haphazard mass of ruptured flooring, studs, planks, heating ducts and what-have-you let out a groaning noise and a few hundred pounds of rubble cascaded down, nearly burying me. A section of iron pipe swung down and smacked Ox in the head. He went down like he had when Vasilev gave him that barrage of left jabs and finished him with a right cross that would have shattered a cinder block.

Goodnight, sweet prince, as they say.

I suppose, had you been watching, it might have been comical, like something out of an old Columbia short—me covered in pulverized brick and looking like I'd been dusted with flour and poor Ox, dead to the world. If it had been one of them cartoons I'd watched when I was a kid, his eyes would have rolled back white and said NO SALE like an old-time cash register.

Well, it was nearly an hour before he woke up, spooked and ready to swing.

"Hell is this?" he wanted to know. "The hell am I?"

It took some time to explain things. Ever since the Russian cleaned his clock and he took to the bottle, his brain just hadn't been right. His memory was patchy on a good day, I'd guess you'd say. True to form, he couldn't remember the past twelve hours.

"Trapped, you saying, chief? I ain't liking that at all."

Gladys managed to talk him down and after that, he pretty much sulked in the corner with a bottle of Grey Goose.

"We'll get out somehow," I promised him.

"Sure, chief, sure. Don't know what you were thinking bringing us down here in the first place."

Oh, boy.

Blueberry Tom was our main concern. He was surely getting no better. Gladys finally suggested that we get some sleep, save on the candles. She was right: maybe some rest would clear our heads and we could think of some way to get out of there.

I dropped off pretty fast after a few medicinal blasts of vodka. Curled up on the floor, I must have been out for hours when I felt someone shaking me. I thought it might have been Ox looking for more Kool-Aid, but it was Gladys.

"Be quiet," she whispered in my ear. "Something's happening to Blueberry."

I listened. At first, all I heard was Ox snoring, but then, yes, I heard *other* things ... a cracking noise like sticks being snapped, or bones. That was followed by a muted kind of grinding. It was all kind of wet, rubbery-sounding. Gladys struck a match and lit the candle. There was Ox, sleeping it off in a corner, his head atop the rubble that nearly buried him. And about four feet away was Blueberry Tom.

In the hours since we went to sleep, he had blown up like a frigging balloon. And as we watched, the buttons of his coat popped free one after the other. I could hear the seams of his coat ripping.

"Can't be," I said. "Just can't be."

But it was, God help me, but it was. He was flopping about, these weird spasms passing through him. Those nodules on his face were bleeding. But worse than that, his face was yellow as cheese, his eyes bulging and pink, his mouth elongated into a sort of oval like he was trying to scream. That fish-smell was coming off him stronger than ever. Nose-reaming, it was.

And then, something else. We both heard it and I think we figured we were imagining things—a kind of whispering came out of Blueberry's mouth; a soft, sweet, humming voice like that of a child. *"Dah-dee-dah,"* it said. *"Dah-dah-dee-dee-dah...."*

111

My skin crawled and I felt Gladys grip my hand. Hers was hot, sweaty, and shaking. In the guttering candlelight, we saw that his mouth did not move. It was still strained open in that oval, as wide as it could get. The voice was coming from *inside* him.

"*Dah-dah-dah, dee-dah-dah....*"

Gladys and I kept watching him. We didn't dare look away in case something crawled out. We didn't hear that eerie voice again, but the noises coming from inside him were enough to make your stomach crawl. Whatever that worm had done to him, it was apparently still doing it.

After ten or fifteen minutes, it stopped, and he just lay there, mouth open, eyes staring. Maybe we should have gone over to him, seen if there was something we could do, but we were too scared by then. Whatever was going on, it was just damn unnatural.

It was at least an hour before we dared douse the candle.

I'd like to say here and now that things got better, but they didn't. Gladys and I sucked down a bottle of vodka so we could relax and stop shaking. I guess it did the trick: we fell asleep together like that. We woke many hours later in a boozy stupor, a state we were both used to. We could hear Ox walking about with that heavy tread of his.

"Something," he kept saying. "Gotta be something. Can't be in my head. No sir, not in my head. I ain't sick no more."

Gladys scratched another match and lit her candle. We saw Ox staring up at the hanging ceiling. He kept shaking his head back and forth. Blueberry Tom was moving again, making violent jerking motions like a V-8 slipping gears.

"What is it, Ox?" Gladys asked.

"The voice," he said. "Heard a little kid's voice singing to me. Heard it in my dreams. Heard it when I woke up."

We didn't bother trying to explain to him that what he heard came out of Blueberry Tom. It was hard enough trying to explain simple things to him like how he had to put some food in his stomach from time to time or how he couldn't go to the bathroom in his pants, let alone something like that. Gladys finally got him to sit down and she held his hand, talking to him in that easy way she had like he was a frightened child who did not understand the big bad world around him.

Me? I just sat there, staring off at Blueberry Tom, horror stories making the rounds of my mind. I thought of all the doctors I had seen through the years when the courts stashed me in the monkey house for detox. They checked my insides and my outsides, strapped me down and stuck needles in me, talking, always talking in those pale white clinical voices, asking me why it was I was trying to kill myself and trying to pick the lock of my mind so they could get at my childhood and find out why I was such a wreck. I wondered what they'd make of Blueberry Tom.

Gladys had no sooner gotten Ox calmed down and he had curled up with his head in her lap like a sleepy puppy when those noises started coming out of Blueberry again. But now, they were much more violent: ripping, tearing noises, sounds like dogs gnawing on bones, slurping noises. His body jumped like a carp with a hook in its mouth. All of it made Ox whimper.

By then, it had been well over twenty-four hours since the worm slid up his nostril. Maybe it was forty-eight. Time had no meaning down there in the darkness without the sun and moon. I was scared spitless. So was Gladys. Whatever happened, we knew we'd have to deal with it. As cruel as it sounds, I was thinking that maybe we should kill Tom. Slit his throat with a broken bottle or bash his skull in. Then, when that worm came out, smash it to paste.

As it was, feeling how we were, we didn't dare put out the candle. The idea of being in the dark with the thing old Blueberry was becoming was more than any human mind could handle.

I'm not sure how long later it was, but I think we were on the third candle. That's when he sat up. Something clenched like a fist inside me at the sight of it—Blueberry Tom was gone. In his place was a lolling, flaccid thing that didn't seem to have any bones. He moved like a snake moves, undulating, coiling, like a spongy human tadpole. His mouth was still open wide … in fact, it was open so wide the corners had split open from the stress. Something moved inside it. I only caught a quick glimpse of it, but it was glistening and dark like the flesh of a leech. His right eye was a scab of blood, his left completely missing. The socket was torn open, exploded, call it what you will, the cavity big as a softball. In it, set back, was another eye black as treacle.

That's what we saw.

Gladys let out a cry and maybe I did, too. I don't know. I only know that my guts were doing the slow crawl up the back of my throat.

Blueberry kept wiggling about, moving with those flabby gyrations. The flesh of his throat was burst open and in it, I saw no meat and tendons, but bloated white segments like those of a maggot. It was the worm. It had swollen up, grown inside him until it was nearly as big around as his neck itself.

And I knew why.

God help me, but I did.

It had been eating him: those sounds we heard were the sounds of it feeding on him, eating him from the inside out. Stuffing itself with his flesh. And now it was gigantic and it wore his skin like a wrapper.

He looked over at us ... or *it* did.

And what happened then was just beyond anything I could have imagined. From the yawning pit of his mouth, that glistening thing I had seen emerged. I don't know what it was exactly ... something like a feeding tube or what you might call a proboscis, I guess. It was long and fat, thick around as Blueberry's mouth, a soft and squishy kind of appendage that tapered to a suckering disc at the end. It was oily and beaded with little bumps, oozing a snot-like slime.

It just hung there from his mouth, pulsating, like the trunk of an elephant maybe, but made of a pulpous kind of flesh.

Disgusting doesn't even cover it.

I smelled that sweet, yellow cake smell again. It was enough to make you want to throw out your guts. As I breathed it in, it made me feel dizzy and loopy, the way you get from laughing gas. For just that moment as it filled my head, I didn't hate the worm at all ... in fact, I hoped I'd be next. That sounds insane, but it must have been some sort of hormonal thing, a chemical weapon it used that took away your fear and inhibition, made you want to be part of it. And in my head, I swear I could hear that singing childlike voice, *dah-dee-dah ... dah-dah-dee-dee-dah ...* echoing out and making me feel warm and fuzzy.

Then, all that was canceled out as it exuded that awful fishy odor, making me nauseated. Something which increased as it began to move, slithering about like a python. As the three of us sat there, feeling paralyzed and hopeless, the proboscis-thing began eating Blueberry

Tom. With a moist smacking, it sucked the flesh from his face ... it devoured his lips, gnawed on his nose, rending the cartilage to meaty threads that it vacuumed up. Within seconds, it seemed, Blueberry Tom's face was stripped, ingested, leaving him looking like something from a dissection table.

Lastly, it sucked his remaining eye out with a slobbering sound.

The three of us were shaking, terrified, sickened, but we did not move. Maybe we didn't dare. And that's when Ox lost it. He let out a wild scream that was pure terror and pure rage, pulling himself away from us, jumping to his feet and launching himself at Blueberry Tom. He was fast. Too fast for us to stop him. Gladys and I made a grab for him, but he got away as we cried out his name.

He went right after that proboscis and what it was connected to like he was back in the ring. With a flurry of devastating rights and lefts, he smashed it back and forth. Each time he pulled a fist back, strands of sticky goo were stuck to it. Then, as he realized the stuff had him like glue, that trunk opened up and squirted something in his face that looked like Silly String. It webbed him up. As he tried to pull it away from his eyes with clawing fingers, it webbed his hands to his face. Then he dropped to his knees.

I don't know what I was expecting, but there was a ripping sound and the worm burst from the remains of Blueberry Tom like a cat from a sack, its proboscis engulfing Ox's head. It was a gigantic maggoty thing now that it was free, made of swollen white segments and sweating a vile gray jelly. Blueberry Tom was still connected to it by strands of tissue, but he was little more than a worm cast, a shell that had been cleaned out.

The worm took Ox and took him fast. Like a snake unhinging its jaws to swallow a mouse or a large egg, its elastic flesh stretched itself over his head, then his shoulders, sucking him into itself right up to the belly. And by then, he was no longer moving. There was nothing we could do. Gladys was hysterical and it took all my strength to hold her back, because Ox was like a son to her.

The worm made those same grinding, snapping noises as it digested him. Within about ten minutes that were like a living horror to us, Ox was gone, just a huge bulge inside the worm that it was slowly, efficiently breaking down. And when it was done, I knew, it would be twice the size it had been.

Then it would come for us in turn.

There was no way it wouldn't.

Gladys and I just sat there, holding onto each other as it worked on Ox, moving with weird, flabby contractions, making the most horrible sucking and slobbering noises. Being who and what we were, we opened that last bottle of Grey Goose. We drank the entire thing as that blobby worm horror kept feeding, looking like a ballooned seed pod.

What happened next is kind of fuzzy. As much as we drank, we just couldn't get drunk. That's a fact. We were reaching out for the oblivion of alcohol that made our awful existence bearable, but we couldn't find it. Maybe it hit me harder than I thought. I must have blacked out. Maybe the booze and stress combined put my lights out. But when I opened them, Gladys was screaming.

There were worms crawling on her.

I saw it. They were everywhere—on her face, in her hair. She was tearing them free with her hands, but that didn't stop one of them from sliding up her nose and another entering her ear with a juicy sound like a kid sucking up a strand of spaghetti.

They were on me, too.

I picked five or six free and that's when I saw that the giant worm had split open, revealing its pink, meaty insides. Ox's white bones were scattered about as if it had vomited them out. And spilling out of it was what looked like a pool of jelly, only it was yellow like the broth of chicken soup. In it was a tangled ball of what looked like hundreds and hundreds of noodles—immature worms.

One by one, they were swimming free and coming after us to complete their horrible life cycle. I lost it. It was too much. I ran across the room and jumped up, grabbing the biggest timber I could find. A mountain of rubble and bricks and sections of flooring came down. I got free of it, but it buried the worm. I saw light. It was daytime out there. I leaped up, took hold of a pipe and hoisted myself free, frantically crawling and fighting my way up until I had gotten free of the ruins.

That's it.

That's the story I wanted to tell you. You're probably thinking that

I imagined it all, that it was just some bottle-influenced delirium I was in, a product of slow-cooking my brain in alcohol these many long years. Maybe. Then again, maybe not. All I can tell you is that it happened the way I said. It's been three days since I escaped that cellar or crawlspace, whatever it was. I'm just trying to warn you that under this city are what you might call mutant worms and that, one of these days, they'll rise up to hunt the last of us down.

Yeah, you go ahead.

You walk away.

I warned you. That's all I can do. My friends are all gone now and it's just me alone in the streets. But I got good eats—pork and beans and Spam—and lots of good sauce to take my pain away. But I'm alone. Oh God, but I'm so alone. Or maybe I'm not alone at all. Sometimes it feels like there's something crawling in me and I thought last night, I heard a sort of grinding inside me. And the pain, oh Christ, the pain of it.

You smell that?

Can you smell it?

Sweet like yellow cake. It's nice, ain't it? Real nice. Reminds me of birthday parties when I was a kid. It makes me hungry, makes me long for better times.

Dah-dee-dah, dah-dah-dee-dee-dah.

That beautiful voice. It makes me feel all cozy and easy with things, part of something much bigger than myself, bigger than the whole world.

Dah-dee-dah.

Dah-dah-dee-dee-dah....

Goodnight, sweet prince, as they say.

FALLOUT

Two weeks after it took Neil Stroheim, it returned. It hovered above the grassy hilltop at the outer edge of Porterfield—a fuming white-yellow cloud that seemed to sparkle like mica when the sunlight caught it just right. There was something about it that made people want to look at it. It caught the eye, harnessed the imagination, and created a nearly mindless fear in them.

"It can't be," Molly said, balancing Kaitlyn on one well-rounded hip. "It can't be back already. It hasn't been a month yet."

Billy K., standing there with the rest of them on Fuller Avenue, which wound around Porterfield like a rope, just shook his head. "Our idea of time and it might not be the same thing. You think, George?"

George shrugged.

"Only one reason it would come back—it's hungry," Gus said. "And you know what that means."

Somebody told him to shut up, and someone else told him if he didn't watch it with his predictions of doom and gloom, he was going to find himself missing teeth. Nearly the entire population of Porterfield was there, all those that had survived the war, roughly sixty people. They were scared. Grumbling. Arguments broke out. A couple of the younger guys got in pushing and shoving matches. Billy K. broke those up.

"Now, you people knock it off," he said. "Quit acting like animals. George didn't come down here to listen to this. Did you, George?"

George sighed.

Long before the bombs fell, he was a nothing and a nobody. He missed that. He was an introvert by nature, the sort of guy who could while away the afternoon with a paperback novel or making charcoal sketches on his art pad, dreaming beneath a tree. But that had all changed now. He was the center of attention. For the first time in his life, he mattered. Everyone wanted to know what he thought about things, how he felt, and if he needed something—any goddamn thing—they wanted to be the one to give it to him. It wasn't that they liked him. It was because they were terrified of him.

As he looked over the crowd gathered with their beady mouse eyes bright with terror, he thought, and not for the first time, *I could really exploit this. I could be king. I could be their fucking god if I wanted to.*

But he did not want that. He just wanted to be left alone. He didn't want them kissing his ass or doing him favors, groveling in his presence and slinking around his legs like hungry cats. The only reason they acted like that was because of Red.

Now Molly came up to him as he knew she would. She had handed her baby off to her sister and got up very close, so close that her full breasts pressed against his arm. She was an attractive girl and after the baby, she'd worked very hard to get her body back in shape so she was toned like she had been when she was nineteen. She had smoky blue eyes and a full, sensual mouth.

"Hey, George," she said, her hot breath at his ear. "Why don't you come see me tonight? We can have fun."

Billy K. heard her because he was only a couple feet away. "Hey, that's a good idea, George. I'll bring over one of my chickens—got a real fat hen you'd like—and Molly could barbecue it for you the way you like it."

"Not tonight."

"Please, George, *please,*" she whispered, practically begging. And he knew that if the others weren't there, she would have done exactly that. She licked her lips and made sure he saw it. She would do anything to save herself and her daughter.

If you think I like any of this, Molly, you're wrong.

"I can't."

"Why doesn't the damn thing just blow away?" Winnie Rose asked. She was old and her memory wasn't so good. She asked the same thing every time the cloud showed up.

Of course, it was a reasonable question, George knew, because the wind *was* blowing. It wasn't a tempest or anything, but it was strong enough to blow leaves down the street and push waves through the long grass of the hill. Hell, even the tree limbs were moving. So, it was definitely strong enough to blow away a cloud … so why wasn't it?

Because it's not by accident, it's on purpose. It's here because it wants to be here.

He stared at it. It was like a great, hazy ball of plasma two hundred feet across, shining, slightly phosphorescent. He couldn't look away. He began to see things in it, suggestions of forms and movement. It was like staring into the static on a TV screen. If you looked long enough, you began to see patterns and faint images.

"What are we going to do, George?" Molly asked in her breathless voice.

"You know what he's going to do," Gus Peeples said.

George nearly laughed. Gus was pretty much a zero as a human being. Before the bombs came down, he was little better than the town drunk. He brewed sour mash in a shack out in the woods, drank himself blind, spent a lot of time in the county lockup, and would steal anything that wasn't tied down. But he was a realist. He knew the score. The rest might pretend that everything was going to be okay, but he knew better. And knowing better, he never tried to get on George's good side.

Despising his very existence, George detached himself from Molly. "I better go get Red," was all he said.

And in the crowd, several people began to whimper.

The citizens of Porterfield had gotten very good at deceiving themselves. It had become something of an art form in the town. They openly told each other that the reason that most of them had survived was because of the mountains. They rose high on all sides, blocking the deadly radioactive emissions that had devastated other communities. The mountains, they claimed, turned the winds back upon themselves and Porterfield, tucked away in a deep-cut valley, was spared. The radiation level was near normal in town, but beyond the mountains it was cooking hot.

This was what they made themselves believe, George knew.

And it was also because of the mountains that the well water was still fresh and pure, the creeks in the valley ran clear and were filled with fat trout, the crops came in abundantly, and the livestock was almost freakishly healthy.

But that wasn't the reason, of course.

The mountains certainly helped, but they couldn't stop fallout from the sky, deadly black rains, and radioactive seepage in the soil. There was another agency responsible for blocking these things and it had come back again, two weeks after it had taken Neil Stroheim as sacrifice.

When George got home, he paused on the walk, sick to his stomach, and tired, so godawful tired. There was a white picket fence around the house, hedges squared off, grass lush and green and expertly cut. Fruit trees bloomed, red tulips and wild rose bushes blossoming outside the living room window. Very nice. So nice that it looked like a photo from *Better Homes & Gardens.*

It had been going to seed just a few years ago because George had no practical skills whatsoever. He knew nothing about plumbing, electrical, drywall, masonry, or lawn care. The only reason it looked so good now was because Billy K. took care of it. Billy K. would do anything for him. Maybe he'd beat him up in high school and couldn't stand the sight of him, but now he practically fawned at his feet.

When he got inside, Darlene was waiting for him. She was wearing shorts so he could see her long, tanned legs, a midriff shirt so he could admire her flat belly.

"I heard it came back," she said. "Is that true, George?"

"Yes."

She took him by the hand and led him to his recliner. When he settled in, she massaged his shoulders. He was glad she was behind him so he didn't have to look into her vacuous eyes. There had been a time when she continually criticized everything he was, told him how she'd wished she never married him. Now she was a Stepford wife. She lived in fear of him, constantly cringing and boot-licking. She couldn't clean the house enough for him, make enough of his favorite foods, and please him in every possible way.

I liked it better, he thought, *when she hated me and slept around on me. At least, she was real then.*

"Do you want some lemonade, George? That's what you need, a tall, cool glass of lemonade. You just relax, I'll get it for you."

It was pointless to tell her he didn't want any, that she needed to quit fussing over him. She returned with the lemonade.

"Is it good, George? Do you like it?"

"Yes."

"Do you want a snack, George? I can get you cheese and crackers, some cheese dip, or knock out some of those wontons you love."

"No, I'm good."

"Finish your lemonade, George. I have the bed ready for your nap. I'm making steaks on the grill tonight, the bacon-wrapped filets you like. I baked a blueberry pie for you," she said, blathering non-stop and the more she talked, the higher her voice got until it sounded nearly hysterical. "You should see how the berries are coming in! They're as big as grapes and so juicy and sweet—"

"Darlene, just relax, okay?"

"Oh, you're stressed." She came around and kneeled before him. "George, it's not your fault someone has to go into the cloud. That's just the way it is. When it's all over, I'll be here waiting for you." Meaning, of course, being his devoted wife, it would not be her. "Let me help you relax." She reached behind her and undid the tie of her shirt, tossing it aside. She put his hands on her breasts. "Doesn't that feel good, George? Oh, you know how excited you make me."

"Darlene, wait, I—"

But she did not wait. "Let me make you feel better, George. It's what a good wife does." She unzipped him, gripping his penis and stroking it until he began to grow hard. "You'll like this, George." Then she took him in her mouth, running her lips up and down on his shaft until he was fully hard and glistening with her saliva. "You'll feel better now," she said, pausing, then engulfing him again, her head moving frantically up and down, then pulling her lips off with a loud smacking. "Then you can have your nap until supper." Then she was back at it until he went rigid and came in her mouth. At which point, she took him in as far as she could, gagging and shaking, but making sure it was as good as it could possibly be.

She was a good actress, but her eyes were dead. For all the passion in them, she might as well have been sucking on a cold bratwurst.

"There. Isn't that better, George?" she asked.

He told her it was and she toddled off to the kitchen, not bothering to put her shirt back on in case he wanted to look at her breasts.

She's probably gagging into the sink, he thought.

Sighing, he zipped himself back up and went out into the back yard. It was time to see Red. The very idea made his heart beat faster. A hot worm of fear coiled in his belly.

"Does it have to be this way, George?"

He turned and Darlene was standing in the doorway, her free, pointy breasts like missiles poking out from silos.

"You know that it does."

She swallowed. "Can't it ... can't it ever be normal again?"

He ignored the question. She was like a little girl asking him why Santa Claus couldn't be real.

Beneath the crabapple tree and its beautiful pink blossoms, Red was waiting. Red was a reddish-brown lab. He was four years old. There was a time when old Red would have come vaulting over to him, jumping all over him, absolutely ecstatic that he was home.

But Red didn't do that anymore.

Now he watched George with huge dark eyes that were glassy like those of a stuffed moose, a vapid evil reflected in them that made him cringe.

"It's time again," George told him.

Red gave two brief wags of his tail.

"But you knew that, didn't you?"

Red appraised him. His eyes were very un-doglike. They were scrutinizing, starkly intelligent, and unbearably cold-blooded, like those of a reptile. When he put them on you, they made something inside you squirm.

They made George uncomfortable. Very uncomfortable.

Red stood up. He cast a wary eye towards the house where Darlene was singing happily as she worked in the kitchen, then he looked at George, as if to say, *She annoys me, too. Would you like her to be the one?* He trotted over and let himself be petted, but he was strictly going through the motions and George knew it. Beneath Red's soft, luxuriant fur, he felt like a mass of cold meat. Utterly loathsome, as if whatever dogs were made of, he was made of no more. George pulled his hand away in disgust.

Red appraised him with a discernible lack of pity or warmth. A sour smell of age came off him.

George remembered how Red had been before he went into the cloud: a kind and gentle soul as his breed tended to be. Now, he was no longer outgoing, affectionate, or eager to please. Not a loved pet, but a creature that *kept* pets.

Red was the only dog in town. There had been others and cats, too. But Red did not like the way they yipped and whimpered in his presence, so he got rid of them.

"I guess we better go do this, buddy," George told him, feeling low and dirty.

Red led the way and George followed. The dog made him feel subservient. Worse, like a toy to be played with when it amused him to do so. But it was something he had to live with.

Now Red stopped within feet of the back door. Darlene's singing stopped in mid-note as if her throat had been slit. The door opened and she came shuffling out, a hollow-eyed zombie. There were tears in her eyes.

"Do ... do I have to, George?" she asked.

"You know you do. We all have to be there."

They both followed Red. By that point, they were no more human than Red was really a dog.

FALLOUT

Before the cloud came, things were bad. Two-thirds of the town had died from radiation poisoning. The water was contaminated. Outbreaks of influenza and infectious diseases claimed dozens every day. There was so much soot and dust in the atmosphere that the sun was barely seen for weeks. It got cold. The elderly and those with weakened immune systems died at an alarming rate. The crops withered. Trees dropped their leaves at midsummer.

The survivors hung on, but just barely, eating canned food and drinking bottled water. But it didn't take long before the stocks became exhausted.

Then, in the eleventh hour, the cloud came.

It was yet another scary event. George was one of the first to see it. He had Red with him. Red did not like the cloud. He barked at it, snapping and growling. A sweet-tempered animal, he acted as if he had gone rabid, foaming at the mouth, aggressive and feral, completely unmanageable. He bit George when he tried to restrain him.

Then he ran at the cloud.

Before George could stop him, he was sucked into it. George tried to go after him, but something like a wave of force knocked him on his ass. The cloud would not let him enter it no matter how many times he tried. His old, dear friend was just ... gone.

After that, no one dared approach it. Two days later, Red reappeared. It was like some kind of catalyst—the sun came out, the grass turned green overnight, flowers bloomed and trees blossomed. Everything came alive again. Livestock appeared in the fields. It was spooky, weird, disturbing, but no one dared look a gift horse in the mouth.

The cloud went away.

Then, a month later, it came back. Everyone was well-fed, healthy, and thriving by that point. By then, there was no doubt that Red had changed. The dog that went into the cloud and the one that came back out again were not the same. He was no longer the friendly pooch everyone knew and loved. There was something perfectly alien about him. His eyes were like the slick, sucking black mud at the bottom of a cold pond.

He watched.

He waited.

126

He studied.

Then he began to communicate with George. Not by words, but by sending pictures into his head. He made it very clear what the cloud wanted. George told the others at a town hall meeting. He nearly got beat up for suggesting such a thing.

"You're saying your dog's talking to you," Billy K. had said, scowling the way he had in the 10th grade right before he punched George. "You're a fucking loon, George. He's just a dog. A stupid damn dog."

There was uneasy laughter at that.

"No, not talking exactly," he tried to explain, his face reddening in embarrassment as he saw all those faces he had known for so many years looking at him with pity or out-and-out derision. "Kind of like he puts images in my head."

One of the farmers, maybe Charlie Hope, coughed and said, "Jesus Christ, somebody get this guy some medication. A dog of all things."

But he's oh, so much more than that, George wanted to tell them, but didn't have the heart or—words—to. Whatever happened in that cloud, Red was no longer Red. The very thing that made a dog a dog had been taken from him, replaced with something cold and calculating and blatantly malevolent. They all knew it, even if they didn't want to admit it. The way he watched them all the time, like a cat contemplating disemboweling a mouse. He scared them. No one ever petted Red anymore; they were afraid to touch him.

Winnie Rose, in her own inimitable way, had put it best one afternoon after stroking the dog out of long habit, then yanking her hand away as if she had touched maggoty carrion. "Like cold clay," she said, her mouth trembling. "Dear God, like cold clay somebody molded into the shape of a dog."

They all began insulting George, deriding him, giving him a full ration of shit. He wasn't angry: he knew they did it not out of scorn, but out of fear, because they were all afraid of Red by then.

It might have ended with George getting thrown out into the street, but then Red showed up. He walked up the aisle between the rows of people sitting in their folding chairs, a terrible smell wafting from him that reminded George of the way vomit smells when you have a stomach bug—sour and sickening. Whenever he sent pictures into George's head, that stink became very strong as if he was secreting a vile hormone.

People drew back from him.

They could sense his power, the darkness brooding inside him. He moved with that determined, stealthy, alien sort of stride, going right to George, brushing up against him, feeling hot and repulsive.

Then he turned and put his huge, terrible eyes on those gathered. His lips curled back from his teeth. A droplet of black saliva dripped from his mouth. Outside the hall, the wind began to moan with a mournful sound, the sky went dark and it began to snow.

People cried out.

They tried to get out of their seats, but they couldn't move. They were paralyzed. Red had them and they knew it. He walked from one to the other, sniffing them. Then he stopped right before Mimi LaCasse. Tears rolled from her eyes, her mouth open in an agonized, silent scream. She was a retired teacher and she had had nearly everyone in that room as a student through the long roll of years. Nobody could help her. Red licked her hand. Then she stood up and walked outside, her eyes completely blank.

She went into the cloud and the sun came back out.

That was six months ago. Since then, Red had chosen ten people to follow her.

Now it was time again.

When they reached Fuller Ave, in full view of the cloud, the entire town had turned out. No one dared refuse Red's invitation. A few had in the past, but after Red made them go into the cloud there was no more defiance from the others.

Clutching his arm, Darlene whimpered, "Please, George. Not me. Not me. You know how much I *love* you and how *good* I am to you."

Yes, he knew, all right.

As he passed through the crowd, everyone gushed and was beside themselves at his presence. They touched him as if for good luck. The farmers promised him smoked hams and bacon, fresh eggs and plump chickens, tomatoes and cabbage and potatoes. Tradesmen wanted to work on his house. Housewives wanted to make him pies and fresh bread. The smoldering, desperate eyes of single women, and some not-so single, offered him other things. It seemed like they were all coming at him at once like puppies begging treats.

It made his head swim with vertigo. Didn't they know, *couldn't* they know, that he had no say in the matter? It was the dog, the goddamn dog. He—or whatever grew in him like a cancer—held the power. Only him.

Red walked out in front of the crowd. Not with the carefree stride of a happy dog, but with the silent, stalking movement of an apex predator. No one was speaking by then. They didn't dare draw attention to themselves.

Red, goddamn Red.

George felt himself getting misty and weak in the chest when he thought of the dog Red had once been ... playful and bouncy and comical, loving everyone and everything. All those wonderful afternoons they'd spent fishing, lazing about by the edges of bubbling creeks, gnawing on salami and cheese. Red had loved beef jerky and had a weakness for sharp cheddar cheese.

But that Red was dead now.

What had replaced him was a monster.

George looked from the cloud—which was spinning faster now, seeming to pulsate—to Red, who stood by him, a deadly and impossible heat radiating out from him in waves.

Who's it going to be this time, Red? Who do you want as sacrifice?

The thought just played through his head, but Red apparently sensed it because he looked at George the way a spider must look at a fly before it sucks its blood out. Images flooded George's brain, an absolute barrage of them that made him light-headed, woozy, and giddy in a very unpleasant sort of way. He saw the faces of those who had gone into the cloud, the way they looked when they were chosen ... numb, rubbery, vacant, as if their personalities had been wiped clean—Mimi LaCasse, Jeff Preachley, Dorothy Reya, Neil Stroheim, Tub McGill, all the others.

Then an image of Franny Sweisser appeared in his mind. Franny had decided the dog was evil and decided to do something about it: he went after him with a tire iron. Nobody knew what Red did to him exactly, but Franny wandered about town for a week afterwards like a mannequin, drooling and mindless, still gripping the tire iron, pissing and shitting himself. His eyes had glazed over like frosted glass. When Red finally sent him into the cloud, everyone was relieved.

"Red," George found himself saying, gasping. *"Red...."*

Then, suddenly, he *knew,* he understood exactly who it was going to be this time. It came into his head as adrenaline rushed into his belly leaving him feeling sick and shaky. Whatever had happened to Red in that fucking cloud he would never know, how he was changed and mutated and morphed into a monstrous thing. No, he would never know that any more than he would understand what Red's relationship to the cloud now was.

But he knew one thing: what Red wanted this time was the ultimate horror. The faces of the townspeople paraded before his mind's eye, one after the other and it made him recoil with complete repugnance.

"No," he said. "No, Red. You can't do ... *that.*"

He stood there, barely able to stay on his feet, the world whirling around him. Red watched him with sardonic amusement, his eyes leering and filled with a primal wrath.

"What is it, George?" Billy K. finally asked, because he couldn't take it any longer. "Who does he want?"

George tried to swallow, but found that he couldn't. "He wants all of us this time."

The crowd began to panic. Mothers and fathers clutched children to them. Brothers held onto sisters. Grandparents stood in front, thinking they could physically block what was coming. There was murmuring, sobbing, swearing and oaths of violence against not just Red, but George.

But no one moved.

They didn't dare.

Everyone figured—and rightly—that the first one that broke and ran would be an immediate target for Red's malice. He would make an example of them. Maybe he was going to make an example of *all* of them, but nobody wanted to be the first.

The dog watched them carefully now, waiting for them to queue up. If they didn't, of course, he had ways of making them.

"Please, George," Darlene sniveled. "Make him stop. Oh God, *make him stop.*"

George looked at all the faces of people he'd known, loved, and been friends with, even the faces of those he could not tolerate or had no use for. They were still human beings and he could feel their pain, their hopelessness. And what hurt him deeper and more profoundly than anything, were the kids. They did not understand. They wept with their parents as children must have when they were taken off to Auschwitz or Bergen-Belsen or one of those terrible places.

No, it ended here.

This fucking madness stopped if he had to snap Red's neck in his bare hands.

Red sensed what was in his mind and he looked at George with barely-concealed contempt, letting him know that defiance would not be tolerated.

George stepped between the dog and the crowd. He could feel the heat of Red's anger welling inside his head. It brought sharp spikes of pain that made him wince. But he stood his ground.

"No, Red. I won't let you. Do you hear me? I won't let you."

For a moment, something seemed to melt in the dog's eyes and George saw the old Red, the good Red, the sweet old friend he hadn't seen in some time, but then it was gone, replaced by a grinning, malign force of evil.

The sun dimmed as if it had been turned down, the sky filled with bloated, ugly gray clouds. The temperature dropped thirty degrees in a matter of seconds. What the cloud and its avatar—Red—had given, it was taking away. A steely silence gripped the crowd. People shivered, but they did not speak as the world they knew trembled at the edge of extinction.

Red stared at George, who did not move and certainly did not back down.

The weird, spooky twilight cast a shadow of the dog on the ground that was horribly misshapen, a distorted snake-like shape that slithered and writhed in black loops, something that was probably indicative of its true nature: the cold-blooded life form that inhabited the carcass of the dog. The shadow it threw was not only animate, it was hellishly three-dimensional, swelling like a leech filling with blood, a black and seeping vermiform shape that crawled through the grass, its fore-end widening like a great funnel and its hind end lashing with ophidian convolutions.

George let out a short, sharp cry as it wriggled toward him, backpedaling and falling on his ass. Red moved forward a step or two, his eyes gone the red-purple of infected wounds. Yellow serous tears dripped from them and his lips retreated from his fangs which had grown unnaturally long.

As the crowd pulled back, Red hovered over his former master, appraising him with a cold, deadly concentration. His eyes made George squirm inside. It felt like his blood was boiling and his skull was filled with ice. *He can make things happen,* a voice told him. *Things worse than anything you can imagine. He can show you what he showed Franny Sweisser.* But somehow, he knew Red wasn't going to do that. It was as if he found George's newfound rebellion amusing.

Breathing his foul breath upon him, Red licked his face and his tongue felt like a cold shank of liver. George screamed; he couldn't help himself and the dog seemed to grin, pleased that it had triggered the very reaction it had sought.

Red stepped back and away while hands pulled George to his feet. He moved back and forth before the crowd, making a low hissing sound in his throat. His haunches were raised, his fur standing on end in sharp spikes. Beneath the fur, his flesh seemed to creep with avid waves, rippling unpleasantly as if whatever was inside him wanted out.

The crowd shook with fear, moaning and gasping, whimpering or crying right out. The toxic intensity in Red's eyes held them and they found that they could not look away as he moved with a swaying, boneless motion, back and forth, back and forth like a watch on a chain, fascinating them, bewitching them. George saw that their eyes followed his motions exactly as those of a kitten will watch a toy on a string swung side to side before it.

He was hypnotizing them, George knew, mesmerizing them somehow. He had power over them and that power was inescapable.

But it didn't touch George for some reason. So he stood his ground in-between the people of Porterfield and the demon from hell that tormented them.

"You're not taking them, Red. I won't stand for it," he said, approaching the dog. "If you want to send somebody into the cloud, send me. Do you hear me, you fucking mutt? *Send me.*"

Red stopped with his hypnotic movements. He froze up. For one second, he looked terribly confused the way a cat might if a mouse flipped him off right before he killed it. This open disobedience was unconscionable, maybe even shocking to the monster living inside him.

He growled.

His eyes blazed.

Something like black slime hung from his mouth.

Yet, he did not strike George down or make an example of him. It was as if he couldn't for some reason and it threw him into a frenzy of yipping and yapping, quivering and contorting.

Then he stopped.

He sat down.

And the cloud which had been static on the hilltop began to move. Since they wouldn't come to it, it was coming to them.

It engulfed them and there wasn't a damn thing they could do about it. It fell over them like a fog at sea, yellow and sparkling and fuming. It sucked the world into itself and became the world. Now everyone was going to find out what had happened to the others.

George stood there, staring at the dog who now was so still, so incapable of movement, it was as if he was dead, stuffed and mounted. The world around him had gone hazy in the guts of the cloud, tendrils of mist snaking about. The crowd looked like ghosts.

And then they began to scream.

George saw them—eyes bulging and bodies shaking and hair standing on end. There was a cold energy in the cloud and it was being directed at them. Whatever it was, he could feel it crawling over his skin like static electricity. And then their screams became a horrendous, cacophonous wailing, a howling of agony and he saw why.

They were floating.

Gravity had been canceled out and they were lifted up, legs kicking and arms thrashing, dangling like marionettes and their cries were shrill and sharp as they began to rotate like the cloud itself, around and around in a swirling vortex, seeming to spin faster. And as they did so and their shrieking became wild and perfectly insane, the most awful, grisly thing began to happen: they were coming apart. *Literally.* Arms were pulled from sockets, legs divorced from hips, heads popping free of necks.

George was in the eye of the storm, so to speak. He felt the intensity of the field that held them and pulled them apart the way cruel little boys pull the wings off flies or the legs off a daddy longlegs. They became a maelstrom, a sucking whirlpool of anatomy.

He trembled there on rubbery knees, mouth hanging open, a soundless scream of horror breaking free in his mind as body parts and torsos whirled around him, caught in some noxious gravity like planets trapped in their orbits around a sun.

And that sun was Red.

He was the epicenter of it.

A mist of blood moved with the limbs and heads, glistening like red beads. And the most terrible thing about it all was that the people were not dead. They should have been, but they were not. Molly's head zoomed past him, still screaming. Darlene cried out. Billy K's head chased his torso. Limbs were still quaking, hands still clawing and clutching as if they were attached to bodies, mouths begging for help.

And it wasn't just the new arrivals either—George saw the heads of Jeff Preachley and Tub McGill and Neil Stroheim, all of them, in fact, caught in this gruesome whirlpool of remains cycling around him. This was limbo. They neither lived or died, went forward or back, but were held in this purgatory at the moment of their deaths which would go on forever and ever.

Red still had not moved.

With great effort, George found that he could. It was like moving against a hurricane-force wind. He reached into the field and was nearly yanked from his feet, but his fingers brushed the cold clay of faces that passed by. Hands reached out for him. Heads begged for death. Bubbles of blood broke against his face and arms.

But he knew what he had to do.

His mind was pulling into itself, his thoughts disordered and scattered, his sanity dissolving. Only his instinct kept him going, pushing him toward the final goal in his life that would bring release for the tortured souls around him. When Franny Sweisser's arm came past, his hand still clutched the tire iron as it had that final week of his life. George seized his wrist and pulled the arm free. It was terribly cold. It hit the ground and began to decay and break apart almost instantly.

George snatched up the tire iron and went to finish what Franny had begun. Filled with anguish and a torment that literally was beyond comprehension, he approached Red. Tears ran from his eyes and there was an echoing sibilance of white noise in his head. If you loved something beyond life itself, you had to set it free.

Crying out, he brought the tire iron down.

He thought there'd be an explosion of gore, but there wasn't. Red had been gone a long time. A very long time and the memories of him lived sweetly in George's suffering mind. The creature he hit with the tire iron was just a moving mass of meat. Its head did not just split open, the entire body cracked wide like a dry husk of corn ... and then something black and sinuous rose from the dog. It was shiny and black like wet neoprene. It had a huge, bell-shaped mouth at one end and an undulant eel-like body. The mouth darted out at George and then it fell into the grass, losing solidity and becoming a shadow that was leeched into the soil.

The cloud was gone.

It evaporated like a rain puddle as the thing in Red dissipated. Then, all around George, the remains of the townspeople decomposed rapidly with a crackling, fizzing sound. The world was dead and gray, the grass dead and crunching under his step. Bushes were withered to sticks, trees leafless.

This was what Porterfield was like without the intervention of the cloud.

George, feeling woozy from high doses of radiation, reached down and scooped up Red.

It took him some time to reach the creek outside town, fighting his way through the ruins of Porterfield and the irradiated countryside. By the time he got there, he was throwing up blood, his body feeling like it was constantly pierced by white-hot needles.

But he made it.

This was one of the places where Red and he had whiled away lazy summer afternoons, so it was only fitting that they return together to a place they loved best. There was no more green grass or bright orange and yellow wildflowers, no dangling emerald limbs of weeping willows. No creatures scurrying or bees buzzing. Everything was dead, parched, and crumbling. The creek still ran, but it was a dirty gray in color and a sickening heat wafted from it.

George dug a grave for Red with his bare hands, using what remained of his strength now that acute radiation sickness had overcome him. He placed Red in the crude trench and covered him, then he lay down over the grave and closed his eyes.

COFFIN BIRTH

It was raining when Baby tunneled out of Mother's grave to claim the world that was about to become his playground. That there had been a devastating nuclear conflict above was lost on him. He was a newborn. He did not understand such things any more than he understood that it was a unique combination of radioactive seepage and embalming chemicals that made him open his terrible yellow eyes, giving him not only life but twisting him into a new, feral lifeform with an insatiable hunger.

For three days, he fed on his mother's remains before clawing his way to the surface.

The world above was large and dark and threatening. He was small and pale and vicious.

He crawled through the graveyard with the inching locomotion of a maggot, driven by appetite. Around leaning headstones and crumbling funerary crosses he went, swimming through the leaf-caked pools of sunken graves until he reached the wrought-iron fence.

Yes, the city was before him.

Wearing the night and rain like camouflage, he crept through gutters and slithered over sidewalks.

It wasn't long before he was seen.

A bag lady pushing a squeaking shopping cart stopped and stared at him as if she couldn't believe what she was seeing. She stood there, blinking her rheumy eyes, raindrops spattering the plastic garbage bags wound around her like scarves.

"My ... my *baby*," she said. "Oh, my poor lost baby."

Baby did not disagree; it was her delusion and he would exploit it to the fullest. He was nothing if not crafty. He began to wail like an infant, tugging quite carefully at her heartstrings. She reached down for him and he allowed himself to be picked up, cuddled and fondled.

"You poor, poor thing," she said, brushing mud from his face.

Baby nearly giggled at that, but stopped himself at the last moment, knowing she might find his laughter disturbing. The bag lady stared down at him with a momentary sense of horror as if she knew exactly who and what he was. Baby gurgled cutely, then began to sob. It was important to manipulate her maternal drives carefully. He knew this instinctively.

But he knew much more: as she cuddled him, he looked into her mind, paging through her memories. In a matter of minutes, he understood many things about his new world.

"I've missed you so much," the bag lady said, crushing Baby against her, kissing him again and again with her dry, cracked lips, enveloping him in a foul stench of rancid body odor and cheap wine, both of which barely managed to disguise the charnel stink that clung to him. "They said you died. They said I'd never see you again. But they were wrong, weren't they? Oh, my poor sweet precious angel. Mama loves her baby more than anything on this earth."

The bag lady—whose name had once been Doris McCallister—took Baby away to her digs, a basement flat that stank of cat piss. It was dim, dreary, and filthy. But Baby had been in worse places. The bag lady threw together a makeshift crib for him using a water-stained cardboard box (after emptying out the rat turds) and stuffing it with dirty blankets. Baby found it quite comfortable. He particularly liked the lettering on the box—*Devil's Own Hot Sauce, 12 Bottles*. The irony, of course, did not escape him.

"We'll make baby so happy," she said. "My sweet little chubkins."

She wiped rain from him and plucked wet leaves from his downy hair, but her hands were so dirty that she left dark streaks on his face. Baby did not mind. Let her care for him, cuddle and love him. It could only end one way.

"Here, my love, Mama has some nice milk for you," she told him.

It was a can of sweetened, condensed milk she had heated over a candle flame. The stuff smelled horrible, but Baby lapped some of it up to keep her happy. It was nasty. Absolutely nauseating.

"That's better, isn't it?"

Baby cooed.

"The men started all this," the bag lady said. "They always did awful things. I won't tell you what my father did to me. What my husband made me endure. Bad things, very bad things. I don't like men. They're parasites on this world. We won't let you grow up like them, will we? No, you won't fight and drop bombs and kill people and destroy cities. My boy will never be like that."

As she talked, she picked at the numerous open sores on her arms, many of which were necrotic. She had radiation poisoning, Baby knew, and she wouldn't last more than a few more weeks at the outside. He could sense the minute fragments of fissile materials embedded in her flesh at the microscopic level. Already they were cooking her from the inside out like a juicy turkey in a roasting pan.

Baby salivated. And when she peeled a strip of flesh from her forearm, he licked his lips with a long pink tongue. My God, must she tease him like that? Already his cravings were rising to unprecedented levels. His stomach growled. Sweet juices of hunger filled his mouth.

The bag lady kept talking and talking, spinning endless reams of wool, piling it up around her like the years. She talked of her broken childhood. Her marriage to Earl, a hard-drinking, hard-hitting man. Her bouts in mental hospitals. How she took to the streets, scavenging, picking through dumpsters and trash cans. Eking out a marginal living and being truly content for the first time in her life. And, of course, she spoke of all that insanity about Earl throwing her down the stairs and her losing the baby … but none of that was true, was it? Because her precious little chubkins was right here with her now.

Her voice droned endlessly and Baby could barely keep his eyes open. After a time, he didn't bother. A refreshing little nap and then he'd feel more like killing her. Were they all like this? Were they all just gullible, mindless sheep? If that was the case, Baby figured that he would be their king within weeks.

After a time, he opened his eyes from a cozy, comforting dream of chewing the meat from his mother's rib slats and the bag lady was still blathering. Enough was enough.

"Did my chubkins have a good nap?"

Baby didn't bother cooing; he unsheathed his claws and took her scalp off with a single blow. My, how the blood ran down her face in rivers of the richest, reddest wine. Through blood-seeped eyes, she saw Baby's white, pitted face which was bloated and porcine. He opened his jaws and tore out her throat, hot blood spraying in his face. He lapped it up before battening his puckering mouth to her neck and sucking the blood out of her with a most appalling, slobbering noise.

Finally, she had stopped talking. The incessant buzz of her voice had ended and there was peace.

Baby took his time skinning her, dividing up the meat and tasty giblets beneath. He wasn't satisfied until he had devoured every last meaty scrap. It took him three days, but he relished every bite. He saved what was in her skull for last—it was wonderfully tender and succulent, the flavor delicate and buttery. As he licked the last dried stains of blood from her polished white bones, he contemplated his next move.

It was cold and rainy out in the world, so, using her sinews, he stitched himself a fine bunting from her discarded skin and ventured out into his kingdom.

The pickings were slim for days. Baby fed upon a few stray rats, a plump kitten he found wandering about. He slept down in the sewers to keep out of the black rain. The days were too warm, the nights disagreeably cold. He was mad with hunger by that point.

Then providence favored him.

A bull terrier, a real solid, savage little beast, caught Baby's scent and tracked him. By that point, Baby had been in a few tussles with dogs—that he invariably won—and he decided he didn't like them. Cats, he could respect because of their independent character, but the servile nature of dogs offended him. Silly, slobbering piles of meat.

Baby would have left the terrier to his own devices had the creature been smart enough to go away. But it kept following him, so Baby let it catch him. Although it initially whimpered in fear at the sight and smell of him, its breed was both aggressive and malicious by nature, so it attacked. It was amazingly fast, actually sinking its teeth into Baby's plump thigh, so Baby snapped off one of its forelegs and engulfed its head in his jaws. The crushing of its skull made a delicious wet snapping. After that it was easy. It was a male, so Baby emasculated it and gnawed its testes to pulp. They were quite juicy and soft, but with a bit of a sour aftertaste to them. No matter. Its brain was unremarkable. Baby explored it thoroughly before eating it. Its subservient drives were despicable. Its meat was substandard, though its belly held some luscious morsels. Baby enjoyed its blood the most. He upended its carcass and squeezed every last drop down his throat.

It was as he was doing so, a rope of dog intestine tossed carelessly over one shoulder, that he realized he was being observed. Two people stood there, a man and a woman. They were haggard, roughhewn things, survivors in a terrible world of attrition.

"What the hell is that?" the man asked, putting a flashlight on Baby that blinded him.

"It's … it's Boss!" the woman cried. "That thing killed Boss!"

Baby realized he was in a real spot; the problem being that he was full, lethargic, and gassy. Normally, he could have launched himself at them, gutting them easily, but he was sluggish from his feast. That's when he heard a clicking sound and the man fired a gun at him. The first round zipped over Baby's head. The second thudded into the split carcass of the dog.

This was trouble.

They both had guns and they charged in shooting. For the most part, their rounds were wild. They were keyed-up, nearly hysterical, firing blindly. Baby rolled through the muck of the street and skittered along the curb. A bullet went through his left leg, another thudded into his back. He let out a resounding roar at the intrusion of pain, moving faster, finding a sewer grating and pushing himself through with his elastic, pudding-like body. He fell into the darkness, splashing into a tunnel below. The rank water washed him nearly a city block before he managed to pull himself up on a concrete ledge, scattering rats as he did so.

The bullets.

He did not like bullets.

The holes they had punched into his hide were painful. The blood ran and his nerve endings felt like they were being twisted out by the roots. As he rested, listening to the water rushing past, the subterranean dripping of seepage, he concentrated on repairing himself. It was not beyond the remarkable powers of his metabolism. With concerted effort, he slowed the flow of his blood, squeezing off blood vessels and capillaries. He pushed out the bullets, rushing sugars and proteins to the wound sites, sending his biology into overdrive. Within an hour, he was repaired.

But exhausted.

Lying there in a pool of sewer slime and his own secretions, he slept for twelve hours.

When he woke, Baby was not only hungry but angry. He was fearsome in either state, but combined, they created a diabolic black rage in him. He would have expiation for the damage to his body and the insult to his ego. He would have blood. He would have meat. By divine right, he would demand sacrifice for this.

When it was night, he crept out into the streets. His sense of smell, like his night vision, was nearly supernatural in ability. He located two survivors sharing a bottle in the remains of a drugstore. He slaughtered them both. He ate very little of them, not particularly caring for alcohol-seasoned meat. It was disgusting.

It quieted some of his rage, dulled the yearning ache for butchery in his loins, but it hardly satisfied him. Stronger, his wrath at a low boil, he went out into the streets again. It didn't take him long to find the remains of the dog. They were scattered in every direction by rats, other dogs, and various nameless scavengers that had been born from the seething pit of radioactivity like Baby himself. He could smell them. Some of them were monstrous things that he knew he must avoid at all costs, at least until he had grown to his adult stage.

He cast for scent in every direction until he found the trail of the couple that had injured him. The rain had washed much of their spoor away, but there was enough to track them with. He'd have them yet.

But he could feel a change coming over him. The time was not yet to pay them a visit. First, he needed to be full, to be strong, to be ready. He went back to the drug store and fed upon the two men he'd killed. Their meat was at first sickening from the taint of alcohol, but the more he ate, oddly enough, the more he liked that taste. When he had reduced them to a quivering stew of macerated flesh and cooling blood, he rolled in them, perfuming himself. He continued to slurp up their remains, feeling that odd sense of change coming over him.

But he felt something more.

From each of his victims, he took away something. From the bag lady, it was her memories and view of the world, the very basic knowledge of what human beings were and how babies should act. From the rats and kitten, he absorbed a vestige of survival instinct. From the dog, an innate cunning—offer your victims some bright eyes and a wagging tail and it was that much easier to ingratiate yourself to them. And from the two drunks, he'd picked up a taste for alcohol.

He reached over and picked up a bottle of gin and drained it. Yes, it was quite good. It made him feel giddy. Optimistic. Unencumbered by trifling things like worry and doubt.

He would have more of it soon.

But until then, he went out into the streets until he found a church. It was a place of worship. One day, he decided, it would be him on the altar and his sheep would line up in rows simply to be anointed by his piss. But that would be in the future. For now, he secreted himself in a dark corner of the chancel. Exuding a fibrous silk, he webbed himself up in a cocoon. Then he went to sleep. As he slept, the change began. It was time to ascend to his next life stage. Baby's shell split open and a larger version of himself emerged.

When the sun set that night and the cold dankness set in, he went out to track down his enemies.

Baby had learned, by degrees, to be careful. One did not simply stand out in the street devouring one's prey; that was asking for trouble. Especially with these damn sheep that were always begging for a fight. There was something rebellious and suicidal in their souls, in their very makeup that made them want to challenge monsters wherever they found them.

That was part of being a predator, he realized. Knowing when to strike and when to hide, when to be aggressive and when to be a harmless little lamb.

So, he was very cautious as he approached the digs of the couple that had pumped bullets into him. He hid in the darkness, covering his own high, animal stink with whatever was handy—garbage, rotting animal matter, sewage. He rolled in all these things until he was caked with dirt and leaves and abundant slime.

He saw the man leave the building. He had four dogs with him, well-trained brutes that responded to his every command. In fact, they were so well attuned to him that they did what he wanted without him even opening his mouth. Baby had to admire such cold military efficiency.

He could smell the man and the dogs quite clearly. The man was angry at losing Boss. The woman had told him to leave well enough alone, but being a man, he took the dogs out to hunt Baby. *Idiot.* Off he went with his excited curs, leaving the woman quite vulnerable.

After a reasonable amount of time, Baby approached the building. All doors were locked tight, windows boarded. No matter. Baby located a fresh-air duct through which he could smell the juicy vitality of the woman, the sweet scent of her hormones, and the rich fertility of what was between her legs.

Now.

Baby became a flaccid thing, a worming amoeba-like mass that squeezed itself through the duct. He got into a few tight spots, especially at the elbow bends of the duct, but greased by his own excretions, he wiggled his way through.

The woman was in the kitchen. By lantern light, she was wrestling blobs of bread dough, which in form much resembled the thing that was coming to kill her. Baby moved silently. Had the dogs been there, they would have heard him long ago. But they were gone and the woman didn't stand a chance.

Baby slid from the duct in a snotty, oozing mass, slowly reconstituting as he prepared to attack. When he was some six feet from her, she sensed something. He could smell the hot brew of her biochemistry, a fear response of rising blood pressure and accelerated heart rate. Stress hormones were released. To Baby, they were like sweet, running sap.

She turned quickly and saw him there. She let out a quick scream, grabbing a carving knife and throwing it at him. She missed. He advanced. The smell of her terror was delicious. As he wriggled closer to her, her fear increased. She could not believe what she was seeing—the same horror that had torn Boss apart: a revolting, swollen, maggoty form, an embryonic monster like a hybrid between a fetus and a segmented worm.

She turned and fled, tossing things in his direction as she did so. Pots. Pans. A hammer. She seized a butcher's knife, realizing that Baby had her cornered. And despite his lewd, repellent girth, he was quite fast. His yellow eyes were huge like raw duck eggs, veined and moist, tears of clear serum running from them. His mouth opened wide, then wider still to reveal a jagged collection of teeth.

She screamed again and slashed at him with the knife. She was fast, actually slitting him open. He thought he might lose her there for a moment, so, instinctively, he gripped his phallus and directed a burning stream of urine at her. Its effect was instantaneous: dopy, drugged, her muscular control failing, she dropped to her knees.

Then Baby hit her with the force of a battering ram, knocking her flat. He bit and clawed at her, licking one eye from its socket as she wailed and thrashed beneath him, digging her fingers into his soft, flabby flesh. His mouth engulfed her own, sucking in her lips and tongue, shearing both in a blossom of blood and swallowing them. His claws shredded not only her flesh, but her clothes.

It was then that Baby was struck by an urge he had not known before. It was not just a lust for blood, but an appetite for what was between her legs. The woman screamed her mind away, her head whipping from side to side. Her final sensory impression was that she had been mounted by a huge, plump maggot as it slid its cold, slime-dripping, bifurcated organ into her and pumped madly away, quivering with peristaltic contractions as it filled her with its squirming seed.

When Baby was done, the woman was gone. Her mind had fractured into a thousand mad bits and the blood ran from her in hot rivers. Still excited, despite the act, Baby went after her like a starving man at an all-you-can-eat chicken buffet—wrenching off legs and wings, sinking his teeth into tender thighs and glutting himself on juicy breasts.

Finally, after rolling in her cooling remains, he urinated on her carcass, the walls, the furniture, marking his territory. Then, well-fed and well-satisfied like a diner leaving a most excellent restaurant, he burst through the door and faded into the darkness.

As with his other victims, Baby learned a great deal from the woman. Who she had been. Her trials and tribulations. Things about her husband. Her friends and family who had died from fallout and disease. But he learned another tidbit that was most interesting—the woman had been abandoned as a baby and had grown up in an orphanage. This was a place (Baby understood) where the unwanted were accepted with open arms.

It was a place where children were to be found in abundance. He also learned that there was one such place still operating in the city, plenty of homeless waifs wandering about after the war. The woman and her husband visited it often, bringing food and supplies to the sisters that ran it.

Baby thought about children.

Why, they were soft and meaty, a rare delicacy if one could locate them. He began to plan to that end.

It was not without its challenges. In order to gain admittance, he would need to play the same card he had with the bag lady: he must become a poor, defenseless waif once again. That took some doing. It would mean shedding over a hundred pounds of weight he had accrued since molting. Luckily, he was a master of his own biology. It took some time and Baby was not pleased by losing what he had gained, but he would emerge that much better after his next molt with a full belly of child-meat.

Sometimes, he had learned, great gains required great sacrifices.

The feast would be worth it.

Reduced to the wailing, harmless infant that had tunneled from his mother's grave, he presented himself on the steps of the orphanage. It was a waiting game hoping to be discovered. And not without its dangers. Rats took an interest in him. Several wild dogs and cats eyed him up.

Finally, he was discovered by one of the sisters, wrapped in a fuzzy blanket and brought inside where it was warm. A harmless, shivering bundle of joy, he was bathed and cuddled, the sisters ah-ing and oooh-ing over him. He presented himself as a lovely child with his sparkling blue eyes and silky blonde hair. He was pleasantly plump, but not so plump that he looked well-cared for. No, he was a pathetic, pitiful creature that needed love and a safe warren.

The sisters fed him some nasty canned milk, as the bag lady had. They poked him lovingly with their fingers, commenting on how very soft he was. They rocked him to sleep and were absolutely enamored when he smiled up at them upon waking.

"What a treasure God has delivered unto us," said Sister Millicent. "Such a darling."

"A blessing," said Sister Angeline.

Oh, Baby had them. There was no doubt of it. He had wound them up in his web as surely as a spider with a fly. They were his. He was their angel and they never for a moment suspected the horrible monster he was. The saving grace—the pink frosting atop the cake, as it were—was that they did not have a dog. Fooling dogs was near on impossible, with their keen sensory acuity. That's why Baby hated them. When he ruled this city, he would exterminate them like the vermin they were.

There were six children in the orphanage: two other infants, one toddler, and three others ranging in age from four to twelve. An absolute feast for the taking.

Baby's appetite was a raging monster.

That night, he slipped from his basinet. Oh, he was cunning and stealthy. Because of what he had taken from the two drunks in the drug store, he had a devilish thirst. He crawled into the chapel and guzzled altar wine. Its alcohol content was not quite what he would have liked, but he drank a great deal of it until he was satiated and more than a little buzzed.

Then, he returned to the quarters where the children were birthed. He took the babies first, smothering them and sipping the sweet, sweet wine of their blood. The toddler was no trouble. The other, older children, however, proved to be problematic. He killed two of them, but they fought like tigers. The third screamed and he broke its neck, tearing out its throat and glutting himself on tender throat meat, the rarest cutlet of all.

But the sisters came.

They screamed, too. One of them, Sister Angeline, slipped on the blood on the floor and died from a heart attack. Baby killed the other two. They barely even fought. For many hours, he lounged among their remains, stuffing himself beyond endurance until he was, once again, a swollen, blubbery mass, a corpulent maggot well fed upon corpses.

Oh yes, the world was his now for the taking.

As he nibbled on sweet meats from the toddler's belly, he could feel the need to molt arising again. He was so fat from feeding, he knew it had to be soon because his current skin was stretched to the point of bursting. He was quite vulnerable at this stage. What he needed was a nice, dark place where he could web himself up for several hours.

The problem was, he simply didn't have the energy to crawl down into the cool, relaxing confines of the cellar. He was overstuffed with his numerous kills, replete with child-meat, slothful from all the wine he had drunk. Simply extending one clawed hand to strip away a choice baby-cutlet was exhausting.

His laziness proved his undoing.

By that point, full and intoxicated, he had completely forgotten what he had done to the woman. It was a trifling amusement at best. But her husband, upon finding her butchered remains, did not forget about him. Using his dogs, four of them now that Boss had been dispatched, he tracked Baby's scent from his digs to the church and finally, to the orphanage.

And when Baby opened his bleary eyes, a distended, obese mass of flesh, the dogs closed in. He tried to rise to the occasion, readying his claws and teeth for the disemboweling, but he was simply too fat, too drunken, too sluggish as the need to molt plunged him into a torpid lethargy.

To Baby's credit, he killed one of the dogs, neatly eviscerating the mongrel, but then the man pumped three bullets into him and all his pure, beautiful blood began to pump out. The dogs went wild with a killing frenzy. In his weakened, distended condition, they savaged Baby, tearing him into pieces until there was no fight left in him.

But even then, they did not stop.

No, they were like sharks in a feeding frenzy, awash in a bloody sea of chum, biting and tearing and dismembering. Within five minutes or so, Baby was reduced to an unsightly mess of organs and bones, flesh and bubbling slime and scattered anatomy. Even he, with his great biological gifts, could not put all his pieces back together again. They quivered and wriggled, but finally died as Baby exited this world with a black wail of absolute wrath and horror.

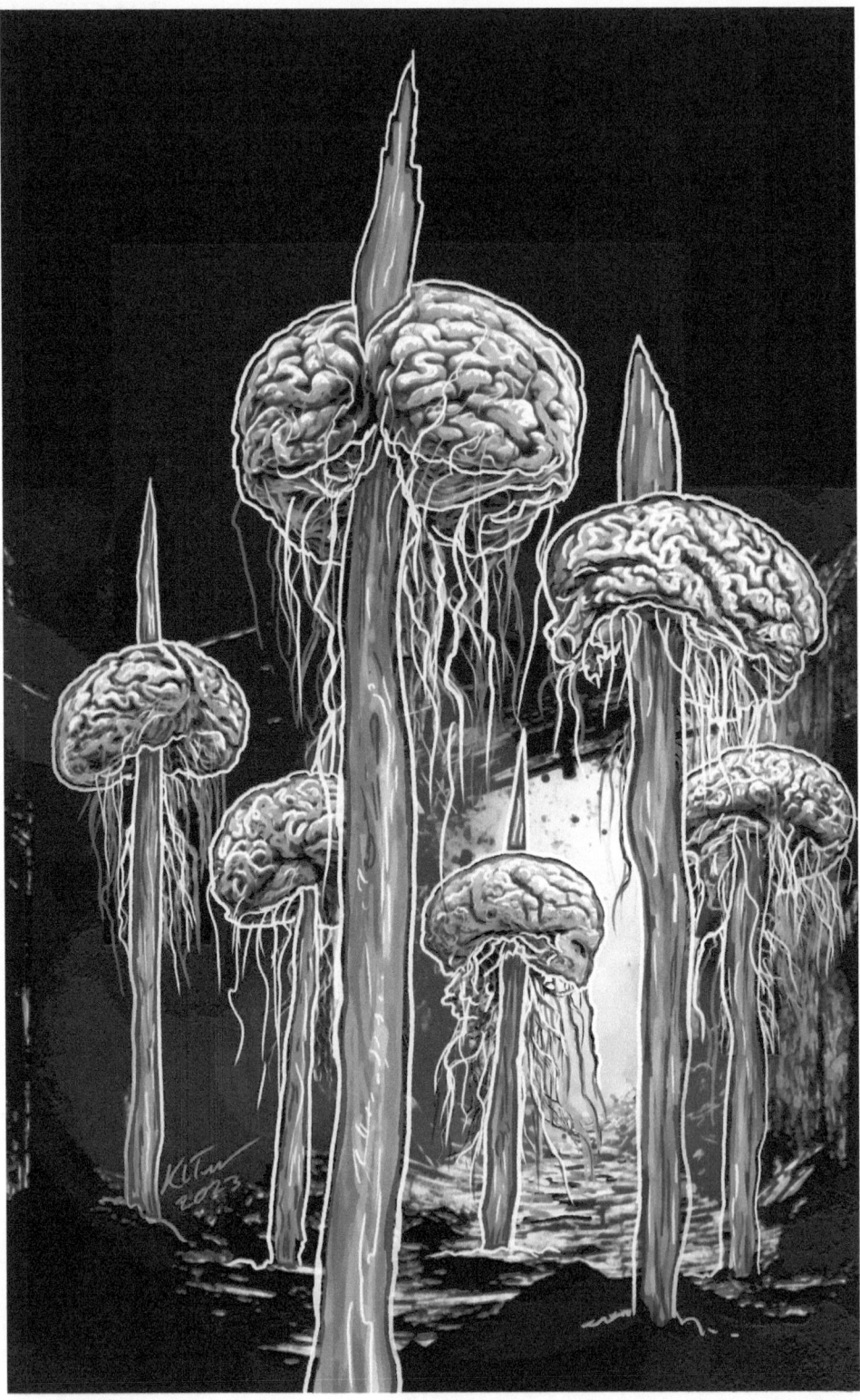

BRAIN DEATH

It was an insidious thing, that was for sure. Rico and the others had survived the bombings, the resultant fallout, the bitter day-by-day struggle to stay alive. Hell, all things considered, they'd made a good run of it.

But now this.

It got Shaya first.

Good, practical, salt-of-the-earth Shaya, whose heart and soul and sense of right was bigger and far more powerful than any multi-megaton weapon used to bring society to its scabby knees. It was she who found each and every one of them, a mother mallard gathering her ducklings, feeding and sheltering them, and, most importantly, giving them a reason to go on when there no longer seemed to be a point.

"What do you make of it?" Rico put to Regina, their unofficial medic because of her background in the Army Medical Corps.

Regina swabbed Shaya's sweat-beaded face with a cool rag. "Without a lab to run blood work or throat cultures, nasal swabs … Christ, it could be anything. My guess is some kind of infection, probably viral."

Rico sighed. He went to the window of the cellar and peered out between the boards into the night world. The locals were already getting worked up, screaming and howling like animals. It was going to be another long night of random violence and insanity as they tried to exterminate each other.

Regina kept wiping sweat from Shaya's smooth brown face. She'd been a tall, statuesque woman, firm-limbed, strong and cunning when she needed to be. An Amazon with the soul of a poet. Now she looked shrunken, as if whatever matrix held her together from the inside was rapidly breaking down.

"We were always so careful, too," Rico said.

Shaya had insisted on it. She carried a Geiger counter to check background radiation, made everyone wear gas masks around the infected and face masks at the very least when they were in unknown territory. They washed and bathed, deconned regularly. But even with all that, something had happened.

Ketch, who was sitting atop a few crates of military-issue MREs, said, "Two days ago, that's when she got sick … am I right?"

Regina nodded.

"Day before that, we went into that food pantry on Twenty-Third, did we not?" He had their attention now and nodded. "What did we find there?"

Rico, of course, knew what he was talking about. It was quite a find —a nearly untouched stash of canned food and dry goods. There were enough goodies there to double their stockpile and keep them alive for another few months. Sunny and Joe Jack had found it, being their apex scavengers. They had a nose for such things. When they got together, they could find just about anything. They were like a dousing rod for supplies. The bad part was that another group had gotten there before them and they found their bodies.

"You remember the bodies," Ketch said. "How they looked."

Rico remembered. There were six of them and they'd been dead several days. No big deal; the city was full of corpses. But these were unique—nobody had ever seen anything like it before. Their craniums were split open in huge, mouth-like chasms. And that was bad enough, but it could have been explained by some weird predator or scavenger. What couldn't be explained was that their heads were soft and flaccid as if the skulls beneath were made of a soft, pliant rubber.

Rico and the others all stood around, looking at each other, trying to make sense of it. They couldn't even guess what might cause something like that. A parasite? Some sort of microbe? Radiation? Nothing seemed to fit.

Shaya and Regina decided to find out.

They couldn't leave something like that alone.

Using surgical gloves, face masks in place, they examined the heads of the bodies in some detail. They were ... *ghastly*. That was the word that jumped into Rico's mind. Using tongue depressors from Regina's pack, they pried open the wounds that looked very much like blubbery lips. Shaya gasped. She ignored the questions she was pelted with as she examined the other heads with Regina in a like fashion.

"What is it?" Rico had asked, anxiety jumping in his belly like frogs.

"Their brains," Regina whispered. "They don't have any brains ... they're gone."

Now as he looked over at Shaya, his muscles were tight and coiled as bedsprings. "You think she has what they had?"

Ketch shrugged. "Could be."

"Then we could all be infected with it."

"A distinct possibility."

Regina sighed. "It's a little early to be jumping to conclusions, isn't it? She could just have an infection. Don't be wigging out on me. Not yet." She looked from Shaya's sweating face to Rico and Ketch in turn. "So let's keep speculation to ourselves for the time being, shall we?"

Which meant that she didn't want them scaring Joe Jack and Sunny with any wild stories. She wanted them to play it cool. No diving into the deep end of the pool. Not just yet. Rico appreciated the common sense of that because, really, they had no idea what was going on. The problem, he knew, would not be him, but Ketch. Ketch had something of an abrasive personality, particularly when he had too much down time. All that pent-up energy. He tended to direct it at people in a negative way. He was a great survivalist, topnotch in a fight; he just wasn't exactly a team player.

"Does that suit you, Ketch?" Regina asked, as if she had read Rico's mind.

"You know me," he said. "Whichever way the wind blows."

Yeah, like hell.

That was the plan, anyway. But with what happened next, it really didn't matter.

155

Breakpoint.

That's what Regina called it. In that, something was happening or about to happen. She'd been watching Shaya carefully these past few days, mothering her, studying her symptoms, rarely sleeping. About seven that night, she announced that Shaya's temperature was pegging at 105°. It was a bad sign.

"She's still fighting it, whatever it is," Regina told Rico. "And I don't think she's winning."

Shaya did not look good at all. She was drowning in her own sour-smelling sweat, shaking violently and chattering her teeth. Now and again, her face twisted up in a grimace of pain and her head would thrash side to side.

"Is there anything we can do?" Rico asked.

"We have to get that temp down. It goes much higher and she's going to die." Regina thought it over. "Since an ice bath is out of the question, we'll do the next best thing."

She grabbed two bottles of rubbing alcohol from the storage room. They stripped Shaya and gave her a rubdown with the alcohol by candlelight until her temp went down two degrees. Her skin felt unpleasantly oily and hot.

"She's okay for now, I guess. We'll do it again in a few hours."

But Rico did not believe she was okay.

It had little to do with the way she shivered or the spasms that made her jerk and twitch. No, this was something else—she *looked* different. Something had altered. Then he realized what it was: her face had changed. She'd always had a very good face with high cheekbones and a prominent aquiline nose, a strong jawline ... but now it was as if her face was sinking into itself, the way the faces of corpses sometimes did when the facial muscles relaxed in death.

He didn't call Regina's attention to it.

Not just then.

She was reclined in her chair, eyes closed. She wasn't sleeping. He could see her eyes shifting beneath the lids. But he didn't want to disturb her; she needed whatever rest she could get. He walked over to one of the boarded windows. The natives were getting restless out there. They had lit bonfires in the street. Dozens of them were rushing about, shrieking and fighting. They had several well-bloodied captives across the street. Several crazies were prodding them with hot sticks from one of the fires.

Rico sighed.

When the sun came up, they'd slink back to their dens. But for now, they were active and dangerous. If they ever learned where Shaya's people were hiding, they'd never stop until the door was bashed down.

He sat in his chair, waiting. Even he wasn't sure what for. He must have dozed, because some ninety minutes later Regina was shaking him.

"Something weird's happening," she said.

He saw it himself: the change in Shaya's face was morbidly apparent. From her forehead to her chin, her face was flaccid as if there was no skull beneath it. It looked like her flesh had gone to gray putty. When Regina touched it with a gloved hand, ripples ran through it like it was made of pudding.

"Christ," she said.

She took a tongue depressor and prodded one of Shaya's cheekbones. It sank into it as if it was made of raw dough. Donning a surgical glove, Rico pressed his thumb into her forehead. It sank in, too. In fact, the indentation remained for thirty seconds or more before gradually pushing back out.

"She's got it," he said. "Whatever those people had at the food pantry."

Regina nodded wordlessly.

They both stepped back and away from Shaya. Whatever it was, it was beyond anything they could handle with a first-aid kit. This was the sort of thing that required specialists and cutting-edge medical laboratory facilities. In other words, she was going to die and her spiking temp was the least of their worries.

"We should tell the others," Rico said.

They were sleeping in the backroom. Ketch had finally gotten tired of making barely-concealed innuendos concerning what Rico and Regina were going to be doing when he closed his eyes. Sunny and Joe Jack were exhausted from a day spent scavenging. They'd returned with a case of soup, a box of candles, and two brand-new military NBC suits still in their boxes.

"Why? What good will that do?"

"They deserve to know."

"And they also deserve to sleep."

"But—"

"But nothing, Rico. There's nothing to be done. We've all been in close proximity to Shaya. We either have it by now or we don't. And we can't get out of here until morning."

Outside, the crazies were hooting and hollering.

As much as Rico didn't like it, they were trapped with Shaya at least until first light. And then ... well, when the sun came up, they'd see.

But what happened next came several hours before dawn.

Rico came out of a thin, uneasy sleep to find Regina standing about three feet from him. There was a look of horror on her face.

He sat up, his brain foggy from sleep. He wondered momentarily what had woken him—but then he knew. It was that awful pulpy crackling noise. It was coming from Shaya. Her body was vibrating on the cot, limbs trembling, fingers whip-snapping as if she was undergoing a seizure. Her head was arched on her neck, mouth open. He could see teeth and gums. Pink saliva ran down her chin.

And her eyes were open.

One of them was staring at the ceiling; the other looked toward the wall. The crown of her skull had enlarged to a phallic mass like the cap of a mushroom. Blood trickled from it down her face.

The crackling sound was coming from inside her head, from within that mass that seemed to palpitate like a heart. It was a thick, meaty sort of sound like something was eating her from the inside out. Swallowing down the bile in his throat, Rico likened it to the sound a chick would make as it pecked its way free of an egg.

"What the hell is that sound?" a voice asked.

It was Ketch. He was standing there with Joe Jack, and Sunny behind him, both of whom looked very pale.

But there was no reason to answer his question because the crackling reached its peak and Shaya's head split open. And what came out of it made Sunny scream and Joe Jack nearly fall right over.

Regina and Rico pulled back.

There was nothing else *to* do.

Shaya's cranium cracked fully open into a blood-soaked cleft and her brain squeezed out with a moist, rubbery sound like a snake from an egg. It wasn't forced out—it emerged independently. It pushed itself out completely, still connected to the inside of her skull by snotty strings of tissue, but animate and horribly alive. It sat atop her ruined head, pink and glistening and throbbing. It looked far-too large to have fit inside her head in the first place, as if it had inflated itself upon release.

Ketch had a .9mm in his hand.

He brought it up to shoot, then lowered it. Brought it up again, then lowered it just as fast. It was indicative of all of them: no one knew what to do. They'd fought some awful mutants since the war, but nothing like this.

The brain continued to throb as if it was filling itself with blood. Then there was a slithery sound and wormy tendrils—dozens of them—slid free of it, clusters emerging from both sides of the cerebrum, squirming from deep pockets like countless writhing, mating worms.

Ketch again brought up his gun, but Regina put her hand on it. "No," she said. "If you bust rounds, the crazies out there will break that door down."

The odd, incomprehensible thing was that as soon as he brought the gun up, Rico heard a brief, high-intensity whining sound like a whirring drill bit. It was sharp and painful to hear. As soon as Regina touched Ketch's gun hand, it disappeared.

Hell was that?

"We have to do something," Ketch said. "We can't just let this … this happen."

But she was right and they all knew it. If the crazies battered down the door, they were in the shit. They didn't have the firepower or the ammo to fight off dozens, let alone hundreds, of them. And that's what it would come to.

"Just wait," Regina told them.

"For what?" Joe Jack asked.

But she had no answer, of course. Neither did Rico or Sunny. So, they waited with weak stomachs as the brain-thing pulsated, its convolutions quivering with minute contractions, its feelers exploring the wreck of Shaya's head like questing fingers.

It was Sunny who finally did something.

She simply couldn't take any more of it.

Before anyone could stop her, she pulled the butcher knife from her belt, let out a war cry, and charged the brain, blade held high. Rico shouted. So did Joe Jack. When she was within mere feet of the brain, its pulsations became so loud it was like a beating, blood-filled heart.

Sunny froze.

Joe Jack did, too, as he made a grab for her.

And a split second before they did, that shrill whining sound came again, rising up to hypersonic levels, much louder and much more devastating than before.

Rico could move, but just barely.

The noise made his head hurt. His skull felt like it was vibrating. The pain squeezed tears from his eyes and made sweet saliva gush in his mouth. Waves of nausea made him double over. Vomit filled his throat.

The brain-thing was directing the noise.

It was using it as a weapon.

It seemed to flex like a muscle, then it flew through the air, propelled by some unknown force. It moved incredibly fast. Sunny waited for it; she had no choice. As it was momentarily airborne, the cerebellum, the lower portion of its anatomy, opened in a puckered horizontal gash and it engulfed the top of her head, snapping over it like a rubber glove. It drove her to her knees. There was a positively revolting suctioning sound and her eyes rolled back white.

She didn't fall over or even cry out.

No, in fact, her body shuddered, then her mouth opened and she moaned almost orgasmically as she licked her lips with a wet, pink tongue.

The whining noise had faded by then.

Rico and the others were freed from their spell, but they felt drunken and loopy. Joe Jack—who had a thing with Sunny—came out of it first and pulled his gun. A blast of that high-pitched whining noise was directed at him. He dropped the gun and fell to the floor.

Ketch and Rico helped him to his feet.

He could barely stand. He acted like he'd just been shot up with Demerol. When he tried to speak, his words were garbled and drool ran from his mouth.

There's no way out, Rico thought with more than a little panic.

The crazies out there were gathering in numbers, anxious to murder anyone, including their own, to satisfy their bloodlust. And here, in this place where everyone thought they were safe, was something even worse.

Finally, they pulled back into the storeroom. They were not about to watch what was happening to Sunny. The brain did not try to stop them. The last they saw of her, she was gyrating madly, panting, tearing at her own flesh with her nails, her orgasmic cries louder and louder as the brain tapped into her hypothalamus, accelerating her libido, unchaining the primal lust at her core as it fed upon her gray and white matter.

Her cries of lust echoed through the cellar and there was no escaping them. The mutant was devouring her brain, giving her the ultimate in pleasure as it sucked up what was in her skull.

It was obscene.

It was sickening.

Yet Rico knew there was a carefully calculating intelligence behind it. He remembered a psych class he'd had to take at community college. The instructor said there were basically two ways to control the human species if all else failed—through the sex drive and the hunger drive. If people were horny enough, they'd do just about anything for release. They'd engage in the most degrading behavior imaginable. And even those who were strong enough to overcome that, could be controlled with hunger. If they were starving, they'd literally do anything for food. His point was that corporate America with its perpetual onslaught of marketing and advertising, manipulated these drives at every conceivable level.

Sex and food. It basically came down to that with the human animal.

Whoever Sunny had been before, she was no longer. She was being erased and eradicated bite by bite … and she was loving every minute of it.

"What the hell are we going to do?" he asked, trying to shut out her cries.

"I don't know," Regina admitted.

"We're getting out," Ketch said. "We're going to pack up as much as we can carry and we're leaving."

Regina shook her head. "We can't. Not at night. You know that."

"Like hell we can't," Joe Jack said. "I'm not listening to that all night! I'm not listening to that fucking thing pervert her! And if you're Sunny's friend, you won't either."

That was it, then.

Rico knew Regina better than the others. They'd been friends longer. She did not give in easily. But in this case, regardless of how dangerous it was, she did not disagree.

Joe Jack led them out.

There was a calm determination to him. As strong as his feelings for Sunny were (and Rico was certain that if it wasn't love, then it was damn close), he marched them out into the other room and he refused to look at her, or what she had become.

The mutant brain did nothing; it continued to feed.

Rico and the others flinched slightly at Sunny's appearance. Her eyes were glazed white, a bubble of mucus at her left nostril expanding and deflating with each rapid breath. A string of drool hung from her mouth, swinging side to side with her motions. She no longer moaned, only made a liquid gurgling in her throat. She moved with jerking, mechanical motions like a macabre human puppet.

She was slowing by the minute.

Joe Jack moved quickly past the degenerate caricature of his lover. He removed the planks that barred the door and threw the heavy deadbolts. Then he unlocked the door itself. Guns in hand, they followed him up the steps. When they reached the sidewalk, they crouched in the shadows.

The crazies were out in force.

Dozens of them paraded in the streets, circling fires and jumping up and down on the hulks of wrecked cars. They squealed and shouted, dancing and fighting and fucking like a warren of animals. A woman whose naked body was a Rorschach blot of splattered blood walked within ten feet of them, swinging a man's head back and forth by the hair.

Being that close to them made Rico's stomach suck up into his chest. They had been civilized human beings once, but four years of savage survival had turned back their evolutionary clocks. If civilization began again tomorrow, they'd have to be hunted down and destroyed like mad dogs.

He could smell the wildness of them—a hot, feral stench like a wolf's den littered with bones and scraps, scented by urine and the secretions of primeval glands.

The idea that he'd once owned and operated a sandwich shop that specialized in gyros and Italian beef seemed pretty preposterous now. Its reality seemed as plausible as Tolkien's Middle Earth. And just as absurd was the idea that he'd had a wife and two children. Two hours before the first warhead exploded above the city center, he'd said goodbye to them as he'd left for work. Lila was bustling about, getting Nola and Josh ready for the bus so she could throw herself together for another day at the bank. She'd given him a quick peck on the cheek and the children waved. A few hours later, they were all dead. The neighborhood—in fact, that entire section of the city— had been blasted into a mangled dead zone of twisted girders and rubble along with the school and the branch of First Federal where Lila worked.

Gone.

Just like that.

Even the bad days with his family where the kids acted up and he fought with Lila were better than a minute of this insanity.

"You with us, Rico?" Regina whispered in his ear.

"Sure," he said, banishing memories of what once was and would never be again.

"Move and move quiet," Ketch told them.

They slipped through the shadows, hiding and ducking until they found a building Ketch knew about. It was safe and defensible.

And it was the first bit of luck they'd had all day.

They stayed there for four days as they formulated plans to break out of the city for good. Joe Jack had an uncle with a cabin on Cranberry Creek, some two hours outside the city. It was a long way, but it was a destination he'd been talking about for months. Now, finally, they were going to try.

It was a weird four days.

Things were changing fast.

Rico could feel it in the atmosphere: that something in the very makeup of the city had been altered. And if he needed evidence of that, they began to see it in the streets—bodies scattered in every direction, the remains of crazies whose heads had been reduced to a soft, featureless pulp. Their skulls were either blown open violently or split open like Shaya's and the corpses they'd seen at the food pantry. And like them, their brains were missing.

It meant, of course, that the freakish, monstrous brain mutation was spreading.

Regina and he had long talks about it, trying to apply logic to something that was so grotesque it defied reason. Why did certain brains (like Shaya's) mutate into monstrosities and others (like Sunny's) simply provide food for them? As much as they discussed it, they came up with nothing. They supposed they'd never understand the pattern behind it or the exact mechanics.

Like many things in the ugly wreck of the world, it just was and you'd drive yourself crazy trying to figure it out.

The bottom line was that they'd found dozens and dozens of bodies like that. And each night there seemed to be fewer and fewer crazies in the streets. Rico never thought he'd miss them, but in a way he did.

They were a known quantity, but the brains were something else again. Something that was stalking the human race.

The revelations did not end.

Their third day in the building, as they plotted their breakout, something happened that made them realize that people as such were definitely an endangered species. They went out and patrolled the neighborhood and counted some twenty bodies before they gave up. Every one of them was missing their brains.

"We need to get out," Regina said, staring at a pair of them that were curled up like dead spiders. "We don't dare wait any longer."

"Then there's one thing we'll need," Joe Jack told them. "Something that will make it much easier."

"What?" Ketch wanted to know.

"A Jeep." He motioned them forward. "Sunny and I found it. It runs and there's gas cans stored with it."

His voice cracked when he mentioned her name. Her death hit them all hard, but it devastated him, even if he refused to discuss it.

Working vehicles were a rarity. In a country where there had been millions, now there were very few that were not broken down or smashed up by the crazies. Word had it that there were plenty outside the city, but there were also batshit-crazy militias, religious cults into human sacrifice, and horrible mutations.

But much of that might have been exaggeration.

Once they got out there, they were bound to find out. For now, there was the Jeep. If it was in perfect working order like Joe Jack said, it would solve lots of problems. It was stored in a garage six blocks away. It took them about thirty minutes to get there. It was in a garage, as he said, along with ten five-gallon plastic jugs of gas.

Ketch, who knew a few things about cars, started it up and let it run for a while, listening to the engine. Satisfied, he shut it off and took the keys.

"Well, let's pile in," Rico suggested.

Ketch shook his head. "No, not tonight. It'll be dark in an hour or so. We'll hike back with our stuff at first light and get the hell out of this shithole. I don't want to try and get out of the city at night. And I don't want our ride parked in the street where the crazies can get it."

It made sense.

His plan was to head straight up 32nd and hang a right on the expressway. It would take them right out of the city and connect with Highway 17 would bring them, eventually, to the vicinity of Cranberry Creek.

Everyone agreed.

The city was eerie and silent as they legged it back to the building to organize their things and get some sleep so they could move at dawn. Usually, they came across a few stray crazies or some street people whose minds were so stewed from decades of drinking that they didn't even know the world had shit its pants.

But there was no one.

Not so much as a stray dog.

About two blocks from the building, they found another body. It was like nothing they'd seen thus far.

"What the hell happened to it?" Rico asked.

Regina just shook her head.

"It's just decayed or something," Ketch said.

"I don't think so."

It was twisted up on the sidewalk; maybe a man, maybe a woman; there was no way to know. Some hideous mutation had turned it into a monster and Rico was pretty sure it hadn't happened post mortem.

But it couldn't have been alive like that, he thought. *Nothing like that could have walked.*

It was lumpy and green, rotting with ulcers and tumescent growths. It looked as if there were bunching roots and fibers beneath the skin, networks of them like the veins of a leaf. In fact, it seemed to be composed of them, its flesh membranous in places, in others, furry like moss. Its mouth was yawned wide, yellow teeth jutting from shriveled gums. Its nose was rotted into a triangular cavity, its eyes black and misshapen pits.

"All right, enough. Let's get the hell out of here," Ketch said.

"I saw this before," Joe Jack told them. "Sunny ... Sunny and me found a body like this a couple weeks ago. We thought, I guess, we thought it was just being eaten by some kind of fungus."

There was no more to be said about it.

They all saw that the top of its head was missing and that there was nothing but space in the skull. That was plenty. They didn't want to see anymore.

They took Ketch's advice: they got the hell out of there.

That night, long after midnight, as everyone rested for the big day, there came a knock at the door. At first, Rico thought he was dreaming ... then it came again. Not the furious, manic pounding of a crazy that wanted in, but a gentle rapping.

Joe Jack was the only one that was really awake. Ever since Sunny's death, he slept very little and what sleep he did get was filled with nightmares that made him cry out.

Rico woke, looked around, and saw Joe Jack standing by the door in the candlelight. The knocking came again—*rap, rap, rap*. The sound of knuckles on the outer pane.

"You should go away," Joe Jack said, as if he knew who it was.

Rico was about to ask him what in the hell was going on, when a voice spoke from the other side: *"Joe Jack, please let me in. I'm all alone.... I'm so alone...."*

Rico felt the hairs at the back of his neck stand on end. It was an unearthly, chilling voice. And the worst thing was that he recognized it. Despite its hissing, guttural delivery, he knew it was Sunny's voice.

"She won't go away," Joe Jack said in a hollow, oddly childlike tone. "I told her she was dead, but she won't go away."

"Joe ... Jack, open the door," came the voice, wavering and weird like a moaning gust of wind blown along the eaves of an old house.

By then, Regina and Ketch were awake. They wanted to know what was going on, but Rico couldn't find his voice to tell them. It was full of sand.

Joe Jack shuffled closer to the door like a sleepwalker. He looked dazed and mindless like a man in a dream as he reached for the lock.

Both Regina and Ketch shouted for him to stop, but it was Rico, who was closer, that grabbed hold of him. Joe Jack, without hesitation, punched him right in the face, knocking him back and down.

"DON'T OPEN IT!" Regina shouted.

Too late. He threw the locks and the door blew right open as it had for Roderick Usher when his sister came out of her tomb.

What stood beyond the threshold was no less terrifying.

It was human in form only, a distorted, grisly thing like the corpse they had found. Eyeless and crooked, it was a mildew-green, pulpous mass of morbid fungi, bulging with toadstool-like bulbs that palpitated horribly. It was made of the same tangled, ropy rootlets as if it was undergoing some loathsome, hot germination.

The top of its skull was missing and riding the cavity was a huge, pulsating mutant brain. It was pink and gray, its convolutions quivering like bulging muscles. Masses of wriggling yellow tendrils hung from it like blood-engorged roundworms. They made a terrible, gelatinous sound that reminded Rico of noodles sucked into mouths.

"Joe Jack," he managed in a dry voice, "get away from it."

But he knew it wouldn't happen.

The brain would not allow it.

Slime dripped from it and it stank like a heap of decomposing compost. It took one, then two squishing steps forward, yellow-green feelers sliding from its body and face, squirming in the air. A nest of them sprouted from the empty cavity of its skull like hothouse orchids, connecting with the brain.

"Sunny," Joe Jack muttered. "Oh God, Sunny."

"I'm here," she said.

Ketch was on his feet by then, but there was no way he could get a shot at Sunny with Joe Jack in the way. Everyone shouted for him to get away from it, but he was no longer in his right mind. He seemed to actually believe that the horror in the doorway was the woman he loved.

And then she was on him, closing the gap instantly.

She embraced him, pulling him against her and he screamed. The sound exploded from his mouth as he went the same color as her, as if his veins were suddenly pumped full of chlorophyll. Whatever she had done to him, he was immobilized instantly, dropping to his knees, a snotty emulsion of green slime bubbling from his open mouth like mint jelly.

The mutant brain—now easily as large as a turkey roaster—jumped onto his head, leeching itself to him. Right away, there was a cracking sound which must have been his skull splitting open like a walnut, followed by the sucking, slurping noises.

Joe Jack began to moan with ecstasy as he must have once upon a time with Sunny before their world became a nightmare.

Rico thought that Sunny's body would fold right up without the brain parasite. The inside of her head was empty. Yet, she didn't. She stood there, trembling, breathing. She had no autonomic nervous system and still, she lived, she breathed.

It was Regina who rallied them.

As before, they retreated into one of the back bedrooms, grabbing anything handy—guns, ammo, knives, hatchets, food, water, the first aid kit, anything they could quickly lay their hands on and stuff into their bags and packs. They went out the window and took the fire escape to the alley. The plan was to get to the Jeep.

But that didn't happen.

There were dozens of green walking corpses in the streets. And many of them had massive parasitic brains suckered to their heads. Others had empty skulls and yet, they walked.

The sewers.

When things got dangerous above ground in the past, they had become the favorite system of conveyance for Sunny and Joe Jack, Rico knew. A way to cross sections of the city without having to deal with crazies or violent street people or the numerous predators that hunted the streets. Ketch didn't like it, of course. He had one weakness and that was claustrophobia. So, he complained about it, but when he saw just how many green corpses were out and about, he became a believer.

Rico led the way with a flashlight in his hand.

Regina and Ketch were right behind him. He wished Joe Jack was still with them. He knew the way. Sunny and he had mapped out the arteries beneath the city, but Rico figured if they went straight on and didn't take any side tunnels, that they couldn't possibly get lost.

Famous last words, a cynical, defeated voice in his head told him.

The air down there was close and suffocating, a mephitic under-smell just beneath it of putrescence, foul gases, and subterranean dankness. There was a near-constant dripping, the sound of things scampering away just beyond the light.

Their splashing footfalls echoed through the brick tunnels with volume. If anyone or any*thing* was ahead of them or behind them, their location was no secret.

They marched through about a foot of standing water and rotting leaves. Dead, nameless things floated by.

"How far we going to go in this?" Ketch asked.

"I figure a couple blocks," Rico told him. "That'll take us in the general direction we need to go. Hopefully, the streets will be quiet when we come up."

"You really believe that?"

Rico wasn't sure what he believed anymore. There had been a time when he figured he knew how the world worked: you were born, you lived, you worked, you died, and hopefully in the process, you did some good things, achieving something that would live on after you. But then came the war. Then came the death of everything he had known and held sacred. All of which led to this particularly disagreeable, desperate moment.

Yet, for all that, as beaten as he felt and as threadbare was his hope, he did not stop moving. He did not so much as hesitate. To do that would mean giving up and if he gave up, it meant everything he had gone through had had no meaning.

It doesn't, you know? In the end, nothing really does, he heard the voice of his father say.

But he wouldn't listen. The gaseous miasma in the air was actually sickening. It wasn't exactly the smell of rot and rancid decay, but something stronger, an effluvium of spiritual putrescence, disease, and suppurating wounds. At any moment, he expected some monstrosity to crawl into the light, a massive and shapeless thing like a gigantic, grinning maggot.

Imagination.

It was just overheated imagination. That's all it was. He could put a lot of labels on it, but it all came back to the same thing: he was scared to death. Fear, pure and unreasoning, lived in his core, it was a leech that was attached to his soft white underbelly, slowly sucking the blood out of him.

He was glad the others were with him or he would have lost it, completely lost it.

They moved forward easily another thirty minutes and Rico saw light ahead. He figured that was a good sign, but something in him recoiled at the idea. He felt an odd pressure in the back of his head. At first, it meant nothing ... but then he began to think that he'd felt it before: when Sunny attacked the brain and was immobilized, and when Joe Jack let the thing she had become into the apartment.

They're here.

Somewhere, there's one of those brains.

I can feel it.

It's like it's sending out thoughts to find us, to connect with us.

He stopped and looked at Regina and Ketch in the flashlight beam. He saw nothing on their faces that told him they were feeling it.

"What is it?" Regina asked.

"Nothing."

But why am I feeling it? Why me?

He didn't know. He had something the others didn't, an adaptation in his brain, an alteration, a deficit, a gift. But it was there and it was making damn well sure he knew about it.

"You're acting fucked-up," Ketch told him with his usual subtlety.

Rico nearly laughed ... but he was afraid it would come out sounding shrill and manic like the laughter of an insane man. He assured them he was fine. He started moving toward the light again. *Should I tell them? Should I tell them that we're walking into trouble?* But there was no point. Whatever was throwing out a net for them would get them whether they went forward or back. The pressure in his head increased—not to a painful level, but more like the pleasant sore buzz of a muscle after a workout—and it told him that he must seek what sought him.

"It's definitely brighter up there," Ketch said. "I think we might just find a way out."

Rico wanted to tell him that he was wrong. But if he did that, he'd have to explain *how* he knew that and even he didn't know.

Water continued to drip, their boots splashing through standing puddles of it. The air was heavy with an overpowering fetid stink. The tunnel ahead was blocked off by fallen rubble, but there was a crevice that opened into a huge grotto and this was where the light was coming from. It was like an immense cavern: the floor uneven with piles of debris and pools of spreading water. Above was the wreckage of a building, a tangled mess of girders and timbers, sections of shattered flooring. Sunlight shone through holes in it, its beams filled with gray mist.

The pressure in Rico's brain increased. *This is it,* it seemed to be saying to him. *This is what you've been seeking.*

The fear that nipped at him since they entered the sewers began to spike. It was utterly irrational, but it gripped him in a hot, sweaty fist, squeezing him, making his breath come fast and his guts roil and his eyes bulge from their sockets. His instinct was riled and then he saw why.

"Shit," Ketch said behind him and Rico could hear him bringing up his shotgun.

Regina made a gasping sound.

The light picked out dozens and dozens of the green corpses, if not hundreds. They were not moving, just standing there like soldiers waiting for orders to march. There were no parasitic brains atop their cleft skulls. The feelers that poked from their bodies were not moving either..., just hanging limp like noodles.

What did it mean?

What did any of it mean?

"Servitors," Regina whispered. "That's all they are. They can't move without a brain steering them."

Rico took three steps toward the nearest group of them. They did not move. They did not even flinch. They were completely unaware of him. A stick floated by and he grabbed it, throwing it at the nearest one. It struck it, but still the thing remained motionless.

"What do you make of that?" he said. "They're asleep or something. Dormant."

"And they could wake up at any time," Ketch said.

"No ... wait." Regina was cocking her head. "Listen."

Rico heard it, too. A sort of low throbbing noise. Together, they stepped forward and saw the source: there *was* a brain, a massive pink brain exploding with yellow tendrils like worms crawling out of it. The brain was not only making the throbbing noise, but it was vibrating. It was easily twice the size of the biggest brain they'd seen thus far.

And it wasn't alone.

They were everywhere.

Clusters of them were gathered like pink, pulsing mushrooms, filled with obscene life and a limitless power that made Rico feel weak in his stomach. That pressure in his head seemed to increase and he knew it was because he was on the same mental wavelength as the brains. Ketch and Regina were scared, shocked, and disturbed, but they weren't plugged into it like he was. The brains were not awake, nor were they sleeping exactly. They were just dormant, gathering their energies for some important task. He kept picking up stray thoughts that flared briefly in his mind as confused, formless imagery.

He moved amid the forest of green corpses.

He was afraid, but more curious than anything. He knew the servitors could not wake until the brains did. He was safe. At least, for the moment. Both Regina and Ketch called for him to come back, but he ignored them. The mutant brains were part of something much larger than themselves and he could feel it: they were cells in some vast neural network and he could feel his own thoughts threading its synaptic connections, exploring, learning, but ever wary because he knew the sheer power of it could blow his own brain apart like a cluster bomb if it was directed at him.

The network was inactive as a whole, but that wouldn't last. Zero hour was fast approaching and, somehow, it had to be unplugged before that happened. But how to accomplish that? He studied the brains in detail. At the moment, they were relatively harmless like hibernating snakes. They rested atop heaps of rubble in pools of slime, quivering masses of gray matter … and in his mind, he likened them to protozoa because—

Then he knew.

Oh Christ, *yes, yes, of course!*

One of them about three feet from him began to writhe and palpitate and there was a squishy, juicy sound as some foaming, yellow secretion oozed from the longitudinal fissure that separated its two hemispheres. It gushed and flowed, the brain shivering, a roiling, festering jelly of flesh. This was followed by a wet ripping like meat pulled from bone and the two undulating hemispheres pulled apart, connected by strings of tissue that popped with bubbles of blood.

Protozoans ... of course, binary fission. Just like in biology class, you remember.

They were dividing.

That's why they were dormant and helpless, their servitors like hand puppets with no hands in them. Once the division was complete, there would be well over a hundred of them. In a week, they would double and double yet again.

"KILL THEM!" he called out to Regina and Ketch. "THEY'RE FUCKING DIVIDING! WE HAVE TO KILL THEM ALL! WE DON'T HAVE MUCH TIME!"

Neither of them asked questions—they went for the kill. They blew dividing brains into fragments with their guns, spraying gore and flesh in every which direction. Every time one of them was destroyed, Rico was certain he heard a pathetic wailing in his head, the way he imagined a spider would scream as you stepped on it. When they ran low on ammo, they filled their hands with knives and hatchets, slashing and chopping, segmenting the brains into squirming clots of meat that they smashed under their boots into smears of pink-gray mush.

The result was immediate: the throbbing noise slowly died away and the servitors began to fall apart. They rotted and steamed, bits of them dropping off, flesh dribbling like hot tallow, limbs falling free. All of them melted down, fizzing and popping and putting out geysers of green-black fluid like swamp water.

Yet, through it all, Rico sensed that the network was not dead. It was injured, it was incapacitated, it was bleeding and it was in pain, but it was far from finished. It still lived. It was still galvanic with energy. Slimed with blood and meat like a firehose of gore had been turned on him, he knew there was a bigger threat, a central nervous system that still existed and if it wasn't exterminated, it would just begin again.

The original disease cell still lived.

There was a heaped wall of broken bricks, lathing, and joists before him. He ran at it with the hatchet in his hand, knowing, knowing. His head drummed with the noxious laughter of his enemy. As the others shouted at him and he scrambled up the mountain of debris, he could see the thing in his mind—maybe not see it, but *feel* it, the immense thrumming, voltaic heart of the thing that could drain his mind dry, tap him like a battery, squeeze every last drop of humanity from his rent carcass.

If he let it, that was.

If he let it.

It sat in a hollow: an enormous super-brain, a monstrous and grotesquely bloated mass of gray matter, wallowing in a steaming, seething, bubbling pool of cerebrospinal fluid that sluiced around it. It was pulsating, sweating rolling droplets of slime, pink and gray with huge pumping blood-filled arteries.

It directed its mind at him and it was like hot needles piercing his brain, bells gonging, searing blades slicing deeper and deeper and he screamed with agony, with invasion, with the cold, oily feel of its mind drilling into his own, alien fingers digging through his head, seeking purchase, a seam that could be widened, a loose thread that could be yanked open, a weakness to be exploited.

But by then, he had dived on it, sinking into its spongy mass and the fluid it put out burned like acid, but the hatchet in his hand came down again and again, slicing, dividing, slashing it open, chopping through gray matter into white matter and deeper, deeper into the diseased nucleus of the thing. Blood and inky fluid exploded in his face, cauterizing him, stinging him, taking away his sight and feeling, but still the hatchet came down. The brain's dying tendrils which were like whipping purple-red, suckerless tentacles wriggled over him, cutting into him, burning out his guts with their acidic secretions.

And the hatchet came down one last time and the mutilated brain screamed with a piercing, droning whine that cracked his skull open, but it was dying.

He sank into its rancid, pupating depths and died with it.

Ketch and Regina never bothered trying to pull his blackened carcass from the steaming, smoldering remains of the mutant super-brain. They climbed up and out of the sewers into the sunlight. They did not speak. They wandered for some time until they found the garage with the Jeep in it.

Silently, they drove from the ruin of the city.

CRABMEAT

The toxic beach.
The toxic beach.
Doug's eyes kept opening and closing, his mind spinning, showing him things that were real and absurdly unreal. He was breathing. He was alive. Yet, he was afraid to move, as if his insides were made of fine, fragile white glass that would shatter easily.

"I think he's coming out of it," a voice said.

Spears. He looked down at Doug, unshaven, bruised, his face streaked with grime. His eyes were bloodshot. There was a tic in the corner of his mouth that jumped whenever he was under a lot of stress, Doug knew, which was nearly all the time now.

Spears gave him some water from one of the bottles they coveted and treasured. Fresh water, like a lot of things since the war, was a precious commodity.

"You okay, buddy?"

Doug nodded. He held the cool water as long as he could in his parched throat. Finally, he swallowed it. He looked around. They were still on the beach. He could hear the waves crashing, feel the wind blowing off the sea.

Did you really think something had changed? he asked himself.

"What happened?"

"You went out cold. You just sort of folded-up."

Doug remembered now. The hunger. He was so damn hungry. They had precious few stores, just some crackers and peanut butter, and those were rationed very strictly by Spears. He was a good guy. He was doing everything he could to keep them alive, but the three of them were slowly starving to death. A dollop of peanut butter and a couple crackers a day was simply not enough to maintain a human body. They were thin, clothes tattered, fighting to stay alive hour by hour.

"I was dizzy. You know how it gets."

When he said this, he looked over at Vicki. Her eyes were blank. She sat there, arms wrapped around her knees, rocking back and forth in the sand.

"Vicki," she said in a monotone. "My name is Vicki."

It was all she ever said. Before they found her, she had been through some terrible trauma, maybe it was the bombing itself and maybe something that had happened afterward. There was no way to know.

The three of them were sidled up against a wall of scrub brush, the beach just below them. In an hour or so, they'd have to crawl back up the rock face into the cave. It was not safe to be on the beach at night.

"I think tomorrow," Spears said, indefatigable as always, "I'll scout further down and see what I can see."

He was always hoping to find a house with provisions. It was a dream they all shared, Doug knew. There was plenty of food in the city, but it was a nuclear wasteland, hot with radiation. That's why they stayed to the beach. The wind coming off the sea blew the strand clear of residual fallout and the hills blocked the beach from the city.

"I can go with you," Doug said.

"No, son, you're in no shape. You stay here and keep an eye on Vicki. I don't want her wandering off."

Hearing her name, she blinked her eyes rapidly. "Vicki," she said. "My name is Vicki."

Night.

Doug sat near the mouth of the cave, smelling the brine of the sea and listening to the distant crashing of the waves. He remembered what it was like when he was a kid, running out into the surf with his friends on hot summer days. How cool and refreshing the ocean was. He wished he could swim again, but Spears wouldn't allow it. He wouldn't let them within ten feet of it. When the tide came in, they hid in the cave.

"There's radioactivity in the water," he'd told Doug more than once. "There was a fellah living down here with me. His name was DeFleur. He'd been a marine scientist type with Scripps. He knew his bacon, all right. He tested the water right after the bombs fell and it was hot. He tested it three months later and it wasn't as bad, but still dangerous to people."

DeFleur was gone.

He'd gotten too close to the water's edge, Spears said, and the crabs got him. Though they were large, they could be exceedingly fast when they sensed prey. And Doug knew all about that.

Trapped, he thought as he stared out the mouth of the cave at the sea, the moonlight gleaming on its surface. *We can't go into the sea and we can't go back beyond the hills.*

He could hear things out on the shore. They made horrible croaking sounds like frogs, a perpetual chortling noise that was awful to listen to. It came and went, and in-between, there was only the crashing waves.

"You okay over there?" Spears asked in a whisper, so as not to disturb Vicki.

"Fine. Just watching."

"You should get some sleep."

"I will."

Spears was like a father, always watching, always worrying, always thinking of ways that could keep them alive a few more days. Back in the day, he'd been a fisherman and owned his own crabber. He knew his stuff. Crabs of any sort fascinated him. It was in his blood, Doug supposed. Even the mutants intrigued him.

Doug didn't like to think about the crabs.

Because when he thought about them, he naturally thought about Olive. He'd loved her the moment he'd met her, years ago. After the war, they'd survived, leaving the city. They'd discovered Vicki wandering up a country lane. She was like a stray they took in. She was so pathetic, in such terrible shape, there was no way they could have left her there.

Near to the sea, they'd hooked up with Spears. He'd been a godsend. Working class tough, inventive, improvisational, he was the kind of guy that seemed to know a little bit about everything.

And yet, you didn't listen to his warnings.

Doug felt his guts twist up inside him. In his mind, he went through the horror again and again. It had been a fine moonlit night like tonight. Vicki and Spears were sleeping. Olive and he had slipped out of the cave. Their intention had been to make love in a secret place. It had been months since they had and the desire was overwhelming.

Stupid, stupid, stupid. What the hell were you thinking?

But that was the thing, wasn't it? They hadn't been thinking with their brains, only their raging hormones. They went to the edge of the scrub and that's when one of the crabs had shown, a monstrous thing like an armored tank. It had seized Olive in its claws. It had moved so fast, so incredibly fast. He heard her bones snap as she screamed, her blood exploding into his face. The crab took Olive into the water. He'd gone after it, but three more crabs closed in. He'd fought and managed to lose three fingers and a lot of blood before Spears had rescued him, fending the crabs off by tossing a bucket of Coleman lantern fuel at them and lighting them up with a flare. It had driven them back into the sea.

Spears dragged him back up to the cave. Doug was hysterical, bleeding and fighting, finally losing consciousness. But before he did, he could hear the tearing and crunching sounds of the crab feeding on his wife.

Now it was just the three of them.

"Get some sleep," Spears told him again. "You need it."

Doug laid down, forcing his eyes closed. His mind thought of nothing but Olive and his stomach thought of nothing but food. Finally, physically and mentally exhausted, he went out.

When the bombs fell, there was absolute obliteration and absolute chaos. Doug found himself on the ground, coughing, gagging, finally throwing up. The world around him was a swirling storm of dust and smoke. He could not see. He could barely breathe. He kept gagging, spewing out black grit and tangles of blood. His mind could not seem to focus, to make sense of any of it.

What the hell is this? What happened?

He could hear sirens in the distance. People shouting. Screaming. Dogs barking. It was so hot, he felt like a sausage in a frying pan. Why was it so damn hot?

The sunlight had gone a dirty amber in color, dust blowing around in churning clouds. He forced himself to sit up, realizing he was literally covered in a thick, chalky powder like pulverized brick and stone.

As the wheels of his mind began to spin again, he realized with a stab of fear that something not only terrible had happened, but something catastrophic. He was too dizzy to stand. His mouth tasted like blood. He crawled toward the house and discovered a ramshackle pile of debris— splintered timbers and broken glass, shattered bricks and what might have been a collapsed wall. The dust blew clean for a few moments and he saw that Peggy Chun's house next door was likewise flattened and it was burning.

As he tried to wrap his brain around it all and make sense of it, a memory from early childhood came to him, something from history class. They'd been studying the Cold War of the 1950s, the duck-and-cover drills kids practiced in school. In the case of a Soviet atomic attack, you were supposed to jump under your desk and cover your head. Hell, there was even a cartoon film they'd been forced to watch where a comical turtle pulled himself inside his shell.

Oh no.

Oh, Jesus H. Christ. It can't be.

But in his bones, he knew that it was. The dust continued to blow, but it was gradually thinning. He could smell the smoke of fires burning. Hear more screams. In the distance, there was a rumbling as if a building had fallen over.

The remains of his garage were scattered in the yard. His car in the driveway was covered in what looked like an inch of ash. Not that he could have used it anyway: the big oak on the boulevard had gone right over. It lay there in a spidery mass of denuded limbs. The upper boughs were either gone or withered to blackened sticks.

They did it. They really goddamn well did it.

He realized his phone was in his pocket. He pulled it out, but it was dead. It wouldn't even turn on and it felt hot to the touch.

"HELP!" he called out. "IS ANYONE AROUND?"

No one responded.

Dazed, aching, he got to his feet and started walking. Olive was at the library. He had to get there. He had to find her. The further he got into the city, the worse it became. Nothing was standing—not buildings, houses, or trees. Telephone poles had come down, wires tangled like cobwebs. Cars were burning, a delivery truck overturned. An SUV was smashed by fallen rubble.

It was a wasteland, an absolute wasteland.

After a time, he began to see other people. Like him, they were walking, stumbling forward, shocked and mindless. When he called out to them, they did not answer. Their clothes were rags. Some had horrendous burns on their faces and arms, but most were coated in that chalky white powder so that you couldn't even tell what their race, gender, or age was. They wandered about like ghosts haunting the cemetery of the city.

Doug walked and walked.

There were burned bodies everywhere. Some of them were still smoldering with a nauseating stench. He saw the remains of what might have been a dog carbonized to a blackened husk, a burning baby carriage.

Maybe a mile later, the city a scattered, broken jigsaw puzzle around him, he came to the river. The suspension bridge had collapsed, girders poking from the water like the serrated plates of sea monsters. The river was filled with bodies, what seemed thousands of them. Many were burnt, looking oddly like bobbing black logs pulled from fire pits. Many others were broiled red like lobsters. There were so many of them, he could've walked over them to the other bank and never got his feet wet. The water was steaming. He could feel the heat coming off it.

They must have thrown themselves in to avoid the heat, he thought, *only the water was boiling.*

He stepped around the blackened remains of a woman clutching a baby. There were bodies heaped everywhere. Most had their clothes burned right off them. They were bloated, blood expelled from mouths and nostrils and anuses. Swollen blue tongues protruded from mouths, eyes blown from their sockets or filmed white.

He stood there, shaking, dried up inside. There was so much death that he was overwhelmed by it, shocked into numbness. He could not feel anything anymore. There was just too much. It was like a giant had ladled out human porridge in every direction.

He finally sat down before he fell down.

People were wandering around, most starkly mad. Their retinas were burned out, eardrums punctured. They called out for loved ones, walking corpses whose blistered skins hung in flaps and sheets. A poodle with most of its hair scorched down to an oily nap lapped at the throat of a dead woman.

This is it.

This is the world now.

Back to the Stone Age.

The smell of cremated flesh and burnt hair in his nostrils, half-melted bodies scattered around him in a jackstraw tangle, he began to weep, the tears cutting clean trails down his dirty face.

This was what the puppet masters of the military-industrial complex had given the world and their mindless flag-wavers.

He hoped they were all goddamn well happy now.

Although his mouth was filled with blood from his bleeding gums and twice, he'd gone down to his knees and vomited more of the same, he started walking again. He didn't know what else to do.

An hour later, he reached the library. Olive was there and she was alive. They clung to each other for some time. Finally, she said, "Doug … we need to get out of the city. We need to get out of here right now before it's too late."

He woke up shaking. Out of the mouth of the cave, he could see that the moon had moved halfway across the sky. Something had woken him, but he wasn't sure what. He tried to swallow, but his throat was so dry it felt baked and swollen. The wind had subsided to a low droning and the waves were no longer crashing, just lapping gently at the beach now.

Spears and Vicki were sleeping.

"Doug."

Was he still dreaming? He heard his name called and he knew without a doubt it was Olive. No, no, no, he was delusional. He was hallucinating. It was the lack of food—his head wasn't right. It wouldn't have been the first time in these weeks since her death that he'd heard things that weren't real.

He went through the reasons in his mind: guilt, trauma, depression, despondency … all that combined with starvation could do funny things to your head. Olive was dead. There was no point in denying that. There was no possible way she could have survived the crab attack. Just no way.

He breathed in and out slowly, trying to calm himself. His heart was racing. His palms were sweating. And he was alone, oh so terribly, terribly alone.

"Doug," the voice said again, a whisper from out on the beach. *"Come to me, Doug. I need you. Please don't let them eat me. I don't want to die like that again."*

He pressed his hands to the sides of his head. He was breathing rapidly, beads of sweat rolling down his face. She was not out there. She could *not* be out there. But that voice, oh dear Christ, that voice. It echoed in his head and he could hear the desperation, the fear in every word.

"Stop it," he said beneath his breath. "Stop talking to me."

"But, Doug, I'm alone…. I'm so afraid."

He began to whimper, pressing his lips tightly together so the others didn't hear him. Maybe they couldn't anyway because it was all a dream. It had to be a dream. But then the voice called to him again and it took everything he had not to go to the cave mouth and see what was calling him.

The voice of Olive echoed across the beach, bouncing off the high sandstone cliffs. It was ghostly and surreal, finally fading away until it was replaced by the clicking noises of the crabs, a wet snapping that went on and on as if they were signaling each other up and down the beach. *Click-click-click-clickety-click.* It was the sound of their pincers and the vibrations of their shells, a horrible sound that filled his head, filled the cave, reverberating back and forth until he could no longer think. *CLICK-CLICK-CLICK-CLICKETY-CLICKETY-CLICK—*

Now he could see them massing at the water's edge, their spiky shells white as ghost-flesh, pincers raised, snapping and snapping as they moved in and out of the water. They crawled over each other and fought with their thrashing claws and he was certain that they were looking up at the cave with raised eyestalks.

"At it again, eh?" Spears said. "Goddamned things. What a racket."

Doug calmed slightly at the sound of his voice. He wasn't alone after all, not really alone. Spears had his hand on his shoulder and he said, "C'mon, Doug. Lay back down. They'll go about their business sooner or later. We're safe up here." And Doug realized that he was sitting at the mouth of the cave, his legs hanging out into the air. He didn't remember going out there, but somehow, he had.

"Doug."

"Okay."

He laid back down, pretending he couldn't hear them clicking out there, hissing and fighting, feeding on things they'd dragged from the water and on each other with tearing and crunching sounds.

Two days later, Spears had a heart-to-heart with him. "We're in a rough spot, Doug. You know it and I know it. Crackers and goddamn peanut butter aren't going to see us through. We're starving a day at a time and it's affecting us all. I'm dizzy like you are. My head's wrong more than it's right and we're wasting away." He laughed with a short, barking sound. "Was a time when I was a big fellah, near on three hundred pounds. I liked my grub. Boy, did I like it! Turn on the tube, watch me a game, and order a pizza. When I wasn't doing that, I was grilling burgers and steaks and barbeque chicken out on the Weber. But now look at me ... Christ, I bet I don't weigh one-seventy."

Doug nodded. He had a feeling where this was going and he did not want to hear it. "So," he said, licking his lips, "what are our options?"

"We need food, man. *Real* food."

"We can't eat the fish and the birds are too hard to catch."

"I ain't talking about fish and birds, son. You know that's not what I'm talking about."

Spears looked over at Vicki, who was playing with weeds abandoned by the tide, tying dried strings of them into chains like she might have done with daisies as a child. Her eyes were empty. Her mouth caught between a smile and a frown. She was so thin her arms looked like sticks.

"We need meat. That's all there is to it and there's only one way we can get it. You know what it is."

For one insane moment, Doug thought he was going to suggest cannibalism, that they eat Vicki, and he nearly tittered at the very idea. That's how far his mind had gone. *But we can't eat her, it wouldn't be right. Hee, hee. More meat on a McDonald's hamburger than that girl.* But, of course, that wasn't what Spears was suggesting. Doug knew what he wanted to do and it made the idea of cannibalism seem acceptable.

"The crabs," he said, without meaning to.

"Yes, the crabs."

"No."

Spears sighed. "I'm a man who knows those scuttlers better than most. I know how it can be done. We kill one of them and we'll have more meat than we know what to do with."

Doug felt his stomach roil. "I won't eat one of those things. There's no fucking way."

"Then you're gonna starve to death?"

"Yes."

"Don't talk like an idiot. If you don't give a damn about yourself, then think about Vicki. I can't bear the idea of watching her die a day at a time. Can you?"

Doug shook his head. No, of course not, but there had to be a better way.

"I did some exploring in my walk yesterday," Spears said. "Just down the way beyond the cove, there's a stretch of dunes. I found the fresh molts of three big crabs. You know what that means, don't you?"

Doug didn't. He knew they molted, of course, but beyond that all he knew about crabs came from the menu at Red Lobster.

"It means, son, that out there somewhere we've got some soft shells wandering about. Not hard-shells. We'd never stand a chance of taking one of them, but a soft-shell: a crab that just molted. Shell hasn't hardened yet. We can pierce it with a spear. Kill the bastard and cook it up, fill our bellies."

The very idea was revolting. Nothing disgusted Doug the way the giant mutant crabs did. A big part of that was what happened to Olive, of course, but even without that, they offended him. The way they moved … that clicking … the smell that came off them; it all sickened him. And to eat one, no, the idea made him want to throw up.

"I need your help on this."

Doug swallowed. He knew he couldn't say no.

"All right."

"Now you're talking."

So, they went crab-hunting.

Spears was completely in his element. Doug had never seen him quite so excited. He was back on turf he understood—crabbing. It didn't seem to matter that the quarry in this case were absolute monsters, their genes twisted by radiation, they were still crabs.

Their mission was to find the crabs (which was easy), then locate a soft-shell (which might take some work). Spears said soft-shells were very vulnerable until their shells hardened and that other crabs were notoriously cannibalistic, so they were very wary after a fresh molt.

Vicki was a problem. They couldn't take her with them, because they feared if the crabs came after them that she just might not run. She was easy prey. Far too easy.

In the end, they took her up to the cave and Spears tied her ankle to a crate and told her to sleep.

"Lay down, Vicki. Just lay down and close your eyes," he said.

"Vicki," she said. "My name is Vicki."

"Of course, it is. Now you just get some rest."

She obeyed like a dog and Doug felt his heart break (if there was anything left of it by that point), wondering what horrible things had been done to her. But, following the war, she was a lone woman in a savage world of predators that walked on two legs and he could just about imagine what had been done to her, probably countless times. And there was no doubt in his mind she was a delicate creature. Some women might have gone through what she did and became tougher, meaner, but Vicki was a sensitive soul.

He recognized that instantly because he was one himself. The experience had made her wilt, fold-up, draw into herself much as he had drawn into himself following Olive's death.

Sometimes he didn't even know why he kept breathing, why he didn't just throw himself into the sea. But he knew: Spears. He kept them all going. He simply would not give in or give up.

He led Doug on a merry chase through the sand dunes down the beach. He showed him the cast-off shells of the crabs, huge molts half-buried in the shifting sand like the fossils of prehistoric monsters. Though they were harmless, Doug was sick to his stomach even approaching one, everything inside him pulled tight as a wire.

"See how it's cracked open in the back here?" Spears said, jabbing it with the bowie knife he had wired to the end of a heavy stick to be used as a pike. "That's where it came out. This shell was too small to hold it anymore. It needed some breathing room."

By God, it was bigger around than a child's swimming pool. How big was it now? And how much bigger could it possibly get? Doug felt himself growing dizzy again. The molt had a decidedly dank, rotten smell to it and that combined with the burning sun above and the briny smell of the sea, the decaying weed and dead things stranded by the tide, made him want to drop to his knees and vomit.

But Spears was far from done with his anatomy lesson. "See the red-tipped claws? Right here, son. Do you see it?"

Doug did. The pincers were mammoth, jagged on the inside. The sun gleamed off them. He touched one of the spikes and it was sharp enough to cut his finger. He looked at the blood on his fingertip and thought about Olive. Was this the monster that did it?

"Red-tipped like that, you know this was a female and she's the girl we're after."

They came across two or three crabs hiding beneath the sand, their antennae and eyestalks the only thing protruding. They gave them a wide berth. They were sluggish during the daytime, but you had to be careful because a meal was a meal to them. They kept an eye out for suspicious mounds in the dunes. Most of the crabs were in the water, but not all.

Doug trudged along behind Spears, certain more than once he heard Olive's wailing, lonesome voice coming from the sea, echoing eerily off the sea cliffs, but every time he looked at Spears, he could see that he hadn't heard it at all.

Imagining things.

You're just imagining things.

You need to keep your head screwed on right.

He was starving. The lack of real food was making his mind funny. He was hungry, hungry all the time.

Finally, after about two hours, about the time Doug was ready to suggest they get back to Vicki, Spears climbed a dune away from the sea and down there in a little protected hollow was the crab.

It was the size of a small car, white as a winter moon, its limbs a glossy pink. Its antennae were twitching, its eyestalks retracted. In some perverse, grotesque way, it was almost beautiful. Doug hated the crabs, they disgusted him, filled him with horror … yet, he could not help thinking that there was something fundamentally appealing about this one.

Mad images paraded through his head—he saw himself going down there and putting his hands on its pristine flesh. It would be soft and smooth the way a woman's thigh was, pleasing in a tactile sort of way. As he ran his hands over it, it would make a breathless cooing sound, the way Olive had when they made love—

"You with me, son?" Spears asked.

"Of course."

Spears seemed suspicious of that. "I need your head in the right place or we'll never pull this off. You reading me on this?"

"Yes."

"All right. Here's how we're going to do this. I want you to go down there to the far side of the hollow. Make some noise. Stomp your feet, draw her attention. When you do that and she's focused on you, I'll jump on her and ram the spear right into her heart. I know exactly where it is. It'll be quick."

"You want me to be the bait."

"Exactly, Doug, exactly."

Funny, but yesterday the idea would have been unthinkable, appalling really, but today it seemed reasonable. He wasn't sure why. He really wasn't, but he felt a terrible need to get close to the crab down there. It was more than a strange impulse, but a deep-seated need he could not ignore.

With that in mind, not feeling particularly suicidal or particularly brave, he circled the hollow, reaching a vantage point where he could see the crab in the distance clearly and there was a fallen tree he could scramble down. And if he needed to get away fast, he could use it to climb back out and not trust himself to the loose sand of the dunes.

He reached the hollow and the crab was unaware of him. He picked up a piece of driftwood and pounded it against a rock, stomping his feet at the same time. It drew the crab's attention nearly immediately. It— *she*—turned to face him, eyestalks erect. Spears had told him that crabs could not see well, but they could detect motion.

And he was detected.

The crab raised its pincers.

It moved two or three feet in his direction and he wondered if it was going to charge, but it didn't. It hesitated. It did not seem aggressive at all. It seemed ... *curious.* It waited there, its soft shell the color of fresh marrow, its eyes not the beady jellied black of crabs, but a sparkling blue like Olive's eyes had been. It was perfectly ridiculous of course, just as it was ridiculous to believe that he could approach it and it would not harm him.

But it won't. I know it won't. It's just as lonely as I am.

Now something perfectly impossible happened: it changed colors. Its shell went from the purple of twilight to the red of boiled lobster to the orange of an autumn sunset. And as it did so, he could hear Olive's voice speaking in his mind, his thoughts blazing like hot embers. *Oh, Doug. God, I'm so tired of being alone. I'm so tired of being away from you.* And he understood that perfectly as the colors shifted in his mind in the most delightful ways, making him feel warm inside. Protected, Joined. Loved.

"Olive," he said. "Olive...."

Then Spears—whom he'd completely forgotten about—jumped on the back of the she-crab like a primeval hunter. Doug cried out, but it was too late. The crab scuttled around in a loose circle, claws lashing.

And Spears brought his makeshift pike down with everything he had, penetrating the soft shell with a sound like a knife jabbed into a pumpkin. Red-black blood jetted into the air in a fountain and Spears brought the deadly pike down two or three more times.

The crab screamed.

It screamed like a woman in agony.

It screamed with Olive's voice, the way she had the first time she died.

It skittered about, blood-spattered and weakening, then finally dropping into the sand, its legs curling up. Spears kept the pike buried in it until it stopped moving.

Doug raced through the hollow, screaming, crying, completely out of his mind. *Olive, Olive, Olive.* This was the crab that had killed her. And in killing her, had absorbed not only her life force, but her personality. All that she was had been in the crab and Spears had destroyed it *and* her.

He knocked Spears off the shell, shouting at the top of his voice, but nothing he said made any sense. When he came at Spears again, the bigger man knocked him down. "What in the hell are you doing, you goddamn idiot?" he cried.

But Doug honestly did not know.

He felt weak and sick inside. He brushed tears from his eyes and wiped his mouth with his fist. He was scared, beside himself with fear and angst and rioting emotions. There was no way he could explain to Spears what had happened and what he had done by ... by *murdering* the she-crab. His mouth was filled with sweet-hot drool and he gagged out tangles of it. His mind was coming apart and he knew if he didn't scream, his psyche would implode and get sucked away into a whirlpool of delusion. Spears stood above him, angry, uncertain, ready to slap some sense into him if that was needed.

"I'm all right now," Doug told him.

"You're far from all right, son," Spears grumbled.

What came next was horrifying. Spears climbed up out of the hollow and retrieved the nylon bag of tools he had stashed up there. In it, was a five-pound hammer, a crowbar, and several saws. He got right to work. With Doug's help, they flipped the crab over and Spears began sawing into the body, removing huge shanks of meat. He shattered the thin shell that had formed over the legs and pincers, peeling and sawing more meat free.

Doug just watched him work with the glee of a butcher until he simply could not take it anymore, stumbling off and vomiting into the sand.

Spears easily harvested two hundred pounds of meat from the she-crab. He built a bonfire of driftwood on the beach near the cave and roasted slabs of meat on iron pokers. The smell was first appetizing to Doug and then completely repellent. Spears and Vicki stuffed themselves with it, but he could not touch it. It amounted to cannibalism in his mind: they were eating all that remained of Olive and he simply could not bring himself to do it.

"Come on, boy," Spears kept baiting him. "It's delicious. Eat some. You need to get some meat in your belly."

But he couldn't. Vicki, of course, could not understand why it was wrong and Spears would never accept that they were devouring Olive, tearing out hot, greasy handfuls of her flesh and cramming it into their mouths chunk after chunk. Their eyes blazed with triumph, their jaws tearing and grinding, their chins and fingers oily with she-crab meat.

It was an atrocity beyond reason.

And they kept eating, day after awful day while Doug watched with horror. Didn't they see? Didn't they understand? Couldn't they hear Olive crying out each time they took a bite? She cried and screamed in Doug's head and he writhed in the sand while Spears held out dripping globs of her flesh, telling him he must eat it, he must fill himself with her fat-dripping flesh.

Finally, his mind soft as a gourd, his stomach retching with painful dry heaves, he cried, *"Don't you see what you're doing? You're becoming like them! Like the crabs! You're eating her and becoming cannibals! Can't you fucking see that?"* But they just stared at him with glistening, beady black eyes and that's when he realized they knew very well. They wanted to be like the crabs. Monsters. Predators. Flesh-eaters. Horrors that could scuttle over the toxic beach and swim in the dark depths, feeding and mating and breeding and bringing forth their terrible spawn in seething numbers.

And all the while, they kept eating; gluttonous, voracious monsters, tearing into Olive's flesh, greedy for it, their teeth chewing and their mouths slavering and as they did so, Olive screamed in his mind at the pain of it. *"Help me! Oh, dear God, Doug, help me!"* she cried and he could see her eyes in his head like flickering blood-lanterns. *"Make them stop! Make them quit biting into me! It hurts! It hurts! IT HURRRRTS SO BAD!"*

But they were not even human and they would not listen to him. They were blind, ravenous things that had crawled from the primal sea-ooze, creatures that only understood the politics of survival, of hunger and feeding and the sweet, rich taste of meat. They offended him and he wanted to kill them, but the very idea of putting his hands on their chitinous flesh revolted him.

Chomp-chomp-chomp, slurp-slurp-slurp, they went as they ate and ate and in Doug's head, Olive screamed and wailed with an ear-piercing, mind-splitting agony that echoed through his skull like a manic reverberation from the dank depths of hell—

"Stop it! Stop it! Stop it!" he implored them and they grinned with grease-slavered faces, puckering mouths sucking juices, strands of she-crab hanging from their teeth as they gorged and gorged, swelling into bloated, monstrous forms.

And day by day, they were even less human.

When they had finally eaten every last scrap of Olive, every last juice-dripping succulent shred of her, they became restless. He did not like the way they looked at him. The hungry gleam in their black glittering eyes, how he woke from sleep during the dark watches of night to find them wide awake, nocturnal things that studied him with famished eyes or how they gathered at the cave mouth, excited by the clicking sounds out on the beach.

Doug was in trouble and he knew it.

If he didn't do something about them, they were going to attack him. They were going to tear him into pieces and feast on him, stuff their guts with his remains as they had done with Olive.

But he tried to reason with them, to connect with whatever humanity still existed in the cold crustacean depths of their minds. "This has to stop," he told Spears, calmly, with great control. He did not rave or babble mindlessly like on those days when Spears forced him down and bound his wrists. No, he was a study in control. They had fed on the woman he loved, but even that he could forgive them for if they only admitted their sins and stopped the terrible regression that was taking them over. "You need to quit acting like those awful crabs. You need to be human."

But it did no good.

Spears acted like he was to be pitied. Vicki's blank eyes looked upon him as if he was some pathetic, miserable thing. When she crawled about in the sand on all fours like a crab, picking at weeds and stranded, rotting sea-life with pinching thumb and forefingers, he brought Spears attention to it. Telling him that she was becoming a monster. He wouldn't listen, of course.

Several times as Doug explored his jutting ribs with trembling fingers, his thoughts scurrying like mice in his head, his stomach stabbing him with sharp pains, he saw Spears change—his face became a flaccid ever-shifting cauldron of pink flesh with a yawning, triangular mouth, eyes protruding on segmented stalks, hands morphing into jagged pincers.

"STOP IT!" Doug shouted at him. "STOP DOING THAT!"

Spears made a hissing noise and Doug ran away down the beach, panting and shaking, his mind as emaciated as his body.

After that, Spears was careful around him.

He spoke quietly and carefully, but with an undercurrent of quiet contempt. Doug began to hear him whispering with Vicki and he heard his own name mentioned more than once. They giggled. They shared terrible secrets. They knew that *he* knew about them and day after day, his mind soft as putty, he watched them and they watched him. He tried to think, to come up with a plan, but his thoughts were fuzzy and incoherent. Like his vision, they were wavering and indistinct.

One night, so weak he could no longer stand, they thought he was sleeping, but he fooled them. He was wide awake. He saw them leave the cave, scuttling down the cliff face and crossing the beach on their jointed legs. Something had been deposited by the tide, a huge, foul-smelling fish, maybe a shark or a large tuna. As he watched, they began to feed on it, tearing it apart with their claws, digging into its briny, mucid depths, slurping and chewing and sucking up strands of corpse jelly, stuffing themselves by moonlight. Soon, gigantic crabs joined them and Doug nearly went insane at the sounds of feeding, the cacophonous *Click-click-click-clickety-click,* that echoed in his skull, filling the world, making it vibrate like their shells: *CLICK-CLICK-CLICK-CLICKETY-CLICKETY-CLICK—*

Another night, oh so stealthy and sneaking, he followed Spears and Vicki to a secret, dreadful place where the largest, most vicious mutant crabs gathered. Atop a dune, he watched with shriveling horror as they clustered about a huge, bubbling pool of nauseous slime that steamed and fizzed like liquid flesh, pink and yellow and waxy. The crabs moved in and out of it, bathing in it, rolling in it like hogs in mud wallows and Spears and Vicki joined them in the secret, midnight rite, moving among them *as* them.

Doug stumbled back to the cave on his pipestem limbs, simultaneously weeping and giggling, repulsed to his very core, knowing that soon the change would be complete and they would feast on him, picking his bones of every last scrap of meat.

Something had to be done.

And he knew exactly what.

Spears went out scavenging.

At least, that's what he claimed. But he always took Vicki with him now and that was more than a little telling. He said many times that he did not trust Doug to watch her, but that was a lie. They were going off to frolic in the surf, to pick at dead things as their kind liked to do.

Doug waited for them to return.

He waited with an axe from the cave.

He'd had enough. It had to end.

There was very little left of him by that point, and he was not about to wait until he was so sapped of strength that he would not be able to fight them off. It's what they were hoping for, biding their time. Olive told him so. She told him lots of things and she was the only one he could really trust. *Olive. Dear, sweet Olive. God, how I love you. Do you ... do you remember teriyaki shish kabobs on the grill? Do you? The pitchers of sangria? Those long summer nights? Do you do you do you remember?* She assured him that she did, but right now he had work to do, a terrible task that needed to be accomplished.

Ssshh!

Here they come!

Yes, Spears was coming down the beach now with Vicki trailing behind him. They stayed well away from the water which was patently ridiculous, but they probably thought he was watching and were trying to fool him, throw him off guard. Confusion, confusion, confusion. When would the games end? *Not until I finish them, Olive. Not until I do what has to be done.* In his head, he could see Olive, the she-crab, showing him all those beautiful colors. Each brilliant, chromatic shade was a different emotion that she wanted to share with him.

He charged out, going after Spears. Vicki screamed and ran right out into the water. Of course, she did; it was her natural element. Doug raised the axe high. Spears, that evil, calculating, mindless beast, was a forest that he was going to fell, a tall gnarled tree that needed to be brought down and split into kindling.

"I KNOW WHAT YOU ARE!" Doug screeched at him. *"I KNOW WHAT YOU'VE BECOME FROM EATING MY WIFE!"*

Somewhere in the distance, he thought he heard Vicki thrashing in the water, screaming and flailing, but it was Spears who he faced and Spears who must die. But he was strong and vital from the meat and he ducked away from the first cutting blow of the axe. He dodged the second, too, then he tripped over a rock, feet tangling and he cried out as the axe bit into his shoulder. Blood exploded onto his neck and chin, rushing down his arm. The axe sank into his leg, grinding into bone and Doug, in his weakened state, could not pull it free. Spears, bleeding and feral, pulled his knife and sank it into Doug's thigh. When he fell over, it went into his ribs and then deep into his stomach.

God, the pain, the erupting agony. Doug nearly blacked out, but when the axe came free from his weight leaning on it, he raised it again. Spears tried crawling away, but Doug brought the axe down and cleaved his head open.

Done. It was done.

Doubled over, blood gushing from him, Doug looked around for Vicki, but all he saw was the misty sea and the swath of beach that bordered it. She had gotten away.

He crawled through the sand toward the cliff, listening to Olive sobbing in his head. He had let her down, but he tried, he had tried so hard. Through his blurring vision, he could see the cave mouth up there, but he was far too debilitated by that point to reach it, paralyzed by convulsive spasms in his guts, damaged beyond repair, devastated by days without food.

He lay there, listening to the waves and smelling the salty marrow of the sea, flocks of gulls winging above him.

Night.

It was night.

He woke to the sound of his own whimpering or maybe it was Olive's. He knew the crabs would come out of the surf and sand if they hadn't already and they would find him as they eventually found everything. Yes, oh yes, he could hear them out there—*click-click-click-click*—gathering, swarming, active as the moon rose full and fat above him, limning him in silver light, making the surface of the water glow.

You need to die now, to let go, Olive told him and, as always, how right she was, how very right. Why did he keep living with most of his blood gone? He must have lost many pints by now.

He heard a splashing out in the water.

They're coming now. They're coming.

He focused his eyes and he saw multitudes of giant crabs down the beach. The moonlight turned them into surreal, impossible things like VW Bugs driving out of the water. They would find him. They would strip him to a skeleton. His bones would bleach in successive days of sun and salt. Gulls and cormorants would pick away at what was left.

The splashing again.

Oh no.

Oh Jesus, no.

A massive crab emerged from the water, its mottled carapace plated, spiky with sharp protrusions, whip like antennae rising into the night. It skittered towards him on segmented legs, reaching out with huge serrated pincers that were clicking open and closed, anxious to grip something, greedy to scissor through flesh and bone. His death knell was a constant jarring, mind-shattering *click-click-click-clickety-click. CLICK-CLICK-CLICK-CLICKETY-CLICKETY-CLICK—*

As it seized his leg with one beaded, water-dripping cheliped, slicing through skin and muscle, crunching through bone, he screamed away the last bits of his mind in a hysterical expulsion of terror and agony.

The crab had him.

The crab owned him.

It dragged his carcass to its mouth and began to tear strips of meat from his belly. And despite his screams, he heard its voice very well, its unnatural hissing sibilance lancing through his brain: *"Vicki,"* it said, *"My name is Vicki...."*

BRIDE OF THE TERMITES

As Luanne lay there bleeding, pulling her broken body ever forward, she remembered that long ago, before the war, she'd had a husband and children. The scary part was that she could not recall what happened to them. She was dying. She supposed that the answers to a lot of things would be known to her soon, or, there'd just be bigger questions.

Crawl, she told herself. *Just … crawl.*

Her inner voice was the motive force that kept her going even though she was in incredible agony from the beating. Typho and his rat pack really went after her this time. They'd beaten her before, kicked her unconscious many times, but never like this. Now she was ruined. Blood was coming out of her mouth and ass. She felt … *loose* inside as if things that were supposed to be connected had broken free.

If she could just make it into that old rotting shed. It was only about fifteen feet away. She could get inside, close her eyes. It would be a good place to die. She didn't want to die out in the streets where the rats and wild dogs would get her.

Crawl.

She smelled bad ... like shit and piss and infection, a rank odor that was partly because she hadn't bathed in weeks and partly because her bowels had let go. And they had pissed on her. After they beat her guts out, Typho and the others had pissed on her. And they had laughed about it.

The shed. She had made it.

Trying to ignore the pain, she pushed open the door and crawled inside, over the splintered floor. There was nothing in there but cobwebs and a few moldering sticks of furniture. The wind blew the door shut behind her and she lay there, coughing out blood.

That Typho.

That goddamned Typho. Doing this to her because she'd helped herself to some canned lasagna. She'd been weak. She hadn't eaten in days. Typho didn't care. He claimed that this part of the ruined city belonged to him and everything in it. The food stores. The water. The people. She was poaching, he said. *Poaching.* She had been beaten before by touching something without asking. He owned everything, even the air, she supposed.

Now it didn't matter.

Now there would be peace.

Her eyes fluttered closed ... then, minutes later, maybe an hour, she opened them. The pain had lessened slightly into a cold numbness that seemed to pervade every inch of her. What had woken her was a tickling on her skin as if someone was dragging a feather over her.

Oh no, she thought. *A rat.*

But it wasn't a rat. It was something else, something that made her recoil in revulsion: a huge insect about six inches in length. It was a glossy white, its abdomen composed of closely-packed ring-like segments. It was its legs that were tickling her. It seemed to be tapping her arm repetitively. Its head, in contrast to its body, was a shiny orange-yellow with tiny black eyes and a set of wavering antennae.

She wanted badly to swat it away, but she had no strength. Even breathing was painful. Her lips were crusted shut with drying blood, her vision blurry. She was probably in some sort of delirium. The bug wasn't there at all. It existed only in her mind.

This was what a feeble, fading voice in her head told her.

Her eyes closed.

When they opened again, there were six such insects on her. They looked familiar, as if she had seen them in a book sometime in the past. They were all madly tapping her with their legs, appraising her with their eyes. She felt an absolute instinctual fear of them.

She wanted to scream.

They were on the walls of the shack, too. Dozens of them and they all seemed to be looking at her, studying her.

Just let me die, she thought. *Wait until I'm gone to eat me.*

And the most perfectly insane thing was, she had the strongest feeling that they understood her, that they were not just dumb bugs, but something special. Something unique.

As they intently scrutinized her, she drifted off into oblivion.

When Luanne came out of it, it was many days later. How many, she could not be sure. She was only aware with some inner sense of a great passage of time. The amazing thing was that she felt no pain. Not a stitch of it. How was that possible? Maybe she was too far gone. Was that how it was when you were about to die? Did you feel liberated from your pain? Permeated by a feeling of wellbeing and euphoria? Was that it?

She was not alone.

The bugs were still there, only there were many more of them now. They were not on her: they gathered around her in orderly ranks. Some of them had larger heads the color of blood with huge mandibles. Yet, they made no aggressive moves.

They watched patiently.

Her mind was as clear as it had been in days, maybe weeks. She knew what the insects were—termites. There was no mistaking it: they were termites.

But so large, so strange.

Mutations.

They were mutations.

That had to be it. But not sickly and weak like the others she had seen, but vibrant and healthy. The radiation had not harmed them. It had … *evolved* them into a new order, a higher species.

It was as if they were venerating her somehow like she was royalty. She was more convinced than ever that they were intelligent. She tried to tell herself that such a thing could not be, but the more she argued with herself, the more certain of it she was.

She found them fascinating.

She was no longer repelled by them. They were fellow creatures in a devastated world. She knew that her body was healed, that even her internal injuries and broken bones had been knitted up. She did not know exactly how, only that *they* had done it. Even the dried blood at her mouth had been cleaned.

They repaired you, she thought. *They helped you and … and now you must help them.*

But what did they want? That was the question. She knew she was well enough to hop to her feet and run out the door. She didn't think they would try to stop her. In fact, she was sure of it. That wasn't their way. They weren't keeping her as a prisoner. No, they were fawning over her, worshipping her in their own way. They were all sort of standing, balanced on their hind set of legs. As they looked at her, their heads nodded to the left, then the right like puppies awaiting their master's voice.

They wanted to listen, to hear what she had to say.

So, she started talking.

"We survivors are in a real world of hurt," she told the attentive crowd of her benefactors. "We human beings made a mess of this world. We really did. Now we try to live, to go on day by day. Get enough food to eat. A safe place to lay our heads at night. We want to start again, put the world, *our* world, back together again. But how do we do that and should we do it at all? If we started, will we just be dooming future generations? Will we just be creating the same monster that killed us in the first place? Will we be on the same path to Armageddon? Maybe all roads lead to the same destination when we walk them. There's a word for what I'm trying to tell you … *cyclical,* that's it. A cycle that will repeat itself again and again until we find a new road to walk."

The termites listened with rapt attention. Never in Luanne's long, hard, frustrating life had anyone ever took this sort of interest in anything she had to say. But they were captivated by all that she said, like she was the second coming of Jesus. A prophet delivered unto them.

"The scientists said we developed from a lower order, an ape-like ancestor. That we evolved from animals and somewhere along the line, we accidentally became intelligent, aware. Some people don't believe that." She laughed. "You know why? Because they don't *want* to believe it. They like to delude themselves that they're God's children, made in his image. What's that saying? God's a neurotic, intolerant, greedy sack of shit? No, I know we came from animals. We were nothing but a terrible accident. I grew up with animals. I was used and abused by them. I read about them every day in the newspaper. *Animals.* Beasts on two legs. All organized into tribes that hated anyone that was different, anyone who thought different, anyone who didn't believe what they believed. *Divisive* is the word. It was the only thing we were really good at other than killing each other and stealing what they had. And all of them tribes, oh yes, *all* of them manipulated by the rich and powerful. Nothing but sheep that were easily led, puppets dancing on strings to a tune whistled by their masters."

Her captive audience seemed to bristle a bit at that. She figured they were part of a colony that co-existed and served one another, lived for the good of all. The heretical, hypocritical, destructive culture of humanity probably sickened them.

"But where does that leave us? I don't know. Should mankind be allowed to rise again? Should the same pack of selfish, greedy wolves be allowed to destroy the world a second time? I don't think so. Which brings me to my situation. What Typho did to me. Because there's always a Typho, isn't there? Always some paranoid, aggressive piece of shit trying to lord over the rest of us. I was an easy target, because I've been an outsider all my life. I never fit in any appropriate box, so I became a victim like I been a victim my entire life."

She swallowed, because more of them had gathered now. Hundreds clustered around her, filling the shed. So many, it made her skin crawl, but at the same time she was in awe of their community, their togetherness.

"Now, you apparently fixed me. I don't know how and I don't know why you bothered. But here I am. That's all I got to say."

The insects muttered in low, droning reverberations as if they were discussing what would come next. As Luanne waited there, they moved in closer and closer, not in a dangerous way, but as if they needed to touch the living god among them.

She had never felt such love before.

Whatever the termites had done to her when they repaired her, she came out of it with her sense of smell highly activated. It was an amazing thing. She could smell the close dankness of the shed, of course, but more so she could smell the richness of growing things outside, flowers blooming and sweet sap running. The foul smell of a scavenging dog a few streets over. Unburied corpses in the distance. She could cast for scent in every direction like a bloodhound.

And she could smell *them*.

The colony had a peculiar odor that was not exactly sweet or sour, acrid or bland, but a low, oily smell like chemicals. Formaldehyde, she thought. Faint, but there. Kind of like pickles or the juice they were preserved in.

So, when one of Typho's thugs came for her, as she knew one of them would, she could smell him. She knew by the stink of hormones and glandular secretions that it was a hoodlum called T-Bing: a gigantic ape that routinely beat people to order for his master. Another rabid dog.

She could smell his hate.

But she smelled more than that. She was aware of his fear, too, because beneath that wagonload of black flesh and acid attitude, he was a frightened little boy who had always used his size and strength to intimidate and menace. It hid his numerous insecurities. Because deep inside, he was weak and shivering.

He kicked open the door of the shed. The entire structure shook as it did sometimes in the wind. He filled the doorway.

"Figured you'd be here," he said. "Just knew. Typho say, go get that ugly bull dyke bitch. See if she still alive. If she is, put her lights out, T-Bing, cancel her ass good and proper. Don't want that big, stupid lesbo stinking up my streets."

Luanne nodded. "And what did you say?"

"I say, it done. Sure as shit."

He stepped forward, a nickel-plated 9mm in one massive fist. She could smell two things on him immediately: indecision and obedience. He didn't want to kill her, not really, but he would because that's what his master said.

"Nothing personal, bitch."

He brought up the gun and then lowered it when he heard a peculiar, high-pitched whirring. "Hell was that?" he asked, fear creeping into him like worms into bad meat. "You hear that?"

She did. It got louder. So loud that it incapacitated him like a directed sonic weapon. He cried out and dropped the gun. He let out a strangled cry and dropped to one knee, pissing himself.

Then one of the soldier termites dropped onto his head. Another attached itself to the back of his neck. Three more climbed his legs. They vaulted from their holes with smooth efficiency. The colony was under attack by an intruder and they knew exactly how to deal with it. T-Bing screamed and thrashed, his fear amplified to the point that he was nearly insane with it. As he fought and cried, the stingers of the soldiers pierced him rapidly again and again like the needles of a sewing machine. They stitched him into a paralyzed, flaccid heap of flesh that could only lay there, drool running from his mouth and his eyes wide and white with terror.

By then, forty or fifty of the soldiers had appeared. Then fifty more. A hundred more. They swarmed over him, stinging him, juicing him with paralytic toxins until he was as senseless and dopy as a fat, juicy spider taken by a hornet.

The soldiers looked to Luanne.

They waited for her orders.

"Can he still feel pain?" she asked them.

Their jointed, wavering antennae telegraphed to her with that same sibilant whirring that his nerve endings were unimpeded. Not only was he aware, but he could feel every piercing stinger sliding in and out of him like a hot pin.

209

"Bring him to me," she said.

Like ants, they were incredibly strong and could lift something like thirty times their own body weight. Which would have been like her being able to lift a pickup truck over her head. It was little effort for them to drag a 350-pound man ten feet. They accomplished it in seconds, dumping T-Bing at her feet. She studied him with a combination of pity and hatred. He symbolized everything that was inherently wrong with the human race. He was a pile of trash.

"Render him to bones," she ordered them. "And do it slowly."

There was no hesitation.

T-Bing could not scream because his vocal cords were inoperative, but his eyes mirrored his agony as they took him apart piece by piece with their scissoring, razor-sharp mandibles. They peeled his skin free in sections, then they went after his connective tissue and muscles. The smells radiating from him were those of a dying animal, sharp and foul and sour. His mind snapped long before they were done. One of the last things they took were his eyes.

When he was a gleaming rack of bones before her, Luanne was pleased.

She very rarely left the shed, but when she did, seeking out those stragglers who had long before been her friends, she found that she could no longer communicate with them. Her ability to use verbal language had diminished as she became part of the colony. The termites did not communicate the way human beings did. They made a variety of sounds —whirrings, trillings, hissing noises—conveying state of mind and being without cumbersome speech. Their mode of communication was partly telepathic and partly chemical, a purely organic system that was symbolic by nature, an exchange of detailed imagery that was far more descriptive and perceptive than simple spoken language.

When Luanne tried to talk with others, she found herself struggling to form the words that would properly illustrate what was in her mind. It was not only frustrating, but infuriating to a great degree, because simple spoken language could not adequately convey what she was thinking, why she thought it, or how she felt about it. Which was how the termites did it. Each single thought was accompanied by complex images that were intuitive, intellectual, and emotional at the same time.

Her old friends simply stared at her as strings of monosyllabic blather foamed from her lips, words attached to words and strung into incomprehensible sentences that made no earthly sense. It was like trying to talk to someone in the depths of a Tourette's episode.

Eventually, she gave up.

She was no longer part of their world and their language was bland, insipid, terribly rudimentary. The language of grunting apes. Listening to it not only annoyed her, it repulsed her on some primary level.

After two or three tries, she gave up.

She never left the shed again.

Though she no longer ventured out into the world or had congress with her own species of any sort, she received all the gossip in the streets. It was a simple matter to send her mind out and feel what the stragglers felt, hear their thoughts and fears. She knew how many were dying of radiation poisoning. The hottest parts of the city. Those exposed to the worst dust storms of fallout. Mutations that had been seen. Where food was to be found, uncontaminated drinking water, safe shelter. Which communicable diseases were making the rounds.

Most importantly, she heard about Typho and how his army of gangbangers was steadily being decimated. Dozens had disappeared in the night. Many others had been found belly-up in the streets, swollen like barrels as if they had been bitten by venomous snakes.

Typho had maybe eight or ten loyal dogs left, but that was it, and they were a terrified lot, ready to bolt at any moment as the noose tightened around their throats. The street people grew less and less afraid of him by the day. He had sent four of his thugs to deal with Luanne and none of them had returned. The word on the streets concerning her was most disturbing.

Finally, he had to make a show of it. So, scared as he was, he came for Luanne in person to show how fearless he was, original gangsta to the gills.

"You bitch," he snarled at her when he entered the shed, the single gold tooth in his mouth gleaming. "You ain't been nothing but a source of bullshit to me from day one. Now I'm gonna sort you out personal-like."

The only reason he hesitated pulling the trigger of the Glock in his hand was because of the conical towers of carefully-terraced earth that had been raised around her. They looked like termite mounds he'd seen in a book once. He wrinkled his nose at the smell coming from them. It made him confused, his head woozy.

"Gonna ... gonna kill you," he muttered as the scent, such sweet and heady perfume, turned his hand to soft butter and the Glock fell from it. "Gonna ... gonna ..."

By then, two soldiers had dropped onto his back. They stabbed him with their stingers, and he dropped to the earth, making muttering sounds as his mouth filled with saliva that overflowed it and spilled out.

Dozens of soldiers swarmed over him. He was stung, bitten by pincers, destroyed both physically and psychologically. Luanne watched them work on him, smiling as he was emasculated by their tearing mandibles. When they took him below much later, he was little more than a drooling sack of meat.

How long it went on, she did not know. But she lacked for nothing. They brought her food, bottles of water. Cared for any and all wounds, whether that was a simple scratch or a hangnail. They made her comfortable. They cleaned and groomed her. They sang her to sleep each night with a rhythmic droning that was like a choir of children. They worshipped her. They listened raptly to whatever she thought at them.

She was their queen and never had she been so perfectly contented.

But she began to notice a strange feeling in the colony. A sense of expectation, a barely-concealed excitement. A thrumming of not only activity, but of rising hormonal levels that smelled like flowing honey and springtime. It began to affect her, too. She felt younger, stronger, vital, positively juicing with vitality as if every cell in her body had been rejuvenated. There was a burning heat in her, a hunger in her loins she had not felt since she was a teenager.

She was overwhelmed by lust and charged with erotic energy. She could think of nothing but the act, the joining, the mounting, the congress of flesh. The entire colony was flush and seething with it.

Then she understood.

One afternoon when she was trembling with the need of it, out of her mind with it, practically salivating with the idea of it, a dozen, then two dozen termites crawled on top of her. These were not the fearsome soldiers that protected her nor the drones that saw to her every need and want, but pulsing, fertile males from down below in the very hot marrow of the colony. They had come to mate with her.

Of course, she was still very much human in most respects and the idea not only revolted her, but she found it absurd. Inter species mating? It was biologically impossible. She could no more mate with these creatures than a mouse could mate with a scorpion.

Yet, *yet,* the images they sent into her mind, that were practically dripping with desire for her, told her that, yes, it was not only possible but inevitable. They must join. The future of the colony was at stake and she must perform her ancestral duties for the good of all, the one and the many.

Her instinctive human revulsion of crawling, leggy things was dispelled by her ravenous appetite for what they offered. She not only wanted to breed with them, she *needed* to, before she experienced some catastrophic meltdown via her raging hormones.

She didn't know what to expect, only that she was ready for it. The males were violent in their attentions. They literally attacked her in a buzzing swarm, impaling her with their sharp penises which were like hypodermic syringes, injecting her with burning loads of semen. They were not particular as to where they stuck her—in the belly, the ribs, the legs and neck and groin. One of them jabbed her in the lips and another jabbed her in the left eye. The pain was intense and unbearable: she writhed and convulsed and cried out in a combination of agony and pleasure. It was like having dozens of red-hot needles jabbed into her at the same time.

They shared images with her as they mounted her: visions of the colony, of procreation, of mountains of glistening spawn. And the unpleasant knowledge that what she was undergoing was known as traumatic insemination.

When they finished with her, they left her there, shaking, swollen, contused, blood leaking from injection sites. She was blind in one eye, her lower lip swollen like an inflated tire. She was sick to her stomach, vomiting out a thin gruel of bile, completely debilitated by the act.

Sobbing, nearly insane, she could feel their sperm moving through her like worms, migrating to her ovaries.

Yes, she was the queen.

But like all great things in life, there was a terrible price to be paid for it.

After that horrible, degrading, and agonizing experience, she was never quite the same again. The way she thought, the very mechanics of how her mind worked, had been changing for some time and now she saw the world in an entirely different way.

Her thoughts were only of the colony.

How to increase it.

How to fill the world with her kind.

There was nothing else.

The drones attended to her as they had never before. Impregnated, she was a holy relic that they cared for with tender attention. As the weeks passed, her abdomen bloated with spawn, enlarging to five or six times its normal size and then enlarging again until she became a huge pulsating sac of eggs, a vibrating, soft mass that weighed several hundred pounds. Her arms and legs became vestigial sticks. She looked like a head attached to an inflated, rubbery bag. By then, of course, she could no longer feed herself. But the drones took care of that, chewing her food into a globby predigested mush enriched with specialized proteins and hormones that they vomited into her mouth.

Then eventually, they dragged her far below into the maze of tunnels that comprised the very beating heart of the colony, depositing her lovingly in a birth pit they had dug out especially for her.

Typho was there—an armless, legless, eyeless shuddering sack that the workers and soldiers fed upon, chewing him apart bite by bite. It was his flesh that they fed her upon, sweetening it with their own secretions and hormonal discharges until she grew fatter and fatter, an obscene and bloated, semi-human, segmented blob that pulsed constantly with the action of the larva within her.

Despite it all, he still lived.

They would not let him die.

When the glorious day arrived, she pumped out hundreds and hundreds of slimy fertilized eggs from a central orifice with a wet, smacking sound until she was literally buried in their pulpous masses. Each one throbbed like a heart, finally hatching a single white grub that knew instinctively that it must seek food. With her remaining eye, exhausted, flaccid as a squeezed-out pastry bag, she watched as her beautiful larvae traveled to the well-chewed, yet living carcass of Typho and began to feed on him, glutting themselves on his flesh, sliding in and out of him like plump white maggots.

And it was in this way, as the diseased world of men slowly ground to a halt, that Luanne ultimately found her special place and purpose, breeding an army that would eventually exterminate the last of her kind.

Even though she was insane, there was satisfaction in that.

215

CONJOINED

Wendy knew it had to happen sooner or later, so when the three men cornered her there in the alley, she realized she had two choices: she could either lie there and take it, hope they didn't hurt her too badly or kill her afterwards, or she could fight.

She chose the latter.

Once upon a time, before the idiocy of man had crippled the world, she had taught school. It was an ofttimes difficult and demanding job, jumping through the hoops set by an uncaring administration, unrealistic parents, and restrictive, cumbersome state and federal guidelines (because everyone had to put their nose in, especially if they could squeeze tax dollars and appropriations out of it), but she had done a good job. Instilling in her students good morals and ethics, molding them into decent human beings even if their selfish, senseless parents often corrupted this very thing.

But now, with the way things were, she saw that there was no longer anything like decency or morality—human beings had degenerated into the drooling, aggressive animals they had carefully (or not-so carefully) concealed beneath the veil of civilization.

The beast was out of its cage.

And it was hungry.

That's where she was at that very moment: facing three horrible beasts that might have once been fathers or sons or brothers.

217

There was nowhere to run, so she pulled the hunting knife from her belt and prepared to fight. The trauma and torment of the past few months had morphed her into a small, wiry, but vicious fighter. She barely resembled the young, attractive woman she had once been. She had killed no one. But she had stabbed several when they tried to take what was hers.

The leader of the trio was a balding, middle-aged guy with a face crusted with sores and embedded dirt. His associates were younger, but they all had the same shiny, predatory eyes.

"She gonna fight," the older guy said. "You see that, Ethan? Little whore's gonna fight and deny us what's ours. She gonna make a game of it." He laughed with a grating sound. "Now ain't that something? Listen, sweet pie. You just let us have our fill and you'll be with us. You can be our woman. We'll protect you."

Wendy didn't even bother replying to that. She was geared to survival. She knew, in the end, they would probably get her, but she had become good with her old knifey and she was certain she could do some damage to them before that happened.

Then maybe, mercifully, they'll kill you.

The idea was not as unpleasant as it should have been. For, really, what was there to live for? Civilization had split its seams and it would never, ever go back to what it was. It would take hundreds of years before anything remotely like law and order would emerge. And until then, there would only be cruel, dehumanizing survival. Scavenging for food and fresh water. Fighting. Hiding. Seeing how long you could go before you picked up a deadly germ or succumbed to radiation sickness.

What kind of life was that?

No, better to make a stand and die here and now.

One of the younger guys stepped forward, the one called Ethan. His nose was pierced with a stud, his hair and beard thick and almost luxurious. When he smiled, his teeth were actually white. There had been a time when he was probably good-looking.

"Listen, it doesn't have to be this way," he said, holding out his empty hands to show that he was harmless. His voice actually sounded kind of reasonable. "All we're trying to do is survive day to day, just like you. We're trying to put together kind of a community. There's a chance if we do that."

Wendy swallowed. "And you think rape is the way to accomplish that?"

"Oh, just take the bitch," the older guy said.

"I won't let them rape you. You have my word. You can come with us. We have food and shelter. Clean water. That's what I'm offering."

Again, his calm, soothing voice and looks were disarming, but she knew better. He was just edging his way in closer. It had probably worked many times in the past. When he was five feet away, a crazy light filled his eyes and he leaped at her. Wendy ducked, pivoted, and slashed his left hand open.

"Shit," he said.

The other two were coming now. They advanced slowly, trying to flank her. She stood ready to kill. There was nothing else.

Then something peculiar happened.

Wendy felt a building energy in the air like right before an electrical storm. She smelled something quite like ozone. Whatever was going on, it was galvanic and rising, static electricity running along the backs of her bare arms.

"Hell is this?" the older guy said.

Sweat was running down his face in rivers. It was shiny with it. "Hot," he said. "Goddamned hot." His sweat seemed to boil on his skin into steam … and then he cried out and burst into flame like a struck matchhead. He blazed up, stumbling in circles, screaming once before hitting the ground in a carbonized, smoldering mass. The other two were perspiring now. They tried to flee and comically smashed into one another. They barely recovered from that when they were both engulfed in flames. Before they fell over, they expanded from superheated gases within their bodies and popped like ticks. Their scattered remains burned and crackled.

The stench of it was horrible.

Wendy was terrified, waiting for the force to be directed at her, too. But it didn't happen. That energy in the air dissipated and was simply gone. She backed away, moving toward the mouth of the alley, but slowly as if she might stir something up if she went too fast.

"Hello," a voice said behind her.

She whirled around, her heart pounding in her throat.

There was a girl standing there.

She was maybe seven or eight years old, a pale little thing with huge black eyes. What struck Wendy (outside of her intense eyes) was the way she was dressed. She was wearing a light-blue floral print dress with short puffy sleeves. It looked like something from the 1950s right down to the Peter Pan collar and decorative buttons. She was out of place and out of time, like a ghost from a fifties sitcom.

Cradled in her arm was a perfectly horrid little doll. It had a white, mottled face with a crooked mouth and black plastic shoe button eyes.

"My name is Ginny," the little girl voice said. "Do you want to be my friend?"

Trembling with horror and dark madness, Wendy realized that the voice didn't come from the girl—it came from the *doll*.

"You seem nice," the voice said, "and we like nice people. We want them to be our friends. Tell me you want to be our friend or something very bad might happen."

Her entire body shaking, Wendy could barely find her own voice. When it came out, it was low and scratchy. "Yes," she managed. "I want that."

"Oh, good," said the voice. "Then we can play together. What's your name?"

"Wendy."

"Oh, I like that. It's nice."

Dazed, confused, and more than a little terrified, Wendy followed the girl and her doll across town to an immaculate little frame house enclosed by a freshly painted white picket fence. The grass was bright green, red and yellow tulips growing in neat little rows. There were carnations and zinnias, manicured bushes overloaded with plump raspberries and tall sunflowers that gently nodded in the breeze.

It hasn't touched this house, this yard, she thought. *The war, the fallout, the blight ... it hasn't even come close to this place.*

Birds sang in the apple trees, bees buzzed among the flowers, hummingbirds hovered about a feeder.

For all its prim beauty, it was a nest of dragons. The terror Wendy felt at the sight of it was deep-rooted, organic.

"Do you like my house?" the voice asked. "Here, you can have anything you want."

Then they were inside, a creaking screen door on a spring slamming closed behind them. Inside it was spartan and neat. Under ordinary circumstances, it might have been homey. But it wasn't. The atmosphere was somehow synthetic, like a museum display. It made her skin crawl.

In the kitchen, she sat at the oval table, because she knew it was what Ginny wanted.

"Did those bad men hurt you?" Ginny asked.

"No. I'm okay."

"They were mean. We don't like mean people. We make awful things happen to them. But you're nice. We know you're nice. You'll be our friend."

It was beyond disturbing, like being trapped in a living nightmare. Wendy still didn't know if Ginny was the girl or the doll. The very idea that it could possibly be the doll made her want to laugh hysterically. But she didn't dare do that. If Ginny could torch those idiots, she could do the same to her.

The girl had a perpetual blank stare to her eyes. When she put them on you, it was as if there was nothing behind them, like they weren't even connected to her brain. She was more of a doll than the doll. Her eyes did not blink, her body did not move. A single drop of perspiration slid down the side of her face, but that was about it. She was practically catatonic.

Wendy's education and teaching experience told her the girl was either in shock or she was non-verbal. But if that was the case, then how did she throw her voice into the doll? Unless, of course, she didn't. The idea was terrifying ... but what *if?* All Wendy could say for sure was that the girl looked like a child that had suffered trauma, unbelievable trauma.

"You look hungry," said Ginny. "When is the last time you ate?"

221

Wendy shook her head. "I … I don't know."

"We have lots of food here."

To prove this, she opened the cupboard and it was filled with neatly stacked canned goods—Chef Boyardee ravioli and Beefaroni, SpaghettiOs and Campbell's soup, Dinty Moore Beef Stew and Bush's Baked Beans—as well as an abundant supply of Kraft Mac and Cheese. Commonplace things before the war, but now rare commodities that people fought and killed for.

"That's some of our food," Ginny told her, "but you don't want something from a can. You want something special."

Without touching it, the cupboard door gently closed.

"You want pizza, don't you?"

Trying to keep the fear from her voice, Wendy said, "Yes. I'd like pizza."

Again, there was that energy in the air. A bead of sweat rolled down the girl's face and the fine hairs at the back of Wendy's neck stood up. The surface of the table wavered and when it solidified again, there was a large pizza sitting there. It was on a cardboard round, oozing with cheese, the fresh mushrooms on top lightly browned, the pepperoni curled into little cups.

"It's good," Ginny said. "It's from Carbotti's, our favorite pizzeria."

"But … how?" Wendy heard herself ask.

The doll giggled. "I told you: here, you can have anything you want."

Wendy hesitated. This was all so wrong in so many ways, she couldn't even catalog them with her whirling mind. But the pizza … dear God … she could feel the heat coming off it as if it was fresh from a brick oven. She could smell the oregano and basil, the well-spiced sauce, the fresh mozzarella and pepperoni.

"You don't like it?" Ginny asked, sounding disappointed.

"No, it looks great."

Wendy's ravenous appetite won out. She pulled a slice free, strands of cheese hanging from it. Biting into it was like heaven. The thin crust was perfectly crispy, the toppings making endorphins fire in her brain. Never had pizza tasted so very good. It was unbelievable. She never thought she'd see a pizza again.

As the doll watched her and the girl stared with her dead eyes, Wendy wolfed down five slices. In the process, without asking, an ice-cold Coke appeared before her. She finished her sixth slice, drained the Coke, and leaned back in her chair. She was pleasantly stuffed as she hadn't been in forever.

"Boy, you sure were hungry!" the doll said, at least, the voice that came from it did, though its crooked mouth never so much as twitched. The doll moved. It looked over at the girl. "Now eat."

Mechanically, the girl took up a slice with a trembling hand and finished it as the doll watched her.

"Another," she said.

The girl ate another slice. Her expression did not change. There was no pleasure in it for her. She looked positively bovine like a cow chewing cud.

"That's better," said the doll. "You have to keep up your strength." It turned to Wendy. "I have to remind her to eat." She giggled with a squeaking sound. "In fact, I have to remind her to do everything."

The hollow inside Wendy was nicely filled, but she was still scared. Scared, maybe, as she had never been before in her life.

"We're glad you're nice, Wendy. We're so glad. Do you like being our friend?"

"Yes, yes, I do."

The doll wiggled in the girl's arms. "You'll be happy here with us. Anything you need, you get. That's the way it is for our friends. We take care of them. People who are bad and not our friends have to be punished. We don't like mean people, do we?"

The girl just stared.

"And our friends never, ever have to worry about the awful things out there or the bad people. They don't come by our house. They don't dare. A few mean people tried, but I made nasty things happen to them. I made them crawl. It's funny when they crawl."

Wendy swallowed. "But what about the radiation? The contamination? The germs?"

"They don't come here. We're protected and so are you."

Wendy just nodded, finding it nearly impossible to make sense of any of this. She was secretly delighted that she was safe, but terrified

223

that she would do or say the wrong thing. Ginny was incalculably dangerous. Essentially, she was a monster with the mind of a child. Wendy knew she would be safe like a pet, like a favored dog, as long as she pleased Ginny. But when she didn't, the consequences would be terrible.

"Now you're tired and you need to rest," the doll said. "Now we all need to rest."

The girl led her upstairs, pointing to a door at the end of the hall. Wendy did not hesitate. She went into the bedroom and closed the door. There was a princess canopy bed in there with shimmering pink curtains. She stood there, staring at it, instinct running wild inside her, telling her to sneak out the window, escape, do something. If she didn't, sooner or later, Ginny would get tired of her and make a horrible example of her.

But escape would be risky.

Going against Ginny's wishes could be deadly.

Sighing, she pulled back the soft comforter and sank down in the bed. It was a feather bed. Deliciously comfortable. She lowered her head onto the pillow.

She didn't want to sleep. She was too keyed-up, but then her eyes closed and she went out. Later, she discovered, when Ginny decided you needed to rest, you had no choice.

Wendy slept for four hours. When she came downstairs, the girl and her doll were waiting for her in the dining room. Dinner was waiting. Roast turkey. Mashed potatoes and gravy. Buttered rolls. Cranberries. Stuffing. Pumpkin pie. And, oddly enough, macaroni and cheese and stacks of pancakes drizzled with syrup. These latter items were Ginny's favorites, so they were served at every meal.

"We love Thanksgiving," the doll said. "Don't you? It's our favorite, so we have it a lot."

"It looks good."

"It is! Eat! Eat!"

Though Wendy was not particularly hungry after the pizza—it was more calories than she generally had in a week— she ate. It was all very good. Without a doubt, it was probably the finest Thanksgiving dinner she'd ever eaten, everything exquisitely prepared as if by a professional chef. She had two plates because it pleased Ginny to see her eat. She even had pie and a couple pancakes, because Ginny insisted.

Afterwards, she was sick to her stomach. If she kept eating like that, she was going to be big and round, something that you never saw anymore. America's obesity epidemic had been cured by the war.

Yes, you'll become an overfed puppy, she thought. *Another pet for Ginny.*

The girl did not eat at all and Wendy could sense the tension in the air. Ginny did not like it when the girl did not eat.

"You'll get skinny and weak. I don't want you to get skinny and weak. So, you have to eat. Eat a lot. I want you to eat until you can't eat anymore."

The girl did not move. A few beads of sweat rolled down her face and Wendy was almost certain that she was fighting the will of the doll with everything she had. She suddenly began to jerk with rolling spasms, her face contorting, tears rolling down her cheeks.

"If you keep this up, I'll throw you away," Ginny said.

"No, please, don't do that," Wendy told her.

"If she's a bad toy, she gets thrown away," Ginny insisted. "Those are the rules. Bad toys go into the gutter."

The girl's shaking hand seized a drumstick from the turkey and wrenched it free. She struck at it with her teeth like a crocodile, tearing out chunks of juicy meat and well-seasoned strips of skin free that crunched in her jaws. She scooped up mashed potatoes with her hands, shoving them in her mouth until gravy dripped from her chin. She swallowed two rolls in rapid succession. Cranberries were smeared on her face like blood. She picked up the pie plate and fed from it like a dog, stuffing more and more into herself as the doll giggled and the girl gagged.

"See how bad she is, Wendy? She's not nice at all and she makes me mad. Should we punish her?"

Wendy shook her head. "Maybe she's just tired."

"She's not tired! She's bad! Real *bad!*"

The girl vomited out a glistening mass of undigested and unchewed food. Ginny screeched. The girl's face became tight and corded. Her eyes rolled back white as food fell from her mouth. Blood trickled from her nostrils.

"Please, don't hurt her," Wendy said because she simply could not bear any more of it. "Please, Ginny. *Please.*"

"Oh, all right. But she better learn her lesson or I'll make spiders. I'll make lots of them."

It went on day after day, a nightmarish and surreal existence. The rest of the world was like a festering, infected wound, but in the perfect little house, everything was … perfect. The meals appeared like clockwork. Beds were made. Baths were drawn. Freshly-laundered clothes laid out. Everything was gleaming, clean, and well-ordered. Nothing was amiss.

And it was as close to hell as Wendy had ever been.

Hour after hour was spent walking on eggshells, stepping lightly, *very* lightly around Ginny and the girl. It was important to smile and be happy because Ginny did not like grumpy, unhappy people. It was a stifling, artificial existence and Wendy spent every minute of it waiting for the house of cards to fall.

She thought about escape.

She did not believe Ginny could read her thoughts, so her mind was the only truly private place she had. Anywhere in the house, in the yard, she could feel the doll watching her. She did not believe it was her imagination.

At lunch one day—grilled cheese sandwiches, and plenty of fucking pancakes and mac and cheese—the doll said, "The war was bad. It was too bad it had to happen at all. But sometimes terrible things have to happen so people learn their lesson."

Wendy felt herself go weak inside as if the blood had been slowly leeched from her. The cheese in her mouth tasted rubbery. She set her half-eaten sandwich on the plate. The sight of it suddenly made her sick to her stomach.

"What lesson was that?" she asked.

The doll put its shiny black eyes on her and she instantly felt hollow inside. It was like something conjoined to the girl, a malignant growth, a tumor in the shape of a doll. It seemed to be breathing rapidly. Had it opened its crooked mouth and showed her the triangular teeth of a shark, she would not have been surprised. It was the closest thing to pure, living evil that she had ever seen.

"People were bad, so, so very bad. Do you remember how they hated each other? How they did mean things to each other? All the killing and hurting and awful things?" the doll said in that squeaking, childlike voice. "They were all so mean. That's why I started the war. They had to be punished. They had to be … *cleansed*. Like a table, they had to be wiped clean."

Wendy felt her heart drop into her stomach. Oh, good Christ, it couldn't be so. Nobody had that much power. But, then again, the doll was not a nobody or even a somebody, it was a *thing*, a monster, a demon imp.

She tried to control her breathing. She tried to keep her horror from etching dread onto her face. "But some people survived. Some did."

The doll's mouth seemed to grin. "But I'll get them, Wendy. I'll get all the bad ones. I'll punish them." She giggled. "Aren't you glad you're a nice person?"

Wendy tried to swallow, but there was no spit in her mouth. "Yes," she said. "I'm glad."

They played a game. It was *Candyland*. Wendy had played it dozens of times as a kid, but not this version. This one came entirely from Ginny's mind and it was disturbing to say the least. The things she remembered on the board like Molasses Swamp, the Gumdrop Mountains, and Lollipop Woods had been replaced by Black Rain Swamp, Fallout Mountains, and Mushroom Cloud Woods. The winding path of colored blocks had been replaced by what looked like tombstones and the two innocent children at the start had become skull-faced wraiths in shrouds. And at the very center of the board where there used to be the Gingerbread Plum Forest, there was now:

Wendy could barely breathe looking at it. A simple, harmless children's game had become something obscene beyond words.

"I don't think I want to play this," she said, her guts twisting inside her at the sight of it and the very real possibility that she had just pissed Ginny off.

The girl shook with minute tremors. Her dead eyes bulged and sweat rolled down her face. The doll's face seemed to scrunch up, her crooked grin wider than ever. "Why not, Wendy? The rest of the world had to play it, why not you?"

Wendy wiped her eyes with the back of her hand. "Because I already played it, Ginny. It's not a nice game. It's not very nice at all."

There.

She said it. Let that little monster kill her right now. Let it end before this nightmare went any further. She felt a surge of joy at the very idea. Scared, yes, but vindicated somehow. She had drawn a line in the sand. Now she'd see what the doll thought of that.

She'll beat you like a naughty puppy, she thought. *She'll break you like a misbehaving toy.*

But, amazingly, the doll did nothing. For some time, it did not speak. It did not move. It looked like the toy it was—inert and harmless. But the girl's lips curled back from her teeth and her breathing became very loud. A drop of blood slid from her left nostril.

Then the doll quivered slightly. From deep inside it, there was something quite like the warning growl of a mad dog, followed by what could only have been the chattering of teeth. Many teeth. "Oh, poor, poor Wendy," it said. "You'll ruin everything if you act up. If you make me mad, why, then I'll have to throw you away … you don't want to go into the gutter, do you? It's an awful place."

"No. I don't want to go there."

"That's good, Wendy. It's very dark there. Things move in the gutter that shouldn't move at all." Ginny watched her for a few moments. "I'm glad you're being nice, Wendy. But now you have to play the game."

With a shaking hand, Wendy selected a card from the stack. Unlike the usual cards that featured colorful blocks telling you how far to move, this card had words:

MOVE SEVEN SPACES IF YOU DARE

She moved her game piece as instructed, luckily missing the block called Bloody Hearts. She knew for a fact it was called Candy Heart in the real game. She remembered as a child wanting to eat one of the pink hearts, all of which said, *I Love You.* But these didn't say that. No, each heart—a human organ now—said, *I Hate You, Burn in Hell,* or *The Gutter.*

"Oh, you're lucky," Ginny said. "It's a bad, bad thing when you get your heart ripped out."

Now the girl chose a card and showed it to Ginny. Then she moved her game piece six spaces. "Neck and neck," the doll said.

Wendy selected a card. It read:

LUCKY GIRL MOVE TEN SPACES
BE VERY CAREFUL

Inside, Wendy was crying hysterically. But she would not let the doll see it. This was twisted and insane, but she would not give that monster the satisfaction of seeing her grovel in fear. It was important that she maintain her dignity in the face of adversity. If she made it easy for Ginny to break her, she would torment her constantly. She had to make this hard on her. The end would be the same—she couldn't possibly hope to fight what was in the doll—but she had to make Ginny work for it.

"Your turn," the doll said.

Calming herself, something which was nearly impossible, Wendy reached for her card, her guts knotted with terror. She picked one. It read:

MOVE TWO SPACES ENTER THE FOREST

She knew that in the real *Candyland,* she would have landed on the Peppermint Stick Forest space. But there were no peppermint sticks on this board. They had been replaced by what at first looked like gnarled, dead trees, but were in fact human cadavers, blackened and fragmented, driven into the ground. It was called Ride-By-Nights Forest. Being a teacher, she got the reference right away. It was a poem by Walter de la Mare from 1913, "The Ride-by-Nights," concerning a whimsical, magical flight of witches. She couldn't even imagine what its context was within the game itself.

"You're in a very bad place," Ginny said. "You have one chance, though. Pick another card. Pick one carefully."

Wendy's scalp was hot and itchy. She brushed aside a droplet of sweat at her temple. She picked another card, the doll watching her with sadistic delight. She turned it over. On it, there was a skull-and-crossbones in black. Written beneath that was a quote from the poem:

"UP ON THEIR BROOMS THE WITCHES STREAM, CROOKED AND BLACK IN THE CRESCENT'S GLEAM; ONE FOOT HIGH, AND ONE FOOT LOW, BEARDED, CLOAKED, AND COWLED THEY GO."

Wendy opened her mouth to ask what it meant, but there was a distant roaring and crashing. They were no longer in the house—they were out in Ride-By-Nights Forest. All around them were the black, grotesque forms of the irradiated cadavers.

The doll laughed with a wizened cackling.

The girl was shaking, her mouth contorted in what looked like agony. Drool ran from her lips.

There was a huge, resounding explosion and a huge mushroom cloud rose in the distance, illuminating the forest that seemed to go on to infinity. It hung there like a gigantic flare, throwing out a blinding yellow-orange glare that guttered and danced, making the cadavers seem to move.

Wendy could hear a panicked, fragmented sobbing coming from

her throat, but she was barely even aware of it. The light dimmed to a smoky, strobing glow that created leaping shadows in every direction. Through it, she could see figures moving through the forest of burnt remains. They were hunched over and grotesque, semi-human shapes that moved with the surreal slowness of nightmares, seeming to glide, moving closer and closer.

"Ginny," she said, with more control than she thought possible. "Make it stop ... dear God, make it stop...."

But it did not stop—it increased. The burning fireball in the sky continued to flicker with that ethereal orange glow like a candle in the skull of a jack-o'-lantern. The world had become a shaken snow globe village, but instead of snow drifting down it was black ash, which Wendy knew were the cremated remains of the victims of the global nuclear holocaust.

The mushroom cloud was reflected in the plastic buttons of the doll's eyes, which seemed pleased, if that was even possible. The girl was having some kind of seizure, blood running from her nostrils and ears. It looked black as oil in the intermittent illumination.

The winds came, dark and seeking, gathering clouds of dust and dead leaves in whirling cyclones. And in the spoking light, Wendy could see eerie figures. They moved through the forest, black shapes, ragged and fragmenting in the wind. Some seemed to crawl. Others crept among the cadavers which leaned this way and that like totem poles. And still others leaped up into the air and were scattered to and fro in the wind.

The Ride-By-Nights, she thought with mounting horror. *That's what they are: Ride-By-Nights. Wraiths created by radioactivity and the perverse imagination of the doll.*

The air was filled with debris. The shockwave of the detonated bomb created hurricane-force winds and the cadavers were in motion, rattling like castanets, heads bobbing and limbs flailing. And then, one by one, they exploded, shattering like glass, bits and pieces and razor-edged fragments of them blowing in every which direction.

Through the storm of ash and dust and churning smoke, one of the figures appeared ten feet away. It was like a golem: something carved in the rough likeness of a human being, but not human at all. It was a corrugated thing with a fissured face and bright, gleaming crimson eyes. Steam and smoke blew off it.

"If you move, it'll see you," Ginny said. "And if it sees you, it'll break you into pieces like a bad doll."

It was a Ride-By-Night and Wendy knew it had come for her. It had come to take her to the gutter where the toys Ginny had broken were dumped. More of them were coming now, shapes of rippling black mud. The wind carried their smell and she flinched … roasted flesh, burnt hair, rotting corpses, piss and disease and suppurating wounds. It was what the world smelled like after the bombings, the scent of the death of humanity.

"Stop!" Wendy shouted at the doll and the girl, maybe both and neither. "Ginny! Make it stop! Make them go away! Do you hear me? You have to make them go away!"

The girl was in a mindless stupor as always, but maybe more so, a tormented waif dusted in black ash. And the doll was not speaking, emoting, doing anything. It looked, if anything, just like a stupid toy. One of the Ride-By-Nights was so close, Wendy could see it reaching from the slithering shadows with a flesh-oozing hand.

She grabbed the doll and threw it to the ground. It still did not speak. She kicked it and stomped it, beating it as if it was a living thing. As she did so, the wasteland and its occupants began to fade and she heard the doll scream in her head with an explosive cacophony. Then its voice was speaking, a dry and creaking tone that sapped the strength from her. *Do you really think you can destroy me, Wendy? Do you really think you have what it takes to put me down? I, who have broken the back of humanity? I, who used their own weapons against them? I, who crawled into their heads and made them slit their own throats? Do you really think you can?* And Wendy realized the doll was in her hands and she was trying to tear it apart. Stuffing hung out of its side and one eye was missing. Its crooked grin was more crooked than ever and she could feel the power thrumming inside it that burned her hands and made her drop it.

As she pulled her scalded hands away, it was as if blades of ice impaled her. She was, again, on the floor of the living room, crawling on her belly. The doll was in the girl's hands.

In a hissing voice, it said, "Next time we play the game, it will be your last."

She barely made it to the bathroom before she threw up.

The following days were horrific ones. The food that was offered rotted black before Wendy could get her fork into it. When it didn't, it crawled with green worms. The doll sensed Wendy's sympathy for the girl so it punished the child repeatedly. It force-fed her carrion until she vomited. It pierced her with needles. It burned her. It tore the hair from her head. It beat her senseless with invisible fists.

The horror went on night and day.

When Wendy tried to intervene, the doll played roughly with her. It broke her fingers. It made bones snap and jut from her legs in compound fractures. There was no end to the agony it visited upon her. But always, always, it fixed her so she was fresh for another slate of suffering.

Exhausted, agonized, starving, she dreamed of destroying Ginny, of burning her to ash. And the doll seemed to know because every time thoughts like that entered her head, it giggled. And once, it pulled her mind from her head, sinking her deep inside its depths so she could feel what a cold, undying, soulless thing it indeed was. It was like drowning in a pool of black sewage.

"You're not a very nice person," Ginny told her. "I think you're mean and awful. Something very bad is going to happen to you."

But Wendy could not even guess what form it might take, only that she was now a puppet of the doll and it pulled her strings as it pleased.

Then one fateful day, they went for a walk.

Wendy had become a hopeless, beaten thing by then that stumbled along next to the girl as they toured the wreckage of the city. She saw a reflection of them in a dusty store window and they looked like a very bedraggled mother and her sickly child with its doll. The image made her sick to her stomach.

"What do you think we'll see today, Wendy?" Ginny asked. "Do you think we'll find someone to play with?"

"No."

"Oh, yes, we will. I just have a feeling."

Of course, the feeling was correct. As they walked down yet another lonely street, they came upon two teenage boys squatting before a fire. The boys were startled to see them. They immediately reached for their knives, but then relaxed. They seemed nice and that made Wendy hurt inside.

"Just leave them alone," she said.

"But I won't. I want to play with them."

The boys offered them their fire. They had some water and a few cans of food and they offered this as well. Whoever they were, their parents had raised them right. They had not degenerated into mindless, selfish beasts like so many of the others. They had not forgotten what it meant to be human.

"Do you want to play with us?" Ginny asked them.

Their inviting smiles of friendship faded fast when they realized the voice had come from the doll. They looked at each other and at Wendy, maybe suspecting it was some kind of joke. But that didn't last long, because they both instinctively sensed that something was not only very wrong, but that they were in the presence of evil.

They both made to run, but, of course, Ginny would not allow it. She seized them with her mind and made them stand straight as posts, their mouths hanging open and their eyes filled with terror.

"Which one, Wendy? Which one should it be?" Ginny asked.

Wendy just stood there, completely powerless to stop the atrocity that she knew was coming. "Please leave them alone," she pleaded. "Don't hurt them."

The doll watched her with its one remaining shoe button eye. "I like it when you beg, Wendy. Beg more. Beg on your knees."

Beyond simple things like pride and well-entrenched in humiliation of every sort by then, Wendy dropped to her knees. "Please, Ginny, *please*. You can punish me. You can kill me, if that's what you want. Just don't hurt them. I'm begging."

The doll giggled. "Oh no, Wendy. I like you. I won't kill you. But the problem is that I'm oh-so-hungry and I must feed."

Wendy was only too aware that she did not say *eat*, but *feed*. The insinuation of that was too terrible to contemplate.

"No, Wendy. I'm not going to eat them." The doll laughed at the very idea. "You're so silly! Now, why would I eat big boys like this? No, no, no. I need a different kind of food. A special kind of food. I need to feed on their life force. So, go ahead, Wendy, pick which one I should drain."

"No … no, please."

"Pick, Wendy, or I'll take both of them."

Wendy felt like her guts were being pulled out of her. Tears flowed from her eyes and she willed her heart to stop. She wanted to die right there on the street. It would have been a blessing. *So, is that it?* she wondered. *Is that what powers the doll? Did she feed on the life force of the millions upon millions that had died in the war and its aftermath?* A vampire. She/it was a vampire and it was time to recharge her batteries.

"Well, Wendy? Choose."

There was no way to avoid it. She knew that even if she made a mad grab for one of the knives the boys dropped and slit her own throat, the doll would fix her. She would never let her escape this, the ultimate horror.

Wendy stood up. Sobbing, angry, defeated, raging, too many conflicting emotions to make sense of, she squeezed her eyes shut and pointed toward the boy on the right.

"Good choice," Ginny said.

The other boy ran as the doll leeched his friend or brother or whoever he had been. It happened quickly. He shook violently, crying out, and then he melted. His eyes oozed like slit egg yolks. His face split open. Everything inside him spilled from a yawning crevice in his torso. Then all of it, like him, became a flowing wax that steamed and dripped from a pile of smoldering bones.

"See how easy it is, Wendy?" the doll said. "Now you're no better than I am."

The girl got sick. She collapsed one day and fell onto the kitchen floor.

Wendy never learned her name. Maybe she had been Ginny before the doll found her. The doll was a parasite and the girl had been the host. As she fell ill, the doll stopped talking. Things stopped happening. There was no more food or sunshine or comfort.

Wendy preferred it that way.

She wanted to die as the others had—from the cold, the germs, the fallout. She just wanted it over with. She nursed the girl the best she could, but she failed by the day. She trembled with fevers. Her breathing became shallow. Then, one evening, she stopped breathing altogether.

It was done.

It was all done.

She covered the girl with a blanket and it was the best she could do for her. This was Wendy's chance. The doll had been silent for days. The girl had dropped her to the floor where she still lay. As Wendy left the house, she gave it a wide berth. She would be free now, really free.

But as she opened the door, the doll sat up. "Now, Wendy, just where the hell do you think you're going?"

Wendy screamed.

But it didn't last long.

The girl's name was Suzanne. She stumbled through the streets, dizzy with the agony of hunger. She had not eaten in nearly five days. Her clothes hung in rags. Her face was smeared with grime and blood, one eye nearly closed from a battle she'd had with a man who tried to rape her and a woman with him who thought such things were great sport.

She knew that if she didn't eat soon, she was going to drop. It was getting very hard to find canned food. Those who had it protected it with guns and killed anyone who tried to take it.

Just a bite, she thought. *Just a few bites of anything to keep me going.*

She came around a corner and froze.

A woman was standing there. She was very thin, dressed in a dirty sweatshirt and jeans. Her eyes were unblinking like huge open sores, red and bleary. The strangest thing was that she carried a doll in her arms. It was an ugly little thing with one eye and scraggly hair. Its mouth was stitched in a sardonic grin.

And it spoke.

"My name is Wendy," it said. "Do you want to be my friend?"

LITTLE MONSTERS

He was a man with a gun in a terrible new world and they were hunting him. As far as he knew, he was the last man on earth. The last normal man. There had been a time when there had been billions. Now there was just one and his name was Merrick. Not that such things even mattered anymore. There was no point in names. There was really no point to a lot of things, yet he did not give up and he did not give in.

It was night and he was on the prowl.

That's what he called it in his mind: *prowling*. He was a cat on the prowl, carefully moving from neighborhood to neighborhood. He had not seen any of the imps tonight, but it didn't mean they weren't around. They had gotten very good at camouflaging themselves in the shadows. They were hunters. They knew how to set traps and deadly ambushes. He knew he could never, ever underestimate them just because they were small. They were like little dolls next to him. He could crush them … but they were many and he was one.

He could never underestimate their numbers.

Or their viciousness.

He had seen it in action too many times.

No, the trick was to be careful and quiet.

He had to keep in mind that he was a minority. A very, very small minority and they were a large, aggressive majority.

Hidden behind the burned-out shell of a car, he was about to move when he saw some of them. So small. So deadly. Four of them moved up the sidewalk across the street and they made his skin crawl. They made horrible hissing and slithering sounds as if they were part reptile. He did not move. He did not breathe. Their hearing was remarkably acute. Almost supernaturally so. If he cleared his throat or scratched a match, they would hear him. During the daytime, they were nearly blind in the brightness, but at night they could see like leopards.

They had their strengths and weaknesses.

He waited silently for nearly fifteen minutes until he was sure they had gone. Even then, he moved cautiously. The streets were washed down by thin, silver moonlight. It was beautiful. Even though what it illuminated was the graveyard of the city—buildings reduced to crumbling headstones, houses laid flat like burial slabs, apartment complexes fallen into themselves like sunken tombs—it was still beautiful. It had been so long since he dared go out at night, he'd forgotten just how beautiful moonlight could be.

But he didn't have time to admire it.

The night was *their* time and he was extremely vulnerable. Trying to fight them or outmaneuver them in the darkness was as foolhardy as Van Helsing hunting Dracula after sunset.

He moved along a street of dark ruins, trying to stay to the shadows. He placed his feet slowly and expertly. All it would take to bring them was a stray leaf crunching under his boot or a tin can accidentally kicked. His place, his hideout, was about six blocks away and that was a long way in their hunting grounds.

Now and again, he heard scurrying sounds.

It could have been them or it could have been rats. There were many of both since the city had fallen. He made it one block, then two. That's when he saw the light. It came from a fire in a vacant lot. He moved along a row of wrecked cars until he was close enough to see what was going on.

Imps.

Oh Christ, dozens of them. They were gathered around a bonfire, shrieking and hissing as they circled it in some crude dance, throwing their hands to the sky, bodies whirling, heads tossed back as they cried out. There was probably some ritual significance to it, but he didn't want to know what it was. Everything about them sickened him. What they had been before the radiation and what they were now.

He was in a real fix.

He had two choices: either he snuck past them across the street, hoping with the racket they were making that they would not hear him, or he went around, cutting back and circling. But the latter meant going six blocks out of his way, most of the streets being completely blocked by wreckage in this area. He didn't dare try to cut through the wreckage itself; that was far too noisy and the last thing he needed as he climbed hills of rubble was to fall or trip and twist his ankle. Besides, he had seen them more than once coming up from their holes in the debris of collapsed buildings.

No, he was going to have to chance sneaking past them. He quietly unleathered the .9mm Colt at his hip and then stealthily, he crawled from the shadow of one car to the next. It was slow going and at any moment, he knew, they might leap on him and tear into him with their claws and vicious mouths.

Merrick generally didn't go out at night. It was far too dangerous. But he had screwed-up and lost track of time. It had happened before. At least this time, he had a good reason for it.

He'd been over on 12th and Hoover, scavenging, always on the lookout for a food stash or some weapons. Anything that would give him the edge in survival. As he explored, he came upon a wild dog pack. There were six of them, five tattered mutts led by an absolutely evil-looking Rottweiler. He was upwind from them or they would have scented him sooner. Since it was daylight and he had no fear of the imps, he wasn't exactly being quiet.

Then he spotted them down the street.

The Rottweiler, apparently, was the baron of the pack. It growled low and gutturally at him, ropes of nasty white foam hanging from its jaws. It was a signal to the others because they came bounding after him. He had the .9mm. He could have dropped them, but he saw no reason to waste bullets if he didn't have to. He ran for two blocks with them closing in. It was then, as he turned to fight, that he saw the hidden stairway cut down through the sidewalk, leading to the basement of a hardware store. The door was half-open. He grabbed hold of the little railing, swung himself over and down the steps, slamming the door shut behind him.

It was a dangerous move.

For all he knew, he might have entered a nest of imps, but that's not what he found at all. He was in a survivalist bunker. It was something he'd always dreamed of finding. Flashlight in hand, he searched for survivors, but, of course, there were none. What he did find were cases of medical supplies and MREs, camo clothing and boots, rain gear and sleeping bags, body armor and guns—.38 and .357 revolvers, .9mm Berettas and assault shotguns, an old M-14 semi-auto with a scope that had been converted to a sniper rifle, and even a pair of factory-fresh, full-auto M-4 carbines still greased with protective Cosmoline. There were cots and blankets, anti-radiation suits and dosimeters, propane-fueled cook stoves and water purification apparatus, pellet stoves and cases of water, flashlights and batteries and lanterns—

Well, the list went on and on.

Someone had planned very carefully for the end. It had probably been some highly paranoid nut, but Merrick appreciated their attention to detail. It was the greatest stockpile he'd yet found.

His first priority was to protect it.

He went up into the hardware store, the dogs long since moved onto better pickings. He found a heavy-duty lockset with a deadbolt, grabbed some tools. He replaced the locks and pocketed the keys. Then, as added protection, he put a reinforced padlock bracket on the outside and secured it with a Masterlock.

Those goddamn imps would never get in.

But by then, the shadows were growing long. Hence, his current predicament.

They were roasting a dog.

From his vantage point, Merrick could see that it had been a large animal, maybe a German Shepherd or a Great Dane. Being that it was skinned, it was hard to say. It was spitted above the fire and the imps were slowly turning it, the smell of burnt meat and hot grease not as disgusting as it should have been. There had been a time, years ago now, when the animal lover in him would have been offended, but those days were gone. Most of the dogs were feral now and would attack without provocation. When civilization ended, they answered the call of the wild and had never looked back.

If it came down to it, he told himself. *You would eat dog. And they would gladly eat you.*

He moved along the line of cars at a low crouch, his eyes watching for perimeter guards. The imps were tribal in structure, staunchly militaristic by nature. They had leaders and warlords. They sent out scouts and posted guards. You could never underestimate the complexity of their hunter-gatherer societies. They survived by hunting dogs and each other, different clans waging war against one other. Essentially, they were like ant colonies.

He crept further and further down the row of cars. He saw no guards. Only when he was an easy block away from the fire did he relax and wipe sweat from his face. He could still see the fire in the distance, hear them hooting and howling like prehistoric savages, which, in effect, was exactly what they were.

He'd found the remains of their fires more than once. When he searched through the ashes, he commonly found the bones of dogs, but he also found the tiny bones of their kind. Which meant they were also cannibals.

I'd kill them all if I could, he thought. *If there was a way.*

He stayed to the shadows of the ruins.

He only dared cross a street after many minutes of careful reconnaissance. Just because they were gathered around the fire didn't mean that scouting parties weren't out. They knew about him, of course, and they hated him on sight. They were small and he was big, like a giant or an ogre that they had to slay like medieval peasants.

He feared many things about them. Primarily, that they would take him alive and feast upon him as they had with the dog. But he also feared their spears. They were very good at making them and were deadly accurate with them. They dipped the points in their own shit to create infections in the bodies of their enemies.

There had been a time when he had gone house to house, killing them in their lairs. But after he spent hundreds of bullets and had one frightful battle after another in darkened cellars, he had given up. As many as he killed, that many more seemed to replace them. That's all they were good at: killing and hunting and breeding. He'd cut the throat of a little pregnant female once and in her death throes which were violent and bloody, she had aborted her fetus ... just the sight of it had made him stagger out into the sunshine and vomit.

After that, he'd given up.

There were just too many.

About a block from his place, he stopped. He didn't initially know why, but he was gripped by an unreasonable fear. It was instinct. It was warning him against an impending threat. He could feel it along his spine.

He waited, studying the shadows.

He moved in closer.

What he saw at the street corner was a cairn of stones. He was certain it had not been there before. It troubled him. Somebody had piled it there. It had to have been the imps; there was no one else now. He did not for a moment believe it was a meaningless heap of rocks. They did nothing without a reason. It was marking something.

It's marking your place.

They know where you hide.

Was that possible? Were the stones a marker to alert other tribes that this was where the monster lived? Like a skull on a stick to mark the boundaries of a tribe of headhunters in an old movie. He was nearly sure of it.

They had tracked him down.

If that was the case, they would be attacking his place every night until they got in. He was compromised. He would no longer be safe.

After a time, he saw that they were all around him, hiding in the shadows. They knew he was out and they were waiting for him to return, lying in wait.

Silently, he put on his leather gloves in case he had to kill one of them. It was necessary since he couldn't stand the feel of them.

Hidden behind a row of overgrown hedges, he waited for sunrise. He didn't dare move until then.

One of them, a scout, came for him as the first streaks of blue were visible in the eastern sky. It came with a soft, barely discernible rustling as of leaves on a tree. Merrick had not been asleep really, just in sort of a numb fugue from his exhaustion. He saw a dark figure come around the hedges. He could hear the rasp of its breathing. Smell the stench of its hide—a suffocating, noisome odor of the dead things it had been feeding upon.

It was completely unaware of him.

His outline was blurred, melting into the shadows of the hedges. He could see the creature clearly in the fading moonlight: a squat, bowlegged pygmy with a scaly, leprous yellow face. It was completely naked save for a sash of dog skin. And it was female: high, pointy breasts jutting from a well-muscled chest greased with animal fat. Around its throat was a necklace of what looked like teeth.

She repulsed him beyond reason, a feral monstrosity shaped roughly like a human being but with the predatory cunning of a beast of prey.

She paused, sniffing the air like a wolf.

Greasy strands of dark hair hung in her face. She tensed visibly, sensing something that she did not like. Her spear, the shaft decorated with feathers, was held high for throwing.

Merrick controlled his breathing.

He did not move nor flinch a muscle.

He was part of the hedge. He believed it and so did she. He only needed to draw her in a bit closer. His eyes were locked on the smooth roundness of her hips, the small cones of her breasts. It had been a long, long time since he'd touched a woman. Felt her breasts. Put his mouth on her. He realized then, that despite himself, the imp female was arousing him.

Jesus, he thought with a wave of nausea. *What the hell's wrong with you? She's not even human.*

She moved in closer until she was nearly on top of him. Then she knew. In a moment of revelation, her snake eyes found him. She had enough time to utter a short, hoarse, glottal hiss before he seized her, striking like a rattlesnake with lightning speed. One gloved hand covered her thick-lipped mouth and flattened nose, enveloping them with crushing pressure, blocking her air supply. He pinned her arms to her sides, squeezing with maximum pressure. She writhed wildly, a hot and oily mass rippling with muscle as she tried to worm free.

Slowly, slowly, her struggles grew weaker and she finally went limp.

She stank like a wet dog. Strands of her filthy hair were stuck to his sweaty face. He could feel the lice jumping in it. Copious amounts of slimy drool oozed from her mouth. His glove was wet with it.

When he was certain she was dead, he gripped her head in both fists and twisted it violently until her neck snapped. Only then did he gasp for breath.

With a silent cry of repugnance, he lowered her corpse into the grass. He had attacked her with manic ferocity and he honestly wasn't sure whether that was to save his own life or because his own sexual arousal had sickened him.

He stared down at her twisted little body. He figured she had been about eighteen inches tall. Average. The males sometimes got to two feet, the children the size of Barbie dolls.

In death, a sour, musky smell issued from her that reminded him of the reptile house at the zoo.

He waited for the sun to come up. In fact, he prayed for its rays to purify him, to burn the smell of the imp off him.

He remembered seeing the mushroom cloud.

He had been miles away at the time in the very outskirts of the city, but he had seen it like so many others—a gigantic rolling ball of orange fire and yellow smoke rising above the skyline, connected to the earth by a massive pillar of purple and red encircled by white rings of irradiated steam. As it climbed, becoming larger and larger, sucking up dust and debris and flashing with sparkling colors, it was a thing of beauty. Beautiful and deadly at the same time like a red widow spider or an

Australian tiger snake. It hovered above everything, rotating and gushing with white smoke. It was a new and malefic god to replace the old, tired ones and he watched it being born.

After that, of course, there was unbelievable devastation in the form of hurricane winds, firestorms, and fallout. The city was broken, shattered into a million pieces. He had tried unsuccessfully to reach his neighborhood, where Angie and Chris had been waiting for him. But his neighborhood was gone. The streets blocked by burning wreckage. He made many attempts to find his family, but it was pointless: the blast had incinerated the entire area.

In the following weeks, as what was left of the city's infrastructure collapsed, he saw thousands slowly die of radiation poisoning. Those that were spared were killed off as one plague after the other made the rounds.

Month after month, he was amazed that he did not die. He wanted to, but his existence was horrible. Without his wife and son, it was pointless to go on. Yet, he did. The more he wanted to die, the more he lived. He moved from one commune of survivors to another. Most of them were collections of crazy people, minds broken by the nuclear holocaust and what was left mangled out of shape by one form of fundamentalist religion after another.

Well over a year later, civilization as he had known it dead, he hooked up with another small group that was led by a retired Air Force colonel named Van Howten. He was a survival expert who taught them all to live in the new, damaged world. He taught them how to shoot and kill, of course, to protect what was theirs from roving gangs and criminal elements, but he also instilled in them the importance of remembering that they were human beings, that they needed to help others and share food with the less fortunate.

Van Howen died during a cholera outbreak.

When it was over, there was just Briggs, Wong, and Merrick. They got by pretty well for over a year and that's when the imps first showed. Every day, it seemed, there were more of them. They waged war against them, but there were so many. The imps killed Wong first, then Briggs. Merrick escaped with his life, but only after killing an easy dozen of them with his knife and bare hands. They were savage to the extreme. They would sacrifice dozens of their own, just to kill a single normal.

Merrick got very good at avoiding them and taking them out one by one.

It had been going on for years now. He had not seen a single normal human being for at least six months. He believed he was the last one, and he would not go down without a fight.

There was an old folk song that said, *Be the first to praise the sun, the first to praise the sky.* And that's who Merrick was all these years later. When the sun came up, its golden rays bathed his skin, making him feel human again. Allowing him to breathe easy. It chased away the shadows and creeping night terrors. It made him want to fall to his knees like a superstitious primitive and give thanks to it.

But there was no time.

Things needed to be done. He crossed to the cairn of stones at the corner. It was no haphazard structure, he saw, but one carefully engineered with four large foundation stones at its base which supported three smaller ones with two atop those, and a single one at the apex. And that one was dabbed with red paint in a crude cuneiform symbol.

No, not paint: blood. Their blood.

Yes, and it probably wasn't done lightly. The blood and the symbol probably had some religious or ceremonial significance for the imps. Something that only they and the other tribes would recognize.

The very idea was terrifying, yet fascinating.

On a hunch, he walked down the sidewalk past his place toward the end of the block. He found another such cairn on the opposite corner, equally marked. He rounded the block and cut down the alley where he found yet another cairn.

It all made a rudimentary sort of sense.

The three cairns, if seen from above, would have formed a triangle and his hideout would have been at the dead center of it. As he thought, his place had been marked by them.

He'd known for years now that they existed at a simple tribal level, but this proved that there was more to it than that. He had seen the cuneiform symbols many times, he realized, without attaching any significance to them—on walls, doors, the sides of houses, even scratched in the dirt. Sometimes there was only one or two, but often a series of them. It was something symbolic for them. Communication. Trail sign. Ritual. Probably all these things.

And if some part of him still doubted that, it doubted no longer with what he found at his front door.

The doorway to his place was well hidden by thick laurel shrubs that had grown wild and bushy, making it nearly impossible to spot from the street. That's what he liked about it.

But it was hidden no more, of course.

Curled up on the threshold were two imps whose hands had been tied behind their backs with leather thongs. Their throats had been slit. They laid in dried pools of their own blood, some of which had been used to paint more symbols on the door in a weird spiraling pattern.

Sacrificed, Merrick knew.

Offered up to whatever malign god they worshipped. For good luck. Prosperity. He remembered reading years before about primitive clans offering blood sacrifices to ensure the success of the hunt.

It was all interesting and more than a little frightening, but what concerned him most was that the door was open a few inches and the lock was bashed free.

He expected them to be lying in wait, but they weren't. As he stepped inside, flashlight in one hand and the .9mm Colt in the other, he could smell the evil stink of what they had left behind.

The windows were boarded up securely so no one could see his lights at night, so he guided himself with the flashlight.

They had trashed the place.

His clothes and bedding were slashed to ribbons, his furniture torn open. His stockpile of food and beverages had been raided, cans burst open, spaghetti and beans and soup spilled to the floor along with dry goods, noodles and flour, sugar and coffee. Water bottles were emptied out, as were cleaners and detergents. His guns and ammunition were sunk into the mess along with his matches and batteries.

There was nothing they hadn't touched.

Even mirrors were shattered, plates and glasses broken into bits. The only thing missing were his knives, two axes, several screwdrivers and hammers. Things that could be fashioned into weapons.

They had urinated on everything, the vile ammonia smell of their piss pungent in the air. They had smeared the walls with shit, ripped apart his books and magazines, taking special pains to deface the breasts and vaginas of naked models.

How they must have hated him.

No, he told himself. *It's more than that—it's fear. Fear of who you are, what you are, and the level of destruction your kind are capable of. You're a menace to them.*

He supposed fate had favored him by leading him to the bunker last night and making it so he couldn't return. If he had, he would have been dead by now. The imps would have had the head of the giant on a spike.

As disappointed as he was, as frustrated and angry, he found that he did not necessarily hate them. Not the way he had before. Maybe it was because after five years (or was it six?) of this madness, he was beginning to understand them. Like him, they were in a constant fight for survival. But they were not animals. Not exactly. Mutants, yes, but not without a certain level of primitive intellect.

And unless something changed dramatically and soon, they were poised to inherit the earth. And why not? They were nature's solution to global nuclear annihilation. They were survivors in every way. They bred like rabbits. They grew from infancy to adulthood in a matter of months. Maybe they only lived a few years, but they required far less resources to survive than his kind did. What it took to feed him in a week would last a pack of them a month.

Oh, he was still going to kill them.

But it would not be out of hate, but necessity. The last gasp before his kind went extinct.

There was nothing worth taking. They had destroyed everything. Merrick left it all behind and went back out in the streets, making for his new digs at the bunker. Everything he needed was there. If it hadn't been for finding that wonderful cache, he would have had to start again. The very idea exhausted him.

For a long time now, he had toyed with the idea of setting up three or four different hideouts in the city so he'd always have an alternate place to go. Either that or making for the countryside (even though he knew for a fact the imps were there, too). But he'd done neither and he probably never would. Just getting through the day was more than enough.

And what about when they find the bunker? he asked himself as he moved up yet another lonely street. *Because you know they will.*

That was something he did not want to think about.

Right now, he needed food and rest. These two things encompassed his every thought.

When he reached the vacant lot where the imps had their bonfire last night, he decided to look around. What he found was both disturbing and enlightening—charred bones in the firepit. Some of them were from animals and some from other imps, but he also found the bones of a normal: a skull, ribcage, a femur. Which meant there were other normals around.

And the imps are hunting them to extinction.

If only he could find out where they were hiding. To be with his own kind again … *God.*

If nothing else, it gave him a reason to go on.

The bunker was wonderful.

Locked in behind that heavy-duty door that would have taken a tank to breach, he felt safe and secure. He set up a cot with a sleeping bag and pillow, had himself an MRE meal of beef stew followed by some sugar cookies, and an orange Gatorade to wash it down. Then he slept for six glorious hours and made use of the chemical toilet.

Whoever had stockpiled the bunker had not been an illiterate type. There was a room in the back with bookshelves from floor to ceiling. Hundreds of books, everything from paperback westerns to poetry collections, Dickens to Hemingway and Shakespeare.

He decided for the next couple days he wasn't going out at all. Everything he needed was here. He would make an intensive inventory of all he had, eat, read, sleep, do some hard thinking.

The idea that there were other people in the city excited him. They were in hiding, but they had to be out there somewhere. The best idea he could think of for finding them was to canvas the city, leaving messages for them in plain sight on the walls of buildings. On sidewalks. Fences. Whatever it took. He would use markers or paint so they wouldn't wash away.

That first night, he had a cheese tortellini MRE and some MRE bread. Things were about to get better and he knew it.

He stuck to his plan.

In the coming week, he hiked about the city, leaving messages everywhere. After he'd left about twenty-five of them, he began returning to each and every one and was distressed to find that there were no replies.

He longed for the days when cars still ran. It would have made everything so much easier. Some of them had after the war, but he discovered that gasoline had a limited shelf life. After the first six months, the gas was no good anymore. Something in it had broken down.

No matter; his feet still worked, and he put on many miles in his search for others. It wasn't without its own concerns and paranoia, though. He realized that some of the survivors might be dangerously crazy by that point or predatory, in that they might kill him to get what he had.

So he was always careful.

But he never stopped. If there were others, he simply had to find them. He had to track them down and befriend them, show them that he was no threat but a benefactor, that together they could be strong. And if he could find enough of them, they could seriously put a dent in the imp domination of the city. It was probably fanciful thinking at best, but he saw himself as a great uniter, someone that would bring them altogether and create a strong community that would put the imps on the run.

"What I do is good and necessary and righteous," he told himself again and again. It gave him strength and was a nice antidote to his own cynicism that seemed to have gotten worse month by month.

Then one, fateful day, he heard a woman singing.

Was it possible? Was he hearing things? Had he lost his mind completely?

He stood there, frozen, barely even breathing, his hand sliding to the butt of his .9mm. He was at least three miles from the bunker, in a part of the city he had never been to before. It looked much like the rest of it —ruins, rubble, some neighborhoods standing intact, while others were flattened. The shockwave of the bomb had done that. Like a tornado, it smashed a house to rubble, but did not overturn a glass of water left on a picnic table a short distance away.

But the singing … it went on and on.

He didn't recognize the song. He thought it might be opera, but he was too far away to know for sure. Practicing great care, his eyes looking for ambushes or hidden figures, he tracked the singing to its source: a building whose face was scarred from the blast, but relatively unscathed other than that.

He stood on the steps, the handgun greasy in his fist. He wondered how dark it might be inside. The imps didn't come out into direct sunlight, but they were quite active in dark places.

But the voice … this was what he'd been waiting for so desperately. If he didn't go in there, didn't take the chance, it would haunt him forever.

He thought of the weapons back in the bunker. The shotguns, the M4s. They would have been handy in a situation like this. He had not taken heavy firepower because he did not want any survivors to get scared off by too many weapons.

Now, he regretted it.

You could come back tomorrow better armed, just in case.

No. He would not do that. This was the chance he'd been waiting for and he couldn't turn away from it if it was within his grasp. He thought of others he could fight with and help. Men who could be his friends and women—

No, that was the last thing he needed to be thinking of.

He moved up the steps.

The front door was not locked. It was dim inside, but enough light came in through the windows to see by. Still, he kept the flashlight in his other hand. It was some kind of apartment building, he saw. A footpath was beaten through the dust on the floor. That was a good sign. It led to the stairs. The singing was coming from above.

Feeling tense, balancing uneasily on the edge of his fight-or-flight instinct, he went up the steps. In the corridor above, a dirty yellow light came from a window at the end. The singing went on. He followed it to its source: a door at the end. He stood there a moment or two, uneasy, filled with conflicting emotions. It would have been very simple to slip back the way he came, but the urge to see another human being was overwhelming. It owned him. It was the fuel that burned inside him and the rudder that kept him on course.

He wasn't sure how to handle this.

His social skills were so rusty they creaked.

He knocked. It seemed incongruous under the circumstances, yet he felt it important to announce his arrival. The knocking brought no cessation to the singing, so he called out. "I'm a friend," he said. "I want to come in. I mean you no harm."

The singing went on.

Pocketing the flashlight, he tried the door. It was open. That, more than anything, made panic surge inside him. Who would leave their doors unlocked these days?

To hell with it.

He turned the knob and threw it open. It was dark in there, so he brought out the flashlight quickly, spearing the light around. He was in a kitchen. There was a table covered with dust. Cupboards grimy with handprints. Cobwebs hung from the ceiling in thick strands like ancient party streamers.

"Hello?" he said, his voice echoing around him.

The singing continued. It was definitely some sort of operatic aria. The words sounded like Italian. The voice was very clear, very strong. It sounded professional.

He moved into the next room and there was a small African-American woman huddled in the corner in a dirty, torn dress. Her eyes were huge and bright, dazed, her face caked with filth. She didn't even flinch when he put the light in her face.

"Ma'am?" he said and that's when he noticed she was tied, arms and legs bound. He noticed this with a surge of fear as he caught the sudden, overpowering, animal stink of the imps.

Bait! She's being used as bait!

Seven or eight of them charged into the room, growling and chittering, snapping their teeth. Spears were upraised, their tiny naked bodies smeared with black grease in serpentine patterns. Their wicked eyes gleamed in the beam of the flashlight, their matted hair tangled with sticks and leaves.

He killed three of them in the first few seconds, ducking as a spear sought him out, thudding into the wall. He shot a male in the face, spraying blood and skull matter against the wall. He clipped another in the belly.

But the others kept coming.

He knocked two of them aside, smashing one of their writhing bodies beneath his boots. And then two others launched themselves through the air. They clung to him, biting and clawing, drawing blood. He threw himself backward against the wall, crushing the bones of the one on his back and smashing the butt of the Colt against the other that clung to his neck. He hit it again and again until its skull cracked.

As he turned to flee, a spear sank into his thigh.

He shot the imp that threw it and staggered into the kitchen. Several of them were still coming, dragging themselves low to the floor on their bellies.

They didn't follow him out into the light of the corridor. He stuck to the wall, moving toward the light as hot blood ran down his leg.

Oh, how stupid he'd been! How easily led. As he'd been studying them these many years, they'd been studying him. They knew exactly what he wanted and exactly what he needed. All those messages he'd written on walls and sidewalks. They'd found them, no doubt, and had watched him from the shadows as he returned again and again to see if there were any replies.

And they laid a perfect trap with the woman.

By the time he'd gotten down stairs, his leg was wet with blood. He'd pulled the spear free in his flight and that only made the blood run that much faster.

He needed to pause.

He needed to bind it. He had a first-aid kit in his bag, if only he had the time to get to it. But they weren't going to give him the time—he was wounded, and they knew it. They would hound him until there was no fight left in him.

Get out into the light! You have to get in the light!

But they were everywhere, dozens and dozens of them were waiting in the dank shadows of the first floor. Slinking, slithering little forms with yellow faces smeared with night grease, hunters and killers, Paleolithic savages that were poised to take down a mammoth.

He emptied the .9mm into them, dropping one after the other. But more came. And then more. Another spear sank into his shoulder. He pulled it free with red-stained hands, slapping another magazine into his gun.

The front door was still open.

There was a wedge of sunlight on the floor that spilled through. If he could get to it, worm his way into it and pull himself outside, he still might make it.

But they were everywhere.

They were massing like toads, hopping and jumping, seeming to come from every direction. He fired again and again, dropping them one after the other. But the other imps came right over the top of their bleeding corpses. In the past, if he knocked off enough of them, the others would scatter.

But not this time.

They had him and they knew it.

He batted them away, crushed them, beat them down, but still they came. He pulled one off his back and threw it to the floor, ramming his knife into its swollen pink belly again and again, drenched up to the elbow with its hot, reeking blood.

Screaming, his voice drowning in their howling, shrilling cries, he emptied the .9mm into them yet again and still they converged.

"GET AWAY FROM ME!" he shouted to no avail. "GET THE FUCK AWAY FROM ME!"

But his panicked appeals excited them into a mad frenzy. They rushed at him, slashing at him with knives. He fought them hand to hand, gutting them as their blades laid him open. Covered in their blood and tangled in their entrails, he fought on and on. He seized a spear-thrower in his hands, its small body flabby and pulsating, feverishly hot with sweat and oily secretions. He snapped its neck in his rage, tearing it open, yanking its little thrashing limbs free.

They were hanging off him, biting and stabbing, clawing at his eyes. He forced himself to his feet, dozens of riders clinging to him like leeches, and used his size and weight to bowl through them.

More spears sank into him.

A fork was driven into his throat.

Crawl, he commanded himself. *Crawl into the light.*

He made it, he actually made it and as the light touched them, his riders fell off one by one. He could smell the fresh air, feel the sunlight on him. But by then, he was broken and gouged, bleeding from dozens of wounds. As he tried to crawl out of the doorway, they grabbed him by the ankles and pulled him back into the shadows.

He didn't have enough strength to fight.

They had him.

They finally had him.

They gathered around him like a pack of prehistoric hunters, hatchets and spears raised. The human race. This was what the human race had become. Mutated by radiation into imps, regressed to primordial savages. He was a monster, a freak to them. There was no reasoning with them, nothing left to do but scream as they ripped him apart, bathing in his blood. He lived long enough to see them yank his liver out and begin to feed on it with their salivating, voracious mouths.

THE SHAPE

1

The dead man hadn't been lucky.

Despite the four-leafed clover tattooed to his right bicep, he'd still gotten himself killed. He'd been slashed open, burnt, crushed ... it almost looked like he'd fallen out of a burning plane a half a mile up. But that wasn't it. His death had been ugly and brutal, certainly, but it had nothing to do with planes because there were no more planes. Just like there were no more trains or baseball games or TV. Not much of anything when you came right down to it.

No, this poor bastard—we'll call him *Lucky*—had gone out the hard way. We all knew that and knowing it, preferred not to think about it. Kind of like cancer. You know it might get you, but why dwell on it?

The five of us were crouched in a cornfield (six if you count Lucky) watching the little town below us in the valley. There was a sign ahead on the side of the road, its Day-Glo surface blasted with bullet holes. BITTER CREEK, it said. And beneath that: CLASS C BASKETBALL CHAMPS 1996.

I wondered if Lucky had played basketball.

I figured he hadn't. He was so mangled and misused, he looked like something you scraped off the bottom of your oven. Yet his tattoo was unscathed.

259

Go figure.

Carl said, "I figure he ran out of luck."

I laughed. I couldn't help it. Pretty soon we were all laughing. Carl just said the craziest shit sometimes. Janie wasn't laughing, of course. She didn't think death was funny. Even fifteen months after the world stopped breathing, she still mourned its corpse.

Lucky was dead; he was just another body in a world heaped with them and it didn't mean a thing. We couldn't let it. But, crouching there, smelling him, we were all thinking things.

Janie kept staring at him like she wanted to say a few words over his remains. "I wonder what happened to him?"

Carl laughed. "What do you think happened?"

And there was no point in elaborating on that. Down deep, we all knew: *the Children*. The Children had gotten him. When they got their hands on someone, they always left them looking like this.

"All right," I said. "Let's go. Let's get this done."

Morse took a couple pictures of Lucky with his Nikon and nobody mentioned the fact.

He was always snapping pictures of everybody we came across. It was his thing. There was nowhere to get the film developed, but, hey, everybody needs something to call their own. Besides, Morse wasn't a bad guy; he just had trouble forgetting that he'd been a magazine photographer once. Just like I had trouble forgetting that I'd been a husband. Now I was just a drifter. Morse, too. We clung together, watched out for each other. That was what we did. It was enough.

We kept walking up that desolate country road, Janie and I in the lead, Morse and the others behind us.

They followed me because I made them feel safe, and they made me feel like a big man. Truth was, I was so small I could've gotten stuck to the bottom of their shoes. I knew it and maybe they knew it, too. But they didn't mention the fact. That kept me happy and I kept them alive.

"Are we going to do this forever, Rick?" Janie said to me. "I mean, won't there ever be a point when this isn't necessary?"

I lit a cigarette. It was stale. Everything was stale now. "I doubt it."

Carl elaborated for me: "No, ain't gonna happen, baby. Don't you see? The Shape ain't never gonna be satisfied. Not until his belly is full and he's picked his teeth with the last of humanity's bones."

"Shut the fuck up," I told him.

And he did. I did the selecting and they all knew it. Carl didn't want to get on my bad side. He was with me, but that didn't mean I wouldn't send him over.

"Yeah, you better watch what you're saying," Mickey told him, her ample cleavage bouncing as she walked. "One of these days, Carl, you'll be standing in line. Right, Rick?"

Good old Mickey. Nobody kissed my ass the way she did.

The five of us rounded the crest of a hill and, stretched out below us, was a town. It wasn't much. Maybe it had held four or five thousand at one time, but that was before the bombs fell. Just another drop of a town in the puddle of Nebraska. A little place surrounded by cornfields.

As we wound on down the road, a peculiar sense of melancholy grabbed me with both fists. I was so accustomed to seeing one vacant town after another, just grave markers to civilization, that I had pretty well forgotten that they were more than brick and wood, pavement and concrete. This had been someone's home. People had fallen in love here and raised children. They'd grown old and retired in this oasis in the rustling corn. They had loved it here. It had been the sweetest sight to their eyes.

In a way, it put a new twist on things.

At least for a few seconds.

Eventually, of course, it died a lingering death and its corpse was stomped down by my usual apathy. Maybe it had been someone's home, but now it was a lot of nothing. Empty houses and abandoned schoolyards. No more sundown vigils held with cold beers and good friends. No more hayrides and school dances and office parties and backseat romances. All as extinct as mastodon shit.

No one said anything as we entered the city limits. There were no signs of life. Death was in the air. A putrescent blanket that covered us, suffocating us with its heat and heaviness.

"Mmm, that air," Carl said. "Nothing smells quite like Nebraska."

The streets were lined with rusting cars and debris, the gutters clogged with brown leaves and broken glass. The sun was high in the sky in a hazy, filmy pocket, reflecting off the filthy glass fronts of the main drag.

A cop car with flat tires and an imploded windshield stood watch on the outskirts. Behind the wheel there was a skeleton in soiled rags. A silver badge winked on its chest.

We moved on.

Morse started whistling Dion's "The Wanderer" and I heard a few panicky laughs. We were all nervous, I suppose, being on foot like this. I just wished our van hadn't thrown a rod back on the highway. My fingers were tickling the .45 Browning in my coat pocket and Carl had unslung his 12-gauge pump.

"I hope we're alone," Janie said. "I really hope we are. I don't want to see anyone."

Carl suppressed a giggle. "We're never alone, honey. Big Brother Shape is always watching."

"You're starting to get on my nerves, man," I said and meant it.

Carl could be funny sometimes, but other times, just goddamned annoying. He was the only one in my little posse that ever mentioned The Shape. We all knew what it was … sort of … and that it was always watching us, just like we knew what it demanded of us and what we had to do to keep it happy, but we didn't talk about it.

But sometimes, when Carl got nervous, he'd start saying shit. Bad shit. Unnecessary shit we didn't want to be thinking about.

"I hope they're all dead," Janie said. "Better that than what we'll have to do to them."

"Better them than us," Mickey pointed out.

Mickey was right. It had been like four weeks now since The Shape had come and you could set your watch by that mother, because it came every month regular as a woman's period. Count on it. And when it came … or *she* or *he* or whatever in the hell The Shape was … its belly was always empty. And when that happened, you'd best have something ready. Something hot and tasty.

"I can't take this much longer," Janie said, those tears in her eyes again. "It makes me feel … dirty, corrupt. Why in the hell won't it just end? How long do we have to keep on like this?"

Morse started snapping pictures of her like she was emoting for the lens. *Click, click, click.*

"Knock it off!" she snapped at him.

I gave him the look and he did. He even put the lens cap back on, slipped out of my sight real quick-like. Morse had been with me four or five months and in all that time he had not spoken. He whistled and hummed, but he never spoke. Funny, he could talk. We knew that. He talked in his sleep a lot, sketching out his former life. Just never to us, was all.

I put my arm around Janie, but she shrugged it off. Poor Janie. She'd been with me ever since Cleveland. That's where we'd hooked up about six months after the bombs fell. Janie was sweet and kind, girl-next-door pretty with high cheekbones and big green eyes, a honey-blonde ponytail down the middle of her back. Janie had been a cheerleader in her senior year when the world ended. She had been a good girl, honor roll and class president, civic-minded and caring. She'd gone to church, volunteered at the local children's hospital, collected coats for the needy in the winter and canned food for the elderly in the summer.

I think I loved her.

And loving her, wished she were dead.

She was just too good to be thrown into the ashcan with the rest of us. She had morals and ethics while the rest of us had left ours in our other coats. And because of that, she was a thorn in my side. She was my proverbial conscience, always disapproving and disappointed in what I did and was going to do.

She just could never swallow the idea that I did it to keep us alive.

2

Maybe I hung around Youngstown too long.

Maybe I just couldn't believe what I was seeing.

I think back then I had some crazy and utterly fucked-up idea that the end of the world was going to pass like a bout of the flu—civilization had shit its pants and vomited its guts out, but it would pass, it would pass. The fever would end. But when those bombs fell ... and baby, they came down like rice at a wedding ... the world ripped the seat right out of its pants like a fat lady bending over and there was no seamstress that could hope to stitch it back up again.

Four months after the end, I was still there in Youngstown; hoping, I guess, that humanity would regroup and that we'd be able to put Humpty Dumpty back together again. That shows you how naïve I was.

I started thinking different when I first saw the worms.

There were corpses everywhere in the city, piled up on the sidewalks like garbage. There was radiation sickness, of course, but poor sanitation had led to rampant outbreaks of cholera, typhoid, and the plague. At first, the survivors buried the bodies, but after a while there were just so many that people started throwing them out into yards and dumping them on sidewalks. And all those rotting stiffs, well, they became disease vectors bringing in the rats and the flies which further spread the pestilence. The pathogens were in the water, blown on the air, and people continued to die.

And that's where I first saw the worms.

The parking lot of the 7-11 about two blocks from my apartment had been converted into a body dump for some insane reason. There were hundreds of corpses there broiling in the sun, exhaling clouds of flies and a hot, gaseous stench that would put you right down to your knees. I had found a box of untouched canned food at a Salvation Army depot, and I had to pass the body dump. When I did, I saw that the bodies were moving.

They were actually *moving*.

I thought at first it was the gas making them writhe and shudder, but that's not what it was at all. I stood there with my box of goodies, the hot stink blowing over me like breath blown from the throat of a corpse, and I saw a worm burst from the mouth of a stiff ... it was thick as my wrist, segmented, and slicked with something slimy like snot. It was flattened out like a tapeworm. It rose right up and hovered there like a cobra preparing to strike. It didn't have any eyes that I could see, but I swear to God it was looking at me. There was a bulb where its mouth should have been and it kept opening and closing as if it was breathing, the whole time dripping this black fluid like India ink.

I dropped my box of food, cans of beans and SpaghettiOs rolling around on the sidewalk.

That worm just hovered there like it was daring me to intervene. Then another worm slid out of a dead woman's green belly. Pretty soon they were all coming out like they needed to sun themselves. Some of them were no bigger around than fingers, but others were much larger. They came out of nostrils and eye sockets and assholes, slithering forth and rising up, all of them slimy and corpse-belly white.

They soon tired of me and went back to work. They started to eat, tunneling through that heaped carrion, sucking and slurping and chewing. Once they burrowed their way into a body, the buffet was open. That bulb or mouth would squirt some of that black juice into the corpse and the innards would liquefy. The juice was some sort of digestive enzyme, like what spiders inject into their prey—they'd squirt it in and then suck up the dissolved liquid.

It was sickening.

But what was even worse was that I saw a dozen worms slide up out of bodies and wrap themselves together in a fleshy helix. They coiled together like that, making some weird trilling sound, vibrating, a watery mucus enveloping them.

I think ... I think they were breeding and that's what made me run. Because, you see, that trilling sounded almost orgasmic to me, pleasurable.

But it was all part of our brave new world.

Even now, when I close my eyes, I can smell Youngstown. It had a special kind of stink that crawled up your nose and down into your belly, so that even with your eyes closed you knew you were in the city ... rotting garbage and burning wood, fuel oil and unburied bodies. I figured back then, that I should've bottled it, kept it on a shelf somewhere so that if the world ever started turning again, I could pop the cork anytime I was feeling low and take a whiff. Then I could say to myself, yeah, maybe your life sucks, but it don't smell like Youngstown.

After my wife died—a few months into the fun and games, about the time The Shape started whispering to me—I lived pretty much like a spider. I hunted the city, seeking out damp, dark corners and crevices where I could secrete myself, webby and lightless places where the roving gangs of scavengers and the packs of wild dogs couldn't find me. I became good at hiding and stalking and mainly because The Shape was in my head, telling me where to find food and shelter, which damp and dripping cellars were safe and free of rabid rat colonies.

Then one day while I was out searching for weapons (I wanted a machine gun), I got drafted. The Army or what was left of it found me and

I was pressed into service for my country. A half a dozen soldiers jumped me and that was that.

I was part of a clean-up crew.

We tooled around in garbage trucks picking up bodies. They decked us poor sonsofbitches out in white containment suits with helmets and we collected corpses and tossed them in the hoppers like Monday's trash.

The first time the guy with me pulled the lever and cycled the bodies through, when that hydraulic press crushed the bodies, compacting them, I threw up.

You stood there in those hot suits, flies buzzing around you and maggots dropping from your gloves, just filthy with all the revolting shit that oozed from the remains. And that was bad enough, but what was worse was hearing those cadavers compact. Even our helmets couldn't muffle the sound of dozens of putrefying corpses being crushed, bones snapping and flesh being squished to mush. Every time you cycled a load through, this black muddy ooze would run from the bottom of the hopper and rain to the street, squeezed from the corpses like pulp from tomatoes. And the smell of it ... dear God, it was almost more than you could take.

But you took it and mainly because you had no choice.

While we poor bastards tossed bodies in the hopper, the soldiers would keep their guns on us. You tried to break out, tried to run, and they'd cut you right down, throw you right in the back with the stiffs. They were crazy. I saw guys get shot and thrown in the hopper while they were still alive. I remember the looks on their faces when the soldiers made us cycle them through, compact them with the rest of the carrion.

Jesus.

When the honey buckets were full, we'd drive them outside the city to the dump, empty our load in immense body pits where they were burned. A mile from the dump, you could see clouds of black smoke rising into the sky, smell the cremated flesh and burning hair. It was like standing downwind from the ovens at Treblinka.

I worked the truck for two weeks and that's how I met Specs.

He was just a green kid with oversized glasses and a bad lisp. The soldiers were really hard on him, shoving him around and beating him. One night I got sick of it. I broke a bottle over the head of our sergeant—this delusional, psychotic prick named Weeks who thought we had been invaded by aliens—picked up his M-16, and cut down three soldiers with it. Then me and Specs ran. We found a truck and headed for Cleveland.

And Cleveland was just like Youngstown, it turned out.

Maybe worse.

But that's where The Shape told me we had to go. So, we went. In Cleveland they had a real bad rat problem, even worse than Youngstown. At night, hordes of them would come up out of the sewers and cellars and take to the streets in massive swarms like driver ants, devouring anything in their path. They were all rabid and incredibly vicious. By moonlight, you could see them down there, so many greasy gray bodies that you could have crossed the street walking on their backs and never once touched pavement. I saw them take down dog packs and street gangs, leave nothing but bones behind them.

Cleveland also had Red Rains.

I don't know what caused them exactly, but I figured they were like an acid rain—charged with fallout, blood-red, and incredibly corrosive. You got caught out in one and the drops would burn holes right through you.

Specs and I spent a month there, hiding from the gangs and the rats and the Children, of course. I can't explain them adequately either, but the same radiation saturation that killed adults by the hundreds of thousands did something else to the kids. And not just certain ones, but *all* kids, anyone under ten years of age for whatever reason, but none older than that. Maybe the onset of puberty made them biochemically infertile for the change. But under ten, well, it mutated something in them, turned them into deranged night stalkers with yellow luminous eyes and fingers that would actually burn you to a cinder if they got hold of you. They hunted by night like vampires in packs, killing anything they could catch. I think somehow, maybe because they were young and still growing, their cells had absorbed the fallout, made it part of their natural rhythm. I don't know. Only that they were monsters. If you put a bullet in them, they'd literally burn up like atomic piles right in front of you.

It was bad. Real bad. I'd heard that pregnant women were being killed on sight by gangs to avoid any more Children being born.

It didn't bode well for humanity's future given that the next generation were hideous mutations.

So, you get the picture: with the rats and the Children, you had to be wary if you went out by night.

Cleveland was where I also met up with Janie. Sweet, wonderful Janie. She was almost twenty years younger than me and for some reason, she took to me and fell in love with me. I figured in the old world, she wouldn't have looked twice at me even if I'd been her own age, but it was a new world with a whole new set of expectations and priorities and Janie had changed with it.

Anyway, it was Specs and me and Janie then. I told them both about The Shape, how it had been whispering in my head, leading me around by the nose. Janie didn't seem surprised, and Specs? Oh, he believed, all right. He was into all that new age shit, crystals and astrology and you name it. So, when The Shape told me that I owed it something, that it wanted a sacrifice, Specs went along with it. Hell, he was excited about it. Janie said nothing. Nothing at all. Those sad green eyes were on me like I was some kind of animal, but that was about it.

Me and Specs did it.

Specs had read lots of books about witchcraft and Satanism and all that high, happy horseshit, so it all came natural to him. We grabbed some old man, tied and gagged him, then dragged him into a vacant lot one night and tied him to a clothesline post. We piled wood all around him in a big heap and then we lit him up. Specs said it was expiation, that we had to make a burnt offering and that would keep The Shape happy and on our side.

It was horrible.

The old man died screaming, lit up like a candle. I saw his eyes actually boil out of his head and his skin superheat like wax and run off the skeleton into the flames. When he was smoldering, I told The Shape to come and get him. That was the first time it ever appeared to us, took on physical form. It took our offering and when it was done with the old man, it told me it wanted something fresh and alive next time.

A month went by and The Shape appeared again on the night of the full moon. I didn't have anything to give it, so it told me to make a choice. Either Specs or Janie.

So I gave it Specs.

And I've been making selections for it ever since.

3

"Let's just do this," I said.

We walked down the empty, leaf-blown streets of Bitter Creek and I knew we weren't alone. We were being watched and it wasn't by The Shape, even though I could feel my significant other getting nearer. It was funny, but I could actually feel it, feel The Shape out there: in my guts and along the back of my neck like a hand coming out of the darkness. You know how it is: you don't need to see it to know it's there.

Regardless, we were being watched.

I could feel it just fine. I didn't know if the others could. There was someone out there. I just hoped that whoever it was, they were human. Because you couldn't always tell anymore. The end had brought things into being that had no right to exist and it had changed others to absolute nightmares. That was the world these days. Like something Roger Corman had envisioned back in the fifties … mutants and roving gangs, religious crazies and nature run wild.

We came to a town square. Lots of brick-fronted businesses with dusty windows, simple frame houses spread out beyond. The lawns were all yellow and overgrown, the streets plastered with wet leaves. A Mobil station, a video store, a bowling alley, a café … it could have been any of a thousand towns in the country. They were all laid out approximately the same: Main Street or Elm or whatever as a hub, everything else radiating out from it like the spokes of a bike tire. Same old, same old. Just another dismal little town filled with death. They all smelled the same: a pungent yellow smell of age and decay and memory sucking into itself. The moldering smell of a library filled with rotting books … except it wasn't the books that were rotting.

As we walked, sensing the place, letting it fill us like poisoned blood, Janie kept looking at me. I pretended I wasn't aware of it. But eventually, I looked over at her and those green eyes of hers were blazing. Hate? Anger? No, maybe something like disappointment. Those eyes seemed to say, *maybe I love you, Rick, but maybe I just feel sorry for you.*

But there was no time for that shit.

We all had our guns out and we were feeling tense. There was a thickness in the air, the sense that although maybe we were the only ones wading through this particular stream, there were others watching us from the grassy banks, just biding their time, studying us.

About that time, Mickey stopped and cocked her head. "I feel ... I feel like I'm being watched," she said.

Janie sucked in a breath. Maybe I did, too.

"That's just me," Carl said. "I've been watching your ass is all."

"Shut up," she said.

Mickey was an interesting girl.

Maybe she'd never be invited into Mensa or win the Nobel Prize for physics, but what she lacked in book smarts she more than made up for in intuition. Unlike Janie who was petite and fair and porcelain-doll pretty, Mickey was tall and dark and long-limbed. She was pretty, too, but in a blatantly sexual sort of way. She had the curves and the legs, the high tits, the big dark eyes and full lips. The kind of girl who could talk about eating a salad and make it sound positively sensuous and carnal, make you want to dash out and fuck your hand. Here was a girl who'd gotten along on her looks her entire life. She knew what men liked, and she knew she had it. But before you go thinking she was some empty-skulled bimbo, let me say that Mickey was intuitive as all hell. She could read people, she could read situations. And she wasn't liking this one at all.

Morse, of course, seeing her standing there looking darkly beautiful and haunted like she did when she was sensing something, snapped a picture of her. Mickey didn't even flinch. She'd had lots of pictures taken of her in the old days and in most of them she hadn't worn much more than a thong. Sometimes less.

We moved through the streets very slowly, trying to pick up on what was watching us. Outside a little drug store, we found two bodies. *Children.* They were curled up on the sidewalk, reduced to husks like the remains of those snakes you burn on the Fourth of July ... wiry and blackened, crumbling. When Carl nudged one with his boot, it fell apart like cigarette ash. I'd seen it before. Sometimes, the Children just decayed like isotopes, burned themselves up from the inside out.

We kept moving.

And still those eyes watched us.

"Rick," Mickey said, gripping the Glock nine she carried in both hands like a cop on a shooting range, "I'm getting a really, really bad feeling here."

Even Carl didn't have a smartass response for that.

Morse scanned the streets with his telephoto lens, humming under his breath. Janie looked at me and I looked at her. Maybe I was about to take charge like a true leader, maybe I was about to rally my troops, but something happened.

A door slammed.

We all jumped.

Then we went after it. We cut down an alley and came out on another tree-lined street. Houses, buildings, and then a little ma-and-pa lunch counter at the end. I saw movement behind the plate glass windows and went after it. Inside, it was typical—flyspecked windows, a long counter, and lots of empty tables. Everything dusty and wreathed with cobwebs.

And a girl.

She couldn't have been more than eleven or twelve. She just sat there in a booth like she'd been waiting for us. She was out in the daytime, so I knew she wasn't one of the Children.

"Hey," I said. "What are you doing here?"

But she wouldn't answer me.

She was dressed in rags that might have been jeans and a sweatshirt once. Her face was grimy, her red hair clotted with filth. She stank like she hadn't had a bath in months, had been pissing and shitting herself. And judging from the dark stains at her crotch, I think she'd been menstruating, too. No matter. The Shape liked 'em seasoned.

"Take her," I told Carl.

Carl liked that bit. Liked charging into places and forcing innocents down, tying them up. Probably some unconscious storm trooper fantasy he'd been carrying since he was a boy. No matter, he handed his shotgun to Morse and went over to the girl.

"You got a name, sunshine?"

She just looked up at him, her eyes dull and bovine. He put the questions to her about who had survived and where they were and what she was doing alone. She just kept staring, though, either an idiot or mad or simply made that way by the world pissing down its own leg and leaving her stranded in a dead town.

Carl wanted to use his hands on her. He wanted to beat on her until she started begging him not to. That was the way Carl was. He was violent and possibly even sociopathic and he fit seamlessly into the skein of our big bad new world. Really, though, it was probably just frustration. A need to share some of the pain and horror inside of him.

He slapped the kid, warming up. "Talk, you fucking cunt," he said.

But she didn't even make a sound. He might have been striking a rump roast thawing on the counter.

"Stop it!" Janie said. "She's just a child! Don't you dare hit her!"

Carl drew back his hand to start again, but I shook my head and he stopped. He shrugged, grabbed the girl by her hair and threw her to the floor. He planted a knee in the center of her back and dug some duct tape from his bulging pack, taped her wrists together behind her back. She did not fight. She did not struggle. When Carl was done, he yanked her to her feet.

"Rick?" he said. "Request permission to piss all over this wench so she smells a little better."

Morse took a picture of her.

"Request denied," I said.

Well, we had ourselves a little treat for The Shape and that yanked our asses out of the fire once again. You probably think I'm some kind of beast, some kind of degenerate freak doing the things I did. Gathering up innocents for this thing I keep talking about. But that just shows that you don't know shit, you don't understand how it was after the world went fucking *boom!* But I guess if you're reading this, then you know all about it just fine.

I didn't have a choice, you see.

I made these sacrifices (go ahead, call it that if you want), I did the selecting, and I did it not only to save my sorry ass but the asses of my little posse. We took care of The Shape and The Shape took care of us. We were healthy. We weren't riddled with sores and radiation burns like the others. There was no disease in our bodies and our genes weren't going crazy from fallout. The Shape led me on, always pointing me in the right direction and I always found a few treats for him and, in return, we were alive and we were strong, we always had full bellies, safe places to lay our heads at night. No, I don't know how it worked. Not really. Only that being in league with that thing gave us all a sort of protective magic.

But did I like it?

Did I get off making offerings to that monstrosity?

No, I did not. The guilt was rotting me from the inside out. My dreams were sweaty, disturbing ... goddamned ugly if you want to know the truth: people lined up, people I knew and didn't know, people I'd admired and, yes, even loved, all waiting for me to decide who lived and who died. I'd wake up seeing their eyes, accusing and hating. I felt like a guard at Birkenau or Belzec, deciding who went to the gas chamber and who didn't. You think that was easy to live with? That it didn't eat my guts out? You can't do what I did without losing part of yourself, and after I'd been doing it for a year, I couldn't honestly remember the sort of person I'd been before.

But I didn't do it alone.

Mickey and Morse, Carl and Janie were there, too. We were like soldiers doing a really terrible job. We just didn't talk much about it. It made things go down easier that way. I had a lot of graves out there on my conscience, a lot of ghosts trying to claw their way out, and, man, I had to keep them down. Somehow, I had to.

"All right," I said to my troops. "Let's take five."

"We gonna grill this bitch up tonight?" Carl said, giving the girl a little push.

"We'll see," I said.

"Full moon tomorrow night," Mickey told us.

And that's when it would happen. That's when I'd call The Shape up. It was the only night he'd show and if I didn't have some goodies for him, he'd take us. I knew that because he told me so with that scratching, metallic voice in my head.

So tomorrow night we'd make our offering. Oh yes, there was no doubt about that. Because I was feeling The Shape out there getting closer and closer like a noose being slid around my neck and I wasn't waiting for the trapdoor to open beneath me.

"I need to sit down a minute," Mickey said, dropping into a booth and crossing her long bronze legs, making sure I saw her do it.

I did.

And Janie saw me looking, too.

Now that we had found our lamb of sacrifice, I think we all relaxed a bit. We had a safety buffer and the drive wasn't so strong. Mickey and Carl began looking around the café for food, anything we could use. But it had all been picked over pretty thoroughly and what was left behind, the rats and mice had gotten into. We found some dry spaghetti and a few cans of pork and beans, but that was about it. I was tired so I sat there and had a smoke, feeling sorry for myself *and* the shell of the world at the same time. I was looking at the big picture and seeing us and all the other scattered bands as insects crawling over the rotting cadaver of some dead beast. I think, essentially, the analogy worked.

Janie kept giving me these caustic looks, and once again, I pretended I didn't see her. I pulled off my cigarette and thought about all the things I missed. Fresh food, TV, and motorcycles came to mind right away. There were bikes around, but most of them were either wrecked or in pretty bad shape. All the dealerships had been looted after law and order collapsed. People being people had helped themselves to all those little extras they'd never been able to afford. It was tough finding good vehicles, too. Most cars and trucks were either smashed-up out on the roads, abandoned and rusting, or had been stripped of useable parts. You'd see a lot of that. Really nice pick-ups, SUVs, and sports cars sitting around on flat tires with shattered windshields, engines stripped or destroyed. Oh, there were plenty of drivable rides out there, but the people who had them also had guns. Lots of times, you'd just find cars with skeletons in them.

In Omaha, we'd found lots of skeletons like that, some in cars and some just lying right out in the streets. Crazy thing was, none of them had skulls. Which either meant some nut job was collecting them or something else had decapitated those people while they were still alive. Either way, we didn't want to run into whoever or whatever was doing the collecting. Because you just never knew what you might find in those urban graveyards.

"Okay," I finally said. "Break's over."

We all got to our feet and right away, I was feeling that same old bit again, that we were being watched. I just couldn't shake it. It wasn't The Shape and it wasn't that girl, so then what?

Mickey looked over at me, telling me with her eyes that she was feeling it, too. And then I heard a thudding report out in the streets and it took me almost a split second to realize it was the bark of a rifle.

4

A hole opened in the plate glass window.

We all dove down, except the girl and Morse. Christ, stupid harmless Morse. Now he wasn't a fashion photographer doing spreads for *Newport News* and *Spiegel's*, no, now he was a combat photographer. As those rounds chewed into the dusty windows and they fell apart like candy glass, shattering among us, Morse just stood there with his Nikon to his left eye, working his telephoto and f-stop, trying to get a good shot for *Newsweek* or *Time*.

I yelled for him to get down.

I don't remember what I said, something about getting his fucking head down, and then there was another report and a slug caught him right in the telephoto. Lucky shot or really good aim, I didn't know. But I saw the camera fly apart, blood and meat blasting out the back of his skull. He folded up and died without saying a word. People started shouting and I told them to shut the hell up. Somebody out there had a long-range rifle, maybe a .30-30 or a .30.06, and all we had was close-in stuff. We needed those bastards to come to us.

Silence.

No sound out in the streets and none in the café. After a few moments, I heard a couple voices calling out there. Sounded like kids, teenagers maybe. We stayed put, drawing them in. And they came, all right, muttering among themselves. I whispered for the others to get ready and I rose up behind one of the booths so I could get a look. I saw maybe a half-dozen kids and some older guy with a rifle. They didn't bother sending out a scout; they came towards the café in a group.

"Get ready," I whispered.

Mickey had her Glock and Carl had his Remington pump. Janie, of course, wouldn't touch firearms. But she wasn't exactly a pacifist: she had a big butcher knife and I knew she wasn't afraid to use it if she had to.

I watched those peckerwoods converge on the diner.

They were quite a crew. All long-haired and so filthy you couldn't tell if they were boys or girls. They carried pipes and axe handles and baseball bats. From the stains on them, I figured they knew how to use them, too.

The older guy kept his rifle up, urging the others forward. As they made to climb through the shattered windows, we came up shooting. We drilled three of them before the others even knew what happened. The old guy started busting caps and killed one of his own rat pack, but did no other damage. We kept shooting and pretty soon they were all down. Even the old guy. Mickey had jacked a couple rounds into his right kneecap and he was done.

Carl hopped out there first, kicking the rifle away.

I followed with Mickey behind me. A couple teenagers were still alive, vomiting out blood into the street. They smelled so bad and were so dirty, even Janie wasn't rushing to their rescue. They looked like Neolithic savages, filthy and bruised and pockmarked, their teeth rotting from their mouths. The air stank of gunpowder, violent death, and voided bowels.

Carl was kicking the old guy when I got there.

I told him to stop. The old man was going to be another selection along with the girl and I didn't want him dying until the time came. Mickey had done quite a job on his knee. It was blasted to mucilage, one of the bones sticking right through his pant leg like the end of a shattered Pepsi bottle.

"Filth! Trash! Fucking garbage!" he yelled at us. "Y'all ain't nothing but trash and dirt and cunting animals, that's all you is!"

"Shut the fuck up," I told him.

But he wouldn't, so Carl booted him upside the head and put his lights out. Then he taped his hands in front of him so he could crawl, because he sure as hell wasn't going to walk. The teenagers were dead except for one boy, who'd been grazed by a bullet. We bound and gagged him, too. The Shape was going to like the table I set.

Mickey came over and wiped some dirt from my cheek. You should have seen how she did it. She licked her fingertip and then drew it real slow over my cheek.

She wanted me and I suppose I wanted her, too. I mean, really, how could a guy not want Mickey? She was a pin-up girl, a centerfold. She had the tits and the ass and the legs, was darkly pretty and seductive. You could just imagine how many guys had whacked-off over pictures of her in magazines. She was so hot a picture of her in your pocket would have burned a hole in your pants and started a brushfire in your crotch.

But the truth was, she scared me.

She really did.

While Janie always turned her head when I called up The Shape and it took its sacrifices (that word again), Mickey liked to watch. She really liked to watch. Death and violence got her off. Maybe it always had or maybe it was something the end of civilization had unlocked in her. I didn't know, but I was certain that she had some seriously scary psychosexual issues. She not only liked to watch The Shape take its offerings of meat and blood, she liked shooting people. She liked looking at the aftermath of bodies and shattered anatomies.

And right then, looking down at those dead and dying teenagers, she was getting off. Her nipples were standing hard against her t-shirt and I was willing to bet that if I slipped my hand down the front of her cut-offs, I could have slid two fingers into her without much trouble.

She was looking from the bodies to me, the hunger all over her. She looked like she wanted to take a bite out of something or have something take a bite out of her.

I guess it was scary what the total collapse of society brought out in people, all those nasty things they had suppressed so carefully.

Carl went out scouting for a vehicle and I stood watch over our prisoners, making them face the wall so I didn't have to look at them. Janie wasn't talking to me. She always got like that when she knew a selection had been made. She'd draw into herself, wouldn't talk to anybody or look at anybody. She'd get that look about her like she was going into a trance or something. I knew she had trouble with taking lives and giving them to The Shape, but there wasn't a choice. At least, not one that I was willing to make.

Mickey and I smoked cigarettes and she remarked clinically about the condition of Morse's head. She kept talking about the shoot-out, about those kids going down under our guns. The more she talked about it, the more excited she seemed to get. I was about three feet away from her and I could feel the heat coming off her, hot blood making her skin damp.

Janie was lost in her own little world.

She wandered out into the street, arms folded over her chest, eyes glazed and unfocused.

"Janie," I said. "Stay here, don't …"

"Oh, let her go, Rick," Mickey said. "She needs to clear her head. You know how she gets."

I did, but I didn't want her wandering around out there alone. I hoped Carl would get back so he could keep an eye on her. But Janie's safety wasn't the only reason I didn't want her taking off; mainly it was that I had a pretty good idea of what Mickey was going to do when she was out of earshot.

5

It didn't take long.

I smoked my cigarette and watched the streets and Mickey kept talking about how our slugs had drilled into those teenagers, how Carl's shotgun had torn two of them literally in half. She was really getting off on the idea, her voice low and husky and breathless.

Finally, she set her gun down and came up behind me. So close I could smell the musk coming off her flesh. That heat she was throwing was almost enough to make me swoon. Before I could slip away, she put those long fingers of hers on my shoulders and started to knead the muscles there, working them expertly.

"You have to relax, Rick," she breathed at my neck. "You're stiff."

She massaged me for maybe another five minutes and then came around front. I pulled her to me and tasted her lips, felt her tongue slide in my mouth. We were wrapped together like that I don't know how long, licking and tasting. Then I was kissing her neck and tasting the salty heat of her skin.

"C'mon," she finally said.

We slipped behind the counter and into the kitchen itself at the rear. I pulled her t-shirt off and pressed my face into the valley between her large, upturned breasts. Her nipples were erect like pegs and I kept sucking them while she squirmed and gasped. Then she pushed me away and stepped out of her cut-offs. She put her ass up on a counter and slid an index finger into herself, working herself rapidly, arching her back and shaking violently. She made herself come and then she fell to her knees, almost tearing open my pants as she got my cock out. I was already hard. She took me in her mouth, bobbing up and down until I couldn't take it anymore.

I pulled her up and lifted her onto the counter. I handled her roughly and she liked it.

"Yeah," she said. "Oh please, Rick, oh I need it...."

I grabbed her by the hips and pressed those long bronzed legs up until her knees were at her shoulders and then I rammed into her. She came again almost instantly. I pumped into her as fast as I could, just pounding on her because it's what I wanted and what she needed.

What can I say? I betrayed Janie and probably myself, but I never hesitated. I just kept violently thrusting into Mickey and she was just wild with it. She came again and again, the whole time squealing and hissing and telling me to fuck her hard, practically shouting it. I had been sleeping with Janie for some time, but it had never been like this with her. Janie was too refined, too cultured. But Mickey was an animal, grunting and tearing into my back with her nails, begging for me to keep doing it.

And when I told her I was going to come, she wanted it to be in her mouth.

So that was Mickey. A fantasy girl. My private porno queen willing to do anything and everything to make me happy.

Of course, sooner or later, somebody had to show up.

As it turned out, it was Janie.

About the time my swollen penis slid out of Mickey's mouth, Janie showed. At least, that's when I saw her.

"C'mon, Janie," Mickey said. "There's always room for one more."

I thought Janie would burst. She went about three shades of red and told Mickey she was nothing but a fucking whore, a fucking slut, and Mickey agreed completely with her, laughing about it.

It was quite a scene.

But I learned something about Mickey. She'd wanted me because I did the selecting and I had the power; that got her off. But that wasn't all. What turned her on just as much was the idea of destroying what was between me and Janie. Things like that made Mickey's blood run hot.

I zipped myself up and Janie came right at me with murder in her eyes. She came within about two feet of me and I was glad she wasn't carrying that knife. "You're a rotten piece of shit, Rick."

"Janie, I ..."

But she wouldn't hear it. "You're no different than all the rest! Just a lying, slimy, useless fucking piece of shit! Oh, I was stupid enough to think you were different, that you were special, but I was just fucking stupid.

You're no good! God, how the hell could you do this to me?"

And what could I say? I felt so low I could have hidden under a rock without stooping. Christ, Janie was good and special and I had shit on her. I was trash. Maybe I always had been, but at that moment I knew it to be true.

"Janie," I said. "Just wait now, just wait."

"Wait for what?" She was sounding very calm, very in control and that was the worst part. "Wait for you to do this again? Oh no, that won't happen. I've done a lot for you, Rick, things you can't even imagine or won't because of that colossal ego of yours. But those days are over."

She turned away and I made to grab her arm and it was like taking hold of something serpentine and muscled and savage. She swung around, screaming and scratching at my face. *"Get your fucking hands off me! You don't ever touch me, you never ever touch me! Not again!"*

I backed away, literally scared.

Even Mickey wasn't smiling then. She was just kneeling there still, naked and glistening with sweat, her impressive bosom rising and falling with her respiration.

"And you," Janie said to her, acid in her eyes, "you aren't even worthy of living. Have your fun, you little tramp, because your number is almost up."

And then she stomped away and that ugly little scene wound itself out. Carl came back then, just as Mickey was pulling her clothes on. He looked from her to me and burst out laughing.

"You put it in her ass, Rick? That's what she likes best."

"Fuck you," I said.

Well, the tension was a little high after all that, as you can imagine. But there was nothing really to do but to keep pushing on, find a safe place for the night and then when the full moon came tomorrow night, give The Shape what it wanted and breathe a sigh of relief that we had another month to relax.

Janie had stopped speaking to me, of course.

I caught her eyes once and quickly looked away. I'd never seen such hate and malevolence in them before. Finally, ultimately, I'd shown my true colors and now she despised me. Totally despised me. Maybe it was for the best. Although deep down I was shattered, I knew that Janie deserved something better than a slug like me.

I had slept with both girls now, Janie repeatedly.

Trust me; it was no notch on my belt. Because it was always there in the back of my mind, that dread question of what I would have to do if either of them became pregnant. Because if the stories were true, babies always became like the Children and usually right away. *Monsters.* Sometimes they came right out of the womb like that, literally burning their way out and killing their mothers in the process.

Could I let Janie suffer like that?

And better, would I have the balls to put her down if and when it happened?

6

Night.

We holed up in a little sporting goods store and just waited for dawn. There were lots of supplies in there we could use. Sleeping bags and ammunition, military MREs and boots. It was picked over, but not badly. It was a good place to wait out the darkness. Defensible and set back away from the street. If anything or anyone tried to get at us, we'd see them just fine in the moonlight and the street outside would make an excellent kill zone.

I pulled up a chair before the window, cradling the old man's bolt-action .30.06 in my lap. I figured there wasn't much Bitter Creek could throw at me that I couldn't cut down with that.

I was sitting watch. Carl was snoring in the back room with our prisoners. Mickey and Janie were sleeping, too, but on opposite ends of the store. My little band was a little dysfunctional before, but now it was completely splintered and it was my fault. I don't think Janie ever really liked Mickey, but they had a working relationship, they were united to keep us alive, but now that was gone. I could feel the bad vibes smoldering between them. That fire had been waiting to burn for some time and now I had handed it all the kindling it needed. When it finally burned out of control, it was going to be big and nasty and consuming. I figured one of the girls would be burned beyond recognition and maybe me and Carl, too.

Damn.

There was nothing to do but watch that empty, waiting street. Now and then I'd lean forward up against the glass and see the moon above the roofs of the town. It was not quite full, but damn close—round and fat and leering like a yellow eye, its gaze painting the buildings a phosphorescent yellow.

It reminded me of when I was a kid.

There was an older girl named Mary LaPeer who had flowing dark hair and brilliant blue eyes. I was just absolutely in love with her. Mary had a telescope and on warm summer nights she'd take it out in the backyard and look at the moon and stars, sometimes until one or two in the morning. I'd watch out my window, my heart beating with a slow and expectant roll, waiting for Mary to come out. When she did, I'd slip out the window and join her. Mary showed me the moon and Mars and the Crab Nebula one time, but no heavenly body she showed me burned brighter than the stars in my eyes when I looked at her and listened to her talk about the rings of Saturn or the misty yellow orb of Venus.

Mary was five years older than me. She was into science fiction, particularly Robert Heinlein. She used to give me books by him to read— *Red Planet, Starman Jones, The Star Beast,* and *Podkayne of Mars.* I treasured them and read them to pieces.

I was infatuated with her until the day she graduated high school and moved away, off to college. On that day, I cried and cried because I knew I'd never see her again and I didn't. Even now the memory of that pained me. I never forgot those summer nights or the crickets chirping, the soft whisper of Mary's voice and the Milky Way spread out over the sky, Mary telling me that one day, she and I would travel out there together.

Corny as hell, I know. But I believed it and I liked to think on those starry nights, Mary did, too.

Sitting there at the window, peering off into the graveyard of the world, that moon poised above, I remembered Mary and missed her and wanted to sob. Maybe I lost myself in my memories too much, because I think I drifted off.

And when I woke, there was someone out in the street.

I nearly fell right out of my chair. I blinked my eyes a few times to see if I was imagining things, but I wasn't.

There was a girl standing out in the street looking right at me.

She was like a wraith that had burst the gates of her tomb, thin and ragged and flyblown. And that's when I knew she wasn't a girl at all.

She was one of the Children.

I think I tried to call out to the others, but my mouth went all rubbery like I'd just gotten a shot of Novocain in the gums. I made a sound, but not enough for anybody but myself to hear. I just sat there stiffly like something whittled from a log. Maybe I thought if I played dead, pretended I wasn't alive, then that awful little girl out there would just go on her way. But no dice.

She saw me.

She knew I was there. Maybe she saw me move or maybe she smelled me, tasted the fear rising from me and decided she wanted more. In the dappled moonlight, I could see her just fine—the colorless hair falling to her shoulders, the gray skin and horribly seamed face that looked more like an African fetish mask than human features, something worked with a knife and chisel. Her eyes were yellow and incandescent, sunk deep into exaggerated bony orbits like candles burning from the depths of mineshafts.

Breathing hard, the spit dried up in my mouth, I brought up the .30.06 with what I thought was a careful, confident motion. But the truth was that my hands were shaking so badly, I could barely hold onto the damn thing.

The girl out there had not come any closer.

She stood her ground and I stood mine.

I had to shoot her. I had to put her down. I had to spray the irradiated filth in her skull all over the pavement and I had to do it soon. Because whether it was out and out telepathy or something biochemical, when one of them knew where you were, they *all* knew.

But I hesitated.

I knew Carl wouldn't have and probably not Mickey either. But even after all I'd seen and done, the various encounters I'd had with these little ghouls, I was still human enough where the idea of killing a child—or something that had once been a child—turned my guts.

A voice in my head that did not belong to The Shape, but was probably simple old instinct told me, *Look at that fucking thing, Rick, it's not human, it's not a child. It's gray and shriveled and embalmed-looking like something that crawled from a grave. It's walking meat, nothing more.*

283

Great advice. I brought up the gun and I was going to kill that thing because I knew I had to. As frightening as that child was, she was also somehow pathetic, more victim than victimizer even if she was lethal as the glowing rods pulled from a reactor core. At that moment, perhaps sensing my indecision, she brought up her hands, held them out palms up like some miserable waif begging for alms, for a couple dirty nickels to feed her starving siblings with.

Just do it, you idiot.

I sighted her in with the rifle, seeing her for what she really was: a monster. A seething, creeping horror from a pit of radioactive waste. Her eyes were a shiny translucent silver-yellow like shimmering opals planted in the sockets of a skull. There was nothing in them. They were flat and dead, voids filled with a blankness, a blackness that existed, perhaps, beyond the rim of the universe.

I hesitated too long.

Her hands fell away and then one came right back up, pointing at me and her oval mouth opened like the maw of a lamprey, moonlight winking off all those tiny hooked teeth. And she screamed ... a shrill, droning sound like a grasshopper in a summer field, but loud enough to make my ears bleed.

And the others started coming.

I heard Mickey and Janie stir, heard a commotion in the back room that I knew was Carl coming to do some killing.

I took aim again and put a round right into that little girl. It shattered the plate glass window and caught her right in the chest, throwing her back and down and spraying blood and meat twenty feet or more. It happened immediately to her as it always does with the Children: she began to burn up. It was as if whatever was stored up inside her went all at once, potential energy going kinetic. By the time she hit the pavement, about as dead as dead gets, she was already smoking like a bag of burning shit. Some crazy blue fire erupted from inside her and her flesh liquefied like hot grease, steaming and sputtering, her face sliding off the bone and her blackened skeleton trembling in the street for a moment, then crumbling away.

It happened that fast.

But by then, there were other Children.

I never saw where they came from. Maybe from under the rusting wrecks of cars or out of sewers and cellar windows, spilling from chimneys and skittering down the brick facades of buildings like spiders. No matter, they were in the street. A dozen of them with more on the way.

They ringed the front of the sporting goods store, chattering and squealing with delight, eyes shining and lamprey-mouths opening and closing like eels sucking air, skeletal fingers all pointing at me while each and every one of them made that high, keening noise that I knew meant, *there, there he is, one of the different ones, the alien in our midst, kill him, kill him, kill him....*

They started to close in, a ragged and emaciated band, heads tangled with matted hair and faces contorted and vicious.

"Motherfucker," I heard Carl say, "it's the goddamn brats again."

He kicked out what remained of the window and by then Mickey was at my side, her Glock nine in one hand and my Browning .45 in the other like some death-crazy Confederate guerrilla that wanted to die hard with smoking pistols in both fists.

The Children, maybe twenty or thirty of them, swarmed at us like insects, screeching and droning. I dropped three of them and Mickey wasted four others. Carl cut two of them nearly in half. It was sheer pandemonium, the dying ones sending up great clouds of ash and black smoke and the living ones pouring forth right over the tops of them.

But none of them made it through the volley of fire.

A few got within three or four feet of us before we blew them away, opening skulls and perforating chests, but that was about it. I put my last two rounds in the belly of a little boy and he actually stumbled and fell almost on top of me, impaling himself on a shelf of jagged glass, burning up right in front of me. Carl kicked his carcass back outside before we asphyxiated on the fumes.

And about the time the others started to pull away, the street out there blazing bright like the mouth of a crematorium, somebody hit us from behind. I heard Janie cry out and then somebody knocked me and Carl aside. The next thing I knew, the girl we'd captured in the café was diving through the window, rolling across the sidewalk and coming up on her feet. Carl reloaded and was about to put her down, but he didn't get the chance.

A half-dozen of the Children fell on her, taking her down effortlessly, putting their hands all over her and suctioning themselves to her with those sucking mouths. The girl screamed and shook, but she couldn't throw her riders. They clung on, incinerating her, reducing her to a smoldering, insane thing that vomited out loops of cremated entrails.

We shot through her to get the Children.

And then they were all blazing and smoking and writhing, curling up and sputtering like bacon on a hot skillet. One of them broke free in its death agonies and shambled maybe five or six feet in our direction, then collapsed to the sidewalk, shuddering and flaking away, finally puking out some black and bubbling mass before going still.

And that was it.

We'd survived another attack by the Children. We just stood there, gasping and shaking, twenty or more of the little ghouls lying in the street, fused into some blackened, steaming mass of bones and bodies.

"Those are some mean little shits," Carl said.

"We better get out of here," Janie said, refusing to view the carnage. "Those bodies are radioactive waste now."

We went down into the cellar and waited for dawn.

There wasn't much else we could do.

7

The next afternoon, Carl got lucky.

He found us a nice conversion van with beds in it and didn't have to kill anyone to get it. It was parked in somebody's garage, he said. We loaded up our stuff and our two remaining snacks for The Shape and got the hell out of Dodge. We drove about three or four miles outside of Bitter Creek and found a little federal campground. Carl and I got a fire going and Mickey heated up some canned food and we sat there, not saying a thing, just eating and avoiding looking at each other. Now and again, I'd look up and Mickey would be staring at me. And when she wasn't, Janie was. But while it was mostly lust in the former, in the latter it was hate so sharp it could have slit my throat.

It would be night again in five or six hours.

And then it would be time to call up The Shape.

It was getting hungry and I could feel it out there, gathering like an electrical storm, like a tornado that wanted to do some serious damage.

8

I suppose it's time to be straight on a few things.

Like The Shape for instance.

I keep alluding to it without being very specific. What is it? Where did it come from? That's what you want to know and that's exactly what I can't honestly tell you. But let me briefly sketch out the end of the world for you, put things into a loose sort of perspective.

Okay. It started with an exchange of nuclear weapons in the Middle East. Iran launched one against the Israelis and the Israelis responded in part. Maybe it could have stopped there, but the fuse had been burning a long time and it was just too late. Nukes were used in Africa and Asia, Europe. About thirty such weapons were used worldwide. Mutual assured destruction, just like they'd always said. Four of them were detonated in the continental United States—one in New York, one in Chicago, another in Atlanta, and the last in LA. The initial strikes killed fifty million people, the news said—when the stations were still broadcasting, that is. Resultant contamination killed another three million and fallout tripled that within six months. The funny thing was that all of the weapons used against the U.S. came from Russia just like it had always been prophesied. What was funny about that was that the Russians were only responding to three nukes exploded on their soil, only they fired back at the wrong country. The ICBMs that hit them were all from their own former republics.

Considering the madness of the time, it wasn't surprising.

Nukes were being fired by just about everybody in the wake of mass nuclear destruction. The United States, of course, responded by striking Russia seven times. Other weapons were launched from North Korea into China and vice versa. Africa and the Middle East were particularly hit hard by a variety of tactical nukes that killed millions as armies attempted to destroy armies and succeeded mainly in thinning the already teetering civilian populations. By the time it all came to an end, there was no more civilization as such. Just billions of people dying from fallout and rampant infectious disease.

And that, as you probably already know, is how the world ended. Not with a bang, but with a big motherfucking *BOOM!*

Like I said before, I was in Youngstown during all this.

My wife was dying of radiation poisoning and a cholera epidemic was sweeping thousands into the grave every week from poor sanitation that just wasn't poor, but nonexistent. That's where I was. Hiding in our apartment, waiting to get sick myself.

And that's when it happened.

I was sitting there one night by candlelight, barricaded in with my wife's corpse while the crazies roamed the streets below in wolf packs, killing and being killed, and I had decided to end it. I had a knife and I was going to lay my wrists open. I remember how depressed I was, how beaten and frustrated that the world had been ripped asunder by those fucking warmongers and politicians. I pressed the blade to my wrist and then I heard a hissing sound like a gas valve opening. And a voice, a clear and authoritative voice, said into my ear, *"Do you want to live? Do you want to thrive? Are you willing to do what it will take to assure these things?"*

That was The Shape.

I never saw it at the time, I only heard that voice telling me how it had to happen, how it all had to come down. You know the rest … how I was pressed into the clean-up gang and made my run with Specs and met up with Janie in Cleveland, how ever since that first sacrifice in Cleveland, I've been selecting.

But what is The Shape?

There was a very smart guy in Milwaukee that became part of my posse. His name was Price, and he'd been some sort of mathematician before the collapse of civilization turned him into a predator. He had a few theories on my friend. He said that The Shape was the ultimate cosmic chaos, something born of nuclear fission and plutonium saturation from the very blast furnace of creation. Something that was nothing until the radiation brought it into being, gave it body and mind and attitude, if you can dig that. A wraith essentially, a spook birthed from a thermonuclear womb, a supercharged flux of sentient radiation. A brand-new devil for a brand-new world.

Anyway, that's what he told me, and I guess it makes as much sense as anything else. A random series of particles that became organized and cohesive and organic (for lack of a better word) as a result of massive fallout. And let's face it, as crazy as that sounds, this particular bogeyman had been waiting to be born for a long time. All the raw materials were there in barrels of radioactive waste, the cores of atomic reactors, and stores of unstable isotopes. Just lying there waiting to be born. Much like the inorganic chemicals of Azoic earth had waited to become life.

I had always wondered why The Shape only showed on nights of the full moon. Sometimes I could talk to him—or it—in my head on other nights, but only on the nights of the full moon would he show for his latest meal. I figured it was all impossibly esoteric and mystical, something supernatural that my poor little brain could never hope to understand.

But Price had a theory on that, too.

In fact, there wasn't much that he *didn't* have a theory on. From female orgasms to the mating cycles of katydids, Price had a very definitive opinion. He was one of those guys that were just too smart for their own good. I tried to argue with him about a few topics, but that was a mistake. He made me feel like a striped ape wallowing in my own shit. He was a professional debater and he took me off right at the knees, leaving me feeling stupid and annoyed and goddamn uneducated. Annoyed mainly, because he never seemed to see me as an equal but as an object of amusement like a cute little puppy that had learned not to piss on the furniture, but hardly an intellectual equal.

Anyway, Price had a theory on the full moon bit, too.

And he gave it to me in the form of a lecture as always. He said that if you looked through the body of folklore and tradition concerning the moon—he had, of course—then you would see certain underlying principles that were intriguing. The moon, he said, had a history of inciting the human species. It drove men mad, it regulated the menstrual cycles of women, and was forever an object of religious significance. To many primitive societies, the moon was considered a goddess, the creator of time and space, the repository of human souls both dead and unborn awaiting reincarnation. This Moon Goddess ruled the cycles of creation and fertility and death, and this was why ancient calendars were very often based on lunar phases and the menstrual cycles of women which were nearly identical in duration. The moon ruled not only the tides, but human and animal life, rebirth and procreation. That's why Scottish girls at one time would only wed on a full moon and why certain crops could only be planted beneath its glowing eye. Witches were said to draw down the moon, to call up demons and familiars only on this blessed night.

But much of that was superstition, and yet, he told me, there was a germ of underlying truth to it all. For the geomagnetic pull of the moon had a decided impact on all living things and their individual electromagnetic fields and maybe it was at these times of greatest influence—the full-moon phase—that certain doors were open that might be closed on other nights. Maybe witches really did call down demons and nameless monstrosities and maybe those things were much like The Shape in origin and composition. The same geomagnetic forces that made crops and women fertile might also create an ideal environment for something like The Shape to physically manifest itself, exploiting cosmic and lunar energies to give itself substance.

Just a theory again, but I liked it.

Price was a smart guy, as I said.

I think he was dead right about not only the moon's influence, but about the nature of The Shape itself.

Figuring that all scientists and theorists liked to test their hypotheses, I gave Price the chance. I threw together a little controlled experiment of my own: I gave him to The Shape.

9

After we finished eating, there was nothing to do but wait.

It was an insufferably long day waiting for darkness to fall and the moon to rise so I could call up The Shape. I had done it more times than I'd like to admit, but each month, each full moon and what came with it, well, it filled my belly with needles. I couldn't relax. Couldn't do much of anything but wait for the rising moon. Maybe it was because I was afraid that one of these times, The Shape might not like what I offered, might not exactly care for the buffet I had spread and demand a little something more exotic and filling—all of us.

I didn't like doing it. I didn't like any of it. I was not proud of what I had become, a slave to that horror ... but what choice was there? I mean, without The Shape protecting us, how long would we have lasted? If the crazies or the mutated wildlife didn't get us, the Children would.

By sundown, we were all tense, I think.

Carl, as usual, sensed this and tried his damnedest to pump some life into the party by telling us dirty jokes. It didn't work. Janie was in a decidedly blue mood and Mickey was still horny and I just don't know what I was.

Mickey couldn't stop staring at me.

I could see what was in her eyes just fine. She knew that The Shape was coming and the very idea of that was like foreplay to her. After sacrifice was made, she wouldn't be able to control herself. She'd want to do some serious rutting. And she'd want to do it with me. Things in our little group were reaching critical mass, and there didn't seem to be a damn thing I could do to stop the explosion.

About the time I was ready to call up my old friend, Mickey came over. I was standing there, watching the light fading and feeling that sickness in my belly that always came just before The Shape showed. Mickey had been pulling off a flask of bourbon and maybe I should have stopped her. As it was, she came right over and tried to kiss me, grinding her pelvis into me. I told her to stop and the crazy bitch went right down on her knees right in front of the others, started trying to unzip my pants.

Carl started laughing.

Janie was livid.

"Stop it," I told Mickey. "That's enough."

"Don't you want your dick sucked, Rick?" Mickey asked me, just steaming with lust. "C'mon, let me suck your cock."

I shoved her away. As attractive as she was, I found her repellent at that moment. Like some bitch in heat, some animal that had no compunction about performing in front of a crowd.

"Please, Rick," she said.

"Knock it the hell off," I said.

But Carl was liking it. "C'mere, Mickey, I'll let you suck me off," he said, unzipping himself and pulling out his dick which was going erect even as we watched.

Mickey went right for it.

I mean, I know civilization had ended, but come on for Chrissake. Mickey went over there and started blowing him right in front of us. Carl was loving it, of course, and I was just speechless, and Janie? She was getting more offended, more pissed off by the moment.

Finally, she stood up, *"Enough! I've had enough of this shit! Do you hear me? I've had enough!"*

But Mickey's head was still bobbing and Carl was moaning and then, right at that particular moment, I felt something shift around us. The air went heavy, crackled with static electricity. There was a sudden thrumming sound and an overpowering stink of ozone.

The Shape was coming.

But I had not called it.

It rose up near the fire, a whirlwind of shrieking matter, black and buzzing, angry and spinning. An energized cloud of radioactive dust and debris and force. An elemental cloud of sentient electrons, wrath, destruction, and appetite. It was taller and wider than a man, a stink blowing off of it like fused wiring and melting steel, cordite and the breath from foundry ovens.

"Take ... take your selections!" I told it, absolutely terrified. I was always terrified when it showed. But more so now. I had not called it, I had not concentrated on its image and summoned it from the thermonuclear furnace of its birth.

It paused there, sparkling with flecks of luminosity and arcs of electricity. Two leering red eyes looked out from that storm of atomic refuse. The noise it created—like screeching metal and hurricane winds and bubbling cauldrons—was so loud you had to shout over the top of it. When it moved, that buzzing sound grew louder and its body envelope began to spin faster.

It was doing that now as it came in my direction.

At the last moment, as I screamed, I could feel the blazing, cremating heat of the thing and it was like standing too near a smelter full of molten steel. The Shape was still ten feet from me, but close enough to bake my skin and singe my eyebrows. I collapsed at that very moment. But at least I knew something. I knew what it had been like for those others, I knew the horror they must have felt as they were scalded and incinerated, kissed to ash and embers by that abomination.

But The Shape turned away from me, going right for our gagged and bound sacrifices. That poor, crazy old man and the boy could do nothing but watch it with wide, insane eyes as they were vacuumed into that living kiln, that pulsating nuclear reactor.

When The Shape takes them, it takes them fast.

They were sucked in, absorbed and leeched and disintegrated, vomited out the other side. When they were pulled in, The Shape lit up like phosphorus, like blazing witch-light. You couldn't see much when they were assimilated by the thing, but if you didn't look away, you could catch a few glimpses. Sometimes they flew apart like meat in a vacuum chamber and you saw blood and tissue, limbs and organs and I don't know what all spinning in that seething radioactive tornado. I think it actually took them apart at the subatomic level, particulating them, consuming their electromagnetic fields and the very bonds that held their molecules together.

When it had what it wanted—and, believe me, this took about ten seconds—it reassembled them, integrated them, and spewed them out the other side ... but never the way they went in: smoking, blackened heaps that were often anatomically altered. I'd seen arms growing out of backs and heads jutting from bellies, bodies reversed and rearranged from molecular dispersal and realignment.

And sometimes, when The Shape took two at once, they came out like what we were seeing: a steaming and sparking mess of melted wax with bones thrusting out in every which direction. The old man and the boy had had their atoms mixed like the fly and the scientist in that old movie. Their clotted mass cooled fairly rapidly. They had been fused into one, like plastic army men heated and squished into a common whole.

It was sickening and repulsive.

Mickey was staring in rapt fascination and Carl's dick had shriveled right out of her mouth. Janie just sat there, her eyes shining like quartz.

The stink of the bodies was horrendous and The Shape, of course, was enough to make you want to scratch out your eyes before you lost your mind. But what really disturbed me was that I had not called it. *Someone else had.*

I was no longer doing the selecting. And, trust me, my entire ego and mindset was wired into the power that selecting had given me. Suddenly, I was empty and small and weak. It was like waking up and discovering that your dick and balls had been removed, a little sign hung down there saying, *So sorry, friend*. Yeah, it was like that. But squared.

I was sitting there on my ass and watching Janie and that's when I knew. That's when I knew she was controlling the thing.

"Janie!" I shouted.

She looked over at me like I was something squirming and repellent that had crawled out of rotting meat. She hated me. She despised me. I had violated her trust.

"Are you surprised, Rick?" she said. "Are you really surprised? You never did the selecting, I did. I *always* did."

I knew it was true.

Yes, the thing had spoken to me in Youngstown, shown me how to stay alive and what to do. But it wasn't until I'd reached Cleveland and hooked up with Janie that it began to ask for selections. That's when all this really started with the sacrifice of the old man. I thought I had been behind it, Specs thought so, too, but we were both wrong. The Shape had led me to Janie because Janie had the power to raise it, and it knew Janie would not give it a sacrifice to save her own life, only to save others and, particularly, *me*. And she had done it many times, something abhorrent to *who* and *what* she was. She had done it because she had been in love with me.

She still was, except that love had been perverted now by my infidelity, turned into something vicious and demented.

The Shape took Carl and Mickey. It moved so fast they didn't even scream.

They were pulled in and disassembled, changed and slapped back together, spit out as a fused and burning mass. It actually takes longer to tell it than the actual experience. And when they were gone, Janie gave me a look of absolute malevolence, and then ... then she dove right into that whirlwind of devastation, that thing born of breeder reactors and atomic cremators, that living chain reaction of thermonuclear waste.

I screamed when she came out the other end, smoking and sizzling and popping.

The Shape, its belly full, weakened and phased itself out.

Then I was alone.

Absolutely alone.

10

I've been alone ever since.

That was two weeks ago and I've had to live with certain realities that wake me up sweating and shivering in the dead of night. One of them is that I was never, ever in control of The Shape. It was always Janie. Some sort of latent psychic gift, I suspect. Possibly hereditary. Who knows? The other is that, even now, it will not accept my selections. Yet, it will indeed come again this month as it has every month, but the only selection it will accept is me.

And that's Janie's revenge on me: the pain and terror and insanity of waiting for that nameless thing to show … because the waiting is the hardest part, just like Tom Petty said.

But that's all I can do.

Wait and remember Janie, how good she felt in my arms and how her face felt in my hands, how her skin always smelled of lilacs and sunshine corked in bottles. So, that's what I think of. Her face and her eyes, the way she felt when she was under me, her lips on mine and the smell of her hair. I know that I loved her and I know she loved me, but I also know what happens when a love like that is betrayed. It goes from tender warmth and mountain cool to a clean and savage

hate. A hate that is an acid that will dissolve all that I am and leave nothing behind but bobbing, polished white bones.

So, I wait.

I wait for The Shape.

I wait to be the final, and most deserving, selection.

ATOMIC HORRORS AFTERWORD

Like the man who just pushed the button bringing about nuclear annihilation, climatic devastation, and quite possibly the end of the human race, I ask myself why did I do it? Why did I write these stories? The research for them entailed delving into some seriously depressing subject matter, the worst of which being detailed accounts by survivors of Nagasaki and Hiroshima, whom the Japanese call *hibakusha*. It was some seriously harrowing stuff. I won't even get into the awful dreams I had when my head was full of this stuff.

The answer to my own question is that I wrote this book because A), it was suggested by my publisher and, B) because it would be hard to imagine a more horrible situation that would lead (in my fictional world) to the events in the stories.

When I was a kid back in the 1970s, before the Cold War was supposedly over, we watched a film (yes, an actual film threaded onto a projector) concerning nuclear war. It was probably pretty sanitized stuff, but it got into my imagination and I had a terrible nightmare where the sky was on fire. I never forgot it.

Not that it stopped me from watching every single 1950s atomic bomb movie I could find—*Panic in Year Zero, World Without End, The Day the World Ended* etc.—and those monsters brought forth by atomic fallout: *Them!, The Beast from 20,000 Fathoms, The Giant Behemoth, Godzilla* etc. I even watched non-monster movies like *On the Beach, Invasion, USA,* and *Kiss Me Deadly* (which had the most horrifying entity at the end, about as close as cinema has ever gotten to Lovecraft's *The Colour Out of Space)*. Later, I was traumatized like everyone else by *The Day After,* and particularly by two nasty British offerings, *The War Game* and *Threads.* The latter I watched again before I wrote these stories and it had lost none of its unsettling power.

And when I wasn't watching stuff like that, I was reading it. In comic books and in novels. When I was a teenager, I plowed through O'Brien's *Z is for Zachariah,* Frank's *Alas, Babylon,* and Zelazny's *Damnation Alley,* amongst a score of others. I should mention that if you've ever read my post-apocalyptic outlaw biker novel, *Cannibal Corpse, m/c,* that there's more than a little of Zelazny's Hell Tanner in my John Slaughter.

The problem with the movies, particularly the 1950s ones, is that they rarely lived up to their exploitive posters. Hence, these stories, that in one way or another have been fermenting in my imagination for a long time. So, here, if you're interested, is a bit about each story. Feel free to skip this if such things don't interest you.

"Furnace"—Well, this had to start somewhere. I wanted something that drew the reader into the horror of the situation and this works pretty well. I conceived (heh, heh) of The Abomination (anti-Christ, demon child, whatever you want to call it) being born at the same time the bombs came down. With that in mind, it was easy to write.

"Ground Zero"—I've always found so-called preppers and survivalists to be basically idiotic. Really, you're going to survive into *what?* The new stone age? Do you have any idea beyond your Chuck Norris fantasies what that's going to be like? I took one of those types whose head was messed-up from the war and was not exactly in touch with reality to begin with. He thinks he's a badass, but he has no idea how harmless he really is until he meets the father of survivors.

"King of Flies"—Well, here's another problem. You've survived, only the majority of the world's food supply is horribly contaminated. How long do you think you can live off canned food and MREs? Sooner or later, you're going to have to eat what's readily available. Particularly if you're trapped in a cellar, slowly starving to death and out of your mind from it.

"Rat Trap"—James Herbert's Rats Trilogy is one of my favorite guilty pleasures, particularly the second book, *Lair*. There was no way I could write about the aftermath of nuclear annihilation without bringing on some mutant rats. I like the idea of the rats being intelligent and trying to exterminate the surviving humans. Fun irony.

"Doll Parts"—Is it that hard to believe that one of the survivors might be a telekinetic with a warped brain and a mommy fixation? Well, maybe, but my graveyard puppet Adelia was a great epicenter for his degenerate world and those trapped in it.

"Black Widow"—Yeah, I'm not proud: I love mutant spider stories. The idea of Meyer's pregnant wife combining with a mutant spider in the nuclear wasteland appealed to me. And her children, her awful, awful children croaking like toads.…

"Worm Cast"—I've been fascinated by the world of hobos ever since reading William Kennedy's novel, *Ironweed*. They made a movie of it, too, but I like the book so much that I won't watch it because I'm sure they fucked it up. These people live in our world, yet they don't live in it at all. The idea of them surviving a nuclear war intrigued me. And being that they're hard drinkers, the possibility of a worm in a bottle occurred to me right off. A very special, radioactive worm.

"Fallout"—This is kind of the tear-jerker of the collection. I liked George and I liked Red. I liked their relationship. What the entity in the cloud did to poor Red was disturbing, but fun to write about. When something you trust turns to a monster, what do you do about it? You do what George did for the good of all: you kill the thing you love best.

"Coffin Birth"—I've been wanting to write this for years. The original idea I scratched in my notebook was called "Baby" and had the little monster attacking women, ravaging their wombs because such a thing gave him birth. I like this treatment of it better. It's a horror story, but black comedy at its core.

"Brain Death"—Like the rats, I knew I had to do a mutant brain story. The plot occurred to me as I read some brain stories from 1950s horror comics: "The Quivering Brain" and "The Brain-Bats of Venus." Both are very entertaining. Although monster brains are somewhat underrepresented in horror fiction, there's plenty of them in movies and old TV shows. For the former we have everything from the various versions of *Donovan's Brain* to *The Brain from Planet Arous* and the great *Fiend Without a Face* (I'd like to include that cinematic train wreck, *They Saved Hitler's Brain,* but, alas, they saved his whole head). The latter is well-represented by Roald Dahl's "William and Mary" on *Way Out* and *Tales of the Unexpected,* and "The Brain of Colonel Barham" on the original *Outer Limits.* Anyway, the preceding list gives you an idea of how screwy it is inside my head most days. I liked the idea of monster brains with wormy tendrils overwhelming their victims with a non-stop orgasm.

"Crabmeat"—Well, obviously, if I'm going to do brains and rats, I just had to do some crabs, via Guy N. Smith and Corman's *Attack of the Crab Monsters.* I read Smith's crab novels as a teenager and loved them. Corman's crab movie played again and again on Saturday afternoons during my grade school years, courtesy of Channel 50 from Detroit. I borrowed ideas from both, particularly Corman's crabs who absorbed personalities as well as flesh. That was the key to Vicki. I love that ending.

"Bride of the Termites"—I remember watching a nature documentary where they went inside the walls of a termite-infested mansion in Louisiana with tiny cameras. It was horrible. The queen was a great swollen bag of eggs. So fat and pregnant that the workers dragged her around until her limbs had become vestigial things that were worn away. Her abdomen was palpitating with the horrid, squirming life inside it. Yeah, there was definitely a horror story there and it jumped into my mind when I put this book together.

"Conjoined"—This one just popped into my head, origin unknown. The doll being an evil parasite and the little girl being the host is just the sort of thing that occurs to me and my warped brain. Probably because I like reading about insects and the weird symbiotic relationships they have with each other and nature at large.

"Little Monsters"—I got the idea that it would be fun if there was one guy left and everyone else had shrunk down to these little bloodthirsty savages. Sort of a role reversal from the usual trope of the normal people being the little ones in a world of nasty giants.

"The Shape"—This was published many years ago in *Dark Animus* magazine, a great Australian small press mag. Those of you who've read my post-apocalyptic novel *Biohazard* will no doubt recognize the obvious similarities between this tale and the novel. Well, "The Shape" came first. I expanded it into *Biohazard* at the request of a publisher who then later couldn't fit it into his schedule. Ha! Irony!

"Wormwood"—Well, if there's a precursor to the other stories in this book, this would be it. It was originally published by Elder Signs Press in *Horrors Beyond 2,* back in 2007. The Chernobyl disaster was, without a doubt, a modern horror story. I read several detailed accounts of it before I wrote this story. When I learned that the superhot reactor core was buried in the town cemetery, it all fell into place for me. It doesn't take too much imagination to realize that the radioactive dark matter entity was probably Azathoth.

Well, there you go. All the info that's worth knowing or that I can remember. The Abomination and I would like to thank you for buying this book and reading these tales. I'd also like to thank Joe Morey at Weird House for putting this out. I think it makes a nice companion piece to my earlier collection, *Horrors of War.* If I'm able and still above the ground and not below it, there will be others to follow. Here's hoping.

ABOUT THE AUTHOR

TIM CURRAN is the author of *Skin Medicine, Hive, Dead Sea, Resurrection, Blooding Night, Dead Sea Chronicles,* and *Horror of the Blood Devils*. His short stories have been collected in *Alien Horrors* and *Horrors of War*. His novellas include *The Underdwelling, The Corpse King, The Brain Leeches,* and *The Sunken City*. His fiction has been translated into German, Japanese, Russian, Spanish, and Italian.

ABOUT THE ARTIST

Steeped in the enthralling fantasy and science-fiction illustrations of the 1960s, '70s, and '80s, artist and illustrator **K.L. TURNER** brings a bit of old-school painterly style to today's methods. With more than 30 years of experience in the arts, he expertly brings an expressionistic style into his illustrations to create compelling works which captivate and draw the viewer in. His works are found in media and galleries around the world, and celebrated in pop culture. A versatile creative type, Turner is also accomplished in the mediums of photography, sculpture, and the fine arts. Choosing to live and work on the beautiful front range of the Colorado Rocky Mountains where he was born and raised, he continues to derive inspiration from nature as well as cultural influences both at home and in his travels.

NEVER MISS A BOOK YOU WANT!

Join the Weird House mailing list
for the latest news, releases, and special offers!

Scan this code or visit:
https://www.weirdhousepress.com/subscribe/